BLESSINGS OF THE FATHER

———————— Book Two ————————

LV IS FAB

Other Books By
Mitch Reed

Blessings of the Father - Book One—Ties That Bind
O.O.O. - Obsessing on Obsession…the Documentary

BLESSINGS OF THE FATHER

—————— Book Two ——————

LV IS FAB

Mitch Reed

iUniverse, Inc.
Bloomington

Blessings of the Father
Book Two
LV IS FAB

Copyright © 2009, 2011 Mitch Reed

This is a work of fiction. All of the characters, names, incidents, organizations, and dialogue in this novel are either the products of the author's imagination or are used fictitiously.

iUniverse books may be ordered through booksellers or by contacting:

iUniverse
1663 Liberty Drive
Bloomington, IN 47403
www.iuniverse.com
1-800-Authors (1-800-288-4677)

ISBN: 978-1-4401-1768-8 (sc)
ISBN: 978-1-4401-1769-5 (ebk)

Printed in the United States of America

iUniverse rev. date: 08/24/2012

PUNCTUATION DISCLAIMER

Dear Reader:

At the risk of alienating you with my somewhat nonconformist grammatical and punctuation style, allow me to be upfront about it and explain.

I believe that all languages are living, flowing, and yes—evolving. So too in my opinion—should the grammar and punctuation that supports and defines that language. I've simply taken that liberty and freedom upon myself in how I look at my grammar or punctuation. My use of both conforming and nonconforming grammar or punctuation is based on trying to convey a very comfortable or conversational style of writing…a genuine casualness hopefully comes through this way.

Our society today already openly embraces as well as utilizes a variety of nonconformist language shortcuts and systems to linguistically streamline, (shorthand) personalize, (texting abbreviations) or culturally focus (Ebonics). I believe this leaves both grammar and punctuation open to personalization too—so I've gone down my own road accordingly.

Grammatically speaking, I will always write my sentences and statements from the perspective of the naturalness and realism of the spoken, rather than the written word. This is rule number one-as it supplants normal and conforming rules of grammar. I.E. why did I just use this mark: -?

I've assigned enhanced meanings to certain punctuation marks I use in my books. I.E. I use … to denote an afterthought to a preceding sentence or statement. This is opposed to where I use a dash – for when the sentence needs a hard pause before continuing the same thought. I'll often use a comma for a short or soft pause, rather than just ending a complete thought. For the shortest or softest of pauses, I denote this by use of this mark: -

My ultimate goal is to enhance the conversational style of my writing…not to insult anyone's knowledge of punctuation. I apologize now if it doesn't work for you…that's okay-but for me—it does.

Imagine reading my book as if someone is actually speaking the words audibly as you listen to the words being spoken…not merely reading them. You'll hopefully see where I was heading with this new casual style as a result.

Mitch Reed

Dedication

Book Two has been an absolute pleasure to complete, thanks in great part to the collaboration of two of my oldest and closest friends—David Essex and Gary Stein.

I know that often times, authors choose members of their family for this high honor before others, and rightly so. Yet in my experience, I not only have found the suggested contributions of my two dear friends helpful, but all-important to the story's over all vitality and vision. I am humbled and forever in their debt…thanks guys.

But with that being said, I want to thank my sons, Hunter and Ansel as well, for all of their on-going support too.

Mitch Reed

Preamble

Promptly at 9:55 pee, I showed up at Toonland Amusement Park where I made my way to the Tour Center to retrieve my twins, Trevor and Taylor, from their assigned tour guide. The boys were already there…looking certifiably akin to the walking dead. Now I was the refreshed one, while they were the 'dog and pony' show…they were—dragging.

God, payback's a bitch sometimes…isn't it?

After thanking our guide Hilary, she assured me that the boys had behaved exemplary as promised. We bid Hilary a nice evening, then made way for our hotel where Trevor announced they were going to bed immediately…I was shocked.

"Daddy, can you set the alarm clock for us please—we need to be up at six?" Taylor added.

"Six—what? Whoa—hold it—six am? Now boys, do you feel okay—are you sick? Six am with my two sons awake…I had better call the Hotel's doctor right now. Really I know I asked you this yesterday—but now I'm serious…just who are you two? What have you done with the genuine Trevor and Taylor Morgan…my two eleven-year-old sleepyheads who have to be threatened—just to wake up before noon?"

"Oh Daddy—stop it."

"T-man, why do you two plan on waking up so early…pray tell?"

"We have to be at the park right at eight am when it opens—we have an audition Daddy."

"An audition—for what? Just when had you two planned to ask my permission on this?"

Apparently, Taylor had passed the torch back to Trevor as he now explained.

"Hilary told us that the park is having a contest with open auditions in the morning. It's for a spot in their show in Future World tomorrow night. We thought it could be fun to try out.

"Dad, the performance is being done by the Toon-Crooners—that's Toonland's chorale group. They're having a contest for only kids under twelve to join their group for just one performance. Mummy was always trying to get us to sing for others, so we want to try out for her. Taylor and I talked about it a tick or two; we decided that we really did have a lot of fun singing at the house yesterday. We just want to see if we can do this.

"So can we try? Please Dad, please?"

"Of course T-1…but always ask me first—not after you've signed up! You know it may interest you both to know, that I was once a member of that very group myself, back when I worked here."

"Really Daddy, that's wonderful. So we can all say we sang in the same group, just at different times. Don't you love that Dad—I mean if they pick us?"

"Yes Trevor I do. I think it's wonderful if you two get the opportunity, but you need to realize something else if that happens."

"What's that Daddy?" Taylor inquired now.

"T-Man, if you're selected, you boys will have to leave time for rehearsals so you'll lose a lot of time in the park tomorrow—are you both prepared for that?"

"Sure Dad—we've been practicing our keyboards and singing since we were five—so we already figured that." Trevor jumped in with—instead of his brother.

"Alright boys—you're right. You give it your best shot...Grandfather and I will be there to root you on. Naturally we'll want to support you—but do we really have to be there exactly at eight o'clock in the morning?"

"Yes sir."

"Alright then—let's get to sleep. I better speak to Grandfather now. I have to reschedule our portrait sitting too...but I still say, we can sleep in later than six—after all, we're already here at the park."

I awoke at 7:00—the boys were already up! The little buggers had audaciously ordered room service for themselves.

"Are you boys enjoying spending your inheritances?" Apparently, there was a little of my father in me after all?

"Good morning Daddy. We thought you could sleep longer this way... but we're paying for breakfast—so don't worry."

"Oh sure you are...but it's with the money I gave you yesterday! Yet, it was a nice gesture on your part and very considerate—so thank you boys."

"You're welcome Daddy...but I guess we'll need another forty or so each, for today if you can?"

Jeeze, why do I even bother? I asked myself now.

The Transporter dropped us off right across from the audition area. I went to their sign-in table where I signed a mountain of paperwork...two huge stacks naturally...how lovely...not! All of this paperwork—just so my two could walk up to their mic and say:

'Testing, one, two, three,'...then audition.

After completing all the necessary forms, we sat down to wait our turn as we people-watched. I noticed something else at that moment. I pointed it out to Cedric to gauge his reaction as well...every stage mother in the State of California surely had her kid—or kids, here for this audition. That told me that this was a serious amateur competition—I hadn't given that much thought until now.

Some forty minutes later we finally heard the boys' names called—oh happy day…well at least we had some wonderful coffee to sustain Cedric and I through our wait.

We followed a production assistant inside into the rear area of the stage where we were directed to…you guessed it: sit and wait some more…we were getting good at waiting.

We listened to the auditioning kids singing from behind a curtain. While we couldn't see them, they were all enjoyable to listen to while still being amateurs.

Sitting there listening to these unseen kids, I thought again about the true talent my sons possessed. I knew that my boys did not sound amateurish like these other youngsters. Sure the twins were young and sounded juvenile to a degree, but they still sounded very polished and professional…way beyond their years. I realized too, that along with having angelic—yet big voices—six long years of consistent practice accounted for most of their skills.

Finally they were called. When I asked them if we should wait—or go with them for support, they told us they were nervous enough as it was. Adding that if it wasn't a big deal to us, they'd prefer not having us there rooting them on. As Trevor so eloquently put it:

"While we soil ourselves Daddy."

"Its okay guys. Look, we can hear you fine from here anyway—you guys go on and make us proud…I speak for Mummy too boys…so go for it. You two can do this as we're all proud of both of you already…just for trying."

"Thanks Daddy, thank you Grandfather." Cedric and I both nodded our acknowledgements before sitting back down…to wait some more apparently.

The boys disappeared but I could hear them talking sedately to some guy backstage—probably the contest's producer or director. Huh—that was odd. This guy's laughter sounded familiar…but I just couldn't place it…oh well.

I heard a piano start in—then heard my two little pishers begin. They were singing Unchained Melody—incredibly. I could not distinguish who was taking which part but their harmony alone had to be blowing this guy away already.

Assuming this guy knew his stuff, I thought he'd be a good barometer on their raw, amateur talents. In keeping with Miranda's wishes, I wanted the boys to branch out from their insecurities with a garage band once we moved to LV permanently.

My God—the way they nailed this song I knew instinctively that they were in—there could be no doubt about it. After they finished there was a momentary silence—then robust applause followed from the production staff for nearly twenty seconds...the longest I had heard so far. At this point, Cedric turned to me before nodding and beginning to clap himself...so I joined in too now.

Moments later my two sons were walked out with the same guy apparently...who was beaming. Damn...if he didn't look familiar...Holy shit—it couldn't be! I nearly choked on my last swallow of coffee as I screamed to myself.

"Mr. Morgan—I'm Scott Davis, the producer of our contest. You sir— certainly have two very talented sons."

Hearing his introduction—I was already laughing which seemed to confuse him...as well as Cedric. Obviously he didn't recognize me—yet. Although he was looking at me funny now...probably assuming I was out of my mind. True I was over fifty pounds lighter while nearly fifteen years older. Yet I knew exactly what to say to him now.

"Well, of course you'd think that—but if you don't mind, I think I'll have to call you—Scooter as I thank you for your compliment!"

"Scooter? I've haven't been called Scooter...I'm sorry sir—but do I know... oh my God—Marc? Christ—is it really you?" As I nodded my head, giving him his answer...he leapt towards me. Milliseconds later we were already in a deep embrace, hugging each other before then actually kissing each other's cheeks. All of this took place in front of my stunned sons and father-in-law, who himself still appeared to be in shock.

"Guys, please say hello to my closest, dearest, friend from when I worked here—but don't call him Mr. Davis...heavens no—it's strictly—Scooter for him."

"Marc, what on earth have you been up to? I've been trying to find you for like fourteen years? I figured you were still in England all this time...so I finally gave up. Now having met the twins here with those accents—I'll assume I was correct?"

"It's been fifteen years buddy boy. I've been great Scoot...but here in the States. I'm still in the food service industry sixteen years now—and counting. And you I see—were never able to walk away from production and all of this...could you?"

"Yes, I'm still here—so don't rub it in. Now listen bud—despite your pathetically mediocre voice—you've got some super-talented boys here— listen, are they ringers? You know if they're already pro in England, I still have to disqualify them...this contest is strictly for amateurs?"

"Absolutely not Scooter. They've never been paid for performing anywhere. Usually they're at home practicing—or on occasion at their school."

"Damn bud—we've got to do something about that then. You're doing them a great disservice with their level of talent Marc. Christ pal, they're ready to turn pro right now. Hell, I shouldn't have to tell you that—of all people… our very own—first-chair tenor?"

"No Scoot—I'm in no hurry. I love them just the way they are—all mine.

And now on to our second installment of Blessings of the Father, I hope you enjoy Book Two.

CHAPTER 1

▼

AND SO IT BEGINS

MY ALARM SOUNDED OBNOXIOUSLY RIGHT at 7:00 a.m. It seems though that it worked selectively…my twin tornados were still sleeping.

I pulled back the covers and attacked Trevor's ticklish feet with reasonable success as he started to stir. Taylor on the other hand—well that was a completely different story. Apparently, he was not going to open those eyes of his without a fight.

After a couple minutes of 'just a few minutes more Dad' in between tickling his feet, I finally forced him up under protest. As if on some sort of autopilot his protest became painfully obvious as he sounded reverie with three short but pungent blasts out of his own trumpet section…merely to taunt me…I'm sure.

Just the same he was pushing my patience—I was sensitive to people farting in my bed…who wouldn't be?

After regaining my ability to breathe freely while slapping my young son's 'musical…arse' for good measure-I got the boys started on their morning routine as I left for the kitchen.

"Morning Grace, how was your night?"

"Fine Marc, how about you?"

"Too short. I think I could have used another two hours in bed this morning."

"Too bad…welcome to school days—dear old dad".

"Yes, I suppose you're right. You know Grace, why don't you take a little pity on me and whip me up a Latte each morning and have it ready. If you did, perhaps I could shake myself awake a little faster."

1

"You know Marc; I'd always have one ready if you drank it the same way each day."

"That's true Grace but if you prefer just start with a plain Latte then I'll flavor it myself. If I'm then in the mood for something else—I can always have a second cup—all right?"

"That works for me love—consider it done."

"After Paul and I drop the boys off at school he will take me to the office. When the boys get out at 3:10, Paul will pick them up to bring them over to me, there—so don't panic. I want to show them around some…then we'll head home, okay? Ask Sofia to have dinner ready at 5:30; I want to leave time to help the twins with their homework. Hopefully they can get a little TV in before they have to go to bed too."

"I'm fine with all of it love, just don't forget to give me all the telephone numbers in case something arises and I need to ring you up."

"No sweat Gracie—I'll leave them by the telephone for you." I immediately did it so I wouldn't forget. That would bring out the wrath of Grace later on during some emergency, if I did.

Right at 8:30 the three of us dropped inside our limo 'Laverne' and started our short trip over to the boys' new school; The Meadows School.

We went into the administration office where I was able to introduce the boys to their new vice-principal Mr. Riley. After receiving the twins' classroom assignment we were escorted there by one of their staff. I immediately noticed that all the kids—but particularly the girls were eyeing the twins big time while giggling away. I wondered how many of these girls would be getting their homework done tonight. Surely these teenage ladies would be on the telephone talking about the two new cuties in their class to all hours.

I purposely avoided all physical contact now, knowing more about teen peer pressure along with our little slip at Sunday school by giving them parting kisses. I simply verified with them where Paul and Laverne could be found outside after school let out. I now winked at them as I cocked my head towards four very cute girls who were still eyeing them…then I gave them a final wink. They casually looked over; winked back to me then began walking into their room. You could see they were relieved I hadn't said anything other than so long.

I got to my office right at 9:15. After perhaps fifty or so 'welcome back' greetings I got straight into work inside my office.

Robbie flew into my office about two minutes later carrying my coffee brewer and mug along with a humongous stack of messages.

"Wonderful seeing you this morning boss…how are all of my 'Brady' men doing so far?"

"Fine smart-ass…but how was your weekend with all the girls?"

"Marc, I don't believe it—it's a new record, damn how about that. It seems it only took you thirty seconds to start your gay-bashing rhetoric. My word, maybe I should arrange a press release—what do you think?"

"You know Rob while you're writing out your press release, why not save some time by writing out your resignation too?"

"I'd do that Marc but I am 'resigned' to put up with your sorry 'straight' ass for eternity apparently. I believe by all appearances that I'm attached at your hip—by an Act of Congress."

"Don't let 'them' stop you from leaving Robbie, the door is always open you know?"

"Oh my, did someone fall short on getting his full six cups of coffee consumed this morning?"

"Okay Robbie—enough of the cracks. Let's get down to some real work this morning...shall we?"

"Sure we can Marc. How was the barbeque by the way—sorry I couldn't make it? Did the Pagan sacrifice go well—with the dozen slabs of ribs...I almost forgot to ask?"

"It was great Robbie, even though you of course were sorely missed...at my kitchen sink!"

"Are we getting to work now Marc—or do I jump right into the stupid straight jokes?"

"No; let's get to work, enough with the humor, what's on the agenda for the day? I also want to review the latest financials and departmental reports. By the way Rob, are any of these messages of critical importance? Jesus that's some stack you brought in."

"Yes. I've separated them with the important issues on top then the not so crucial ones follow below those. And you had one guy call in like six times. If you ask me he seemed more desperate with each ensuing call though."

"Really, that seems both odd and ominous Robbie—who was it?"

"He says he's an old friend of yours from Toonland. I'm sure he said his name is Vern."

"Robbie, it can't be a Vern because I don't know anyone by that name—I'd certainly never forget a name like that...sadly, neither will Jim Varney."

"Okay boss, let me find the messages then as I saved them together... yes, here they are. Oh—oh I'm sorry, his name isn't Vern...so Marc you were right. His name is Vic...Vic Tremmers."

"Vic Tremmers! Holy shit O'Hara—let me see those. You know Rob, that's a name I haven't heard in almost fifteen years...thank the Lord for that. Damn it all to hell—hide me someplace, will ya?"

"Jeeze boss, you seem genuinely upset—I think I'm going to enjoy this."

"Christ Robbie, I'm so glad it amuses you, because you're the guy who's going to have to blow this guy off—despite the fact that he's a sweet guy—he's like the last person in the world I'd like to get reacquainted with believe me—fifteen years is like five hundred years too soon to see him again."

"Marc, why don't you save me the usual fifteen minutes of trying to drag the story out of you—just tell me about this guy as you've got my curiosity up."

"Fine Rob, but as my corporate gatekeeper you're still the guy who's going to get rid of him—he can be like a flea stuck to a dog's ass when he wants to—but be gentle how you talk to him or he'll go off on you."

"All right boss I get the message…now dish me the dirt on this guy."

"Okay Robbie it's like this—Vic Tremmers is perhaps the world's greatest screw up in the civilized world. Hand me the dictionary. I'll bet you a 'c' note right now that if we could open up the 'F' section for 'f__k-ups'—we'd find Vic's picture there because he's certainly the poster child. If Vic walks into a room of people that know him…they'll all get up and blow out of there in an instant—get the picture? The man is a walking minefield—he's way beyond just being jinxed and believe me Robbie—he usually brings trouble right along with him. Think of him as another variation of Suzie Morton only male and without the intellect or tact!

"As I recall, he went to work at Toonland after coming home from Vietnam where I think he lost his social skills or something else happened to him. I do remember that he's about ten or so years older than me and I was convinced some kind of trauma happened to him in Nam—you know, shell shock or something? And you've heard all those Vietnam Vet stories about Agent Orange illness—right Robbie?"

"Sure boss, who hasn't?"

"Well Robbie, think of Vic as a victim of Agent Fool's Illness or something—the guy just couldn't do anything right except three things. He was one hell of a martial artist in a sort of 'Billy Jack' kind of way…you remember the movie right? His second gift if you will was that he could cook Texas BBQ like nobody's business. His last talent was two-fold. He had a way with horses—I never really ever saw anything like it honestly …he could communicate with them—I swear…but it wasn't just horses. Vic had a similar way or something special—working with challenged people too. I remember when a Toonland visitor would come onto his ride platform with a handicap or disability; he had a way of making their transfers effortless and seem commonplace or an everyday thing. His connection with these guests was off the charts. They all loved the guy. But getting back to the horses for a minute—he knew about as much regarding horses as Forest Gump's friend—Bubba—apparently knew about shrimp.

The sad thing is—he's also one of the sweetest, nicest guys on the planet Robbie, as long as you don't cross his temper. Under normal circumstances you can't help but like him. I've never been any good at pushing him away—that's why you've got to do it for me or I'll be stuck with the guy forever—see my dilemma Rob?"

"Okay boss, you've made your point. I'll do my best to blow him off for you—but what happens if I can't?"

"Then I'll have to try doing it—or get stuck to him again. Alright—let's move on this is depressing me—what's next?"

"Alright Marc, yesterday at Costco you asked me to remind you to call Natalie Garson at Spanish Trail Realty about a new house. While you're doing that—I think I'll take advantage of your long-windedness by getting my manicure done."

"Cute Robbie, what else?"

"We have 'Legal' at ten to bring you up to speed on our due diligence for the acquisition of the Cousin Burt's restaurant chain. At noon you have lunch with the Foundation staff in the boardroom…"

By the time Robbie finished running down my appointments for the day I already felt exhausted…I was that out of shape for the resumption of this morning ritual. I immersed myself into my schedule but still had not heard back from my message to Natalie Garson. Right before three, though, that got covered as Robbie buzzed me that she was now holding on line four.

"Natalie—how have you been kiddo?"

"Fine Marc…how are you?"

"If I told you—you wouldn't believe me! How bout I just say—unbelievable?"

"Hey I guess that will work for a Monday but what was the reason for your call? I apologize for taking so long to call you back but I was stuck in a seminar all morning and afternoon."

"No problem Natalie, your assistant shared that. I know it isn't easy being a successful businesswoman with your agency."

"No you're right—it isn't…but Lord knows it's what I love to do."

"Natalie the reason for my call is for you to be aware I'm in the market again for a new home. I need you to find me either an existing home, or a lot. It must be in a very 'family-friendly' neighborhood however, busting at the seams with kids."

"Did I just hear Marc Morgan right? A family-friendly neighborhood? Aren't you the man who once told me you loved children…as long as they were properly cooked?"

"Yes Natalie—you're correct…that was me…but no more. Here's the abridged version Natalie—I have twin eleven-year-old sons now."

"You what? You are joking right—Marc?"

"No Nat, I'm serious."

"Since when have they carried kids—off the rack at Brooks Brothers… they're stepchildren right?"

"No Natalie—they're all mine. My wife passed away in October over in England so the boys are now with me. I want a more suitable neighborhood for them to develop their friendships.

"You know Marc, I'll never turn away a commission, but what's the deal? You are after all—Mr. Spanish Trail—why should you need to leave your home that took us over eight months merely to find and negotiate with the builder?"

"Come on Natalie—you of all people know that kids are few and far in between inside the Trail…they're as rare as the number of lawyers residing in heaven!"

"Oh my God Marc—you are serious. I thought I was being set up for the latest Marcus Morgan gag or something…I know your reputation on gags after all. I'm so sorry to hear about your wife—forgive me. You know I don't think I ever even realized you were married…hey wait a minute, are you sure that this is all for real Marc?"

"Yes Natalie it is. My wife and I separated years ago. While I certainly forgive your innocent comments—after all how would you know as I've never mentioned it? I'm glad I finally got your attention though."

"You most certainly have—but more to the point—I'm truly sorry for your loss."

"Thank you Natalie, but don't give it another moment's thought please."

"Alright Marc—so lets get down to what you are looking for then. If you could have your choice what's your preference on this purchase, an existing home or a lot?"

"I think a resale due to time but it will have to be near perfect to my style and tastes—otherwise I would prefer a sizable lot to build on this time around."

"Alright—let me just get some basic details. How big is your minimum size on an existing home as well as your desired lot size range?"

"I'm comfortable with about what I have now in the size of an existing house. The lot minimum is three acres, but preferably right at five acres should work out perfect."

"How many bedrooms do you want after accounting for the office, den, maid's quarters, and theatre requirements you have?"

"Dang it Nat—I see you haven't lost your touch. You sure remember me like a book…don't you?"

"No Marc—honestly I don't…I am reading all of this from a book… sorry! But hey, they don't pay me the big bucks for being disorganized you know."

"Yes I'm sure they don't. But to answer your question though I need at least six bedrooms this time on top of those other rooms. I've increased my house staff and I'll still require a guesthouse or Casita with at least two bedrooms too."

"Alright Marc, your at eighty-two hundred square feet now—so we had better look for nine thousand at a minimum. How many of those wonderful cars of yours do you want to fit in the garage this time around?"

"You know Nat—since a forty car garage is somewhat rare—I guess a three car will work…although I'd love more." We were both laughing now as you can imagine with that remark.

"Baths?"

"At least one for every bedroom ensuite plus a powder room or two."

"And you want this home in a family neighborhood?"

"Absolutely Nat…on a street packed with kids near my boys' age."

"Oh—and near your sons' ages? Well Marc let's see—when would you like to go looking for lots? I'm prepared to wager you dollars to donuts, a resale home matching your requirements does not exist in a family neighborhood—but of course I'll look."

"All right Nat. You're the pro, so I'll count on you…I'm just the schlep."

"Oh yeah—you're a schlep alright…a schlep who just happens to own the most unique restaurant chain in the country…that's all.

"You know, we all have to do something to pay the bills—don't we Natalie?"

"Yes we do Marc. As for me—I'm sending my bills immediately over to you then—since you're such a schlep." We were both laughing at her crack.

"When can you get back to me with some info?"

"Marc can you give me till tomorrow mid day? I'm going to define my search filters by utilizing some new software. My new assistant Brenda Sheedy may call you later for more definitive information I could be forgetting now. She will assist me in honing in on all of your variables. I want to advise you candidly though—that you had better assume you'll be building. Will you need a referral for an architect?"

"No Natalie I'd use Milton Stevenson—our corporate guru, he also does custom residential."

"Alright Marc, speak to you manana."

"Fine kiddo—talk to you then."

Moments after I hung up the phone, Robbie buzzed me.

"Boss, we need to talk—have you got a minute?"

"Sure Rob come on in…let me guess—you spoke to Vic?"

"You got it Marc. I'll be in there in a minute."

"Fine—I can't wait—not!"

Robbie walked in seconds later. I already could tell I was about to be 'worked'!

"Boss—I have to admit it—he's the most insistent guy I've ever come across. Nothing I tried—worked to blow him off. I'm sorry Marc, but honestly he was so damn persistent but also a bit curt too…I actually felt boxed in. So it was either break down my guard a little or I would have been forced to allude to some unflattering remark or comment coming directly from you to shut him up. I didn't think you wanted me going down that road of all places—please tell me I wasn't mistaken?"

"No Robbie, I understand. I knew he'd be difficult…so what happened,—what's his story?"

"First Marc—he's thrilled that he was able to track you down after all of these years."

"Naturally Robbie—as am I…only kidding. Christ what the 'f__k' do I do now? How did he find me—do you know?"

"Yes and no. He said something about a manifest that I couldn't follow, so I can't really tell you anything with certainty boss.

"Jeeze Robbie, trust me—this guy's hardly a super sleuth pal."

"That may be Marc, but what else can it be? I suppose he may have read something about the acquisition. You'll recall that we mentioned in our press release that your roots in foodservice date back to Toonland as a youth."

"Great Rob—remind me later to fire the genius who wrote that press release."

"Ah boss…"

…"Yeah I know—I wrote it…but what the f__k it sounded good—didn't it?"

"Sure boss. At any rate he'd appreciate an appointment to see you personally. Apparently he's down on his luck."

"Now there's a real shocker Robbie…how can anyone be 'down on' something they've never possessed—I ask you?"

"Beats me boss but at any rate he's put in an application for a line cook's position we had listed in the paper. We turned him down so now he's appealing to you personally. He says he's the last person who would ever call in a favor but he claims—you owe him one…if you can believe that crap!"

"Jesus—you know Rob—technically he's right—I do owe him. Okay Rob, fair is fair. I'll take his number but you have to keep him at bay for a while. I need some time to adjust to all of this."

"Here's his cell number, but listen boss—cut me some slack…what's the juicy tidbit he has on you?"

"You know O'Hara, sometimes you are one big pain in the ass!"

"Spare me the insult boss…give it up…now!

"Fine. I once screwed up a menu standard at Toonland. Vic stepped up to the plate and took the fall for me while we worked in the same kitchen. Problem was—he was over at the BBQ pits…nowhere close to the scene of the crime if you will. That's exactly the kind of guy Vic Tremmers is, Robbie. He has a heart of gold—yet every time he tries to help—he somehow f__ks it up worse. That's when they transferred him out to ride engineering as I recall—so are you happy to learn this deeply classified information?"

"Yes—as a matter of fact…I am!

"Great. So listen Mr. Smarty Pants, did you happen to pull a copy of his application?"

"Yes of course I did…here, its interesting reading."

"Oh…I'll just bet!"

Robbie handed me the application whereby I began reading it. For starters, I took note of the fact that he had listed fourteen foodservice jobs in the last ten years alone with a smattering of horse training positions in between.

"Okay Rob call him to set up an appointment—the further out the better."

"Yes Marc I'll do my best although I already know his situation sounds pretty desperate."

"Jesus Robbie—who's side are you on?"

"I'm sorry boss—it's just the guy's hard luck has sort of gotten to me."

"Fine—you're forgiven. Explain to him that he has to go through our appeal process first—so I'll hear from them personally anyway…you just put him off as long as you can—all right Mother Cabrini?"

"Okay Marc I'll do my best. Listen—in another few minutes I understand that Paul will be here with the boys."

"Wonderful—that's the best news I've had all day…now get out of here already—you're depressing me."

After all the crappy news concerning Vic Tremmers being once again in my life—even if it worked out to only be an hour meeting—I needed a break.

I went outside to wait for the boys as I was excited to know how their first day went at school. Paul pulled up moments later. The boys got out where they ran right over to me. I received the twin bear hug that they had now received a patent on back from the U.S. Patent office. God could they ever squeeze. They were excited which was wonderful to see. Then after kisses from both, which surprised me too—after all we were in a public place. I asked them the universal parental question which they responded to excitedly:

"It was great Dad; I'm really going to love it there." Taylor offered this up.

"Yeah Dad—it's the bomb." Came from Trevor.

"The bomb—T-1? I don't believe I'm familiar with that term from the Queen's English."

"Oh Dad stop. That's just what all the kids say now-a-days on this side of the pond—you know that silly?"

"Gee Trev—thank you for the vocabulary lesson.

"So did you guys make any friends?"

"Yes." They shouted out.

This was an instant relief to hear as it was my greatest fear and concern after all. With them missing their mates so badly back home in England along with having 'slim pickings' in the Trail, I was concerned that they make some fast friends. Singling out my more sensitive twin—I asked Taylor:

"Any that reminded you of friends back home T-man?"

"No, at least not yet."

"How about you T-1? Any of your new friends near match up to your best mates?"

"Don't know Dad...it was only our first day after all—but we sure liked all of them."

"I guess that's the important thing—isn't it boys?"

"Yes Dad, but you know what else?"

"What Trev?"

"All the girls in the class kept staring at us the whole dang day...American girls are funny aren't they?"

"Yes Trevor—they can be...that doesn't surprise me—you're both identically handsome. You know boys; I remember when I was a little younger than you...I think I was eight or so...yeah I was in the third grade. All the girls in my class were going nuts for Andy and David Williams. They were twin brothers around twelve or so years old...they were singers on TV...they actually had great harmony like you guys and a lot of talent besides...but they all but disappeared for a while. They're awesome to this day, although they sort of have a cult following. Anyways, the girls in my classroom talked about nothing else for weeks, it drove us boys nuts, even if we did hate all of the girls anyway.

"With your situation guys...it's similar, there are two of you just like the Williams brothers...but with those British accents as the icing on the cake—the rest might be history guys—once your classmates hear you two sing...do you know what I mean?"

"Cool, Dad, you won't hear me complain…I love girls but they can be so loopy sometimes…can't they?"

"Yes Trev—but we couldn't have much fun without them so I guess you'd better learn to adjust to them."

"Okay Dad I will. Oh—by the way, all of our friends want to meet you too."

"What on earth are you talking about T-1—why do they want to meet me of all people?"

"Dad during recess we were talking to a lot of the kids, but one kid—wasn't it Bobby, Taylor?"

"Yeah Trevo—it was Bobby…he never stopped asking questions Daddy. God I thought he would run out of questions eventually, because he asked so many—but he never did stop."

"Alright Taylor, let me tell Dad, I started it."

"Fine Trev I don't care—you finish telling Dad."

"Thanks Tay. Anyway Dad, Bobby asked us all the normal stuff, like did we have any brothers, sisters, and where we lived? We do live in Spanish Hills, right?"

"No Trevor, we live in Spanish Trail. Spanish Hills was built later on based on the success of Spanish Trail."

"Oh."

"Don't sweat it son, you're just learning things after all."

"Okay—well anyway, Bobby bragged that his father was this famous doctor that puts plastic on people's faces from someplace he called the 'strip' I think. Then he asked us what you did for a job. So Dad—that's when it all sort of just happened—right Tay?"

"Yeah bro—that did it all right."

"What exactly happened Trevor?"

"It's like this Dad; I just said you owned restaurants. Then Bobby asked me were they like a McDonalds, so I said no—they were like Verandas. Then all the kids just kind of went crazy Dad—how come you never told us Verandas are so famous?"

"First of all Trevor, it's not nice to brag—so I usually don't. Secondly boys, I would have thought that you two realized they're well known after talking to Mr. Davis' daughters? With Verandas all over the country like we've talked about—I assumed you would understand that. Most people including kids your age are certainly very familiar with them for over a decade now."

"Yes Dad—we understood there's a lot of them, but we had no idea how many people really love them. My God, Dad, they love the food, the pond, and Amelia…really everything about them—but especially the ghosts on top of all our singers. You wouldn't believe how our friends carried on Dad…you should have warned us.

"All our friends asked us every question you can think of about your dumb restaurants. When we didn't know what to say to most of the questions…we looked stupid in front of all our friends thanks to you Dad. Now all the kids want to talk to you themselves so they can get their questions answered. And they want to know when we can 'comp' them besides that—what's that mean Dad—a comp?"

I was laughing at the remark along with the subsequent question before poor Trevor could even finish his question. Only in Las Vegas I thought… where else would the typical eleven-year-old know that term—I ask you?

"Listen boys—a comp just means that whatever the item is, say like a nice meal or a show—it's at no charge. The person receiving the 'comp' just leaves a tip. The term is simply short for complimentary."

I noticed that as I finished my explanation, Trevor had an agape mouth while his head was dropping into an imaginary cellar. Just above a whisper he spoke to me now.

"Gee Dad—do we happen to have lots of those comp thingies? I kinda said I'd get them for our friends."

"You what? Trevor I can't believe this. My God, son—without asking me first? I'm afraid you're in the dog house mister…big time—you just cost me several hundreds of dollars—what were you thinking son?"

"I'm sorry Daddy—I didn't know what a comp meant…I really didn't. But can you do something so I don't get laughed at tomorrow for not knowing what they were?"

I had to make a supreme effort not to blow my top over this. I also had to try to see it from Trevor's limited perspective. He was new to the country, Las Vegas, and his school. Undoubtedly he had unknowingly agreed merely to avoid being called stupid for not knowing what it all meant. And I, after all, probably shared the majority of the responsibility for all of this anyway. I hadn't thought to sit down with the boys to explain elementary things like this to them beforehand.

Okay—so it really wasn't his fault I realized. I stewed awhile as I chose my next words carefully.

"You know Trev; I don't believe its fair for you to be embarrassed by your mistake…this time. I also apologize for pouncing on you son. After all you just started school here, so you didn't understand what you we're casually agreeing to with this custom. However, I'm not going to simply let it go without you realizing your mistake in this too. When in doubt—you had better ask my permission first…always! So for the next three months your allowance is cut in half to help me cover this expense. And might I add that if something like this happens again—you will be embarrassed—when I say no at that time.

"You both need to understand something that's important boys—so listen to me good. I love to comp people—but when it is my decision and not someone else volunteering me—without my permission. Are we one hundred percent crystal clear on this rule? Have I made my point Trevor?"

"Yes sir…it will never happen again…I promise."

Trevor's head was still at half-mast. One could tell that he was still crying silently. Taylor on the other hand, just nodded his understanding of my new rule.

"Now that we have cleared this up let's discuss how to handle it. Since there are twenty-eight kids in your class—you won't want to offend anyone, so here's what you'll do. You are going to ask your teacher Mrs. Geary to make an announcement to the class. The entire class is invited to brunch at our Summerlin unit a week from next Sunday at 1:00 pee. In addition, make sure you invite Mrs. Geary too. Assuming she has a husband—ask her to bring him or a guest as well. That should solve our little problem…all right?"

"Thanks Dad. I really am sorry for all of this trouble and doing the wrong thing."

"I understand Trev. I do accept your apology so stop those tears alright?"

"Yes sir. Dad your idea is great—but is there any way we could maybe have it on a Saturday instead?"

"Sure, I guess so Trevor, but why of all things is that so important?"

"Because some of our friends mentioned that they spend every Sunday in Church —they're what you call—LTD's, Dad."

"Son, that's LDS, not LTD. It stands for The Church of Jesus Christ of Latter Day Saints. It means that those friends of yours are of the Mormon faith so your suggestion makes perfect sense son.

I was still laughing at my son's innocent mistake of confusing our many Mormon residents with a Ford Police Interceptor. I could barely contain myself over his blunder but I managed before then continuing my comments.

"Many of my own friends and associates are Mormon son—in fact most of my friends are."

"So can we make it on Saturday then Dad, that way our Mormon friends can be there too?"

"Yes of course Trevor. I want your LDS friends to be able to join in as well. Make the party for the Saturday after next, okay?"

"Thanks Dad. I'm really glad you're my Dad just the same…but remember all of our friends really want to meet you—especially Bobby."

"Yeah Daddy—but good luck with him…I hope you can shut him up."

"Okay boys—but I'm glad that both of you are my sons—so I guess that makes us even…doesn't it? As for your friends, I'll be delighted to answer their questions including all of Bobby's at the luncheon—fair enough?"

"Dad is this invitation coming from just Trevor?"

"Certainly not T-man—it's from both of you. He's just paying the price for his role in creating it."

"Oh. Dad—I guess I need to tell you something too."

"Christ, what? You mean—there's more…you're killing me here, boys?"

"Daddy—relax. I just want to say that it was Trevor who said okay to the comp thingies, but I went along with him afterwards. I guess you'd better take half of my allowance too."

"All right Taylor…thank you for being honest with me though. Remember boys you can always tell me anything—even real bad things. I will still love you just as much afterwards—even if I'm angry with you. Just don't ever lie to me boys—always tell me the truth even if it's hard to. Boys, one thing I'm certain Mummy told you about me is that I do not like dishonesty in people… are we clear here?"

"Yes Dad, Mummy told us that a lot."

"Good. Well boys I do believe it's time to give you both the Grand Tour of our offices…don't you?"

"Yes Dad let's go in." Trevor added.

We went inside my corporate headquarters where I first took them to security for clearance badges. I then proceeded to show them everything. They really went nuts for our showroom in particular. Apparently seeing this mock up of most of our retail items in a typical Verandas 'General Store' out of context if you will, totally intrigued them.

I then gave them a tour of our distribution center by riding along on one of our forklift trucks. They enjoyed their ride tremendously but their favorite feature was our twelve-thousand, square foot walk-in refrigerator.

I then took them into our small packaging department where many of our retail items were finalized into their product packaging. This really surprised them when they saw our employees working away on tables putting all of the items into their respective packages. In this particular room, I knew ahead of time that they were going to be a bit surprised. More so, I suspected that I was going to get a barrage of their questions afterwards.

"Daddy—can I ask you something embarrassing? I'm not sure that I'm even minding my manners too good. I don't know Daddy, so here goes,—why do these people look kind of different to me?"

"Taylor; first of all—you asked your question just fine…so don't worry. Boys these are some of our very best employees. Most of them though have some special challenge or another that they have to deal with, while they work.

Some have disabilities that limit their mobility or the use of their limbs, while still others have some mental challenges. Others have injuries or illnesses like Cerebral Palsy, Downs Syndrome, or Muscular Dystrophy. Some are just finding their way back into a workplace."

"Jeeze Dad—it really makes me feel good to see you helping people just like Mummy use to. I had no idea you were like Mummy in that way—helping so many people. I'm sure it would be easier just to hire people without these problems—but you don't—you give them a job here instead."

"Yes Trevor—we could take that attitude, but you know what?"

"What Dad?"

"By doing that, I'd be missing out on some very exceptional and motivated employees. Besides this is a way for me to give back a little myself. I don't think that you boys know this about me yet—but I had a disability myself when I was your age?"

"You did Dad—wow. What was wrong?" This also came from Trevor.

"Guys, I had a disability that made it very hard for me to concentrate or learn things in school—or anything else really…except magically the piano… it was the sole exception, almost like what the experts call an autistic gift.

"So, I had what they call today A.D.D., which is short for Attention Deficit Disorder. If it wasn't for Gram's support working with me everyday in her kitchen—I would have ended up just another statistic. I have no idea what I would have amounted to without her…your Gram saved me boys. That's the simple truth of it…Gramps too. In short fellas, I had a lot to overcome."

"Wow, I never heard about this, did you Taylor?"

"Never, I guess Mum thought that Dad would want to be the one to tell us bro."

"So you see boys, I understand all too well what it means to have a challenge or a problem. I've been there, so I understand what it feels like—just like all of these great employees inside this room. But I'll tell you something else—it reminds me of something from earlier this morning—I need to always look out for everyone I love or care for, along with those I once called friend—no matter how long ago. So thank you boys for reminding me of that too…but here's one last thing guys:

"By working for Verandas, our employees here in this room, have the opportunity to contribute through their work…rather than being judged or pitied. They have the satisfaction just like everyone else of working hard to earn an honest dollar for their efforts. That's important to everyone boys—not just those of us without challenges. Can you boys understand how important that is to a person's self-esteem?"

"Yes Dad."

"And what happens in this room is special for another reason as well boys. You see, the profits from the sale of these items are earmarked to our own non-profit Verandas Foundation. With these dollars we pay for services for other disabled folks who are unable to work but still need our assistance. Boys do you see those stuffed bears over there in the corner that those ladies are boxing up?"

"Yes sir."

"That's Bernie—he's our company's mascot. Right now, we have a big campaign around the country to have kids adopt Bernie the Bear to fund our foundation—he's our best fund-raising item right now. Bernie's adoptions last year allowed our foundation to send over 400 blind children and teenagers to camp for two weeks last summer. This year, our goal is one hundred thousand Bernie adoptions."

"Wow Dad, that's wonderful. What else have you been able to do with all of these things?"

"That's a great question Taylor. See the gentlemen over at that table by the doors that are packaging up some of Verandas signature take-home products?"

"Yes Dad."

"Would you believe that the sale of those items raised over a million dollars last year? These funds were then earmarked to help folks with illnesses like Cerebral Palsy, ALS, MD, and others. That money allowed us to buy them things like wheelchairs, adaptive devices, or in some cases to pay for surgeries and medical expenses."

"Gosh Dad I thought only Mummy had spent time helping others, I never knew you had a foundation too. I'm proud to be your son Dad, I really, really am…I hope you know that?"

"Trev, I think that what you just said is perhaps the nicest thing anyone has ever said to me. But I'm just as proud of both of you two. I love you both beyond mere words, so come over here you two…I need one of your patented twin bear hugs."

The boys immediately came over to me as we enjoyed a good group hug. I then took the boys around the room where they met and spoke to everyone working. All of my employees were happy to meet them as well as speaking to them at length.

Afterwards, their many remarks to the boys reminded me that they were still getting by without a full-time supervisor since the retirement of their beloved Stuart. I briefly wondered to myself: could a guy not known for his tact—or intelligence, who perhaps himself—was a tad shell-shocked… supervise this group? Hell, he already knew how it felt to be a touch different from the norm. Most importantly, he had always been very kind and sensitive with every challenged rider he ever knew from Toonland. Before my thoughts could go further though—Taylor cornered me with a request.

"Daddy I'd like to ask you a favor—can we give our class a tour of your offices? I want all our friends to know what a great Dad and person you are."

"Sure Taylor—just as long as that tour would not include this room. I don't think that's a good idea…here's why son. First, our employees are simply our employees whether they have a challenge or not. I would not want them put on display for anyone as they're just our employees Taylor—understand?

"Second, I prefer to do these kinds of things quietly, because it's nobody's business. No one needs to know whom we hire or how I choose to spend a portion of my company's profits.

"The only motivation I would ever have to publicize our efforts with a portion of our staff being challenged—would be to encourage other companies to follow suit. And I'm happy to say that we aren't the only Las Vegas firm doing this as it is…nor were we the first to do it either. There are many fine corporate citizens here in Las Vegas…Verandas is just one of many, so we're proud to do our fair share. You'll find that Las Vegas is a city with a huge heart boys—this is just one expression of that."

Yet it was certainly their next question which made me so proud—I was overwhelmed by it instantly.

"So Daddy—how can we help out too? We always use to help Mummy but it looks like you could use our help too?" Taylor asked.

"Yes boys, I remember hearing that from Mummy…but I don't know what to say boys—what would you like to do exactly, to help?"

"Jeeze, I don't know—at least something Daddy".

"Alright Taylor, let me think on this a minute. Hey, I know how you two can help…I just remembered. You see, today at lunch, our foundation was meeting to discuss our biggest project. It's like this; our company has tried to assist our local Cerebral Palsy Foundation for over two years now with a huge endeavor of theirs.

"The CPF desperately needs to build a new residential center for their clients. They've been trying to raise this money for three years already, so over two years ago, we committed Verandas to raise at least five million dollars of what they needed…they need that money, boys. It's going to cost them over eight million dollars to build—which is a whole lot of money. That amount of money takes a long time to raise—while they need the home now…today! So far, we've gotten nowhere at raising the five million we committed to…it's been twenty-six months already!

"For the last two years, we've been trying to come up with a way to really jumpstart our efforts. We need to find the perfect, impulsive product that everyone will want to buy immediately when they see it. An item like that could get that center built in no time flat. I'm embarrassed to say that so far—we have not been able to come up with a suitable product. Just any old product won't do—it has to be an item that can raise that kind of money—quickly, like I said. It's not easy coming up with a real fast-selling product like that, but if only we could. With the right product, we could raise a whole heck of a lot of money—literally millions—even more than they require!"

"So what kind of product should it be Dad?"

"Honestly honey—that's the whole problem and the dilemma we've had. We haven't been able to come up with the right item, Trev. The best fund-raising product so far has been the 'Bernie' adoptions like we talked about.

"Look—why don't you guys think on it awhile? See if you can come up with some suggestions. It has to be something we can sell in all our restaurants to raise that amount of money.

"Maybe you two can give the search a new perspective, because the adults have been totally unsuccessful. Let's go review our menus, then I'll take you guys back to the showroom to check things out in there too. You can look everything over to see what you can come up with…but most importantly guys—draw on your own experiences from back in England or here—use your imaginations."

"That would be great—thanks for letting us help Dad."

"No Taylor, I thank you and Trevor—for your offer of help."

I brought out our menus for the boys to review thoroughly. They asked a few questions too that intrigued me. We next went into our General Store showroom…here they spent some time walking it as they asked more questions.

They asked about lots of things, such as merchandising, marketing collaterals, outside products versus using existing ones, point of sale, product visibility, what was product novelty…even how electricity needs were met. Yet all of these questions came from the perspective of an eleven-year-old's vocabulary, understanding…and more-limited sophistication. So to say the least—it was all rather humorous, while some of their contrived terminology was comical too. As before though, I was amazed at the insight of their questions and their intelligence—at least they were applying themselves here.

The boys then started talking amongst themselves while I excused myself to take a telephone call. When I returned, the boys were still going at it so I stayed out of their discussion not wishing to disturb their creative juices…as they were working on something…then Taylor yelled over.

"Hey Dad, we may have the answer now. Give us a 'tick' more to talk—okay?"

"Sure Taylor, just understand that this could turn out to be a rather long and arduous process…remember our marketing department is past two years already."

"Fine Dad but let me talk to Trevor—we're just about finished now."

Yeah right—you're finished…I'll just bet. I thought to myself rather jadedly. Hell, I knew how difficult this was…with arduous being the perfect description. Here I had my two boys calmly telling me how they were 'almost' finished already…shit, I knew better. These two young kids—sharp as they were—were not going to break our dilemma here in less than an hour's time. There was just no frigging way!

The boys had been talking non-stop for fifteen minutes more when they seemed ready to elucidate their idea. They had also been working on something they were crudely scribbling out on some paper too. This at least impressed me to observe the seriousness of their efforts.

Instantly too, I reminded myself to be very appreciative of these efforts no matter how shitty, rotten, or silly their idea turned out to be…which it would be. After all we had our own two-year search where we had come up empty handed too with some crappy ideas ourselves. So I did not want to implode their confidence or burst their bubble too roughly…so soon. That would only hurt their feelings in the process…so I had to psych myself up to be very tactful now.

"Dad, we think we have something that could work."

"Alright guys, I'm all ears. So who's going to be the spokesman then?"

I was now silently rehearsing the consolation speech I would give them. Meanwhile they looked at each other as Trevor then spoke:

"I think Taylor should Dad. This has mostly been his idea. I did help him some but just the same, he deserves to do the talking."

"Okay T-1, thanks. Go ahead T-man—let me hear all about it son."

"Look Dad, it seems to us that in the Verandas we've been inside of ourselves, plus this showroom—there's a good size open area over there (he was pointing towards the area directly next to the coffee bazaar). If your restaurants are all the same—this is where our two stands could be set up."

Stands? Jesus, where did that come from? I immediately asked myself. I was also wondering, if it was wishful thinking of me to feel as if I was beginning to become genuinely intrigued here? Whatever this was—it was clear that their effort was real even if the idea would later prove—to suck! I now left my 'shock' back in the thoughts I had just rehashed moments earlier as I answered Taylor's question.

"Yes, that's pretty much true of all the units' son. Go-ahead T-man, what kind of stands are you thinking about? The proper name for the stand by the way would be a 'kiosk'—just so you know."

"Alright Daddy—a key…ox?"

"No son…its kee'ozsk, and spelled k i o s k."

"Okay, a kiosk. Taylor now wrote it down on his piece of paper.

"Fine Daddy. So we could put two kiosks by the Coffee Bazaar area but from it—we would sell our new product with your coffee and other desserts."

Using kiosks had indeed been thought of for Bernie Adoption Centers in the past, but hell, at least the boys were thinking. However, any take-home item or coffee we put on a kiosk; would only sell somewhat better…we needed something more novel…a star product!

My thoughts were abruptly quashed though as I then heard Taylor's question as he was trying to get my attention.

"Daddy, are you listening to me?"

"Oh yes honey, I'm sorry. I was just running your kiosk idea through my head—please continue son."

"Okay Daddy—well our idea is to sell that different but wonderful ice cream from England we had at Mandaway Bay."

Holy Shit…I screamed to myself now, as I corrected Taylor:

"That's Mandalay Bay Taylor…but what ice cream is that again? Please go on son—this is actually sounding very promising—really…I'm not kidding!"

"Well Daddy, remember the long queue they had at their kiosk? The wait was over ten minutes before we could even get up there to see the ice cream in the case to order it—and they're called Minis. Well, I bet we could do nearly as well with each of your restaurants selling that ice cream too—and if you sell your coffee with other great Veranda desserts next to it—won't it make it like a little food court we go to at the mall—but ours would strictly be for dessert—featuring the Minis and all your other desserts and coffee? All of these desserts would please any of our customers who don't have a fancy for our ice cream…see?"

"Yes Taylor, you're right…my God, I do remember their long line."

Holy mother of God—did my kid just say what I think I heard? First and foremost—a unique, impulsive ice cream 'novelty' product? One that could sell in huge numbers given our volume of 347 units. But along with that—our own specialty coffees and desserts in a mini food-court atmosphere to attract guests over to it?

Could we have really been that myopically focused on our own existing products that we missed a more obvious 'outside-product' option totally? Stuffed animals and popcorn tins are fine—but they had limited sales appeal—this was different…it was novel in itself as a merchandising concept—plus it featured a 'star' novelty ice cream product…brilliant!

It seemed that we failed miserably, while my two eleven-year-olds,—succeeded—in less than a stupid hour's time...could all of this really be happening? I immediately returned my complete attention to Taylor's continuing explanation even as my pulse was genuinely quickening now.

Yet my pulse was running a close second to my accelerating brain activity. I think my smile had a mind of its own at that moment too—after all I couldn't help it...I was flabbergasted! I mean forgive my crudeness, but after all, I was only now becoming used to being around kids socially as of late. Frankly, maybe I hadn't given them enough credit in general? I needed to realize that kids could be quite smart and thoughtful when they wanted to put out the effort.

"My God T-men, you have an incredible idea here boys, damn. Guys—I think that maybe you've done it—yes I'm sure...you've really done it!" My sons were actually on to something big here—Christ had they actually done it? Yes! I instinctively knew it already.

Somebody pinch me for Christ's sake—I must be dreaming—but I'm not!

Absolutely nothing could have prepared me for the sheer simplicity, yet genius of their suggestion as a new fund-raising crusade. There it was—right under our frigging noses the whole damn time...a Dessert Court with a star product! So much for consolation speeches and bringing them down gently. I couldn't believe the idea they came up with. It was right up there with a Harvard-educated MBA...which I had four in our marketing department...a lot of good it did me too.

None of our marketing people ever came up with an idea as strong as the boys'. My thoughts were now cut short by Taylor's next comment. Again he was trying to get my attention.

"Jeeze Daddy—I'm not exactly finished. May I continue then... or are you still thinking? You're still smiling, but it looks a little loopy if you ask me?"

"Sorry son, I didn't realize—my God, there's more?"

You're damn right you didn't realize Marcus—you stupid idiot. And where's he going with this—now? For God's sake Marcus, stop talking to your stupid self...listen to your sons instead...schmuck.

"Yes Daddy—there is. When the people come into the restaurant, you'll give them this ticket. You can have the Verandas ghosts at the place where they take the names, give this to each guest. Especially for our guests with kids. On the ticket it would say something like this..."

..."Taylor we call the place where we take the names, a reception podium... your ticket we would call a collateral piece."

"Whatever Daddy—can I go on please?" It was obvious that Taylor's patience was tempered by his desire to finish explaining things to me, I think. And Taylor then handed me the ticket they had drawn up…it read:

HEY ICE CREAM, DESSERT, AND COFFEE LOVERS, SAVE ROOM FOR A TASTY VISIT TO VERANDA'S DESSERT COURT. WE'RE RAISING MONEY TO BUILD A NEW HOUSE FOR SOME NICE PEOPLE WITH CELEBRITY PALSY. SO COME TO OUR DESSERT COURT FOR MINIS ICE CREAM, DESSERTS, & OUR GREAT COFFEE. YOU'LL BE HELPING NICE PEOPLE GET A NEW HOME THEY NEED A LOT…WHILE YOU GET SWEETER JUST BY HELPING OUT! THANK YOU FRIENDS. VERANDAS RESTAURANTS.

Perhaps the wording of their message would not earn a Marketing Scholarship to Harvard. And the spelling of Cerebral coming out as celebrity was good for a poignant chuckle. Yet the 'bullets' of their message certainly would garner a scholarship to any Ivy League school. Their message was direct, compelling, and to the point. Where had these two been the last two years I had to ask myself again?

I read it a few more times, but with each reading I became that much more excited. Christ, I should fire the whole damn marketing department— along with myself! I was standing there, just shaking my head in disbelief. This was all from my sons' personal efforts as well as their sincere desire to help me and folks challenged like our employees.

Happily, it was my sincere belief that they had found the right product and concept at long last!

"So Daddy, what do you think of our idea?"

"Honey what can I possibly say—I'm really in shock. You see you both did something incredible just now. I love you both so very much for doing it too. Not to mention that over the years countless thousands will come to thank you both as well."

"So Dad—will it work? Could we raise enough money from it?"

"Yes Trevor, it will—but there's only one way I know of to prove that to you two. We're going to run it by our marketing people…today! Then in the morning, I'll call a few of my friends over at Mandalay Bay. I'll get their feedback along with the phone number for the folks at Minis. We'll then be able to eliminate any doubt about it, but I do suspect already that you guys have it with this. It's a brilliant idea boys; actually I'd say it's an eight million dollar brilliant idea—and then some. I'm just too swollen with pride for both of you…mere words are useless right now guys.

"Look at me boys…I'm tearing up. I'm so damn proud. Now come here and let's have a hug." The hug was silent, heartfelt and over a half-minute long.

"Thanks Daddy, it really makes me feel good to know that we're able to be of some help to you. And especially to help nice people have a better life."

"Some help Taylor? I'm the one who can't stop thanking you guys. This is big—fellas; really! You've come up with an excellent marketing campaign. Along with that, the perfect unique product to feature in it. I can't believe our stupidity for over two damn years—Christ what were we thinking boys?"

"I don't know Dad—how would we know anyway? So are you really going to do it?"

"Absolutely Trev but I'll tell you something else—each of these 347 dessert courts across the country will say:

Verandas' Dessert Courts
Featuring Mini's Ice Cream
Benefiting
The Trevor and Taylor Morgan
Minis Make Miracles Happen Crusade

"Guys, this is my sole contribution to your brilliant concept—you need some kind of name to attract guests over. This way everyone will know they've found the right place from your ticket. I also think naming the kiosks this way is the correct approach as we need something nonspecific concerning the charity in question at any given time. I have no doubt, that it won't be long before we have raised all the money needed for Cerebral Palsy. Then, we'll want to help the other organizations in our foundation after that. With each project, we'll create a new flyer to pass out. This way the kiosks themselves will always remain the same.

"And you know boys; I want both of you to start thinking on those lines too. Think about whom you would personally like to help next. Remember, it can be outside our current list of charities in our foundation, or maybe like something one of Mummy's charities did in the past."

"That's great Daddy; we'll start thinking about that, but is it okay to have our names on the kiosks? I thought you like to keep these things kind of quiet like you said? I wouldn't want anyone to think we were bragging, or to think we're better than anyone else?"

"That's a great point Taylor, but in this case—it's something that's really okay. Let me explain why son. You see, when children do things selflessly to help others like you two have—it's different. You've both have set a great example for others to follow—that's something good to share openly with everyone. It helps everyone realize we must all try to make a difference in our communities. Remember when I told you I would strictly publicize who we hire to bring it to the attention of other employers? You know guys, this is really the same thing—it's just that here we're reaching out to the public directly instead of other corporations. No, this is perfectly fine boys. I think we'll even place a small stanchion sign on the floors. These signs will explain how you both came up with the idea and how it is helping those with challenges have a more fulfilling life as a result of their purchase."

"Are you really sure Daddy?"

"Yes T-man, I am. I'll even wager a bet that you'll inspire other kids all over the country too. They'll come up with their own ideas to help others themselves, but perhaps on a smaller scale that they can handle. Boys, don't you think it would be wonderful if that happened? You would always know that you two got it rolling…it all started with your great idea."

"Do you really think so? God, that would be wonderful Dad. Gee, Mummy will be proud of us too…won't she?"

"Yes Trev, she'll be very proud indeed. You can both be very proud in what we've put in place today…I mean that."

"Rad, Dad."

"I'll assume that's another word in your new vocabulary, Trevor?"

"Yes Dad, does it bother you if I talk like that?"

"Certainly not T-1, you're living here now so you'll fit in more easily, adapting to our own slang words."

"Okay."

"Now, here's what we're going to do. I am going to call in our Marketing department right now for an impromptu meeting in our boardroom. Taylor, I'll introduce you both, and then you'll explain the idea for all of them. Then you two will decide how good of an idea it truly is by their reaction—fair enough?" I was immediately interrupted by Taylor.

"Hold it Daddy, I could never get up and talk in front of all those adults,—I just couldn't. Can't you do it yourself?"

"Son, I won't force you to do this if you're really not comfortable with the idea. It would really make me proud though to have you do it, because after all, you're mostly the brains behind the idea. Of course, you had a lot of help from Trev, but mostly it's your brainstorm T-man. I'm sure everyone will be listening to every word you say…trust me, they will respect you."

"Alright Daddy, but I'm real nervous talking in front of strangers."

"No you're not."

"Yes I am, how can you even say that Daddy?"

"Because Taylor, we had folks over after Mummy's services…just who was it that greeted all those strangers at the front door? Who were those two boys Taylor? Moreover, which two twin, awesome boys sang their hearts out at Toonland, not to mention for the 400 people in our home?

"Trevor and me Daddy—okay you're right I guess—but somehow this seems different to me?"

"Well it really isn't son—it's just business instead, haven't you ever given a report in school—it's no different than that? Besides son, you'll have Trevor and me there for moral support...okay?"

"Alright Daddy."

I walked the boys into our executive offices now. You could easily see the upscale mid-century surroundings really impressed them. When I took them into my office, they nearly about plotzed (had a fit) on the spot. My office was a mini museum of 50's TV commercial memorabilia, vintage vending machines, neon signs, and antique restaurant equipment and accessories everywhere. It was a room that Howdy Dowdy would be comfortable in.

"Jeeze Dad, your office is so rad too."

"Thank you Trevor—but you should really thank Gram...she decorated it—and our house too."

"Wow Dad, she's really good."

"Yes T-1, it's just one of her many talents, believe me."

"Oh, I believe you Dad, Gram's the best—the very best."

I called Robbie in on the intercom, moments later he appeared instantly delighted to see my boys again.

"And how are my nephs today—after their first day of school?"

"Fine, Uncle Robbie."

Taylor got this out through his laughter as he surprised us by walking over to his Uncle Robbie and giving him a tender kiss on his cheek followed by a hug as well. That fixed Robbie's wagon but good...he melted right there on the spot like butter to a frying pan. Eventually he recovered from this sweet gesture of Taylor's followed by another round from Trevor. After he came out of his fog, he began to speak to us:

"Thank you boys. I'll likely not wash my face all week from that 'sugar' you just gave me, you're both special to me already too. Turning to me he continued.

"So what's up Marc, I thought you left for the day with the nephs?"

"Rob, not only haven't we left—we're not leaving until we call an impromptu meeting with Marketing and the Foundation staff...we've got major news Rob. Get everyone who's available in here...stat. Shall we say—twenty minutes from now in the board room?"

"You got it Marc; this is my favorite part of the job after all."

"Why is it your favorite part, Uncle Robbie?"

"Because my dear Trevor, I get to call all of our people on the telephone with the following statement. So and so, Mr. Morgan would like to see you personally in twenty minutes in the boardroom—do you have a problem with that timeframe? They always get real scared when they hear me say that Trevor…especially at the end of a day. Frankly I enjoy that just a little."

"Boy, you're a meanie Uncle Robbie.

"Well boys, mean or not—it always makes my day—see ya."

And he was gone in a flash to start out on his 'fear' campaign. Meanwhile, I went into one of my closets where I took out one of our sketchpad easels. I then had Taylor and Trevor rewrite their 'ticket' in larger print on the giant tablet. Next, I turned the page to sketch the kiosks out, right down to the campaign's name boldly below Verandas' Dessert Court. Lastly, I drew the floor stanchion sign with a caricature of two stick figures representing the boys. I added some of the suggestive copy I wanted to see included on the sign. Ten minutes later, the boys and I walked into the boardroom sitting in the three closest chairs next to the easel. I could see instantly that this environment had brought out every last one of Taylor's anxieties—the kid was an absolute wreck already. He was constantly getting up on his feet as he paced back and forth nervously, getting more anxious by the second.

"Daddy, my mouth is so dry—do we have any water in here?"

"Sure Taylor. Just relax sweetheart, you're nervous I know, but believe me we're just going to talk—okay? Here's what you can do, while you're talking just pretend that all of these people—are naked…that might help. That will make you feel better about it…trust me son you'll be fine.

"You know honey, when I first started out, I would get scared too. I'd get so upset when I had to meet bankers and bureaucrats that I would throw up my guts—mere minutes after walking into their office buildings. Then one day, an employee suggested the 'naked' idea to me. After that suggestion, I never had a problem again. It really works T-man—just try it." As I concluded my suggestion, I handed him the water as he gulped it all down in one pass.

"Alright Daddy, but I wish I had stopped at the loo on our way in here… when I get nervous—I have to 'go'."

"Gee son, that door there behind your brother is the loo—so go use it and relax."

As Taylor left us, Trevor asked what I wanted him to do.

"Trev when someone asks a question, if you want to answer it yourself, just jump on in. Better still—whisper into T-man's ear that you'll answer the particular question."

"Okay, I can do that."

Taylor returned a few minutes later. It was obvious that at least part of him was more relaxed. Within a few minutes of his return to the boardroom our assemblage of marketing mavens started to convene. Some experts I thought. One-upped like me, by my two eleven-year-olds…ah hah!

One of our foundation folks was there as well—the ideal person in fact, Jesse Neilson—our fund-raising coordinator.

As these employees made their way into the room, you could see their relief immediately of not being alone. I'm sure their reticence and silence betrayed their innermost fears and thoughts at that moment. They had to be thinking that it didn't appear to be a mass layoff or a firing squad either, unless of course, twin boys were there as witnesses to the execution.

Robbie was there eating it all up of course. His sheepish, yet devious grin spoke volumes of his gloating. For his efforts, he received a few evil-eye stares from some of my staff I noticed. He was indeed a little stinker…just as his boss could be at times…yet he reveled in it too.

So I greeted everyone on his or her way to the conference table, as I thanked them for making such an impromptu meeting possible. Once everyone was in I began my spiel to my people in earnest.

"Gang, the reason I have called you all together this afternoon is to run something by you. Everyone—this is wonderful news…honestly the best! In essence, our twenty-six month search for our super product is likely over! I believe we've got a sure-fire winner. I am humbled and proud to tell you though, that this is an idea that my sons have come up with entirely on their own…save for the name. Believe me gang, it's hot. You're going to be blown away with its creativity…yet its simplicity too. This concept is so strong, it will likely build up the eight million needed for the Cerebral Palsy residential center,—and much more…quickly, I'm sure. How much more remains to be seen, but perhaps we'll know more before we leave this room today."

"For those of you who have not had the opportunity yet to meet my boys, I'm especially honored to introduce them. The young gent over by the easel is Mr. Taylor Morgan; he will be running the idea down for all of us. He will be ably assisted by his older brother—of four minutes, Mr. Trevor Morgan, to his right."

The group was still reacting to my crack when everyone got up and began introducing themselves to the boys. Each person included their area of responsibility or expertise and when finished, sat back down.

"Alright—before Taylor begins, let me give all of you the background on how this all came about. In short, the boys and I spoke of our efforts for the foundation after they had already asked if they could do something to help.

"So you understand gang, this is nothing new for the twins. The boys have over the last few years assisted my late wife in her countless endeavors with her foundations too.

"I explained to them that one way that they might help out, was to try to solve our dilemma in coming up with our needed superstar product. They gave it a lot of thought while they were in the 'General Store' mock-up…hell it took them nearly an hour to save our collective asses.

My crack broke everyone up at that moment.

"As with all foundation items we sell, I am more than willing to put one hundred percent of the net profits into our foundation's treasury. Also, keep in mind that we don't have a lot to give you today regarding costs, revenue streams, health department issues, etc…but, I can say with authority that none of those issues will hamper our efforts given the product is already being sold here in town…quite successfully, I might add.

"Let me also share with you all—that we will supplement this item's sales with other existing Verandas specialty coffees and signature desserts which we can project numbers for naturally. So what we want today—is your input on the general concept itself, along with your suggestions if any, for anything we may be overlooking, or to offer any improvement upon it. Now, with all of that said, I will turn the floor over to Taylor. Son—we're all ears."

Taylor stood up as he also cleared his throat. He was a little shaky at first, but quickly composed himself reasonably. Yet even as his biased father, it was precious just watching him try to begin speaking after clearing his throat repetitively.

"Thank you Daddy, and all of you for being here today. Our idea is to create a small dessert court area within the General Store featuring our star product—Mini's Ice Cream, along with our coffee, and other Verandas desserts. The dessert court will use two kiosks that we will place next to the Coffee Bazaar in that open area in each unit."

I wasn't surprised in the least to see a full complement of nodding heads from my staff sitting around the table…there was a change in their body language's confidence too. Their bodies were subconsciously reacting to hearing the brilliant concept laid out for them. This more than anything already gave me my answer…the boys had truly done it. I noticed that Taylor was watching the nodding heads now too, which immediately calmed him down further.

"Minis Ice Cream is from England where Trev and I come from…it's really brill. Minis are very unique as an ice cream. Its super cold, super rich, and a blast to eat…it's dry until it touches your tongue. Back home, they are super popular with all of our mates. We thought of Minis, because Dad told us to think of our own experiences. When we saw them at Mandalay Bay the other day, Trev agreed with me that they would be perfect. It's so different from most other ice creams; it should be a fast selling item in our restaurants too. You wouldn't believe the line they had at Mandalay Bay.

"At our reception area, our employees or the ghosts would hand out this ticket to each person being seated."

With that said, Taylor turned the easel to his first page which was the 'ticket'. Everyone began appending to their notes nearly in unison, which of course Taylor did not expect either. This sort of shocked him as he realized that at least these adults were treating him just like any other speaker… yet certainly—not as a child. They were obviously very serious with their interest level. This naturally increased his confidence beyond their earlier head nodding. As such, by the time he saw everyone finish their notes on the ticket, he began again, but he really cut loose this time.

"Now if you will all look real good at our ticket, you'll see we tell them to save room for dessert and coffee. This should not hurt selling other desserts or at least coffee in the dining room according to Dad. Just the same though, aren't we selling them on the idea of having some dessert and coffee anyway with the little ticket?

Taylor took a brief moment to now address me:

"Alright Daddy, this is cool. I'm having so much fun—looking at all the people like they're naked."

He had the room full of suits eating out of his hand as he continued with his presentation.

"Right now, let's take a look at this—you'll see what our kiosks would kinda look like. And Dad thinks we should tell our customers—I mean our guests, to be aware that real kids—Trev and me, came up with this idea. Dad says by putting our names on the two kiosks that will take care of it—so he came up with a name for the entire crusade…Trev and I think the name's brill. Taylor now turned the page on the easel as my group wrote down:

Verandas' Dessert Courts
Featuring Mini's Ice Cream
Benefiting
The Trevor and Taylor Morgan
Minis Make Miracles Happen Crusade

"You guys all know that not everyone likes ice cream, right? So Trevor came up with the brill idea of selling our coffee and other desserts too, right next to the Minis. This is how he came up with making it into kind of a dessert court, so hopefully we don't lose any customers at all…see?

"This last part was also totally Dad's idea. He wants to put a thingy on the floor—I think he calls it a station sign. It looks like this:

Taylor now turned to the next page on the easel.

"This sign tells all of our guests, how—and why, we came up with this idea—and he even wants to put our pictures on it!"

"Now I think I'm done, so do you have anything you want to add Trev... this was your idea too?"

"Yeah Taylor, you forgot to mention that when we raise enough for the Cerebral Palsy home—we'll just start over for another project. We can help all the charities in the foundation this way...and any others that get added you know, by us Taylor."

"Oh yeah, I forgot about that...thanks Trev—Dad, do you want to say anything?"

"Son, what can I possibly add? You and Trevor have done an admirable job. I can't think of anything else, but thank you for your excellent presentation... both of you."

Taylor was beside himself with pride as he should be...while relieved that he was finished, and left standing in one piece still. He blushed and bowed through the appreciative applause while Trevor waved to show his thanks. How many eleven-year-olds could do what they had just accomplished without getting flustered? Nevertheless, apparently Taylor was not quite finished as he again addressed us.

"I guess I should ask all of you if you have any questions either.

"Yes Miss." Taylor pointed to another of my staff.

"I have a comment to offer Taylor, first though, again, I'm Lucie Ortiz. It's my job to analyze the sales potential of any new product for our company. While we have all been listening to your excellent presentation, I have been doing a little preliminary Pro forma. That's a fancy business word for an estimate, on what we could possibly expect to accomplish here. Would you like to hear more about it?"

"Sure Lucie. I'd like to know just how much we could raise—is it a lot?"

"Why yes Taylor, the numbers should be quite impressive. An outsider to our industry would argue—they're staggering. For you and your brother's benefit, I'll try to explain all of this in terms you can follow. For the time being though, I'll just focus on your Minis. After we determine how to best approach our own coffee and dessert selections, we can add that revenue in before we finish today."

"Sure Miss, please go ahead."

"Okay then, the first thing to remember boys, is that we have three hundred and forty-seven restaurants total—that we refer to as 'the units'. They are all open seven days a week, which totals three hundred and sixty selling days each year after accounting for holiday closures. However boys, with three hundred and forty-seven units' total—that actually means in a full year, we have just less than one hundred and twenty-five thousand total selling days, when you add all of our units up.

"The placement of these kiosks is critical too. I must say that your location is excellent, being out in the open General Store—where everyone will see them. And your Dad's idea is excellent too, giving the Dessert Court a formal name along with adding the collateral stanchion signs to support the Crusade's back-story. We use that term collateral, when we give out background or sales information to our customers...like your added idea for the little 'ticket'... that's also a collateral piece. Are you both with me so far?"

"Yes Miss."

Lucie was momentarily shocked by being rewarded with the boys' common stereo response—with all the rest of us listening intently too.

"Next, we'll want to estimate our sales each day. So we take a different top selling item we already sell. We adjust for any obvious differences, then simply pretend it's our new Minis...we call this a proxy, boys. I've chosen our Cinnamon Volcano to use as our proxy as its appeal is similar to the Minis even though it's from our breakfast menu. It's one of our top selling breakfast items. It is always consistently very popular which is what we need for this comparison.

"Boys, by doing all of this, my laptop tells me we'll likely sell approximately eighty-seven cups of Minis per day in each and every unit on average. Now remember though—when I say eighty-seven cups per 'day' in each unit, we still have to multiply that by the one hundred and twenty-five thousand total selling days. When we do that, we get nearly eleven million cups of Minis sold annually company wide...that's truly impressive boys."

"Now boys, if you can share with me how much you think we'll sell the Minis for, I can finish my estimates."

Trevor seemed to be a little faster at thinking this question through, so he jumped in.

"Well Lucie, at Mandalay Bay, they sell their cup for four dollars—but that's a real big cup...they said it was like eight ounces on their menu. I think it would be too much to eat for some of our guests after one of our big dinners here. What if we were to sell a smaller cup—say around four or five ounces, for around three dollars instead, Lucie, would that be okay?"

"Alright Trevor—let's use that figure then. Boys, when we don't know the exact wholesale cost for a product, we temporarily use what we call a food-cost-percentage estimate. Let me explain how that works for a moment.

"Since all of us work everyday with how much food costs, we can estimate the food cost percentage for the Minis too. In their case, where it's already sold at a hotel in town, it's safe to assume a food cost percentage of around twenty-eight to thirty percent, for a five-ounce cup. This includes the cost of our employee's labor, the cup, spoon, and napkin for each sold serving.

"So boys, if we retail the cup of Minis for three dollars and use a food cost percentage estimated at the higher end of thirty percent, this equals an estimated cost to us of ninety cents for each cup we sell. This means for each and every cup sold, the foundation would ultimately keep a remaining profit of somewhere close to two dollars and ten cents, per cup. Now that may not seem like a whole lot to both of you—but remember—I'm not done yet. Given we will be selling almost eleven million cups each year, the total amount is going to be quite a lot of money—see how this works boys?"

The twins were both nodding their heads for a change.

"Okay guys, were ready for the exciting part. I'm going to push this little button here on my laptop. We'll then know how much money we're actually looking at with our new 'star' product—so are you both ready?"

"Yes Lucie—I can't wait—do it now please, push the button already." Taylor wanted to know…like yesterday!

"Yeah Lucie, do it—blimey I can't wait." Trevor's excitement level got another chuckle.

Lucie pushed her button whereby a big smile—along with a slight gasp immediately slipped out of her mouth.

Both Taylor and Trevor by this time were very anxious to hear her answer…they're body language said it all. My math skills quickly had it figured roughly in my head at that moment—but that didn't matter. I was still excited to hear it from another person in the room that I trusted to know the accurate potential for this killer product.

"Everyone—here it is. With the estimated numbers I've factored in for our 347 units—at the end of year one, we will have raised for the foundation—somebody give me a timpani drum roll please.

Immediately most of us at the table were using our fingers to simulate kettledrums.

"Okay boys—listen up. Your brilliant concept will allow us to raise the very impressive sum of just under—twenty three million dollars per year! Congratulations, and well done indeed!" At that moment the boys received a standing ovation from the group present…Robbie was in tears.

My boys were in total shock with their mouths agape. Taylor in particular, seemed deeply affected as well as choked up. Next I heard the word 'wicked' escape Trevor's lips as he slid into his chair while shaking his head.

Everyone was still applauding and very much impressed with the potential numbers to augment our foundation's kitty. The CPF residential home would be able to begin building within months—instead of years…as in the two we had just wasted!

I got up to walk over to my boys as they were still in shock. It was a staggering figure after all...their idea would raise millions...and this figure was just the Mini's!

First Taylor, and then Trevor, started tearing up from their emotional happiness of what they had just put into place. It wasn't surprising after all. My wife's foundations never had the support power of 347 sales locations across the U.S. to sustain the effort...this had a staggering fundraising potential given those numbers.

At this juncture, Jesse Neilson our foundation's fundraising coordinator stood up.

"Taylor and Trevor, allow me to introduce myself again, I'm Jesse Neilson; I work to raise the funds for our foundation's projects. I must tell you both that I've sat here this whole time just listening and taking all of this in. Frankly, I'm overwhelmed by the significance of it all in addition to your efforts...thank you guys.

"You know, somehow we never hit on an impulsive outside product—we never even seriously considered it...but you two did it all...in an hour—my gosh. My hat's off to both of you...really.

"Marc, obviously I'm likely going to require some of the boys time over the next few days. Once we have the folks at Mini's in the loop, I'll want a full-court press on this. I will need the boys for photographs in addition to some press interviews. I intend to go all out on this Marc—with your permission of course...and the boys' approval too naturally."

"So boys—are you two ready to sign on to this whole big thing you started today?"

"Yes Dad." I heard back.

"Alright Jess, yes it's settled then. But please try to keep it dignified for the boys' sake, will you? I really would like to avoid a media circus on this if that's possible?"

"Marc, I can understand and appreciate that...I'll do my best, but don't hold your breath boss—you know the local press all too well. Meanwhile boys, I'd like you both here tomorrow after school for photographs—is that all right?"

"Yes, Mr. Neilson, but only if Dad's okay with it first. Today we learned that when in doubt—we ask Dad first."

I got a big smile from that one, I can assure you...either they were the best listeners I had ever encountered...or I was too gullible for my own good!

"No problem boys, thank you...you have my permission.

"Great—thanks boss. Boys please wear jackets and ties for tomorrow, okay?"

"Yes sir."

"Okay everyone, before we leave this for the afternoon, we should finish our estimates. Lucie, do you have a final figure yet for the coffee and the other convections?"

"Yes Marc. It's conservative too—five million, two hundred thousand dollars more annually. That's a total of over twenty-eight million annually sir...great job boys!"

"All right everyone, I guess we've got this wrapped. And soon, we'll be able to build a nice eight million dollar home for some real nice folks."

The meeting adjourned after a last minute decision to feature our Blue Mountain Jamaican Special Reserve coffee exclusively at the Dessert Court. It allowed us to stop worrying about our profit as a consideration, but instead, to focus on building another super seller for the Crusade...we'd even feature it prominently.

After our meeting broke up, everyone came up to the boys who were still a little overwhelmed by the larger final number their crusade would raise annually. They all personally congratulated them with handshakes and a few hugs from the ladies.

The boys and I left the office after the boys had spent a little more time in the General Store reviewing everything once again.

CHAPTER 2

▼

MY TWIN SAVIORS—WHO WOULD HAVE EVER THOUGHT?

WE WALKED INTO THE HOUSE, where the boys went straight to the kitchen to tell Mom, Gracie, and Sofia the news along with the report of their first day in school.

…"And Gram, you really made Dad's offices look great".

"Thank you Trevor, it's nice to hear that…it was fun for me too…but I'm more impressed with what you two came up with today for your Father. I can't wait to go into Bakersfield to be the first one there to buy a cone. I want you to make sure you have Dad call me the day before that restaurant gets their stand—okay?"

"Yes Gram, sure, but it's called a kiosk and you can't really eat Minis in a cone."

"Oh, then whatever way you eat it—thank you Taylor. And how exactly do you spell kiosk—dear?"

"I don't remember Gram; dang, I'm just the idea kid—jeeze."

We all certainly had a great laugh with that zinger.

"Gram, do you and Gramps really have to leave tomorrow? Taylor and I want you to be here when we get photographed."

"You know boys; let me run it by your Gramps. If we can leave later, we'll be there—alright?"

"Yes Gram—but thank you even if you can't stay."

"Your welcome Taylor, now I would suggest you two hit your books. You mentioned you had homework so I'm confident your Father will want to check it later. Sofia, when did you say dinner will be ready?"

"In an hour Mrs. Morgan, maybe an hour, fifteen."

"Alright—I guess I'll go find his highness to see if we can leave later—has anyone seen Mal lately?"

"Yes Marilyn, I have."

"Well Grace?"

"Marilyn, he's washing his new truck—I'm afraid it's becoming a daily ritual!"

Grace was laughing heartily while the words were coming out of her mouth.

"Again? Christ, Grace—what on earth should I do with that man of mine?"

"In my opinion Marilyn, cherish him, he's a bloody sweetheart."

"Grace that was sweet—but we can't be speaking of the same man?"

"We most certainly are Marilyn."

"Alright dear, you've made your point. I guess I'll mosey on out to his highness, the cherished sweetheart right now…see ya."

Mom found Dad by the Navigator on the driveway. You could see the look of utter disgust on her face seeing him washing the truck—yet again as I moseyed on out to meet them.

"Mal dear, the boys have asked us to be with them tomorrow afternoon for some photographs, we'd need to leave later—can we afford to leave Jake to himself a little longer? I also realize it will mean you not being able to wash the truck for that much longer of a time…can you deal with that?"

"Cute Marilyn, but yes, that's fine. When I spoke to Jake earlier he was doing fine…very much enjoying his time away from you! Fleming's just told me about the wonderful news—damn I'm so proud of them."

"Great Malcolm, so instead of making love to this stupid Lincoln constantly, why don't you go on upstairs to tell them to their faces?"

"You know what Mar—I will…I'll do it right now in fact. Son, carry on in my absence, will you?" What could I do, I kept quiet, nodded my head instead as I started drying the fender while dad took off leaving me with holding the chamois…literally.

"Marc, thank you so much son, you've created an SUV monster…this damn Navigator is his new mistress…I hope you're satisfied now?"

"I'm sorry Mom, are you really upset at me over giving you guys the truck?"

"No, of course not son—it has made your father and I both very happy— well mostly him. But he's a real pill when it comes to obsessing over something like a new car. You know, just like the vines and casks back home…it's—all, or nothing with your Father apparently—as he has no 'in between'."

"Yeah, he is a little obsessive, isn't he?"

"Look son, he's not nuts if that's what you're driving at, but he definitely has his moments?"

"Marc, I'm going back in to watch the news before dinner, see you inside."

"Okay mom."

Later that evening after dinner, the boys were still on their homework, which was extensive due to them starting mid-semester. All of the adults were talking on the patio. I noticed at one point that Gracie and Fleming were clandestinely holding hands under the patio table as I got up to catch a glimpse…instantly I thought of Miranda and I, in that one moment. Dad now interrupted my thoughts.

"Marilyn, since everything is fine back home, how long do you want to prolong going back?"

"Gee Mal, I'm flattered. I thought I was only getting a short reprieve of a few hours?"

"No dear, but how long do you want to continue to impose on our boy, here?"

"Malcolm, I'd hardly call a visit from us an imposition?"

"Yes Dad, I'd have to agree with Mom on that—I'm always honored by your visits."

"Son, it's getting real smelly in here what with all that bullshit you're throwing around…stop it now, or I'll really patronize you."

Everyone was laughing at Dad's comment.

"You know Dad; I've got a good mind to prove that statement wrong by not letting you and Mom ever leave. You know—I've called my real estate agent to begin a search for a new home. Pop, as far as I'm concerned, I'm already increasing the size naturally—so you and Mom can just move right on in too. Hell, you've got your grandsons now…so don't you have some catching up to do…weren't you always bitching about not having any? You know Dad, if you'd ever consider giving up the winery for retirement—you and Mom could be doing a whole lot worse?"

It was amazing to me, but somehow Dad had just ignored my entire heartfelt offer by instead focusing on the financial side of my comment. He was honestly unbelievable at times.

"Son, why on earth would you be looking to sell this wonderful home—I can't believe you sometimes? I'd think this palace would satisfy you to no end, it's an absolute showplace…not to mention that I didn't see your Mother for three whole months while she decorated it…did I ever thank you for that vacation by the way?" Before I could respond to his crack, Mom beat me to the punch.

"You know Malcolm, people have died for speaking so ill of someone."

As the two of them sat there and steamed a little, I chose to comment myself:

"This house does satisfy me Dad, but—only me! Haven't you noticed what's missing in this wonderful neighborhood of mine?"

"I have Marko, there's not a single child within four streets. I worry about the boys having friends." Sofia commented—clearly concerned for her new charges too.

"Bingo Sofe, you're absolutely right...see Dad."

"So you're giving this all up—just so the boys can have a few more kids close by?"

"Right Dad. While I was in England with the boys, it became crystal clear to me just how my sons treasured their many friends, including those among the assorted forty or so kids of the staff that were living directly on the Manor grounds. Given that—don't you think that it's the appropriate thing to do for them? Isn't that what you would do for me at their age—under similar circumstances...Grandpa?"

"Hell son, I'd like to think I would—but then again it seems like such a big sacrifice now...I love this place."

"Marilyn, what do you think honey?"

"I see Marc's point dear—but I'm still thinking about what he said just prior to that...I'm shocked that you're not thinking about it as well!"

"Mar, you're not seriously considering giving up the winery—are you?"

"Honey, ask yourself that question, because I know exactly how I feel about it already."

"Really Marilyn, how?"

"Malcolm, were not getting any younger—well Lord knows—you aren't anyway (and Mom laughed at her own crack). I don't know Mal, wouldn't you enjoy being here everyday to watch your grandsons grow into men? After all honey—we didn't have them for their first eleven years—so somehow I know that I desperately want this."

"Jesus, Marilyn, you are serious—aren't you?"

"Yes dear, I suppose I am. I'll admit though, that until Marc mentioned it, I had never even stopped to think about it once—isn't that odd?"

"Do you really want to consider it Marilyn, because if you do—I guess I'm okay with it too? You know, I'm thinking about something Cedric said to me too, come to think of it. He said that the twins were not only his source of pleasure and pride...they were his salvation too. God, how that man loved his Grandsons.

"You know honey, we could probably get a nice price now for both the land and the business especially given the fact that nearly all of our production goes to Verandas. That gives the business a strong bottom line with even greater marketability. Marc, if we were willing to entertain your wonderful offer, would we be able to count on Verandas' continued business for the buyer for at least the foreseeable future?"

"Dad, that's an easy question. As our house selections, your varietals are already our best sellers—you know that. They're very popular so they garner great compliments along with high repeats from even our most discriminating guests. I would be willing to extend our contract for another five years, as long as the quality and everything else is maintained. If that would help you out in your decision—I'm all for it…just let Eric look over anything before you agree to it on our behalf."

"Yes son—of course I would. Well, I guess that we'll give all of this some serious consideration. Thank you again son, I apologize if you took my normal concerns on this decision to mean I didn't appreciate your very kind offer."

"Believe me Pop, you're the one who should be thanked, I've never seen you so accommodating to Mom's wishes before."

"Son, I'd love to say you're right—so that I can blame it all on Mom's wishes—but I'd be less than honest if I did that. You see son, like Cedric, I'm crazy about my boys' Marc…I love them beyond life itself—that's the truth of it. Just knowing we were leaving in the morning, already had me torn up bad."

"Listen Dad, if it makes you feel any better, the feeling is definitely mutual. The boys made a point of telling me how upset they were that you and Mom were already leaving us."

"Really Marc—no BS?"

"No sir, not a drop—they really do worship you guys. Of course I can relate to that. Think about what I left behind in England a dozen years ago, because I didn't have you two around either?"

Christ, that did it; on the spot my Dad lost it. He needed to excuse himself immediately as he was too embarrassed in front of all of us to show how much my comment alone, had touched him. My Mother taking this cue—excused herself as well, I think to go to him,—but she wasn't in much better shape herself.

"Marc?"

"Yes Gracie."

"If it wasn't impossible, I would somehow make you mine—you are one hell of a son." She immediately got up, wrapped me into those arms of hers, and squeezed me no end. After several seconds along with a couple of kisses, she released me as she returned to her new squeeze sitting at the table.

"Thank you Gracie—but honestly—every word of that was sincere."

"Yes Marc, of course it was—that's why it affected me so. And obviously it wasn't lost on your Mum and Dad either—was it?"

"No Grace, I guess not."

"Now, what about this new house Love—are we still going to have room for Suzie? I took your suggestion and asked her to move in with me…I love her company so."

"Yes, of course Gracie."

"Loverly, that's great then—it's all settled."

I excused myself as I left the three staff members there to chat. I noticed that Fleming had finally warmed up to Sofia apparently, as they were all in a very animated conversation as I was leaving.

I thought it was an excellent time to check on the boys in reference to their homework. They were working on the last of it as I came in.

"Hi Dad, we're finally almost done, there was so much to do."

"I'm sure of that, anything you need help with?"

"No sir."

"Alright then, so may I check what all you've got finished?"

"Sure…knock yourself crackers Dad." Trevor got out as his reply.

They preceded to hand me a mountain of paperwork—well actually two identical mountains, as I started right in on checking it over for the next several minutes.

They had done pretty darn well…but not perfect. I pointed out some errors on Taylor's math, along with a few spelling and math errors on Trevor's to correct.

Once they finished fixing these errors, they returned to their Geography, which they had almost done now. Taylor seemed particularly interested in this subject; it showed in his thoughtful work that I reviewed, as it was perfect.

After they finished, it was already nine-fifteen. So much for some free time before bed. I suggested that they bathe quickly and get to sleep.

"Dad, while we're in the spa tub, could you pick out what you want us to wear tomorrow for Jesse?"

"Sure thing Trev."

I went into their closet, returning with their old school uniforms from England.

"Dad?"

"Yes Trevor?"

"Would we be bragging too much if we told our friends about what happened today?"

"Honestly Trevor—maybe. You need to realize that many of your new friends simply can't relate to what happened today…hell even I'm still shaking my head over it a little. Besides that Trev, all of your classmates are just getting to know you too, so you don't want them to see either of you as braggarts… or worse, do you?"

"No sir."

"That's the right answer son. The both of you need to realize that many of your friends' Moms or Dads, don't run or own their own companies either—but work for others instead…like when I worked for Grandfather or at Toonland. So, if you really want to share some of it with them that will be fine, but less is best in this situation—don't go overboard into every single detail—all right?"

"Okay Dad, thanks."

"No problem T-1—anything else?"

"I want to know something Dad?"

"Okay Taylor—shoot?"

"It's simple, but just the same, I've got to know the truth Daddy—the whole truth."

"Alright Taylor, but last I checked—I haven't ever lied to either one of you—have I?"

"Well—maybe not lie Daddy, but there was stuff you didn't say when you could have. I understand better from our argument about them, but that's not what I mean. I guess what I need to know is—was what happened today—really what happened? I mean, were you just trying to make us feel good about ourselves?"

"No T-man, not at all. You know son, I am a little bit surprised at you with your question here. After all, wasn't it you who asked to help 'me' with my problem? Wasn't it you and Trevor that came up with the Minis idea after I explained our problem? Did I ever suggest or mention that first? Moreover, I didn't suggest the ticket or the kiosks either—so get real here kid—this was all you and your brother's idea—so don't doubt any of it son.

"And sure, I wanted to build your confidence up a little by having you make the presentation…but that was it. Yet all the same son—it was you up there—doing all of it, not anyone else. I wasn't pulling the strings on some puppet…was I? Those weren't my words coming out of your mouth either."

"I am damn proud of both of you…which is the God's honest truth about it. Yet because of what happened today, we'll all get to see a bona fide miracle by this time, next year…won't we? When all of those good folks at Cerebral Palsy will get to move into their new home…with you two boys to thank for all of it! Could I say that—if they were still waiting on me and my staff to be looking for the solution, after beginning our third year of trying?

"Now, I've said it all…with all of that—the whole truth, yet nothing but the truth—so help me God".

"Great—now I really feel good about what we've done."

"Jesus son, I hope to heck you do T-man, because you two are very precious to me…but not just from what happened today.

"You two will soon see how much everyone else appreciates what you've come up with, believe me. You may not even like all the attention you'll be getting soon enough, so let me tell you that right now, too."

"What do you mean Dad—what attention?"

"It's real simple Trev, when the press release hits on Wednesday, you two are going to be inundated for at least a week by the press for one, which is not fun under any circumstances—remember I've been there. As a result of all the publicity—in a way your lives will never be quite the same again."

"They won't—how so Dad?"

"Look Taylor, let me give you just one example of how your lives will be different. Let's just take your friends as an example for the moment. Your friends won't treat you quite the same for a while—but let me explain why. You see, you're going to be in the news, on TV, plus maybe in some of our local magazines…your friends are simply going to treat you differently as a result. Your friends won't exactly know how they should act around you for a while, either. Heck, they may even be afraid to talk to you at all initially—see what I mean boys?"

"Yes Dad, I understand that, but you know what?" Trevor asked.

"What son?"

"If things do get a little loopy, we'll just tell them we're the same two guys we were last week. Will that help?"

"Yes honey, sure it will help. As we've discussed already, I personally think the less you say about it—the better. Just warn them that things might get a little crazy when all of this gets out. Maybe after you remind them that you're both still the same guys, maybe you can nip it all in the bud before it starts…or blame it all on me if that helps, but only do that with your friends, not the press.

"Let me warn you both right now though, Las Vegas' journalists usually eat these kinds of stories up—they love them. They are going to be all over you two, like flies to horse poop for a while—so try to get used to it. And as a National company, we do business in all fifty states, so the publicity might be more widespread. And boys, if that happens, just wait and see what the national press is capable of doing to all of us."

"What will they do Dad?"

"They'll pester us a lot son…they will do that to perfection."

"Oh, well as long as they don't say something bad Daddy, Mummy's foundation always worried about that too. And no one had better say anything bad about my Daddy, if they know what's good for them."

"Gee, thank you Taylor—that actually makes me feel somewhat better about it. I have no doubt you mean business—after all I've seen you in action before, along with the sore hand I had to prove it for about five hours." I started laughing, as did Taylor.

"Natch, Daddy…but my arse hurt for two days—so let's not worry about your poor little hand…okay?"

"What are you talking about Tay?"

"Oh nothing Trev, just the little argument Dad and I had over not telling us sooner about Grandfather."

"You mean—Dad clobbered your bum over that?"

"Go ahead T-man, spill it to your brother, he's entitled to know—isn't he?"

"Yes Trev—Daddy paddled my bare arse hard, he really did."

"I don't believe it—Dad, did you really?"

"Afraid so Trev…still love me?" I asked in mock fear.

"Sure I do, yeah—I mean yes, but I can't believe it. I just didn't think you would ever spank us?"

"Why not Trevor, I think I'm kind of good at it now."

"Ah bro, trust me—he's very good at doing it." Taylor was laughing now.

"And you had to pull your pants down and everything Tay?"

"Well actually Trev, Dad kind of helped with that too." Now I was laughing as well.

"Oh this is just too much, are you guys really telling me this is all true—promise?"

"Yes Trev, every word of it, didn't you notice how I was walking after that argument?"

"No, I didn't bro, but alright, if that's what happened, then it did…but I really can't believe it though, I just can't."

"Listen you two, you're still not even in the tub, where speaking of which, the water isn't even started yet. Sorry guys, but you can forget the baths as it's already too late an hour—you two better just get in the shower instead."

"Oh Dad, do we have to, we really prefer the spa tub?"

"Yes, y o u h a v e to, now get those bums in there before I decide to practice up on my whooping skills—some more!"

I did not have to say it twice, at least not for Trevor. You could tell he was sincerely shocked by this revelation from Taylor. There he was, naked as a jaybird in no time flat…it was a new sense of urgency in his desire to please me. How lovely I thought.

After their quick shower, I got the boys in bed as I said good night.

I returned downstairs to find my folks waiting patiently for me.

"My God, guys—you look like a couple on a mission, what's on your minds? Not that I can't guess?"

"We just need to talk Morgans to Morgan, son." Dad answered.

"All right—shoot, have you decided then?"

"Pretty much, yes Marc, we have." My Dad added.

"Okay, so what's the verdict, do the boys and I get the pleasure of your permanent company or not?"

"Yes, we think so, but we do have reservations."

"Reservations—for where Mom, Palm Springs for the weekend?"

Dad and I were busting, while Mom was not the slightest bit amused? Just the same, I was already thrilled deep within me—the folks would be coming back for good.

"Markie, do I need to slap you silly, or are you going to get serious of your own accord?"

"Alright Mom, sorry—but you did set yourself up pretty good with that… you have to admit?"

"I don't have to admit kaka…I'm your Mother—son…that's all the admission I will ever need."

"Okay Mom, sorry for my insensitivity. I can see you're not in the mood."

"You're damn right—I'm not in the mood, this is serious Marc. Daddy and I are in our fifties now; we don't take anything this serious as a joke. Certainly not with turning our lives upside down—again, at our ages."

"Fair enough Mom…you make an excellent point, so what are your concerns?"

"First dear, the issue is you and your future life. What happens when you find someone new to love—what then? You know dear, it is hard enough selling a woman on two instant kids—let alone two live-in, in-laws. In addition, years from now, can't you image us dear, leaving our dentures out in the open from the onset of senility? Oh and did I mention, adding 'Depends' to the household's weekly shopping list?"

I was simply busting from my mother's hysterical, yet candid comments. Finally I composed enough to respond.

"You know Mom, if you're concerned about that, I will not negate your point—you do make a valid argument. In most houses of second marriages, it could prove to be an issue. But in my situation frankly, it's more likely to be a non-issue altogether."

"How so Marc? Are you trying to convince us you'll never fall in love again? You know, if that were true, I would feel very sad for you indeed, son?"

"Not at all Mom, that's not what I'm saying—I mean that I know myself all too well. You see, if I were ever to fall in love again, it could only be with a certain type of woman. One with a similar personality and near identical values or traits as Miranda's—it's that simple. As such, this woman would likely feel the same way as Miranda, in this very situation. Which is to say, she'd be perfectly comfortable with having you two right here with us. In fact, if she was truly like Miranda, she would be promoting the idea herself... wouldn't she?"

"What do you say to that Marilyn?"

"I say that Marc makes a pretty good point. I can clearly see his logic—he's right. How about you Malcolm?"

"I was going to say the exact same thing, almost to the letter."

"Great! One down and one to go, so what's your other concern Mom?"

"Marc, this one is easier. I'm just curious as to the timing of all this, assuming we're going to do it. I think Dad and I would prefer to wait until after the next harvest before listing everything for sale...we might put out a feeler or two just to see if the market exists right now. But, if it should sell quickly, where do we go until you have room for us in the new house?"

"You know Mom, I'd like to think I get my 'smarts' from both of you, but I can see that you're in a league by yourself."

"Quit the corn dear...answer my question."

"Gee guys; wouldn't you enjoy an extended stay at Aunt June's house?"

I was laughing so hard—it was a good thing I was. However, the look on Mom's face could stop a freight train instantly on its tracks with that suggestion, I can assure you. After I composed, Mom started losing her frown the size of Texas—so I continued. You see, my Mom could also tell I was stalling.

"Look guys, I have a little confession to make. Before I tell you about it though, please consider my reasoning. I wanted to avoid upsetting either one of you because it may seem a little extravagant on its face, but frankly, I don't care.

"I know that both of you know the value of earning a buck and saving it, especially you Dad. Honestly, I have no financial problems after all, so how I spend my money is really my business alone. I would have to seriously screw up, to lose one tenth of what I have working in the markets alone, so remember that.

"Okay—here's the deal. I own another very nice home here, but up on Mount Charleston that I use as a local winter getaway. I also have a houseboat moored at Lake Mead which I naturally focus on during the summer. There—now you know the truth...hey, so I'm not a total spendthrift.

"Now that you know, depending upon the time of year you make your move, you'll have your choice—of my two other homes."

My father of course was silent; he just sat there deep in thought… pondering my wasteful ways no doubt. Mom on the other hand, at least was a little more animated over this news.

"Okay son that works for me—so which one of these homes do you prefer to put us in if necessary?"

"I really don't have a preference Mom, but you probably will, once you see them. If its winter when you get here, the cabin is wonderful with all the snow and clean mountain air. You'll love the scenery Ma; it's a winter wonderland up there, fit for a Johnny Mathis Christmas album, while the view is priceless at nearly twelve thousand feet."

"Alright, then its decided, right Malcolm?"

"Marilyn, what does one man need with three homes in the same general area? I mean, I can understand Marc's B&B in Maui—that's a true vacation home along with being a write off business. But these two other homes are here in the same area—which just doesn't make sense to me, sitting vacant, and having no income."

"Malcolm, don't you dare start something with your son over anything so immaterial—shut up and simply answer the damn question."

"Alright—yes we're decided…satisfied Mar? Son, I want to talk to you some more on this subject later on though—this just seems unlike you."

"Mal there's nothing to discuss. Our son is a multi-millionaire; who lives a relatively modest lifestyle considering that. Most people in his position live a much higher life…besides it is his business how he spends his money…not ours."

"You know what Marilyn; you're absolutely right about that. After all, they're all investments anyway—in town or otherwise. Forgive me son, it's just that our folks lived during the depression…which you don't easily forget. They instilled in me a very conservative approach to spending money—it was the same for Mom, so I'm told. I can't blame them for that, nor should I question your spending—who am I, after all—Milton Freedman?"

"Dad, that's mighty big of you—I appreciate you not lacing into me, but let me add something more. I earn just enough vacation rental income on these two homes to be able to deduct them as rental property legally—so they're really a business tax shelter loss, which at least lessens my tax burden. By being super strict in whom I rent them to, its works out to less than a month each year they're rented out. Beyond that, the overhead on my current lifestyle merely uses twenty-four percent of strictly my interest and growth earnings annually. I never touch any of my salary and bonuses—they go straight into my portfolio, pension, charities, or Uncle Sam. In short Pop, at this point in my life—I am not exactly hurting…you know."

"That's comforting son; it seems you haven't forgotten anything I've taught you then about how to manage your money…have you?"

"No sir I haven't. I have less than one percent of my assets that are non-performing at the moment…these two houses included."

"Good boy—so tell me more."

"Malcolm, it's none of our business so don't pry—what's the matter with you?"

"Dear, I'm not prying; I'm just interested in general. I like to hear Marc express how proficiently he handles his money, along with the responsibility he takes for overseeing and protecting it. It's not an easy job Marilyn; after all, he must have a large booty to manage now."

"Yes Dad I do, close to nine hundred and eighty million of them including the real estate."

"My God, Marc—you've got to be joking?"

"No Mom, I'm not. But I will say this—if all goes to plan, I'll crest a net worth of ten figures sometime early in 2002.

"Well you see Malcolm; you finally dragged it out of him—congratulations…your son is nearly a billionaire—are you satisfied now?"

"No Mar, I'm proud of him. Marc is not only my hero—he's my captain—which he already knows…I could give him another billion reasons besides these!"

"Thanks Dad, you know that always chokes me up when you call me Captain, not to mention everything else you said too."

"And every word of it is true son, now come here—I need a Morgan hug."

As I genuinely hugged my Father—I added what he really wanted to hear in the first place:

"I love you Dadio."

"Me too son." Dad got out through his ever-growing tears.

"Listen guys, since we have this issue all settled—why not turn in…I'm going to?"

"Yes—we are too, Marc, but I think something this special, calls for a toast."

Mom took off, but mere moments later it seemed—she returned to our table and conversation.

"Jeeze Mom, that was certainly quick."

"Yes, I thought so too, honey…but Markie, we need to get a little serious here-for a moment."

"Sure Mom, what?"

Mom then placed a beautifully crafted, pine wine box before me, meant

to hold a single bottle. I stared at the printing on the top of it silently now…
my eyes filling with tears already.

"Son, why don't you open the box."

"Okay Dad."

I opened the box where my eyes fell upon its contents. I eased the beautiful
hand painted bottle out of the wooden vessel to read its lavender label…that
was her favorite color. I read out loud the bottle's words while still shocked
and choked up.

Morgan Winery

Commemorative Private Cellar Issue

Presenting

'Miranda's Magic'

Rare California Port

Aged Ten Years

From The Personal Cellar of Mal and Marilyn Morgan

Bottle Number 001 of 240

I knew instantly where this idea originated from. Mom had made it clear
back in England after all, that something of this significance would happen
one day. Here it was in the flesh, so I was snowed under at that moment as
I struggled to get my words out. Jesus, it was simply overwhelming for its
sentiment and deep honor it held for both Miranda and me.

"Oh Mom, Dad, I just don't have the words, I'm sorry."

I started bawling softly on the spot…it didn't take long for me to have
company either. Once we had gathered our composure some, Mom spoke to
me.

"Now baby, read the neck-tie card—go ahead honey, I think it says it
best."

In matching lavender to the label, its front cover simply said 'Miranda's
Magic'. I opened it up to begin reading it; it was beautiful in its simplicity
yet elegant. It began:

Throughout one's life, you meet many people. Some good, those that
want to be, while still others—that haven't a clue.

Then there are others, that rare person, who touch you and affect your life
and you're never the same again…these are the magical few.

And so it was for me, when I met—my Miranda.

No other woman, before or since, has ever touched me more so, than
she. How can I describe her magic to you—for what now remains is only a
wonderful memory—yet one so beautiful.

My memory begins with a charming and young English schoolgirl, blossoming into womanhood when I first met her in her fourteenth year. Later, I watched as she became a beautiful, stunning bride as she married my only son—forever becoming my daughter, not merely in name, but in love too.

And my memories include unfulfilled hopes and dreams, but with undying love at its core that affects you profoundly. Miranda knew about selfless sacrifice and courage—her last twelve years of life proved nothing less than a personification of both.

Finally, it is about the lasting love, my daughter felt for her husband and their twin sons...that I feel and carry for her—every day—forever. And the hope that one day, my eyes might look upon her grace and beauty once more, when I too, am called home."

Rest well Baby

Love You,

Mommy

I had to stop—I couldn't go on with reading more just yet. It was such a moving tribute after all. This was hitting me at my core—I was truly losing control of my emotions now. After another few minutes, I was able to finish by reading the short bio.

This was on the closing pages and closely mirrored the inscriptions on our planes. Additional tears followed as I finished.

"Mom, Dad, I am so deeply moved and touched by this acknowledgment, that all I can say is thank you both—it came as such a surprise, no wonder I'm bawling buckets." As I now gave them both kisses and hugs again.

"Honey, there's a little bit more to this. We plan to auction the second half of the two hundred and forty bottles off on the Internet...our sources tell us that this auction is going to go viral in collectors' circles with this exceptional Porto. Dad and I have decided that all of the proceeds will go to Miranda's Centre and her foundations equally."

"Jeeze Mom, that's wonderful too, thank you."

"You're more than welcome honey. We are giving you bottles two and three for the boys to always have. And numbers four through eight go to Grace, Fleming, Sofia, and Cousin Beth. I'm sending nine to June and number ten will go to Uncle Teddy. Cousin Andrew gets eleven, while twelve we insist on giving to your driver Paul. The rest will stay in your cellar awaiting your discretion."

"Wow—I know they're all going to appreciate the sentiment—thank you Mom, thanks Dad."

"You're most welcome son. I think Jake did an excellent job with our directives, don't you?"

"Most definitely Dad, I'll call tomorrow to thank him personally."

"He'll appreciate that, he really did us proud with how this came out I think."

Mom then opened a non-commemorative bottle of the same rare port as we all drank in near silence...Mom was right, I'd never had better Porto. Before we knew it, we were all ready for bed.

"Good night dear."

"Night Mom, Dad—I can't begin to tell you both how you have touched me with all of this. And naturally your decision has made me incredibly happy too...think how excited the boys will be when they hear?"

"Yes, but your Mom and I feel the same way Marc, so thank you as well."

After parting hugs along with a kiss to each, we bid each other a nice evening before retiring.

I went to my desk to give my emails one last look before turning in. I nearly collapsed in my chair when I saw it...oh, my frigging God—he found me. There it was—a new email from Vic Tremmers! Now how in the hell did he get my email? This guy was turning out to be quite a Lt. Colombo with his persistence. As I read his email it eventually made sense, but certainly not at first.

"Hey Marc, well how the hell are you? It's been too long a spell. No, I ain't pulling' your lariat—it's really me. Shit—I feel like I've already reconnected with you through this here email...ain't this a hoot?"

Great, I thought to myself. This is keeping him at bay? His next sentence though, really sent me over the edge of reason.

"I can't believe the legs on your boys and girls...when I saw them; I knew I had to get my hands on them, right then and there."

My boys—and girls? What in hell is this poor fool talking about? I don't remember him being this sick. And frankly, he was starting to scare me. Happily, his next comment straightened me out though, as it also assuaged away some of my concerns.

"You see Marc; I've been horsing around with you. I saw your team of Belgian Warm Bloods being unloaded at the airport—I couldn't believe how magnificent a team they were...I guess money will buy you everything...you truly have the finest Belgian team in the United States from what I have seen. As you'll recollect, I've trained Belgians and every other breed along with their riders, off and on for years.

"After any length of separation, I always find myself missing them some. I guess it's the atmosphere around these horses, their spirit, and even their smells if you can believe it. Don't ask me how, but I connect to them. So, as

I said, I've been training horses and I was down at the airport picking up my gear from my last job. It happens as you know already, that I'm between jobs again…shit, it sucks. So you can understand why I had to find out who owned these beauties…I hope you don't mind. I snuck a peak at their Manifest and picked up your name…shit, I almost choked on my upper plate.

"Listen, if you don't have a trainer, or have never thought of them competing, I sure would like to talk to you about it. Just hear what I have to say first—then make your decision. You see Marc; I also work with many local handicapped and disabled kids. These challenged youngsters are a blast. They are Tireless-Always Ready-Daring-Super staffers. Or as I like to call them: T.A.R.D.S. for short. Helping them learn to ride these loving horses in my off hours is a Godsend for me. And it's great therapy for both the ponies and the 'tards'. Yeah—they all seem to like it a lot. Bet you didn't know I have a cousin whose retarded? He's also a blast to be with…he loves to get drunk with me! Remind me to tell you about it some time.

"Let me know what you think of my idea. If nothing comes of it, at least we got to reconnect.

"Alright, I got to get off this here computer at the library, so I'm gonna go. I left all of my contact information below.

Your old friend,

Vic.

Oh joy—my long-lost friend! I thought to myself. But then it hit me—this could almost remain a painless reunion. If I hired him to train the Belgians, rather than for supervising our packaging employees, it would have to be in Logandale for the foreseeable future…that wouldn't be so bad—I could handle that. So I would have Robbie contact him tomorrow to set something up for next week…but now, I just wanted to get some sleep.

Chapter 3

▼

The Boys Settle In

The following morning, I dropped the twins off at school with them looking sharp, let me tell you.

I got back into Laverne where I began to open up my email to begin working, with one from Eric at the top position. Damn, he certainly wasted scant time. Apparently the Minis Distributors in California, Katy and Bob, Nethery, were very agreeable to help us in any way possible. To begin with, they would be able to start us up with serving freezers and kiosks for our first fifteen units. They were agreeable to a sponsorship of leasing us another 332 kiosks with freezers and storage with our long-term commitment for product. As Eric said so succinctly in closing his email—we could not possibly ask for a more workable and fair supplier.

When I arrived at the office, I found several memos on the project already sitting on my desk. The depth of the work contained in them, illustrated that many of my staff had obviously worked all night showing great company dedication. That said it all; everyone was indeed excited to have this problem behind us with a workable solution moving forward…finally. I was very impressed with their personal commitments to getting the endeavor launched successfully, as soon as possible now.

I read everything through—approving it all with only minimal changes here and there.

I went through my appointments with Robbie, then asked him to set up an appointment with Vic Tremmers for the following week along with cancelling his appeal process with our HR.

All in all, I had a very productive day. Right at 3:20, Jesse asked for a minute of my time.

"I asked Paul to call me, Marc, when the boys were close to being here. They are now about two minutes away. While the photographer is setting up, is there anything else I should know?"

"Yes, just one. Jess—the boys invited their grandparents down here for the photos. I think they have it in their minds to get some photos taken with them for their personal use.

"No problem…oh Marc, I almost forgot—you'll have tomorrow's press release by five, in your email for your approval, along with the media kits."

"Great Jess, have fun with the boys, but tell them they both owe me hugs." He left in high spirits…hell he should.

As I got through my remaining appointments along with the remaining issues of the day, I worked at a feverish pace until I was interrupted by my intercom's buzz.

"Marc, Natalie Garson on two."

"Thanks Robbie."

"Hey Natalie, give me some great news girlfriend—because I've had a great week so far—hell, I think I'm on a frigging roll."

"You are? Well, I guess that it's just going to keep getting better because I do have some excellent news—over all."

"What do you mean—over all Natalie?"

"Over all Marc, in the sense that finding a resale is definitely out of the question my friend. I wasn't able to find anything that came close to your requirements once I entered 'family neighborhood' into the equation."

"Well obviously, you also have some better news, so spill it Garson."

"Alright—Morgan, here it is in a nutshell. I found you the most incredible building lot in the entire west valley, no exaggeration. In as much as it is in that fabulous family-laden neighborhood known as Section 10, with all mature and newer custom homes on huge parcels of one half acre and up. The street it's on is beautifully lined with expansive trees and greenery. I've confirmed that the surrounding neighborhood is loaded with kids out the kazoo—many between ten and thirteen. And get this—it has an existing smaller home with stables already there, should you want to move in immediately.

"Now here's the best part Marc—it's five acres, so you've met that criterion."

"Jesus, Natalie, it sounds perfect—but it almost sounds like it's the Saint Cloud Stables?"

"It is—the Saint Cloud Stables, Marc."

"You're kidding me—Kathy's selling?"

"You know Kathy?"

"Shit, doesn't everybody who's owned a horse in this town at one time or another?"

"Gee, I never realized you knew about the place—so are you still interested then?"

"Are you kidding, of course I am Natalie? At this very moment, I'm spending over three grand a month boarding my team of Belgian Warm Bloods in Logandale."

"I had no idea you were still into horses Marc, I assumed all of the cars were your method to wean off of the ponies. Maybe you should continue to operate the stables then…they have one hell of an operating cash-flow of over one hundred and forty thousand per year?"

"Wow! Look Natalie, I've been in and out of horses for the last ten years or so…but I'll have to think on that. My Belgians though, are prize jumpers worth a small fortune. They were a behest from my late father-in-law, so some day I look forward to passing on their off spring to my boys.

"Kathy's property would be perfect for me. I could take my time deciding on how to best utilize the property, or just jump right in. Most important though, I could rebuild the stables with air-cooling for the summer months for my Belgians—they can't normally take our heat. Damn this is perfect. Natalie—you are good—lady.

"Calm down Marc, you haven't heard her asking price yet?"

"Damn Natalie, how high is it?"

"Honestly Marc, it is an excellent price for the acreage's size, but it is a sobering figure just the same…there aren't many five acre residential parcels left in the heart of town, as you know."

Natalie gave me the price to mull over now. After I recovered from the shock, I told her to start writing. She took my opening figure and wrote up an offer close enough to Kathy's asking price, so as not to insult her. It offered Kathy a contract with no contingencies, yet our dollar amount would still shake her up…just a smidge. Natalie said she would fax over the papers to sign and then present the offer later that afternoon as we then hung up.

I was really in euphoria now. First, the property offered me almost unlimited potential to build whatever kind of style of home I desired. Best of all, without a Homeowners Association to agree or disagree with my plans, especially on the lagoon—I would finally be in charge of what I wanted… and not my neighbors or HOA. I could finally do as I pleased without anyone having a say so in my plans, other than the building codes naturally.

Secondly, I could go all out on a single story design if I wanted too. I truly preferred single level homes, but typically found them too compromised in size. Most importantly, it was a great mature neighborhood of strictly custom homes on large, tree-covered streets—with loads of kids!

The stables were intriguing too, I could subsidize my overhead by boarding out if I desired…with Vic available for that too, even if it meant him coming to LV sooner than later. Damn, I was thrilled and truly excited—so it was only natural that I could not control or contain myself…as usual.

Oh what the hell—the heck with it…this just 'smells' right, I thought to myself.

Mr. Impulsive to the rescue, I picked up the phone to dial our corporate Architect, Milton.

I gave him my directives on the beautiful home I had built a thousand times in my mind. I instructed him to go for a Sedona style, single-level home in a compound setting, with the main residence featuring a massive, stone-accented interior courtyard. I suggested that be the main theme of the primary home, while adding several other goodies too—you know—the works. I told him to pull up the parcel via computer, as I gave him Carte Blanche to use what he wanted of the overall acreage…as long as he left the pool design for me.

I gave Milton all of my requirements for room counts, baths, garages, and casitas—as I would build two of those this time around. This would allow me maximum flexibility for my staff arrangements, as well as for the folks and occasional houseguests.

Milt asked probing questions, made a few suggestions on security and other features he recommended, but in general, seemed to like my ideas immensely.

After I had it spelled out for him, we arranged payment while he promised preliminary sketches within three weeks. I hung up; as I had to stop, just to take stock of my life at that moment…I was quite happy, indeed.

I had now finished my work, so I left my office for our small TV production studio, where I would find the boys along with the folks. When I got there, the boys asked the photographer for a break, so they could run over to me for a hug.

"Hey you two—how was it at school today—did everything go well?"

"There's so much to tell you Dad…but it all went great. Dad, can it wait because we're not done yet—we'd like to finish here first…alright?"

"Sure, do your thing; I'll wait for the report Trevor." I then joined my parents.

"So Mom, Dad, what's new—how was your day out messing around?"

"Wonderful son, we went to lunch at Mandalay Bay, where I hit a Royal for a cool thou."

"Marc I swear, you should have been able to hear your Mother screaming from right here."

"Jesus honey, so I screamed—big deal. Yet nothing could compare to the screaming that came out of those twins of yours, when we shared our moving plans with them."

"Great, I'm thrilled to hear that too—now I assume with that royal you hit, you're buying dinner tonight Mom?" I was laughing heartily.

"No Marc, sorry—I'm not. Sofia's got a wonderful dinner in the works— all of your Mexican favorites."

"Say no more Mom—you of all people know how I feel about authentic Mexican food, especially Sofia's."

"I certainly do son—I sometimes think you must have been Mexican in a previous lifetime."

"Yes Mom, if the truth be told, I'm sure I was."

"So dear, how is everything going on the boys' project? We didn't get much out of your man Jesse; he was so busy all afternoon."

"Mom, in two words it's—all good, very good actually."

"Wonderful…but that's three words. You know, Daddy and I hung around the Minis kiosk today at Mandalay Bay after lunch; we were there for over thirty-five minutes. Your Father and I started doing our own marketing research by casually talking to the people eating their Minis—it seems like a pretty basic business."

"Oh really, well that's encouraging to hear, although honestly I am still just a little bit surprised at this whole thing myself. I mean hell; I was at that kiosk with them, you'd think 'my creative light' would have gone on sooner on its own."

"Son, don't beat yourself up over it. Jesse said that your team was always focusing on toys and take-home products. You guys just overlooked the obvious, so let it go—be happy the problem's finally solved now."

"Yeah, you're right Mom…as usual, but good marketing report by the way. I guess this means I'm keeping you on the payroll for another week then?"

"We'll see about that son."

"Anything new with you dear, I mean with your day you know, otherwise? You do seem in a pretty chipper mood, come to think about it?"

"Yes Mom, I'm really excited about something myself—it's major too. I'd like to show you, instead of telling you though—if that's all right with you and Dad?"

"Sure". I heard from both of my parents.

When the boys were done with their collateral photos, I learned that they had indeed taken several with the folks too. They now indulged me to take a few shots with them as well.

Afterwards, we got into Laverne to leave, while I told Paul to take us over to Tenaya and Sahara Avenues. When he got to that intersection, I refreshed my memory on the stables location as I directed him to Laredo and Pioneer. We were soon there, so I had Paul pull over as we got out in front of the Saint Cloud Stables.

"Why are we stopping here Dad?"

"Because Trevor, I thought you two might want to have a look at the site of your future home."

"Where Daddy, all I see are those horses?"

"Exactly T-man, where all those horses are hanging around—that's the site of our new home."

"I'm confused Dad?"

"Trevor, I've put an offer in on this entire horse property so we're going to build a beautiful new estate here. We'll have room for everyone, including new stables for our Belgians just like at the Manor—isn't that great?"

"Wicked, but I thought you said Las Vegas was too hot for them Dad?"

"Yes T-1, it is normally—but not if we build new stables with special air cooling units along with lots of shade trees surrounding the stables. Naturally, I never considered building stables living in Spanish Trail, as they're not allowed anyway."

"Son, don't you mean air conditioning?"

"No Dad, I meant exactly what I said; air cooling…overly refrigerated air would kill them".

"Oh, do you mean using those old swamp coolers that everyone had before central air conditioning became prevalent?"

"That's the ticket Dad."

"You see Pop; these units use small water 'chillers' now, like one of our lobster tanks at Verandas. This variably chills the water going through the filter pads so that when the temperature climbs, the unit automatically compensates. Best of all, they keep the horses healthy, yet they can drop the temperature inside the stable almost thirty degrees. That will work beautifully for our Belgians."

"So what do you have in mind for the rest of the land honey? Since we now know you plan on stashing your Father in the tack room."

"Cute Mom, but no. Try picturing a Santa Fe style Adobe with one main level, centered around an innermost interior courtyard with the same retractable glass walls I have now. It will be a totally enclosed compound with no more stairs or elevators except for the subterranean garage and lagoon."

"A subterranean garage son—isn't that an extreme expense for a private home?"

"Not so much Dad—not for me at least, but you need to realize that I compensate Verandas for storing my cars, it's not some perk…it costs mucho dinero Papi.

"You know what Dad—just the same, I think that you personally, had better hold on to your heart; because I'm sparing no expense on this home. I'll make a prediction that this home is going to be the keeper Dad—I visualize myself growing old here. If for no other reason that I'll never be able to leave behind the pool I'm planning to create on this property.

"You see Dadio; I'll have to grade the lot for the lagoon design anyway, given that; the subterranean garage becomes practical…but for no other reason. It's like this Dad; the lower level pool requires me to go down twenty feet total. When they grade the lagoon, they'll also do the subterranean garage under the house as its foundation, so it shouldn't be too pricey, plus saving me all of my current storage costs.

"Why do you need to excavate twenty feet for the pool—you don't have that now?"

"That's right Dad…exactly. You see, the Spanish Trail architectural committee wouldn't allow it. Trust me; I've built this pool sixty four thousand times in my mind—now I'm just doing it for real.

"By setting the lower pool's surface-level at ten feet below my lot's level, I will be able to create an overall twenty-two feet height, plus an additional pool depth of ten feet in the lower pool. The twenty-two feet of height will create a sheared cliff backdrop panorama, from the highest point to the lowest surface level with three levels over all. The sheered backdrop will surround both pools and wrap around three sides of our lot, by using a corner of it."

"Wow, Dad." Came out of my boys now so I continued.

"Adding to this drama, pool guests descend down a gentle slope gradually for that ten foot drop below the lot level, exposing an unseen sandy beach entry of the lower lagoon."

By this time my Father was sweating along with turning beet red over the financial investment all of this would require. He knew that you never recoup that from a pool.

"Malcolm, for God's sake—stop panting! You know Mal—the boy can afford it…you're not writing the check—so just relax."

"Fine Marilyn, but this is way over the top…who does he think he is—Michael Jackson?" The boys laughed at this hysterically.

"Yes dear—maybe he does." Mom and I now joined in with the boys by laughing at her crack, while my Father was still not amused with any of us. I then continued to aggravate him further.

"You might find it interesting Dad, being British, that these sheared cliffs will loosely resemble the white cliffs of Dover, except I haven't decided on their color yet. Being it will be a hacienda compound, I'm leaning towards the Red Clay tones with gray and rose colored bands of color contrast.

"The over all lagoon effect should be awesome when it's complete as it will be two full size pools surrounded by the dramatic sheered cliffs that I mentioned.

"But of course!" Dad threw in sarcastically as I attempted to continue while he stood there just shaking his head…but I was undaunted.

"The upper pool of the two essentially creates a half convex crescent spillover waterfall into the lower pool which goes from ten feet deep to fanning out to the beach entry complete with waves…which also ecologically filters the entire lagoon. This is just like the rain pool I showed you in Maui at our retreat—remember Pop?

"If you say so, son."

"I say so Pop."

"The lagoon sounds brill Dad—what else is it going to have, the beach with real sand should be bloody terrif?"

"Well Trev, with cliffs twenty two feet high, rather than seven, we have much more flexibility now. That's a substantial difference boys, believe me. All the better for our special features—like our three flume slides."

"Three slides? Oh my God, I can't wait…what will they be like Daddy, do you know already?"

"Yes T-man; one slide will be at 4 feet above the water, just like the two we have now at home. But the second one will be a quick drop ten feet above the water to simulate going over a cliff. And believe me; it will feel just like you're coming out in mid air, free falling because you will be! The third one though, is the star; it will run parallel to the upper cliffs through an underground flume. It drops fast below the surface, and then gives you an aquarium view of the upper pool underwater. It will be fast as you travel all the way down and out of the cliffs above the lower pool for its finish. Trust me guys, with streaming lasers, fog, and eight hundred watts of music, everyone will love it."

"Bloody wicked Dad" I immediately heard.

"Yeah boys, I agree. And you know, I'm moving the whirlpool too. We'll have a swim up bar where our current whirlpool is, in its own grotto with a waterfall curtain. Our whirlpool in the new lagoon will be all the way up top in the upper cliffs tucked in the back next to the underwater flume slide."

"Christ son, you expect an old geezer like me to climb up twenty two feet, just to use the spa?"

"No Dad—if you don't want to climb the steps, I'll expect you to take the elevator up top."

"Oh—the elevator!" My father responded in shock.

"Now where was I boys? Oh yes, I remember now. On the front edge of the upper cliffs at 20 feet up, will be a springboard diving platform camouflaged into the outcroppings. Lastly boys, is your monkey bridge.

"A monkey bridge, what's that Dad, I've never seen one?"

"Yes you have Taylor—don't you remember you loved the one you were on at Toonland on Mystery Isle?"

"Oh my God—we're going to have one of those too, oh; this is so brill… thanks Dad. Bloody hell, I can't wait, how about you Trev?"

"Me either bro, are you kidding—all we'll need is a blooming snack bar."

"Oh, I already have that covered too boys, its part of the two story rumpus room and cabana building that will back this corner of the lot on the three walls…it's a trick of covering and hiding the lagoon from outside our compound.

"Look boys, I appreciate your thanks but remember this is my dream pool too. I've waited years to build it. I don't want you to think I'm only doing this strictly for you two—it's for the whole family's enjoyment, mine included."

"Blimey Daddy, who cares—can we charge admission?"

"Cool it T-man, let's not give your Gramps any ideas."

"Why the hell not son? It might be one way you can recoup the money you'll be sinking into this hole in the ground."

"Fine Dad, can I get you a monkey and an organ grinder too, we'll need entertainment after all?" That finally shut him up.

"Just where then on your beach, do your Father and I pitch our tent, dear—and by the way…when's high tide since you have a wave machine?"

"Funny Mom, but you two will have your own two bedroom/two bath casita with an extra lock out unit. That will have a full bedroom and bath in case you have guests; you know—like Aunt June.

"Really, well that's thoughtful of you, but don't you dare tell your Aunt about the lock out unit. Attila can just keep staying at the Motel 6 on Tropicana dear; she loves it there."

"And boys, I haven't forgotten about your other interests either."

"Are you planting us a soccer field Dad, there's room you know?"

"No T-1, that takes up too much space—but you are getting two other things I know you'll enjoy?"

"What Dad?"

"First Trev, you're getting a North/South clay tennis court. Second, you'll have a combination horse path and ATV track to ride around the parameter of the property."

"What's an ATV track Dad?"

"Well boys, that's a racing track for All-Terrain-Vehicles, or go-carts if you prefer."

"Oh my God, how bloody wicked is that, Taylor?"

"Bloody—bro."

At that moment, three boys started walking by us…before stopping to speak to us apparently. They were all around nine or ten years old, in that range. We all said hello to them. One of them decided to play spokesperson I suppose.

"Hey mister, you've got a nice limo—it's just like the one my mom rides around in sometimes."

"Thank you—so what's your name son?"

"Mordachai, but everyone calls me Mordy—but that's all the personal stuff I'm allowed to tell you mister—you are a stranger, you know."

"Sure, I understand Mordy—so do you live around here?"

"Yeah—sure do, but like I said, I'm not allowed to tell you where—remember mister—you're a stranger."

"That's true Mordy, but besides that—I'm just plain—strange!"

I had our little friend and his colleagues laughing now along with our group.

"You know Mordy, these are my two sons, so if you live around here, we're all going to be neighbors, so do you think maybe you could share your friends' names too?"

"Oh sure, this is Josh, and that's Conner."

The two boys acknowledged the introductions as we all said:

"Nice to meet you". In a random order.

"But what's your name mister—you're funny?"

"My name's Marc. These two boys are Trevor and his younger brother Taylor. And these are my parents, Mr. and Mrs. Morgan."

"Your sons look just like twins Marc?"

"You know Mordy, I'm pretty sure that they are, but Trevor is four minutes older than Taylor."

"Oh, you are funny Marc—wait a minute; your name altogether isn't… Marcus Morgan, is it?"

"Why yes it is—have you heard that name before Mordy?"

"Well duh—if you were the Marcus Morgan that owns Verandas—then yes. Heck, I know that name real good, as a matter of fact, I hear it almost every night at home."

"Oh really; now isn't that strange; how come Mordy?"

"Because my Mom works for Verandas, so she talks about him a lot. His name always comes up at home, I really think she has the hots for the guy—but won't tell him. She's always saying that he has her three main requirements."

"And what are—her three requirements Mordy…or do I dare ask?"

"No Marc, you can ask. Well, let's see. First, she says, he has money. Two, he's Jewish,—and three…he's breathing.

We were rolling now, and I mean rolling.

"But thank God, you're not that Marcus Morgan—right?"

"Honestly Mordy, yes I am, I mean—I think that's me—so who's your mom?"

"Oh Christ, oy vay, I'd better not say—my goose is already cooked when this gets back to her sir, I don't believe this sh…crap. Damn it—damn, damn, damn, there goes my Playstation® again, and I just got it back."

"Really Mordy—you can relax, its okay, you see, I already knew I had those three things, so I won't say nothing to anyone about it besides."

"You won't? Well thank God; because mom is always saying I don't know when to shut my mouth. And just then, I was beginning to believe her; me and my big mouth. Okay, well if you promise—she's Shoshana Grossman, Marc."

"You're kidding? Wow, look I'll keep quiet Mordy, so don't worry, but I'll be damned—my boys just met your Mom yesterday…didn't you boys?"

"Was she the pretty blond haired lady with the accent Dad?" Taylor inquired of me.

"Yep, that's my mom all right; she says she's a pistol, whatever that means…but I wouldn't be talking about her accent—dude, with the one you're carrying there—jeeze."

God, this little person was quite the pistol himself, he had us laughing so.

"Say, how'd you guys get to meet her—you know, my mom?"

"Mordy, we were in a business meeting with her yesterday at the office." T-1 responded.

"Gee wiz Marc, you make your sons work already? You really are strange if you don't mind me saying so. Dang, they don't even shave yet, what are you thinking Marc?"

More laughter ensued.

"You see Mordy; it's not exactly like that. The boys just made a presentation to a group of our people including your Mom. It's about an idea they have to raise a lot of money for some special folks."

"Yeah, I think I remember her saying something about that. She came home all excited last night talking about how some problem was finally solved and finding the right product, or something. She worked on ideas for it while we all watched the tube…this morning she was still going at it in her bathrobe—she didn't look like she slept at all, but that's Mom. I think she said it was Ice Cream, I mean; what's new about Ice Cream anyway?"

"Well Mordy, you'll see soon enough, trust me."

"Okay. Listen we gotta go Marc, cuz were supposed to be home by 4:30 so we'll be late if we don't go. See you around dudes, nice meeting you, and remember, you promised Marc—my Playstation® depends on it." They walked away, while we all had a good laugh.

"My word Marc, as I live and breathe, I can't wait to have that kid to the house for a sleep over with the boys—he is something, I'll tell you that."

"Yes Mom he is—as the apple doesn't fall far from the tree, you hear what I'm saying?"

"Why yes son, I can only imagine having that woman in my Bridge club, for a night!"

"Actually Mom, Shoshana is a semi-professional poker player here in town. Believe me when I say that she knows her stuff in Texas Hold-em—and marketing. She heads up our TV advertising after all."

"Oh my Marc, she is talented then, isn't she?"

"She most certainly is—as well as a great looking lady besides."

"Really...so why don't you ask her out then, son...you have her three prerequisites after all?" As Dad busted up with his intentionally farcical remarks.

"I can't Dad."

"Why the hell not—son?"

"Because she's married Father, that's why."

"Oh, I assumed she wasn't, you know, Mordy never mentioned his father, but did comment that she had the hots for you?"

"So, maybe she does, but I can assure you she'd never act on an innocent fantasy. Nor am I about to break up a key manager's marriage so that I can date her."

"I'm glad to hear that Marc."

"Thanks Mom."

No sooner had we finished this conversation than a boy and girl rode by on their motorized scooters.

They waved hello but kept on going, they looked to be 12 to 13.

"Candidly son, it would appear you have found your kid-friendly neighborhood."

"Yep Dad—it's 'kid central' according to Natalie. If she says it, you can count on it."

Our conversation was now interrupted as my cell phone rang at that moment.

"Hello; Marc here."

"Hi there Marc, it's Natalie."

"Hey Natalie, funny you're calling just now. We're standing in front of the stables as we speak, where I was just quoting you to Dad."

"Yes, I know you're at the stables—now!"

"You do?"

"Yes Marc, apparently Kathy saw you and recognized you immediately. But you didn't see her waving. She didn't want to disturb your conversation with some children so she gave up trying to capture your attention. At any rate Marc, you had better call that architect you have on the hook, because it is all yours—congratulations.

"Natalie, that's absolutely wonderful news, but how did you ever get her to take it without countering my offer?"

"Easy, I showed her the comps while reiterating the strengths of a no contingency offer…along with dropping your name early on in our meeting. Even her agent felt your offer was right on the money by the time I finished my dissertation—so that's the deal. When do you want to close, as I left that and financing options open in the contract?"

"What works for Kathy?"

"She can move within a few weeks, she's got a Ranch in California outside of Nipton she just closed on herself."

"Oh, well how about fifteen days then?"

"Fine, I guess I should assume you're paying cash like last time on the Spanish Trail property?"

"Yep."

"Listen, you should have the house inspected so you know its existing condition, when do you want that set up?"

"Don't."

"What do you mean—don't? Why on earth would you say that, its part of what you're paying for?"

"Natalie, do you honestly think I care what condition it's in? It will be coming down two weeks after I close…tops!"

"Oh, I thought you might want to live in it temporarily. You know, let me see if I can find you a buyer for it as a move-off, it's a raised foundation so that's possible."

"Now that is a smart idea Nat, I might see some money out of that. As for living in it temporarily—not if my life depended upon it Natalie. You want me to go from eighty-two hundred square feet plus another thousand square foot guest house—to twenty-five hundred?"

"Good point Marc—so we'll skip the inspection, what about the septic systems then, are you concerned about them?"

"No Natalie, I'm not—are you going down a checklist by chance?" I laughed to let her know I was joking.

"Not this time Marc, it's just that I know horse property. I'm merely trying to protect you—that's what an agent does."

"Fine. Look, thanks for the protection, but I'm okay with all of this. Just get it closed for me on time Natalie; I already have the plans in the works."

"You do? What if she had rejected your offer Marc?"

"Nat, first of all, why would she do that? And hell, I was prepared to pay list for that diamond in the rough any day of the week. I just knew deep down that I could count on you to get me something off retail."

"Oh. Well at least 'that' makes me feel good."

"You know Nat, you should feel good. Look I'm going to send over some certificates for you and Jerry and the kids to have dinner and brunch on me… but do yourself a favor too."

"What's that Marc?"

"Have a little fun with your commission; you deserve it for this one kiddo—big time. In fact girlfriend, you know what—I'm going to make sure of it. I think a week in Maui at my B & B is in order for you and Jerry…along with the kids, but only if you insist."

"Marc, you're too much, thank you. Enjoy the new home you'll build on this gorgeous lot. I'll call you tomorrow to drop by with the escrow papers, but thanks again for the week of R and R…at your B and B…sitting on my A-S-S!"

"You're welcome Nat." As I laughed at her play on the lettering she used.

"Bye Marc, but congratulations again—you got one hell of a nice piece of dirt there."

"You'd better believe it, but I have 'you' to thank, see yah."

I hung up, while everyone obviously knew what had transpired.

"Dad, does this mean what I think it means—we get the new lagoon?"

"Yes Taylor it does—but wait till you see what we build around that pool, you're in for a treat."

We were all still looking at the property some, when four young riders came by us on their horses. I would say these kids were between eight and twelve. They were siblings for sure. When they were right next to us, the oldest tipped his hat as he said hi.

"How you doing guy?"

"Howdy sir, great day for a ride."

"Do you board here?"

"Yes sir, sure enough, seven years now, you thinking of boarding here too?"

"In a manner of speaking."

"Great place for the ponies sir, excellent footing in the arena, but Kathy—she's the owner, so she watches over them like a hawk."

"Do you live nearby?"

"Yeah, right around on the next street, then up four houses."

"Say; are there a lot of kids in this neighborhood?"

"Are you kidding me mister, there's as many my age, as in my class at school. It drives Mom crazy with all the birthday parties, there's seven in October alone, and those are just my friends!"

"Do you like living here?"

"Are you joshing me mister—it's the best. Where else in this town can you ride your horse down the street and not get spooked by some car? We're from Texas, so this neighborhood is the closest thing to home, at least for us."

"Thanks and nice talking to you...I'm Marc by the way, and these two youngins are my sons, Trevor and Taylor. These other two are my parents, Mr. and Mrs. Morgan."

"How do sir, I'm Travis James, and this here's Sonny, and the two girls are our sisters Beverly and Marley. We're the 'James Gang' from outside El Paso originally, although Marley was born here."

"Why you always gotta say that Travis, I wanna be from Texas too?"

"Cuz you ain't Marley, now hush up." The youngest James was near tears now.

I then addressed all of the kids.

"How do...yourselves—James Gang."

At that moment, my Dad must have had an epiphany as he asked Travis the all-telling question...which I already knew from looking over Kathy's books with my offer.

"Travis, if you don't mine me asking, we were wondering what they charge here for boarding?"

"Well Mr. Martin, we board six in the barn. I think that Daddy says he pays around twenty-five hundred a month to Miss Kathy with feed...that's a special rate because we board so many and Daddy's a vet."

"Thanks Travis, that's good to know as Marc here—has eight to board."

"Whoa—that's a whole posse...but you're welcome Mr. Martin."

With that, the 'James Gang' waved good-bye to ride off into the sunset. Okay, so they rode off toward the stables...so sue me.

"Hey Gramps, he called you Mr. Martin, but you didn't care?"

"No, not really Trevor, he can call me anything he wants to."

At that moment, out of my two boys' mouths in their stereo—we all heard:

"But not—late for dinner, right Gramps?"

We were all busting up now. One thing's for sure; my two didn't miss any opportunity to bust their grandfather's chops...which was always priceless.

Satisfied with our new lot, we got into Laverne as Paul began driving us home. Inside Laverne, I was getting an earful now from my two executives on the day's events in school. They had followed my advice, so they didn't tell their friends any more than necessary, more like what might happen. Everything had gone well; their biggest problem being all their mates wanted them to mention them in any TV interviews...by name.

We got home where I had them hit the books while waiting for dinner. They both had big stacks again—so I was actually beginning to feel sorry for them. Meanwhile, my Dad pulled me into a conversation as we nursed our drinks.

"Son?"

"Yes, Mr. Martin?"

"Oh Marc can it, will ya?"

"Sorry Dad, I thought my timing was impeccable though, but apparently I assumed too much."

"You know son, I've got an idea to run by you...I can even help you with it if you want?"

"You know Dad; let me take a wild guess on this idea of yours—may I?"

"Sure son...take your best shot."

"Dad—you can't stand for me not to have some offsetting income from this money pit we'll be building...I know how you think after all. So, you want me to increase the stalls in the new stables to board out."

"Jesus, no wonder they pay you the big bucks, son, yes that's it exactly, so what do you think?"

"Honestly Pop—I think you're nuts. But seriously though, I don't know anymore. I'm in a quandary over it actually. At first, I threw the idea out as unnecessary even as Natalie suggested it to me earlier in the afternoon...after all; Kathy grosses over three hundred 'k'. Now—I'm not so sure, after all, these stables have been supporting local equine fans for some thirty years now... myself included. Hell, I'd really make the community hate me, if I came in and then just threw everyone's horses out on the street—wouldn't I?"

"It's possible son, but if you're against the idea, just forget it, remember it's your property after all. Don't let your neighbors dictate your lifestyle or what you do with your own private property."

"Yes that's true Dad, so I don't plan on being intimidated. Yet this is going to be home for all of us, so naturally I don't want the boys snubbed here either. Nor do I want to be responsible for destroying the last private equine center in the City proper, either—so I've given it another look.

"Since we plan to have the Belgians here—what would some company hurt? Besides, both of the boys love the horses, they're really into riding them as well as having shown great commitment to their care when they were at the manor...so why the hell not?

"If you think about it Dad, with a five-acre lot, it can be completely separate and distanced from the house so I don't have to smell it every morning anyway. The county has the property zoned ten horses per acre which works out perfectly. Rebuilding the stables on their current site also means my neighbors can't interfere with my plans either.

"Lastly, it sounds like you'd like to oversee this kind of as a hobby, so I'm not opposed to you getting involved handling the books, either.

"I also know of an old friend down on his luck right now. He's a super-experienced trainer, so he could probably really excel at being stable master here plus he works with training disabled and challenged kids in return for their free labor, caring for the horses and stables…which I know you'll appreciate that savings of over eighty percent in direct labor…right? That ought to make handling the financials of it all quite painless…and profitable. For me though, it's a perfect way to give back a little more to the large community of disabled kids we have here in LV…so I'd want to set it up as a non-profit Dad, can you handle that?"

"Sure son, that's noble of you…I can understand it too."

"Tell you what Dad, you think on all of this seriously. I'll get you a copy of her financials to help you create a Pro forma based on the new stables, so that we can really discuss it. I'll leave Mom's okay to you…as I don't want to be in the middle of this with you two. If Mom's amenable, then do the Pro forma so that I can give it some more thought myself—so plan it well Dadio.

"My friend Vic can run it all—with you as financial director. I'm sure once this place is operational, your end of it will be limited to listening to Vic bitch,—plus around two hours of book work a week…so I plan to pay you on the cheap Dadio." As I laughed wholeheartedly at my own crack.

"Gee, thanks son, although I would refuse the money anyway."

"Yeah, I knew you'd say that…Jesus, you're so damn stubborn sometimes Dad. Alright, but you had better budget a salary for Vic of at least fifteen hundred per week…on his current application, he's looking for fifty 'k',—so you'll pay him sixty—which will thrill him. But look Dad, honestly with his equine talents, he's worth as much as Kathy currently earns at six figures… easily. Therefore set him up with a pension for the balance in his benefit package…he can't save a dollar to save his life…so we'll do it for him without him realizing it…it's a trick I learned from Cedric.

"One other thing though Dad—I do not want a full-blown horse ranch here under any circumstances, so keep it limited. I'd only want to board out the neighbors' horses, but let's limit that number to forty for Pro forma purposes on top of our eight, to control things easily…and all boarders must agree to the use of their horses with the challenged kids too, or no dice on boarding…got it?"

"Understood son."

"By the way Dad, Kathy currently draws a net operations income above one hundred and forty 'k' above and beyond her salary. So we should have a nice bottom-line small business here to convert to a non-profit, if you follow it up with a good plan. Talk to Vic, he'll tell you how we can use the proceeds to help his challenged clients in other ways. Listen Dad, before you hear it from him, let me warn you now. Vic has a rather unusual acronymic name for his special staff, he calls them T.A.R.D.S…don't worry; he'll explain it to you.

"Lastly Dad, remember I'm designing a 'private' retreat here for all of us… first and foremost, so think about all of that in your plans too."

"Son I can do all of that, including how to best keep our family's compound private, I was already assuming a completely separate gated entrance."

"Good. Since the arena is the only part of the stables to remain of the existing fixtures eventually, center the separate entrance using that as your land marker. Meanwhile, let's reconvene this meeting at 22:00 in the grotto. You can give me Mom's decision then…drinks are on me tonight Pop."

"Cute son…okay you got it, I'll be there."

Later, we all had a wonderful dinner where Sofia certainly out-did herself with everyone eating like pigs—especially the twins. Damn, I just love authentic Mexican food, as Sofia's Tamales were always incredible, especially the ones she made for dessert.

The twins were back to their homework, while Dad had left to work Mom over upstairs. Since I was left to my own devices, I went into my office to check my emails. It was a damn good thing I did, as I had an urgent one from Jess. He informed me that he had already sent the approved press release out via fax before leaving. As such, the press conference was confirmed for tomorrow at eleven-fifteen am. I returned that one quickly, acknowledging the message.

The next email was to say the least—more thought provoking as it was from our foundation's CEO, Bill Richardson, who suggested that since all of the funds funneled through the Foundation anyway—why not advance the Cerebral Palsy Foundation their necessary money to commence construction immediately since their permits were already approved…but more so—actually close to expiring. He suggested that we phase in additional money as it was needed. I gave his email around ten minutes of pro and con thought before replying my okay to Bill as I answered my remaining emails.

I next called the Meadows School to arrange homework as the boys would likely miss school tomorrow. I was surprised that I actually still caught someone there at that late hour—as I expected their voice mail system.

"The Meadows School, good evening."

"Hi; this is Marcus Morgan, my boys are in Mrs. Geary's class. They're going to miss some school tomorrow, perhaps the full day, how do I arrange to get their homework, I'm sorry, but I forget the procedure?"

"Mr. Morgan, if you'll hold on, Mrs. G's is in a planning meeting right now so you can ask her yourself?"

"Great, I guess my timing's perfect?"

"Yes sir, but hold on, this will take a few minutes; you know how teachers hate to be interrupted." A few moments later, I heard the telephone being picked up.

"Mr. Morgan, how do you do?

"I'm well Mrs. Geary, thank you for asking."

"Are the boys ill, or has this something to do with what I heard in the classroom today?"

"You're correct Mrs. Geary; it's the latter of the two. Could you give me their homework assignments for tomorrow in case they don't get in midday?"

"Sure Mr. Morgan, I would be delighted to help you out. If you want my opinion though, let them have their day off without more homework—there I've decided for you.

"You know Mr. Morgan; they're way ahead of the other children given those marvelous British Schools anyway. In fact, I'm sure we're going to consider skipping them into eighth grade in the fall anyway. They're both quite bright as I'm sure you know only too well?"

"Thank you Mrs. Geary, I appreciate that along with your decision on their homework…thank you again for supporting them."

"One thing more Mr. Morgan—God bless them. You know, I have a young cousin Rebecca, who has Cerebral Palsy. From the little I could get out of them, this all benefits folks with CP, have I got that right? The boys seemed so modest about it all."

"Yes Mrs. Geary, that's right, as the boys are responsible for putting it all together; it's been all their doing. They asked to help my foundation in some way. I then told them what we needed—and a mere hour later, they had it all worked out. Believe me; I'm still blown away myself being the father of these two. You see, my team and I tried for two years unsuccessfully ourselves."

"My word—that's incredible. I would like to have my cousin Becky come in and meet them sometime during class. I want the twins to have the opportunity of directly meeting someone their kindness will be helping, I think that's important. Are you taking them out of town tomorrow?"

"No, we simply have a press conference to announce the program so naturally they're at the center of that too—unfortunately. I'm afraid there's nothing I can do about it either, as it's only right that they're there. I might suggest you mention the 'press' issue to the administration, you know how zealous they can become. If this thing explodes in the media, you might get some uninvited visitors showing up, ready to pounce. Its likely that tomorrow night, you'll be able to catch something about all of this on the evening news."

"Alright, I'll advise the administration now before that slips my mind. I'll also be sure to tell their classmates to watch the news as well then, won't I?"

"I'm sure the boys said something to them, but okay, I guess. Since the boys are working on their modesty skills though, I'm not sure what their classmates know, honestly."

"Fine sir—it's been nice speaking to you, I'll make sure to be watching myself then, take care Mr. Morgan."

"Likewise Mrs. Geary—wait a second, here's a thought. Why not bring Rebecca to the class lunch next Saturday? By the way, I'm looking forward to meeting you formally along with your husband there?"

"As are we. Bringing Becky is a fabulous idea Mr. Morgan...as long as you don't mind...so thank you. I know that Becky will be thrilled to be included. Then again, my husband Rick is dying to meet you too, as he's in grad school studying marketing himself. We're all so excited about the lunch—the class especially."

"That's great. With any luck, that's now going to be opening day for the boys' crusade, at least in that restaurant, so I'm going to predict it will be quite a big day."

"Wonderful, I'll see you there, good-bye."

"So long Mrs. Geary."

I went to find the boys laying on my bed, working on their homework with Dad there assisting them.

"Hey there guys—good news, you won't have any homework tomorrow night because you won't be in school, so this stuff tonight can be carried over to tomorrow night if you want."

"Fine with me Dad, but how come?"

"Because T-man, you, and your brother have a press conference tomorrow morning that you'll be participating in at eleven-fifteen. Moreover, at ten, you have a meeting with the head of the Cerebral Palsy Foundation, Mrs. Dehane. You see, I've decided that you two are going to be the ones to tell the CP foundation the great news personally. But best of all, your idea is so good; we're even going to advance them some money tomorrow to get them started so they can begin building immediately."

"Wicked Dad, that's terrif, but how much money are you going to give them tomorrow?"

"You know, first of all boys, it won't be me handing Mrs. Dehane the check, it will be you two. We thought we'd start it out with a nice round number, so how does one million dollars sound to you guys?"

"Bloody hell Dad; are you kidding, a million dollars...wow?"

"No way Trev, I wouldn't joke about this, I'm for real."

Taylor now jumped in as well.

"Dad, how many pounds are in a million dollars anyways?"

"Honestly son, I would have to check the markets, but let's just estimate it at seven-hundred-thousand pounds sterling, shall we?"

"Oh my God Dad, that's a lot!"

"Yes it is Taylor. But when you're giving Gloria the money, you'll actually hand her two different checks tomorrow at different times. The first check is the real one which you'll hand her in our private meeting. Then, at the press conference later, you'll hand her a giant fake one so the cameras can see it easily. That's how we do it in America boys for a press conference."

"Okay Dad, but I hope I'm not too nervous just holding on to it till I give it to her?"

"Don't worry—you won't be. I have a suggestion about that anyway? We want Trevor equally involved, so why not have your brother hold on to it so that he can give you the real check when you're ready to present it to her? How's that sound to you Trev?"

"Cool Dad, but Taylor and I decided he'll do most of the talking tomorrow...right bro?"

"Okay Trevo, we're cool. Daddy, so do we need to write a speech for the lady from CPF?"

"No, just think about how you want to say it, but be yourselves... which goes for the press conference as well. I'll make sure you have plenty of time to answer their questions, so try not to be nervous. The press can be overwhelming at times when they are yelling all at the same time with their questions. I don't want them doing that or scaring either one of you, so I'm going to field their questions for you."

"What do you mean—'field them', Dad?'

"Just that I pick the person out to ask his or her question to keep them under control Trev."

"Oh."

"Listen guys, go downstairs as Gracie and Sofia are looking for you both. I'm told they have a little surprise for you two. Then you can watch the telly for an hour or so before hitting the sheets...after all, you've both got a big day ahead of you tomorrow."

"Sure thing Dad—but don't worry, I'm not even thinking of asking what the surprise is."

"Great Trev, we're making real progress now, aren't we?"

"Yes Dad."

The boys, Dad, and I went downstairs to the kitchen. Grace and Sofia were there already...with big smiles too.

"Sit down boys, while Sofia and me, serve your dessert."

Grace walked over to the Subzero freezer where she took out a small Styrofoam cooler. As she removed the lid, immediately dry ice 'fog', starting flying out of the container, down its sides and then laying flush over the surface of the table.

"Wow, cool."

"Yes it is T-1, exactly. Trev, that's dry ice which makes it exactly one hundred and nine degrees below zero, so you can't ever touch it or it will burn your skin, okay?"

"Really Dad—no joking?"

"No fooling guys—it's dangerous. But meanwhile, what's in this container more importantly was sent to you, from Mr. and Mrs. Nethery at Minis ice cream. They wanted to thank you for everything you've done to help your foundation, as well as their business too. Can you take a guess what's inside?"

"Oh Dad—this is so easy, what our bloody mate Bobby calls a no-brainer."

"Yes boys, it is a no-brainer in that sense, but then again—it's not...I can assure you."

"What are you saying Dad, you always do this to us?" Taylor of course was speaking his mind now as usual.

"Come on boys—all I'm saying is that each of us can figure out what's inside, because it's obviously Minis. The more important question is—which flavor is it? Now that's an altogether different problem to solve—isn't it boys?"

"Oh, I get it Dad; you want us to guess the flavor...don't you?"

"Bingo T-man...you're friggin' brilliant. So go ahead; impress me with your Minis knowledge. You'll guess first, before we'll jump over to T-1 for his guess. We'll go back and forth until one of you gets it, or we run out of flavors, fair enough?"

"Sure; I'm ready, I think it's that Banana Split flavor Dad?"

"Nope, that's not it Taylor, okay T-1, now you take your best shot."

"Okay Dadio, I'll say it's that lovely Cookies and Crème?"

"Sorry son, that's incorrect...alright T-man, you're at bat again."

"Jeeze Dad, this will take us all night, I want to eat it already."

"Okay my little impatient one...let's just say—it's not Chocolate, Vanilla, Mint Chocolate or that Creamscicle flavor either. So what can it be Taylor...I wonder?"

"I don't know Dad, bloody hell—what is it then?"

"Alright boys—you win…here's your surprise. It's a special, limited edition new Minis flavor made especially in honor of—both of you!"

"No way—wicked…really Dad?"

"Really T-1. Making its very first public appearance—drum roll boys—presenting—The Twin Tornados!" As I reached in and grabbed the two huge containers."

"Bloody hell, our own Ice Cream flavor—how brill is that bro…Jeeze first we get our names on Dad's jets—and now this?"

"I take it, this pleases you T-Man?"

"Yes Dad, I just can't believe it, can you blame me?"

"No son, I most certainly cannot."

"Yeah Taylor, this is too cool. Dad, what's in it—do you already know?" Trevor now inquired.

"Nope Trev, but in a moment we will, as Mr. Nethery wrote you two a letter—here it is."

I opened the letter as I began reading it to the boys.

"Hello Trevor and Taylor. On behalf of all of us at Minis, we would like to present you with this new special edition Minis flavor. It has been created in your honor; we call it 'Triple T' for 'The Twin Tornados'—that's you two.

"It's made with two ice cream flavors, mint chocolate, and butter pecan, two different chocolates, with two different cookies finishing it off. Then we swirl it all together just like the flume of a Tornado with instantly frozen mint chocolate shavings—please enjoy it with our warmest wishes.

"Your Dad will also tell you both what we plan to do to support your crusade to help raise this money."

"May God bless both of you and your wonderful cause as we grow your crusade for the future. Bob and Katy, Nethery."

"Wow, that's a wonderful letter,—just what are they going to do to help us Dad?"

"First of all T-1, they will personally sponsor the cost of all of the ice cream kiosks. That's an awful lot of money boys—in the several of millions actually. In addition, to help you boys out, they are donating one hundred thousand dollars of Minis to your crusade, each and every year. That will raise over $385,000 at retail—isn't that great?"

"Yes it is Dad; shouldn't we send them a thank you email?"

"Yes Trev, I was hoping you boys would say that without my suggestion, so I'm really proud of you two for seeing that responsibility."

"Gee Dad; we're proud of you too. You got this all done so fast, however did you manage?"

"Honestly boys, I did have an awful lot of help from many of our employees …didn't I? Believe me guys, after waiting for over two years, everyone at the office wants this started—like—yesterday…who can blame them?"

"No you can't blame them Daddy. It's true, they have waited a long enough time for Trev and I to show up and save them all from your rotten ideas." The boys were now both hysterical at Taylor's crack…but so was I along with the rest of the adults.

"Now; before we relax and finish-off this Triple T, allow me to let both of you in on the rest of your surprise."

"Jeeze, there's more Dad?"

"Just a little son—but I know this is going to make both of you very happy indeed."

"What?"

"Okay T men, here's the deal, Bob and Katy will be driving up here, the Friday after next to do two very important things."

"What are they going to do Dad?" T-Man was now asking.

"First on the list Taylor, is some training…they're going to come here to the house to personally train you two."

"Train us for what, Dad?" Trevor asked.

"Trev, they'll train you both on how to scoop and serve the Minis properly and very professionally into the cups. More importantly, they'll be bringing along our very first kiosk with them to set up at the Summerlin Verandas. This means boys; we'll have the first Minis' Dessert Court all set up in time for your luncheon party with your mates—now how's that for a surprise?"

The boys were screaming and carrying on with excitement at this news.

"So we'll be able to sell the Minis and stuff at our party?"

"Yep, but not only that, we're going to make it our official grand opening of the first kiosk on that day. We're inviting the Mayor to come, along with the Governor, so what do you two think about that?"

"Wow, that's so great Dad, I can't wait,—so do we get to meet the Governor and Mayor Dad?"

"I can't speak for the Governor because he hasn't confirmed yet, but the Mayor wants to meet you two personally. You see he's a real personable guy, boys, for a Mayor I mean, but you know, there's something else you'll want to know about him."

"What else?"

"Our Mayor's wife founded your very school!"

"No way—really?"

"Yep T-1."

"Wow—I can't wait to meet him then, because he's obviously a great guy, right Dad?"

"You got it tiger."

We all began eating the Triple T, but oh my Lord—was it ever to die for. It tasted like the ice cream version of Irish Crème liquor enhanced by one of those small dark chocolate mints made by Andes. In fact, those mints were one of the chocolate candies in there, along with some other chocolate crumbles and frozen mint chocolate shavings. Nabisco's Oreo and Mystic Mint Cookie bits completed the tasty and complimentary ingredients. I called everyone in to join in…so we all had some as I explained the flavor's name which everyone went ape for. Fleming, who detested ice cream by his own admission, was enticed enough to try it. He was enthralled with it, which sincerely shocked him beyond how we reacted to his pleasure.

Once the boys were finished, I sent them upstairs to the whirlpool bath before any television. Dad meanwhile, was on his third helping of Minis, with Mom getting angrier with each helping he added to his huge dish.

"Mal, I swear, you'll burst one day, mark my words, you sure as hell will."

"You know Marilyn; this ice cream has been made and named in honor of our very own two grandsons; therefore I'm entitled and empowered to indulge on such an auspicious occasion!"

"Oh, you're good Malcolm—so very good."

"Thank you Marilyn—I love you too."

"Hey, that's my line Dad, so don't piss me off. You're already losing allies as we speak."

"Okay son, but damn this stuff is so good…it doesn't even give me gas."

"You know dear, there is a God then—isn't there Mal?"

"Yes Marilyn—for your sake, there is."

I went upstairs to change into my trunks; I had a meeting to take in the grotto after all.

The boys were just about to get in the tub when I noticed something that alarmed me in an instant. Trevor's private was all infected! It was red at the end of the foreskin with it not looking too comfortable at all.

"T-1, come here son."

"Yes, Dad?"

"Honey, what's going on down there with your willy?"

"Oh, I've had it before Dad, so has Taylor, sometimes it kind of hurts badly, but it goes away."

"And why do you suppose you got this on your poor little willy?"

"Hey Dad—watch what you're saying…he's not so little?"

"Sorry…you're right; he is not small for a boy of your age Trevor, that's obvious. What I meant to say was he's a poor little guy because he's got an infection…a bad one at that, by the looks of it. You must not be washing him well, or forgetting to pull his foreskin back when you go to the loo—something's going wrong son."

"I guess so Dad, I'm sorry."

"Look don't apologize to me—apologize to him…he's the one hurting right now—isn't he?"

"Oh, okay, I'm sorry Bartholomew—oh sorry Dad, you two haven't really met—have you? My willy's Bartholomew, while Taylor's is Bunkie."

"Really—I didn't know…thank you for enlightening me Trev." Holding back my laughter was near impossible, but I tried, as I maintained a smile as a compromise.

"Gee Dad—don't tell me that you don't have a name for yours?"

"Son, I'm a grown man—I'm nearly thirty three years old."

"So, Daddy, you've still got one of these, you know?" I completely sidestepped that one. Taylor now added to his brother's comments.

"Get in the tub boys—but Trevor; when you get out—we're going to put a little medicine on Bartholomew. You and I will have a little talk about hygiene while we fix him all up—so no telly either until we fix him up."

"Okay Dad."

As I was departing the bath suite, I couldn't resist the opportunity, so I turned to them and said:

"Okay boys—I guess that Freddie and I are going." I winked at them while I began leaving.

As I was closing the door on them, I heard Taylor comment to his brother:

"You know Trev; his willy really does look like a 'Freddie', doesn't it?"

I was still laughing as Freddie and I changed into my trunks in the bedroom, before I then went into the office to get online for some advice.

I returned fifteen minutes later with a suitable ointment I found in the medicine cabinet, following recommendations from Web MD.

"Okay, Taylor, go get in your PJ's while your brother and I take care of Bartholomew."

"Dad, you can call him Bart for short, ya know."

"Fine Trevor…I'll be sure to call him Bart." As I laughed.

"Hey Daddy, I want to watch too, this way if we ever need to do this for Bunkie—I'm ready."

"Fine, if your brother isn't upset that you're there, you can stay."

"Jeeze Dad, we were just in the Whirlpool together naked, so why would I care, you know, you're so weird about our willies, Dad?"

"I don't think so T-1; but I think I'm just a little bit uncomfortable with all of this willy business altogether, that's all."

"Dad, they're just willies...my God—chill.

"Fine son, I'll chill." We went over the print out as I quizzed both boys—what the hell, Taylor asked to be in there too.

I had Trevor apply the ointment which apparently did not hurt him—it soothed the pain considerably according to his sigh of relief that followed the application of medicine. Thank God, that was over.

I left them to the television before retreating to the grotto for my meeting with my own Dad.

I stopped at the bar to fix myself—my two doctors, before making Dad his usual—a Cape Cod, which I enjoyed on occasion myself.

I stepped into the bubbling, steamy water as I sat down to a wonderful soak with the old man. The TV was on to the late local news, with Dad just being lazy.

"So Dad, here's your drink. So what was the outcome of your discussion with Mom—or should I even ask you?"

"Oh, damn, almost forgot about that, yeah, she wasn't thrilled, but she said it was my decision as long as I limit it to setting everything up then playing accountant on the books once a month. I guess that's an 'all right' by default—you know your Mother? I have to drag an 'inch' out of her at a time...so it's a slow process." As Dad busted up from his crack.

"Okay then Dad, I guess I'll review everything too."

"Son, I'm really okay whichever way you decide."

"I know you are Dad."

"Listen kiddo, what took you so damn long getting here though, I'm almost a prune already, this meeting was called for 22:00,—you're late, so now I think I'd better dock your pay?"

With this set up—I just couldn't resist.

"Sorry Dad, medical problems upstairs. Yeah—Bartholomew has a bad infection."

"Bartholo—who?"

"Gee Dadio, I'm surprised,—I thought for sure you already knew Bartholomew by now. I know you've seen him running about the pool hanging around—head first?"

My Dad was just not connecting the dots on the boys' skinny-dipping reference, so after enough time for him to figure it out, I had to take pity on him...by explaining it to him.

"Pop, Bartholomew, or Bart, is Trevor's penis...for the record; Taylor's is Bunkie."

My father was carrying on now, something fierce.

"Oh, I see. Well son, at least they had the good taste to use original names, rather than to name their dicks after dare I say—someone infamous…like Fred…Flintstone?"

"Oh my friggin God Dad, I can't believe you even remember that?"

"Remember it? How can I ever forget 'Freddie'—son? I must have gotten over six months of laughs at my agency telling everyone that stupid story."

"You what? Christ Dad, you didn't really—did you?"

"Oh, didn't I—Tiger. You're damn right I told it—hell, to anyone who would listen…I was damn proud of that story besides. I even got pretty good at telling it after a piece."

"Listen, old man, you're just lucky your wife never found out about it, or she would have likely skinned you alive for sure."

With my retort, Dad was now rolling, coughing, crying, and turning beet red from laughing so hard.

"Oh Marc, keep living your denial son—this is absolutely priceless—really it is."

"What in hell is so damn funny now Dad?"

"I don't know, but let me just ask you one thing son, okay?"

"Alright Dad, but I am not the least bit amused."

"Fine, here's my question for you."

"Okay, go ahead, D a d."

"Where do you suppose, (God, Dad was hysterical.) I got the idea to share the 'Freddie' story at the agency in the first place?"

He was in a 'fit' at that moment with his carrying on.

"How the hell should I know Dad—where?"

"Well son, naturally from your Mother's Bridge Club, of course."

Hearing this, even though this took place when I was maybe five years old, I was now freshly embarrassed, beet red…yet certainly not amused under any circumstances. And yet I prayed still, that this was simply a razz by my father.

"Oh yeah, I'll just bet?" I yelled in full-blown denial.

"Gee Marc, how much exactly—will you bet me son, because I could always use some cash for the road trip home…I can really clean up here?"

"You actually expect me to believe that my own loving Mother sold me out to her girlfriends Dad? And that she openly humiliated me on some night at her Bridge Club by talking about Freddie, to all of her friends there—with no regard to my embarrassment as I got older?"

"No son—certainly not. Honestly she didn't bring it up on one night at her Bridge Club. It was more like two months at her Club; it became the number one running gag at her club son.

"Dad, you have got to be pulling my leg here?"

"Gee, if I was pulling your leg, just what should I call it son? Oh, I know…let's call him Barney. After all, Barney's never far away from Fred's side—is he?"

Dad's comments were over now, but not his laughing.

Surprisingly, I guess he finally broke me down, because now he had me actually starting to laugh too. How he managed to do that, I haven't a clue, but I was howling now…really howling. I honestly could not help myself; it was so funny looking back on it. Remembering the whole stupid story of my penis' naming as well as, the consequences of this confession now—on top of that.

"Alright Dad—enough already. I said through my laughter.

"Cool it now Dadio; I can't stop laughing for crying out loud."

He started to compose, but the heat I am afraid, was just getting turned up on my laughter thermostat. I went on another whole six minutes, before I could finally compose myself somewhat to stop.

After we were both subdued, my Dad got serious for a moment to teach me what he purported to be a valuable truism of parenting that he seemed sincerely hell-bent on me understanding.

"Marc, I'm sorry, you know, I didn't mean to upset you. Son, I'm convinced it's good that this has happened and come up in a way. You know, you were out of the 'parenting' loop for their first eleven years, so I'm actually glad this is out in the open now."

"Why Dad, have you been depressed up until now?"

"No son, it's more that I'm realizing something fundamental and important about you and the twins concerning the fact that you were absent for their developmental years. I've probably been a little remiss in not bringing it up to you sooner is all?"

"Well go ahead Dad; I'm certainly now listening to every word on this."

"Its simple son, one of the greatest joys in all of parenting, is—making fun of your own children. Yet naturally Marc—it's always on the sly. Not just things like 'Freddie', but all kinds of things really…let me prove it to you."

"How Dad?"

"Alright son, but haven't you figured that one out already? Look, just think about how this whole thing came out tonight in the grotto. You too, were already making fun of Bartholomew, the alter ego of whom; Trevor, of course? Nor could you resist stabbing poor little Taylor in the back too, with the 'and his is Bunkie', crack…could you? You're guilty Marcus, as charged, so what do you have to say in your defense,—before I pass judgment?"

"Sorry?"

"No, Marc, the correct answer is; too bad your honor, because I was certainly enjoying myself at my kids' expense!"

"Really?"

"Yes son—really, look, don't beat yourself up kiddo. This whole experience is new for you, as you weren't there during those important early years. Typically, that's when all of this stuff begins to take place after all. First, its innocent crap; oh Junior made the smelliest 'poopie' this morning Mary. But by the time the kid is five, you're desperate for a little levity, so you're sharing every cute or stupid thing the kid ever did. And you're confessing to everyone you know, and some you do not even know! Marc, kids are priceless to be sure—Lord only knows that I'd sacrifice my left nut for you, son. But that doesn't rule out me having some fun at your expense from time to time, Christ; it's parenting's salvation after all!"

"Damn Dad, I never realized. I suppose you're right, as usual, one thing though."

"What Marc?"

"What in God's good name would I do with your left nut?

CHAPTER 4

▼

SMILE FOR THE CAMERA SON

THE NEXT MORNING WAS A big day in the Morgan homestead, with the house in a flurry of activity naturally. Our whole household insisted on going including Sofia, who was really starting to get more involved with our family and staff…clearly Sofia was bonding to both Grace and Reg.

We all loaded into Laverne, as Paul prepared to get us to the office right on time.

Crews from all the press and local networks were there, but were they ever busy setting up their equipment and feeds.

Good old Mordy's mother—our own Shoshana Grossman in the TV production department of marketing, added bringing out sample cups of Minis, which the press began scarfing down in moments.

She wanted to film the press' reactions for her own TV commercial ideas; I thought that was a smart twist on consumer research.

We went into the executive offices, where I asked the boys to give Grace, Fleming, and Sofia, the grand tour since it was still fresh in their minds. I asked my folks to tag along with them to keep them from getting lost or into trouble.

I buzzed Jess's cubicle, but when he didn't answer, I paged him.

He arrived around seven minutes later—seeming quite composed given his responsibilities that day.

"Jess, are we all set on this?"

"Absolutely Marc, I personally spoke to Mrs. Dehane…she'll be here in a few minutes. Gloria got done with another morning appointment nearby, earlier than expected, so she's on her way now. Bill Richardson will be here in a shake or two as well."

"You know Jess; you'd better page the boys now to get them in here by ten before the hour so they're with us. I want them off the floor and inside this office before Gloria arrives; besides they'll probably get a real kick out of hearing themselves paged? I assume you have the check with you?"

"Yes, both of the checks are ready, here's the real one boss." Jess than handed me the 'primer' check of a cool mil.

At that moment, our Foundation's CEO, Bill Richardson, walked in as we all greeted one another 'hello' quickly.

"Jess, go page the boys. Better make sure you explain where they can pick up a white phone. I've got to make a phone call, Bill why don't you stay here and relax, I've just have one quick call to make."

"Sure Marc."

I dialed my architect, where, after the usual pleasantries I was put right through.

"Milt, its Marc, glad I caught you."

"Hey there Marc, making changes already?"

"How did you know Milt?"

"You must be joking Marc? In my business, changes is what ages all architects prematurely—didn't you know that?"

"Can't say that I did, but I'm not surprised."

"So what's the change?"

"I've got sort of an update—but a little change too."

"Alright Marc, you're on the clock, so start talking."

"Okay Milt, first of all, the property's now officially wrapped up."

"Damn it man, do you mean to tell me that you sent me twelve, five (dollars) on a maybe?"

"Yep, I wanted to get started. But besides Milt—it's not like plans 'expire', if you miss one lot, another materializes."

"Not exactly Marc, but you're close. You have to factor in soils or engineering issues too, you know…but you still make a good point over all. Look Marc—it's your money, but I plan on taking lots of it by the time we're finished designing this showplace."

"Do you hear me complaining Milt, or the sound of me breaking a sweat over the money?"

"No, but I always use that line to get a barometer on my client's sensitivity to cash."

"Fine then—did I pass the test?"

"Yes, you did Marc…you got an A+ as a matter of fact."

"Good—now you're talking. Now here's the little change, I want the stables to be larger than I alluded to initially. I need two opposing rolls of twenty-five stalls now, but still center aisled with opposing tack rooms at whichever end is closest to the doors."

"Why that's not major Marc—Jesus, I thought you were going to say—I want to go Colonial or something? The size of the stables is quite flexible on five acres; believe me Marc...is that all?"

"Yeah, that's it—but I would like you to arrange a scale model too so I can drool.

"No problem Marc, I'll call in Herb Grasse in Arizona to do that—he's the worlds best in residential scale-models if my opinion means anything."

"Don't worry—it doesn't...but call him in anyway. Milt—you know, it's funny, but why does his name sounds so damn familiar to me now?"

Wow! Marc, I can't believe I've one-upped you for once."

"What do you mean Milt?"

"Christ, Marc, don't you have a Bricklin? Herb Grasse was the designer of the car; don't you remember?"

"Christ, you're right; I can't believe I forgot his name. Look, I've got a press conference coming up, so I've got to run."

"No problem, I've got a ten-fifteen tee-time...I mean—appointment myself, so speak to you soon."

"Bye Milt."

"So long Marc." I hung up the phone but immediately had a worrisome thought.

No sooner than the thought crossed my mind—of what was keeping my boys, then they showed up at my door. The folks were completing the rest of the tour apparently instead.

"Boys, say hello to our CEO for the foundation; Bill Richardson, you remember him from our board meeting? We're just waiting on Mrs. Dehane now, but she will be here momentarily."

The twins said hello to Bill, as I figured things out in my mind before I continued my comments.

"Taylor, I'll make the introductions and give Gloria just a tidbit of information. Then I'm going to turn it over to you and Trev—are you both okay with that?"

"Yes boss." I heard from Trevor now.

"Boss...now what's this all about boys?"

"Jeeze Dad, if you'd just relax for a change, while you have a bloody look at our new security tags—you might figure it out."

I wasn't amused as I had a lot on my mind...I was in no mood to play along now.

"Alright I will, but I'd watch that mouth of yours T-1…yet thank you for the vote of confidence."

"Sorry Dad, I was only kidding around."

"Okay Trev—I forgive you, but remember to respect your elders though… always. Often, that runs a fine line between making a joke, or saying something completely inappropriate or worse—so be careful kiddo."

"Okay Dad, I understand, sorry."

I looked at the boys' badges now but noticed nothing momentarily—then the light went on. Their color bar code on the top of their tags designated them in the Foundation's division, as employees now, instead of visitors.

"Bill, would you look at this? Well boys, I see you two are on our foundation's payroll now—so just whom may I ask—hired you…was it you Mr. Richardson?"

"Don't look at me Marc; I'm top heavy already…hell, I was thinking of letting you go actually." We all busted up over that crack, as you can imagine.

"Jesse did Dad; he gave us these before our pictures were taken." Trevor now offered.

"Gee—that was nice of him, but he and I will have to talk about it some."

"Okay boss—but we're ready whenever you are."

"Dad or Daddy will suffice just fine boys—that's one thing I want everyone in the whole world to always know…I'm your father. I don't want to hear the word 'boss' out of either of you two again, are we clear?"

"Gee Daddy; did we upset you…again?" Taylor asked pensively now.

"You personally Taylor—no, Jesse on the other hand—well lets just say that he has some 'serious splainin' to do."

"Please don't get mad at him Daddy, I think he was just following Eric's orders."

"Oh, so that's it. Okay T-Man, now I may be coming around to understanding this a whole lot better. Thanks for that heads-up son, because I was just about to bite Jess's head off …I possibly might have been eating the wrong head for lunch…or maybe it's just a labor law issue we have to contend with, who knows?"

"God Dad, you sure do talk weird at work."

"I'm sure I probably do Trevor, thank you for that though—actually; I'm certain that I do."

Robbie buzzed me that he was escorting in Mrs. Dehane along with a message that Jesse was on his way in as well.

Gloria Dehane entered and greeted us with a warm smile with her hand out to accept mine. Jess popped in right after, as I introduced the boys to

Gloria. We all sat down. Jess, Bill and Gloria chatted away pleasantries on the sofa. I began after they finished.

"Gloria, it's wonderful to have you here, we apologize if the notice was rather inadequate?"

"Gentlemen—not at all. It all worked out pretty well actually."

"I'm glad to hear that Gloria." Bill commented.

"Let me share with you why we're all together this morning Gloria, may I?"

"Sure Marc, I mean, not that I don't enjoy coming here anytime for a meeting or visit. Just the same, I am the slightest bit curious on all the urgency with Bill's call."

"Well Gloria, I'm getting to that, you see my two boys here, are pretty darn smart—after all—they're eleven!

"Look, they've come up with something that concerns you and CPF, so I thought we should all get together. Taylor, why don't you start this off, son?"

"Sure Dad."

"Alright Taylor, what's this all about?" Gloria asked.

"First, Mrs. Dehane, we're here to help you with your plans to build that new home you need. Trevor and I wanted to help after talking to Dad. We now know everything your CPF foundation does to help all of these folks... so we wanted to help too. You see, we just knew we had to do something, to try and help out."

"Boys, thank you both for your kind words, I appreciate them very much."

"You're welcome Mrs. Dehane, but there's more. We worked on it a while before we came up with a solution. It's all going to start next Saturday at the Verandas in Summerlin; with what we want to do...we hope you can come?"

"Sure I can boys." Gloria added.

"Anyway, since Dad and the Foundation want you to build your new home as soon as possible, we have something for you. Trevor and I are honored, Mrs. Dehane, to give you this, to get your new house started now."

With that said Trevor took out the check; passed it over to Taylor, as he handed it to a somewhat surprised Gloria.

Gloria took the check without even glancing at it first, as she commented:

"Thank you boys, CPF will put this into our building fund for our center, as you've requested."

She finally unfolded it now as she glanced at it. Seeing the dollar amount overwhelmed her on the spot. Gloria was trying to maintain her composure, but was losing that battle now as Jess handed her the box of tissues.

"Oh my word—Taylor, Trevor,—what's this all about? What exactly have you two come up with—that you can hand me a million dollars before you even start?"

"Mrs. Dehane, Dad says our idea to raise the money is good enough so you can start building now. There will be lots more checks while your house is being built. We're very happy and glad to help you Mrs. Dehane, so please don't cry."

Gloria got out of her seat as she walked over to the twins to hug them deeply, followed by kisses on their cheeks.

"Boys, you have to tell me what you've done, I'm just in shock from all of this?"

Gloria was finally composing herself while listening intently now to Taylor's explanation.

…"So, it's that simple Mrs. Dehane. What do you think of it?"

"My, that is a wonderful idea boys, how ever did you think of it? Your Father's team has been trying for a long time to come up with something?"

"It just seemed to come to us that it made sense Mrs. Dehane; you see, we ate Minis lots of times back in England. Then we saw it here in Las Vegas last Friday at Mandalay Bay…so we knew it would work for this too."

"Honestly gentlemen, I just can't thank you enough…all of you. Say, does this have anything to do with all those TV trucks and people I noticed in the parking lot?"

"Yes ma'am, we have to talk to those people pretty soon—right Dad?"

"Yes Gloria, we have a press conference set for 11:15…don't you just love spontaneity…surprise?"

"Oh my; this is just so exciting, but I must call my office before I forget… boys I don't know what else to say?"

"Just listen to Dad, Miss; he seems to know his stuff". Taylor obviously misunderstood her comment. Sometimes I had to force myself to remember they were still young boys, even as I kidded around with them now.

"Thanks for that vote of confidence Taylor."

"No problem Dad." He was giggling away now, as was his brother.

"Marc, you're very lucky if you ask me—but that goes double for me as well."

"Yes Gloria, I know, they're something—aren't they?"

"Marc, they really are…but so adorable too, I could just eat them up. Marc; is there someplace where I might freshen up a bit before the press, I'm still shaking for Pete's sake?"

"Sure, the ladies room is the first door outside on your left. Alternatively, if you prefer a more professional setting, Shoshana is filming TV spots all week for our upcoming spring menu. So we can offer you a make-up artist today who's set-up and has extremely good lighting along with everything else you might want?"

"How thoughtful Marc, but how do I get there?"

"We would be honored to escort you, wouldn't we boys?"

"Yes Miss Gloria, please allow us?"

"Why of course boys—after you then."

We got Gloria down to the studio where the make-up artist was prearranged, just standing by to be of assistance to her. We left Gloria there as we returned to Jess and Bill in my office.

Jess had apparently retrieved copies of the media press kits hot off of the press, which I was delighted with, as Jess handed each of us one.

All the material blew the boys away. They especially liked the photos we selected. They really got excited over the photos of the actual kiosks, with their images 'morphed' onto its signage, which sent them over the top.

Trevor then picked up his press kit as he began reading the actual materials, before commenting further.

"Boy, this is amazing. Look bro, it tells the whole dang story…how was it done so fast, Dad?"

"Gee Trev, don't ask me; see if that miracle man standing next to you two can answer that?"

"Jesse, however did you do this so fast?"

"Honestly Taylor, we didn't have much of a choice, as there was really no time to waste…besides, we do our own publishing here in house. It all goes right through our computers, including superimposing your pictures onto the kiosks, which is my personal favorite too. Plus, giving the full account of your idea, as well as how it all came about, will speed up the press' questions besides, Taylor."

"Cool Jesse, but I'm Trevor."

"Oh, sorry Trevor, but with matching Blazers and shirts, it's hard to tell you and Taylor from one another right now."

"That's only because you're not Dad—he's never been wrong—not even once."

"Wow, your Dad's pretty good to be able to accomplish that."

"Yes he is, but after all—he's our Dad."

Gloria rejoined us right as I spied my watch. I suggested we go out to 'meet the press'.

We stopped to pick up the folks, along with our household staff—my surrogate family, in the lobby. We walked outside and directly over to the podium. I then made my opening greetings.

"Good morning everyone. For anyone new, I'm Marc Morgan, CEO, and Chairman of Verandas. It's my pleasure to welcome you all here today. I know that you have all had adequate time to review your media kits along with sampling our wonderful new Minis Ice Cream. I'm confident your questions will address anything unclear so far.

"I want to share with you how we plan to handle everything today, as my sons are entirely unaccustomed to this. And they've only recently joined me here in the States, so please be sensitive to that as well. So, I'll choose the reporter to field your questions onto the twins…but from time to time, I may jump in myself if I feel anything requires clarity."

I then introduced the boys, along with my staff.

"This new crusade of the boys making, will first assist Las Vegas' own Cerebral Palsy Foundation in their efforts to build an adaptive residential center for their CPF clients. So please welcome, Mrs. Gloria Dehane, the Executive Director for the Cerebral Palsy Foundation of Southern Nevada."

The boys had decided that Trevor would answer the first question, so I began. I acknowledged a young lady right in front of me; as she stated her name, paper, and then asked:

"What message are you boys trying to send to other kids out there with your crusade?"

"Miss, when this all started, we were only concerned on how to help these folks out in getting their new home built. Originally we didn't think about doing anything more than that. Now though, I would like to say something else…but not just to other kids like us, but everyone. I think that we should all try to never forget it either. There are always good people out there that need a little extra help from the rest of us."

This reporter then continued:

"Alright, so what would you both like to see this crusade attempt to accomplish for these people?"

Taylor took the microphone now.

"Miss, we've all met people similar to these folks—the people we're trying to help. They also need lots of things called adaptive devices, stuff that makes their challenges, as Dad calls them, easier. These things can help them so that they can get around better, or to eat, or to help them be able to work, or to have a more independent life in general while at home. You know, many of these nice people want to work and stuff, just like we all do, well, you know, grown-ups do."

I moved on to another reporter before our first lady started dominating the questions. I went to a man in the rear row. He introduced himself and his Television station.

"I'd like to know where the boys have met all these handicapped persons so soon. I mean, according to the press release and your remarks, they've just arrived here in the states."

I looked at Taylor who clearly didn't know how much he should confess, so I nodded my implicit approval.

"Actually sir, I've seen and met similar folks here at our building where they work packing Dad's products into packages."

Knowing that this comment got all of the press' attention, I decided to allow the same reporter a follow-up.

"Taylor—you are Taylor right? (Taylor nodded.) So are these adaptive devices to assist these folks—strictly to help them here at work?"

"No sir, our crusade is not about work things that help them here, but wherever they are—or whatever they are doing. And the new home that is planned will be made a special way for them to live easier, with all the adaptive devices included already."

"Folks, allow me to clarify my son's comments. Taylor is referring to adaptive-living devices and equipment which assist the disabled, similar to those used by some of our employees here. Our goal is to build this residential facility, already set up with adaptive features for folks living with CP that will reside there."

I sought out another reporter this time from the middle of the three loosely knit rows. The reporter gave his name and radio station, as I made a mental note of the call numbers for later on.

"Boys, what have you learned from these people at your father's packaging plant?"

Trevor took his turn now.

"We've learned that they just want to be treated like anyone else, by fitting in and not being treated differently. Some have told us that they don't want us to be sorry or anything—they really like working. I guess, just like you probably do sir...or maybe you don't?"

Trevor's innocent remark had everyone chuckling at the obvious implication about the nature of working in journalism.

After the laughter subsided, this same reporter jumped in with an immediate follow-up.

"So who would you two like to see helped after your Dad's employees?

I cut this one off at the pass too.

"Folks, I think I should clarify something—right now. The boys came up with their idea on their own, beginning with offering their help to me—but not for our employees per se...so let me make this clear: This new residential facility is not going to benefit any of Verandas employees. Please be certain sir, to make sure your report reflects that fact."

"Yes I understand Mr. Morgan."

"Ladies and Gentlemen, this residence will be under the auspices of CPF, strictly for their clients who are totally unable to work."

I went back to the front row to another lady reporter. After her introductions, she directed her question to me personally.

"Mr. Morgan, how many employees with challenges, are in your employ at the present time?"

"Here in our assembly center, we employ approximately thirty five with challenges. The numbers company-wide, are somewhat larger as we recognize other ancillary challenges as well. These can include employees that are just rejoining the work force, single-parent households that cannot afford day-care, etc.

She was apparently satisfied with my thoroughness, so I moved back to the rear row, to yet another female reporter.

"How long do you boys think it will take to raise all this money—it's a formidable amount after all?"

Miss, we don't know, we just know we have to do it to make it happen as fast as possible."

I was going to assist Taylor in this response but I knew he was surely in for a shock—as my answer would surprise him the most.

"Barbara, I can give you an estimate based on what our people believe the boys' crusade can accomplish financially on an annual basis. Based on Verandas' 347 units across the country, we've been given an estimate of as much as twenty-eight million dollars annually. If we apply that figure going strictly to this first project—we are at, plus, or minus,—four months from the time we complete setting up all units. As such, we plan to advance incremental money now so the project can get started right away."

"After our goal is met, all additional raised proceeds will be pooled and then get equally distributed among all of our non-profits on an on-going basis. Of course we're going to reserve twenty-five percent, for future special projects from the many foundations under our umbrella. Naturally, we have many worthwhile charities around the Globe that we assist—along with some new ideas the boys have as well.

"I think I'll ask Gloria Dehane from CPF to come up and join me. I'm sure you'd all like more information on the wonderful new facility they will be building—Gloria.

"Now Gloria, before you begin fielding questions, I would like the boys and Mr. Neilson to present you with our first check for this worthwhile project—gentlemen."

The boys went to retrieve the presentation check, as they carefully carried it over to Gloria. They now held one end, while Jesse took the other to remove the cover as the photographers had a field day shooting their pictures. All of our employees present applauded proudly while both of my boys had smiling, happy faces. Jesse and Gloria weren't exactly depressed either.

Afterwards, we gave the reporters another four questions to Gloria directly, before ending this portion of the conference...before moving on to the television interviews.

We now went out to greet everyone as we headed for the TV vans. I purposely kept the boys nearby throughout this time to fend off any unsolicited attempts by the press to tackle the boys with any further questions.

We did our TV interviews for the next fifty minutes. They all went reasonably well except for one idiot. He closed his report by stating that we had declined his request to speak to any of our disabled employees.

After the circus was over, we went back into the office as we rehashed how we felt it went over-all.

"Dad, that was great, thanks."

"Hey T-man, you and Trevor did an incredible job. I must say I enjoyed just being your faithful sidekick for both of you."

"Okay, but thanks all the same Daddy, don't know—that was harder than I thought it would be."

"You're welcome Taylor, so how did you like it T-1, you're awful quiet?"

"It was cool Dad."

After completing our wrap up, we decided to head home. It had been a demanding, yet important day for us. The boys could have returned to school for a half day, but I decided they were entitled to a full day off.

We were driving home when I noticed the time was just before 1:00 p.m. so I switched on the radio. I dialed in the call numbers from that reporter's station to wait for their next newsbreak to begin.

The national news came first before the local stories followed. At first I thought I might be too early—but when I heard the announcer's next comments, I realized I was smart to snap on the radio.

"Okay folks, now here's an interesting story for parents out there who think our kids just enjoy spending mom and dad's money."

"Welcome to the lemonade stand for the new millennium friends, as you say hello to twin brothers; Trevor and Taylor Morgan. These two, eleven-year-old, enterprising students from the Meadows School are taking raising money for charity, very seriously indeed, they have big plans...as you'll see.

"These twins, plan to raise eight million dollars to build a residential facility for Cerebral Palsy patients—but they plan to do that in just four short months...do the math folks—that's two million a month! After that, they plan to raise another twenty million or so for other charities within a year's time, totaling a whopping twenty-eight million. And they don't plan on selling a single magazine, candy bar, glass of lemonade, or washing any dirty cars either. I will be right back with more of this incredible story after this word—stay tuned."

We were all going nuts; the ladies were wiping tears from their eyes while even my Dad was fogged up. Meanwhile the boys were jumping in place, high-fiving everyone while totally excited now.

The story was well developed, and so far, right on the money—pardon the pun. Finally after endless thirty-second commercials, the newscaster was back on.

"Now back to our story on those twin eleven-year-olds, out to raise twenty eight million dollars. These young entrepreneurs are the sons of prominent Las Vegas businessman, Marcus Morgan, who owns and operates the Verandas restaurant chain.

"The boys came up with their sweet idea of selling an unusual novelty Ice Cream known as 'Minis,' along with other Verandas goodies, from new Minis' Dessert Courts in their father's restaurants. And Dad it seems could not be happier, as all the profits will go into his firm's Verandas Foundation.

"This worthwhile concern benefits numerous charity and assistance agencies the world over, including our local Southern Nevada chapter of the Cerebral Palsy Foundation.

"The boys' Father aptly named their effort, the: Minis' Make Miracles Happen…Crusade. Their Minis' Dessert Courts will eventually be featured in all 347 Verandas restaurants nationwide, where according to the senior Morgan; they are hoping to sell ten million cups a year! As far as this reporter is concerned, that's an idea worth twenty eight million bucks…and a lick. Now onto our local traffic—Tony in Sky view 1280, take it away."

We were all elated. The report was totally accurate, uplifting, while sure to help publicize the boys' crusade by getting loyal Verandas customers into our restaurants.

"Dad, that was so cool."

"It sure was T-1."

"Do you think it will be on the radio again Dad?"

"Trevor, I would suppose so, at least for the remainder of the day."

We got into the Trail, while just as quickly settled in at the house. The boys asked my Dad to watch them in the pool so I decided to join them.

After changing, we got back downstairs where the boys wasted scant time making their beeline to the lagoon—while I stopped at the bar. My relaxed and contented state of leisure was interrupted by the telephone only minutes later.

"Marc?" Fleming appeared at the bar.

"Who's on the phone, Fleming?"

"Marc, its Robbie…he says the matter's rather urgent, sir."

"Alright, I'll take it here, after all the pool table looks strong enough to sustain my weight laying on it, don't you think?" Fleming and I had a nice chuckle as he then left me to my privacy.

"Hey there Robbo, what's up, did you hear the radio spot?"

"A lot is up Marc, and yes, I heard the radio station's report—it was fabulous."

"So spill it Robbie, I can hear panic in your voice—you're killing me here already—what's happening there that's so frigging important?

"The dam has burst Marc; we're getting calls from our units all around the country."

"Jesus, how's that possible? Maybe I'd better get back down to the office, what do you think?"

"No Marc, we're under control, but I can't speak for Jesse of course, as he's going nuts as we speak."

"Alright then, maybe I should come down to assist him?"

"What—and spoil all my fun? Not on your life Marc—don't you move."

"Robbie!" I yelled at my assistant for his insensitivity of joking at Jesse's expense.

"I'm sorry Marc; I guess I got a little carried away."

"Just a little Robbie? Jesus, I'd say. Look, you tell Jesse I'm coming down—correction, I mean the three of us, are undoubtedly coming down."

"Okay Marc, I'll let him know."

I went outdoors with this knowledge, but I wouldn't push it with the boys, even though I had to say something. If they wanted to pass, I was okay with it but I had to do the right thing just the same, by asking them personally.

"Boys; things are kind of going nuts down at the office, I guess I shouldn't have left so soon."

"Are you going back Dad?"

"Yes T-1, I think I really should."

"Dad, does it have to do with our Crusade?"

"Honestly Trev, yes of course it does."

"Okay then, we'll come too Dad—we'll get out. Come on Taylor, we have to move our bums."

"Okay Bro."

When both boys immediately got out of the water, I was very moved by their commitment. This wasn't a casual matter to them. They were truly invested...on a mission it seems. It was most definitely clear now. Their dedication had even—one-upped the lagoon!

The boys were ready in five minutes, which for them was a record, but as it turns out, we couldn't leave until I stole Dad's keys to his Navigator to get us to the office. You see, we left Paul on the driveway to lament his decision of choosing that moment in time to give Laverne her regularly scheduled bath. There Paul stood, somewhat in shock that we needed a lift while he was right in the middle of his favorite pastime—bathing his beloved Laverne…the look on his face was priceless.

CHAPTER 5

▼

ROUGH TRADE

WE FLEW INTO MY OFFICE where we found a nice group of people waiting for us. They immediately ran off a litany of issues, from interviews to just about everything else. It was all positive; at least up to this point...so it was all rather exciting.

"Okay everyone, let's simply slow down here while we smell the roses. What's happening Jess, why don't you take lead, then Bill will follow."

"Alright Marc, here it is in a nutshell—apparently AP was here or got the story from someone who was. It really doesn't matter, because the fact is, the story got carried by AP so now we're getting calls from every market we're in, and the isolated few—we're not."

"And all of it good?"

"Mostly Marc, but there were a minimal number of weird calls, but nothing alarming, just kooky people."

"That's wonderful Jess, don't you boys think so?"

"Cool, Dad." Trevor offered.

"Wicked, Dad." Followed out of Taylor.

"Yes it is guys, but as I see it, this means the word will spread like wildfire now. Unfortunately, we did not count on this happening. This means some of our units might get inundated for the Minis almost immediately. Guests might start to get peeved if we don't have the Minis in stock relatively soon. We must solve this critical issue this afternoon—everything else remains trivial by comparison. We can brainstorm those issues later in the week."

"Dad, I think I've got a solution."

"All right Trev, let's have it then."

"Okay Dad, why don't we just put them on the menu and keep them in our regular freezers until the kiosks are built? With all the stuff Jesse can do with the computer publishing, just do signs for the customers' tables.

"That's a thought Trev—wait a minute, I'm not sure that's going to work though, but I'll run it by Bob.

"Robbie let's get Bob or Katy on the phone if we can, no time like the present I always say?"

"Sure Marc."

Robbie had Bob on the phone immediately. After the usual pleasantries, we got down to business.

..."Now what can I do for you Marc?"

"Bob, we've got a little situation here that we never counted on, it seems that AP picked up our story today. We're afraid all hell is going to break loose, so we need to move forward with our Minis introduction sooner, somehow. The boys are still on a roll thank God, as Trevor has just come up with a quick fix. I want to run his idea by you for your opinion; I think it could work with a little creativity."

"What's the idea, as I wouldn't put anything past either one of those two?"

"Trevor suggests we sell them off the menu temporarily so we can begin immediate shipments. He suggested storing them in our reach-in freezers for the time being. After I agreed with him initially, I remembered the problem with the temperature needs requiring your special freezers. How would the ice cream do if we supplemented our freezers with additional dry ice to drop them lower to what the product requires?"

"Marc, that's smart thinking on your part, the dry ice would work; but I can help you without it. We never have a shortage of storage freezers at the plant, only limited kiosks. All I need is your space availability in each individual kitchen. I'll then begin drop shipping the proper sized freezer to each unit with the Ice Cream, utensils, and dry ice inside for transit—this will get the ball rolling for you. Once the freezers arrive, plug them in for an hour, get rid of the dry ice, set up your product in the buckets we provide and you're good to go.

"After these initial drop shipments though, we'll begin the distribution center shipments to your warehouses as each region receives their kiosks... fair enough?"

"That sounds wonderful Bob, damn I was freaking out over this mess, and it was all over nothing...when can you start shipping product?"

"By Friday, the first drops could go out Marc."

"Thanks Bob, you are a lifesaver, now get us that Ice Cream and we'll love you forever."

"Consider it done Marc, but right now I think I ought to call the factory to fill them in on everything I just committed them to as well. Make sure you say hello to my favorite set of twins,—see ya Marc."

"So long Bob and thanks." I hung up the phone.

"It would seem gang, that we have one less problem, thanks to Trevor's brilliant save—good going son."

"Thanks Dad, glad to be of help—and without Taylor for a change."

After we all stopped cracking up, Taylor threw in a compliment himself.

"Hey bro, was that a shot? Seriously Trev, really nice save."

"Thanks bro, I'm sorry, it was just a joke."

After we prioritized the remaining smaller issues by assigning them out to people around the room, I then adjourned the meeting. The boys and I left for a second time…still feeling elated.

As we were driving home, my thoughts turned to Miranda. I wondered if she already was aware of these developments of how our two young men were following in her footsteps with their crusade to raise this money. I knew she would be proud of them, while I had to hope of me, as well.

Trevor interrupted my thoughts with a question.

"Hey Dad, do you suppose we could go out to dinner tonight at our Summerlin restaurant?"

"T-1, if you boys would like to do that, I guess I'm okay with it. But I think we should check to see what Sofia has planned first, besides, I wanted to watch the news at six."

"Alright Dad, but why not call her to make sure, is that okay?"

"Sure Trev, your wish is my command."

I called Sofia to inquire as to what was afoot for dinner. When she told me her menu, I said thanks and hung up.

"T-1, we'll have to go tomorrow night—sorry. Sofia is making Osso Buco tonight guys—I can't miss that—its one of my personal faves as you guys live to say. I'm sure it will quickly become a favorite of yours and T-man's too."

"Its fine Dad, can we go tomorrow night for certain, then?"

"Sure, T-1, that would be great…but what's the rush?"

"I just want to take another look in the General Store."

"Oh, no problem son."

"What's Osso Buco Dad?"

"T-man, it's an Italian dish of braised Veal Shanks in something you'd think of as a stew of sorts. It might remind you two of a steak and kidney pie from back home, although not being British—it actually tastes delicious, son."

"Cute Daddy—but only because Grace didn't hear that." Taylor laughed.

"Believe me T-man, you are so right...but it truly is tasty I can assure you."

We got home, where of course everyone wanted to know the latest. While the boys returned quickly to the pool, I poured myself a vodka and cranberry for Dad and me. I then explained what had transpired which had everyone excited that our story had made national coverage.

Promptly at 5:45, Dad and I set up my monitors in the great room on all three local major networks; happily he was finally getting proficient with the many different steps and settings. I called the boys in from outside to change out of their bathers as I flipped on our VCRs to tape. All three networks mentioned the story in their opening plugs, so I already knew that we had hit 'publicity pay dirt'.

We all gathered in front of the media wall as we waited. Mom suggested we completely shut off the volume on two sets so we could concentrate better, which I agreed made sense. Naturally, we started with the twins' favorite channel, ABC.

After covering the leading national stories, the female anchor on our first set, led with our story in the local news segment. This thrilled me, but somewhat surprised me. I was already thrilled with our upcoming dinner—this premier placement on ABC had me excited as I turned my attentions to the anchor as she began our feature.

"In top local news today—Las Vegas appears to have two new civic-minded citizens. They have an eye for helping others less fortunate, but with a most unusual twist. Let's go to Larry Morton with the complete story—Larry?"

"Yes Chris, here is an unbelievable story for our viewers, yet all of it inspirational.

"It's normally rare in Las Vegas, to see newly-arrived residents immediately get involved with helping others. Yet it happened today in a big way—on your screen are eleven-year-old twins, Trevor and Taylor Morgan. Yes Chris—I said, eleven-years-old!

During this portion of the report, the screen was split. Larry Morton was reporting on the left side while a picture of the twins and the facility shared the right side of the screen.

"Their ambitious plan is to raise eight million dollars to construct the residential center for disabled clients, seen on the right side of your screen.

This state of the art, adaptive living facility, would benefit our local CPF clients with Cerebral Palsy. What makes this story so unusual is that these boys do not plan to stop there. You see, they believe they can raise the eight million dollars needed for this facility in only one hundred and twenty-five days, so their total goal is twenty-eight million over the next twelve months!

"If you think that this sounds a little far-fetched, you haven't met these two determined brothers. I met the ambitious pair earlier today at their father's corporate offices; he is restaurateur Marcus Morgan, of Verandas fame.

"It seems that Dad's; non-profit foundation was desperate. That apparently was the inspiration needed to hatch the boys' multi-million-dollar crusade. Yet Dad makes no bones about it—he merely accepted their offer of help, then the boys developed their idea from there." Now the report switched to my taped commentary with the twins by my side.

"Mr. Morgan, just how did all of this come about?"

"Larry, it really happened so fast, it's mind-boggling in a way...you see Larry, within an hour's time, they had it all worked out beautifully. The right products, how to market them, plus where to sell it all from...it all blew me away honestly. They put the basic marketing concepts together, so that our marketing people were able to pick up the ball to run with it from there."

"What was your biggest surprise over their idea?"

"That's easy Larry; their brilliant stroke was to bypass our dining rooms. Instead, they wanted to sell the Minis along with our coffee and other complimentary desserts in our General Store retail area from single-focused kiosks, creating a 'Dessert Court' theme. They then drew up a flyer to hand all guests on their way in, focusing on their crusade to raise the money.

"Tell us a little about the Minis, Mr. Morgan, I understand the product is originally from England?"

"Yes, Minis are a flash-frozen Ice Cream novelty that the boys were familiar with back in their native England."

"That does sound novel Mr. Morgan. You know sir, twenty-eight million dollars is an impressive sum of money to raise,—so what other causes is the money going to from the boys' crusade?"

"Larry, the Verandas Foundation assists charities the world over. Beyond that, Trevor here has come up with a new project of his own." Larry turned to Trevor:

"Trevor, what's this new project you want to do?"

"Okay...after we've raised what we need for the CPF folks, I'd like to do something else. Let's use some money to help folks that work, but are living on the streets, shelters, or in their cars because they don't make enough. They can't afford a house or flat, because of all the money that costs to move into. I want to set up something to help those people get that money together. We could help them move by paying that money for them. And they would eventually pay it back in little amounts; so many more people could be helped the same way too. And we could even help them by finding them roommates if needed so they could afford their rent easier."

"Trevor that's a great idea."

"Taylor; where do you and your brother come up with all these great ideas?"

"Back in England our Mum, before she died, did something like Trevor's idea, but not exactly…his idea is better—plus it does much more. So Mummy should share in some of the credit I think—not just Trevor—sorry bro. And it was Dad's idea to help CPF build their home, not Trevor, or me, we just thought of the Dessert Court with the Minis. That did make it all work—but it's not like we invented the things, you know, it's already sold here."

"And that's our story Chris; back to you—this is Larry Morton reporting."

"Thanks Larry, and yes, that was a truly inspirational story. We'll be right back after this."

As the story ended, I rewound the VCRs, as we switched to the other two stations to play their reports in succession. They were equally favorable. Yet the final station's report was different…we liked its approach the best.

The anchor, Gerry Riddell, had a very interesting spin on his introduction.

"This next story comes to us from Bonnie Stewart. They say that a picture is worth a thousand words; so how many 'dollars' is a cup of Ice Cream worth—when measured by the cup? Candidly, it would appear to be a whole heck of a lot—Bonnie?"

"Yes Gerry; it seems that Ice Cream primarily, is the sweetest and fastest way to raise large amounts of money. Just ask twin brothers; Trevor and Taylor Morgan and they'll tell you all about it with unabashed candor.

"These two diminutive entrepreneurs have taken it upon themselves to spearhead raising eight million dollars to build a residential center for the disabled. This adaptive-living home will be for clients of CPF, our local advocate organization for Cerebral Palsy clients here in town. But believe it or not, after they've accomplished raising this formidable sum, the brothers plan to raise another 20 million before they've been at it a year!

"The real story here is how they plan to sell that much ice cream, but first some background.

"The twin boys are eleven-years-old, along with being sixth grade students at the Meadows School. They came up with their 'sweet' plan, after offering their assistance to their father; Las Vegas' leading Restaurateur, Marcus Morgan.

"It seems Dad's Verandas charitable foundation was having the typical problem of how to raise some much-needed cash. They had a residential center they were committed to seeing built. And at an eight-million-dollar price tag for the two-hundred-bed facility, that's quite a formidable sum. Needing this money desperately, Morgan did what any father would do, he simply asked his kids to solve his problem. And solve it, they did Gerry.

"Now before you get the impression that these boys took a year or more of planning to develop their idea, think again. All told, the twins took an hour! These are eleven-year-olds after-all, so they had to have it wrapped up before dinner, according to their father. You would assume that given their lineage, creativity runs in the boys' genes straight from their father, but not so, says dad. You see, Morgan personally led an unsuccessful search of over two years looking for a miracle product to raise this money in short order, before his boys came along with their solution.

"Trevor and Taylor Morgan's; 'Minis Make Miracles Happen'…Crusade offers a sophisticated marketing campaign developed by the boys in that hour's time. It places Minis' Dessert Courts featuring Minis and other dessert items, along with Veranda's famous coffee in all three-hundred and forty-seven Verandas restaurants. All of the net profits from their crusade will go strictly to the Verandas Foundation…and with that many restaurants, Morgan projects over ten million cups of the ice cream alone will be sold annually!

"I caught up with our two ice cream retailers earlier:

"Taylor; when did you know you had the answer to raising all of this money?"

"When I told Dad that the problem might be solved. We showed him our sketch. He looked at it, and then kept staring at it too, he didn't say much… but then he smiled. We figured out that he liked something about it—except we didn't know what, yet."

"And it only took you both an hour?"

"Yes Miss, about, we had to sketch it out for Dad…that took some time too."

"Trevor, are you two always this quick coming up with solutions to your problems?"

"No Miss, our teacher Mrs. Geary—she gives us tough math homework so this was much easier—compared to that…believe me".

"And that's our story ladies and gentlemen. Look for Minis Make Miracles Happen to be available at your favorite Verandas location in the upcoming weeks for a great cause. But lastly; remember our moral here: When in trouble; ask your kids to solve all your problems! This is Bonnie Stewart reporting… back to you Gerry."

"Thank you Bonnie for a most inspiring story."

We all loved this reporter's spin on our story.

We shut off the TVs as we talked for a while about how all of this publicity might really make the difference for the crusade's success.

"Listen boys—you've both singlehandedly saved your father's hide, that's all I can say."

"Do you really think so Gramps?"

"Yes Trevor, you boys have a winner here—there's just no two ways about it."

"Gee, I sure hope all of this really goes the way we have planned it."

"Don't worry Taylor, to quote your father—have faith. That's what he told me you see—twelve years ago. Right after he asked me to lend him a quarter of a million dollars, so that he could build his first restaurant. A nice place he said, where you would eat alongside ghosts no less, catch your own fish for dinner, while the staff all sang,—show tunes just to shut up the ghosts! Boys, back then, I was just a bit skeptical on his concept myself. Nevertheless, I had faith in him…and look what happened. So if your Dad says that this will work, I'm confident it will."

"I hope so Gramps, I'd hate to have it not raise all that money we promised everybody…what if we're wrong?"

"Look T-man, I don't think you have to worry about that, I'll make sure we put our best efforts forward. But, if it doesn't work out to plan—I'll personally do the next best thing."

"What's that Daddy?"

"Simple T-man, I'll write a check out for the difference myself, son."

"Oh my God, you mean you could do it by yourself Daddy?"

"Yes son, I can—but that is no one else's business…understand?"

"Sure I do Daddy—but wow, you know I never thought about that before."

"Good Taylor, that's ideal as far as I'm concerned. You should never obsess over money, or think about money as something that makes you better than anyone else. Nor is it the answer to all your problems, because it isn't, trust me…if someone asks you about money, tell them you don't know and leave it at that…got it?"

"So, money can't solve all your problems Dad, cuz Bobby says it can?"

"No Trevor, of course not—it couldn't stop Mummy's cancer, nor could it save Grandfather. Money is not the end-all that many people think it is… people like Bobby. Now don't get me wrong honey, money's a big help, which makes it nice to have around, but it simply can't solve every problem nor disaster, or make you happy just by itself. If you aren't already happy with yourself before it's acquired, it's worthless to you."

"Okay Dad, we understand." I received from them.

I was refreshing Dad's drink, along with my own, when the telephone rang. Fleming informed me that it was Gloria Dehane calling so I picked up the phone.

"Hey there Gloria, so what's new—anything interesting happen today?" Naturally, we both lost it a little.

"Marcus, you are too much. Listen, I just heard from my National office, the story's running in New York already—isn't that wonderful?"

"Really, well that's great to hear, I would guess it makes a great human interest story in other markets?"

"Yes it does Marc. Listen, when do you expect to be actually selling the Minis?"

"In around a week they'll begin rolling out. To speed things up, we'll be selling them off the menu. Remember, our grand opening for the first Dessert Court will be the Saturday after next at the Summerlin location."

"Yes of course, but I wanted to call just to thank all three of you again for making my life-long dream a reality. God Bless you Marcus Morgan, and for those two geniuses of yours too."

"You are most welcome Gloria. Naturally, I will extend your thanks to the two geniuses as well."

"Thanks Marc, good night."

"Night, Gloria."

I hug up the phone to share Gloria's thanks with the boys.

We now all went into the kitchen to eat Sofia's wonderful Osso Buco. I would have to say that everyone assembled had a wonderful dinner.

After we stuffed ourselves to the gills, the rest of our evening flew by with numerous phone calls coming in from family and friends around the country. Before I knew it, it was bedtime for the boys. I went upstairs to settle them in, but couldn't help but think again, just how proud I was of them...so we talked at length about all of these feelings...before they went to bed quite content, I believe.

I awoke at seven, to the sound of my alarm along with Trevor snoring loudly into my armpit...the poor kid. I went to wake up the boys...strike that—I tried to wake up the boys. They were not very happy, nor were they giving in to my commands, it was time for desperate measures. I went into the bath suite to call Grace downstairs.

"Gracie honey, is breakfast fixed?"

"Of course Marc, it's 7:05."

"What are we having?"

"Blueberry pancakes and syrup, bacon and eggs, and Steel Cut, Scottish Creamed Oat Porridge—why?"

"Could you send a tray up to my room please, I'm desperate for reinforcements?"

"Reinforcements for what—Marc?"

"To get these two boys of mine up, they're playing hardball this morning. I figured the smell of your breakfast ought to do the trick."

"Oh, why don't you just use Miranda's method love?"

"Gee Grace; I guess I must have missed that part of class—what's Miranda's method?"

"Drop their bed sheets and give them each a nice brisk snap on their little sleepy arses, of course."

"Oh I see, well thanks Gracie. I'll either see you with them in fifteen, or you'll be hearing from me for the food momentarily."

"Trust me love, it's a tried and true method", as Grace continued laughing loudly as she hung up the phone.

I returned to my slumbering boys very quietly. The comforter, which was already drawn down the bed from my recent exit, made my approach that much easier. In one fell swoop, I approached Trevor's bottom, giving him a nice ripe slap across his bum. Bingo!

"Ouch Dad, that hurt."

Before even responding, I wasted little precious time in doing likewise with his twin, also having the desired effect.

"Daddy, my God—that hurt."

"Look, T-Men, the next time I say to get up—I mean get up now! Do we understand one another?" I yelled out sternly.

"Yes sir." I received in a rather insulted—yet groggy response.

"Now you two get in the bathroom to get your bums dressed and ready for school or you'll feel my hand again, I can assure you."

They got the message. They made for the sanctuary of the bath suite while I followed them to hop into my steam shower, myself. By the time I was out and drying off, they were already dressed and out of there. I looked up at the ceiling as I said to myself—thanks, Mir.

Later as I was attempting to drop them off at school, my greatest fear presented itself right in front of my eyes. There were news vans in the lot with reporters waiting at the school's entrance. I was actually a little peeved that no one from the school had bothered to call me, to warn us. After all, I had the foresight along with concern to warn them, I would have appreciated the same courtesy returned.

I told Paul to keep going. I instructed him to turn at the next corner to pull over. I noticed that both boys seemed totally shocked at this press invasion, as they were silent for a change. Meanwhile, I picked up my cell phone, retrieved the school's number, and then dialed.

"The Meadows School."

"Yes, good morning, this is Marc Morgan. Are you aware the press are sitting in your drop off lot—waiting to pounce on my sons?"

"Yes Mr. Morgan, we just got word of it ourselves. We were retrieving your number to call you to warn you to avoid the entrance. First though, there is an alternative way to get the boys in without being bothered. Drive around on Scholar Drive; to the rear receiving area next to the Gymnasium…we'll get them in there. We have already radioed our custodian just before your call… can you find your way over there alright?"

"Yes, we'll figure it out, thank you for your assistance…Mr.…?"

"Simpson, sir, and it's my pleasure Mr. Morgan. You know, I saw the boys myself last night on TV, it sure is a wonderful thing they're trying to do—you must be very proud of them?"

"Yes I am, but thanks again Mr. Simpson." I hung up as I instructed Paul where to go.

We got to the receiving area, where I scooted the boys inside through the gymnasium, then all of us made our way into the main building. Mr. Riley, the assistant principal, now walked up to greet us.

"Good morning Mr. Morgan, and Masters, Morgan—sorry about all of this, we didn't get wind of it until right before your call. My word, they really are like vultures…aren't they?"

"Yes Mr. Riley. Look, would you please just make sure personally that the boys get to their classroom safely…you let me handle the press—fair enough?"

"Yes Mr. Morgan, boys; are you ready to get to class?"

"Yes Mr. Riley." The boys hugged me stealthily as I wished them a good day in school…then they were off with Mr. Riley escorting them.

I was truly pissed off now. I made my way through the school grounds on foot while I called Paul on the cell. I told him to drive around to the main entrance, as I went outside to greet the press coming out from behind them… it was the classic diversionary tactic. Let them focus on the limo driving up, while I appear out of nowhere to demand my own answers with them still in their surprised and confused state.

"Good morning ladies and gentlemen, I'd like to have a quick word with you if I may?" This of course got their attention as they all scurried over to me with microphones and videographers in tow. At least some of them recognized me from our press conference.

When they had all assembled, I asked 'my' first question.

"Might I inquire ladies and gentlemen, as to why you people think it is ever appropriate to disrupt an entire School campus? Did you honestly believe that the school or I would allow that?"

A fiery redheaded woman spoke right up who I recognized in an instant—it

was none other than, Condescension—oh pardon me; Concepcion Connors…
the queen bitch…I mean queen, of the Las Vegas press corps.

Concepcion Sylvia Connors was without a doubt, the most insensitive and
disliked reporter in all of Las Vegas—and far beyond a mere bitch!

As a young reporter years before, she had successfully broke a major
corruption story using impressive and creative tactics. It was undoubtedly her
best work, but certainly—her last! Somehow, she had successfully milked it
ever since. Yet the woman was a master at utilizing the English vocabulary
for one thing. She used it expertly, typically to trap less knowledgeable people
within her clutches during her interviews.

Sadly over time, Connors became jaded and convinced that every human-
interest story was some con, just waiting for her rapacious expose'. As such,
her many editors/producers over the years, had sacrificed their integrity for
ratings by offering her more and more free rein. She and everyone associated
with her investigations, known infamously as 'Team Concepcion' locally,
were totally out of control. She was ruthless, brutal, and it was said she made
Joseph McCarthy look milquetoast—but here she was now—staring me
down. Honestly, the woman had personally destroyed more lives, than the
thousands of 'actor-extras' in a Cecile B. de Mille epic film.

Was I a lucky soul or what? Leave it to me to pull the one and only true
barracuda in town—onto this story. Being the eternal optimist that I was
though, I contemplated that I would just do my best Clarence Darrow while
hoping for the best…I was no dummy myself, after all.

"Mr. Morgan, we report the news, that's our job…it's certainly not yours!
Your sons are the hot news under the microscope right now…although I
wonder frankly; should they? Just the same, that makes them fair game
right now, wherever they are—so, sorry if our little intrusion into your sons'
privileged little world isn't convenient—for you. However, we don't tell you
how to run your restaurants, so may I suggest that you don't—tell us how to
do our jobs either."

My I thought she's getting off to such a cordial start…as usual.

"My word. Thank you for bloviating the facts for my benefit…Ms.…?"

"Ms. Connors, Mr. Morgan—Concepcion Sylvia Connors, from CCC
News."

Sometimes I just enjoy playing stupid, so sue me!

"My word—CCC news—is it? Well thank you again Ms. Connors—for
your very enlightening and educational explanation of the facts."

"Yes, well fine Mr. Morgan, I have a question for you now, if you don't
plan to shirk from it?"

"I see Ms. Connors, so why not ask it, or explain it to all of us, whichever.

I know that personally speaking, that I would prefer—just about anything to your otherwise funereal rudeness."

"I would be delighted Mr. Morgan, you see; I've been around, so I know how to smell through a story. I have thoroughly reviewed your press release along with footage of the conference—but I don't buy a word of any of it, sir."

The other press representatives seemed taken aback by her candor—or were they? True; it was an unwritten rule of the press to allow a colleague the floor to continue an effective 'fishing expedition'. But I also had to wonder, had she earlier, thrown another spin to them from her bully pulpit already?

Connors had her hooks in me now, so did they all want her to reel me in if she could? I then noticed something else for the first time, which disturbed me instantly. The reporters' body language, along with their nuances, led me to suspect, that at least some of them might blindly agree with her accusation. It was as if she was merely mirroring their doubts too. Granted I wasn't sure of this, yet it was a gnawing and troublesome feeling all the same.

Was it possible for the rest of our cynical and hard-edged press corps to be that jaded and close-minded too...Christ? I already knew they were a highly biased lot to begin with.

The bitch was waiting, yet I felt up to the challenge...besides, I had the truth in my corner. Then I remembered something that I had learned very early on in my career—sometimes the truth wasn't good enough!

I quickly thought about what this grating reporter was looking for, yet more so, how judgmental she was. As I laid out my defense, it dawned on me that I had already fallen victim to her classic ruse. She had baited my ego... and quite well I admitted silently to myself. Now I would have to spin that to possible advantage.

"My goodness, Ms. Connors, I'm surprised—did you really think you could get me to answer your question—by baiting me? That's the oldest ploy in the book. Say, did you learn that at correspondence,—oh; I'm sorry, I meant to say—correspondents' school?

"Come on Connors; accusing me of something like shirking from a question—can't we possibly do better than that?

"Yet of course, you'll soon be telling me I'm already shirking the question, which is your whole game plan anyway, right?

"Unfortunately for—you, I have no need to shirk anything, as I've spoken the truth...something you would find—much too novel. As such, I have no reservation about answering your stupid question, other than its absurd and inept—like yourself.

"But you know Ms. Connors; first you must help me out some. You see;

I'm not sure what part of our press conference has confused your itty, bitty brain? So enlighten us—what is it that you have doubts about in our story?"

"Alright Mr. Morgan, I'll bite, but this is so droll—oh, sorry—should I use an itty, bitty word instead? It's a preposterous story on its face, but nice try, I give you an 'A' for creativity. The true motives of course, I'm sure we'd all find more interesting, but they're harder to figure…aren't they? So, let's just review the facts rather than your inane hyperbole sir.

"Your sons are eleven—lacking any semblance of either experience or training. You claim that they only moved into town this week…yet you expect all of us to believe that they—and they alone, cogitated this utterly brilliant musing?

"Yes Ms. Connors, I do expect all of you to believe my assertion—as those are the simple facts. Yet; I never said that the story doesn't have a certain farfetched or Pollyanna-ish charm to it—as it certainly does. We covered all of that candidly in the first paragraph of our press release actually—though I doubt you can read.

"Secondly, Ms. Connors, what is my track record professionally? Am I known to be flakey or a promoter? Am I not normally shown to be typically trustworthy instead? Haven't I run an honest and successful business for a dozen years now—so is there any reason to doubt my sincerity in this matter? And in all of that time, have I ever brought dishonor to our fair city, or have I received countless civic honors instead?

"I would hope that both of those things would earn me some credibility—but apparently not with you Ms. Connors—or may I be so bold as to informally call you by your first name…hum, Condescension?

"But you know, your presence here today represents something far more malicious and sinister…the very worst qualities that the public despises most about our local press. You are not only cynical, but sanctimonious, portentous, judgmentally bias, along with being wholly worthless as a caring or compassionate human being.

"With you, there always seems to be an angle doesn't there, or some gimmick or other deception? For you, ingenuousness and altruism are beyond dead—they're extinct.

"I want to remind everyone here today who might surmise otherwise; that this all began with my son's simple words. Words that are lost, albeit true, on our lovely Condescension here—but just the same, these words were spoken by my son: How can we help too Daddy?

"For most people, words such as his would convey a wonderful, heartfelt feeling…yet for you Connors, they hold contempt, scorn, and ridicule—shame on you Condescension—oh, I'm so sorry, its Concepcion isn't it?"

"Lastly, unlike your other colleagues here, you will not be allowed to interview my sons at a more appropriate time—if ever! You do not deserve the honor of being in their presence or company for a split second of time… nor will I expose them to your vitriol and venom.

"What you lack in humanity, you make up for—in your callousness. I have no further use for you—good day Madam!"

That did the trick surprisingly. She was clearly going into her rarely needed, reconciliatory mode. Her quick, sidestepping of the issue, followed.

"Fine Mr. Morgan, I apologize. Now when can we speak to the boys then?"

"My Ms. Connors—you are clever aren't you? You know, typically I would appreciate the question under different circumstances. It implies that my concerns for my sons as well as their school are taken into consideration. Thank you for your thoughtful, yet useless—attempt at reconciliation.

"Naturally, my position stands. In fact you will never speak to them as long as a single breath resonates in my lungs. If CCC expects to speak to them, I'd suggest you call your producer to advise them to send someone else. And—anyone on Team Condescension naturally will be turned away forthwith…oh there I go again, so callous of me, sorry…its Concepcion isn't it? Yet please relay to them that they should send someone perhaps a bit more polite and professional next time."

This was nasty to be sure, but this leech had it richly coming. Yet by shooting down one barracuda, it's amazing how quickly the rest tow the line. What survives is a civilized forum with you in charge, but more importantly—them acting humane. From the rear of the group, I now heard the question I had been hoping, longing, and waiting for.

"Fair enough, Mr. Morgan. How would this best work out for you and the twins then?"

"Who asked that question, please?"

"I did Mr. Morgan, Burt Jacobs, sir—I'm with Fox News."

"Great Burt, you just earned a private one-on-one interview, congratulations. Burt you can ride in with me to my office, the rest of you may call my assistant Robbie to book a ten-minute slot with the boys and me for this coming Sunday at our home from one pm on.

"Now if there are no further 'pressing' matters, pardon my intentional pun, I'd suggest that you all leave these premises immediately. Your presence is most disruptive and inappropriate to all the children here as well as the administration."

It worked beautifully. They quickly backed right off as Burt moved forward to greet me formally…extending his hand when he reached me.

Meanwhile, Concepcion it seems was being surrounded by some of the other reporters. I had to hope it was just conciliatory, rather than assembling as co-conspirators.

Oh well, only time would tell, but there was no time now to worry about it.

"Good morning sir—thanks so much for this unexpected honor."

"And a fine good morning to you—Burt is it? Look, don't mention it; you were both my savior and my pigeon…so you've earned it." I said as I opened Laverne's door as he entered.

"Your pigeon, sir?"

"Yes Burt, in a manner of speaking. You see, I am not exactly unaccustomed to the mind-set of the press. I can cast out and reel in, the human beings from the barracudas, like our Ms. Connors there. I also know what it feels like to call the boss with the confession that I'd been 86'd. It's not fun.

"No it isn't Mr. Morgan; I've seen it happen myself. But from what I saw, kudos to you as no one deserves it more than that piece of work. Although honestly, I won't mince words here either—all of us had at least some degree of doubt in the authenticity of your storyline sir."

"I'm sure that you all did Burt—that's your job after all, but it's a truthful story—so call me pisher if you want…but I can't change the truth. You see, it's the only story I got, so I'm sticking with it. You have to look past your distrust and reporter's mindset on this one Burt…case closed. And as far as that bitch goes, she's a freight wreck; because she actually has the power—not to tell her boss she was 86'd! And I'd be less than honest if I didn't tell you that that scares me somewhat—off the record. With her, one always has to worry; after all, she's got one hell of a track record for burying innocent people. She's laid to rest—more victims than a high school drivers' education movie, my friend."

"What are you worrying about sir; I'd say you put her in her place quite nicely?"

"Yeah, but I'm only wondering if there's going to be a 'round two', naturally. I mean hell; if reasonable guys like you, doubt my honesty—where does that leave the rest of your ilk? What are my chances at the end of the day in this scenario? After all Burt, all I have is my integrity…what else do any of us have?"

"Okay Mr. Morgan, I guess I concede your point."

"Alright, enough of this doom and gloom, Burt, today's your lucky day; what are you waiting for?"

"Thanks Mr. Morgan, I appreciate all of this, believe me. This is only my "third story since joining Fox, so it doesn't hurt to beat my competition either. While they are all waiting for Sunday, we'll be all over the story and out of your hair completely."

"Nice choice of words Burt—I couldn't agree with you more…so what's your first question for me?"

"Okay Mr. Morgan, but this first one is a little personal. Honestly, it will set the tone of what Fox News is most interested in knowing. Lastly, as they say, I'm only the messenger, so I'd like you to know these are not always 'my' questions.

"Candidly sir, our research department has turned up some very interesting facts on you along with the boys…so I've been asked to verify the accuracy with you for the record, so here goes…"

…"Wow Burt, you sure cut right to the chase, don't you? Okay; let me hear them, what's your question?"

"Alright. Is it really true Mr. Morgan, that you were not even aware of your sons' existence prior to this past October?"

"Yes Burt, that's absolutely true—but it's also a very long and complicated story—care to hear it?"

"Sure…yes of course Mr. Morgan—that's why I asked it."

"Okay Burt, but here's my caveat first. I really do not want this part of the story to become the theme of your story. Our reason for talking today is how two, eleven-year-olds helped their father by coming up with a fantastic marketing concept. As a result, this concept will raise millions of dollars for a good cause—end of story. Are we agreed then?"

"Yes Mr. Morgan, I can do that—you have my word. I'll limit the background filler you share with me to no more than twenty percent of my piece."

"Ten percent Burt."

"Ten would be near impossible to produce a good piece of work Mr. Morgan. Maybe fifteen percent could cut it?"

"Fair enough Burt, but I'm holding you to that. Given the little altercation I just had with our lovely Condescension Connors, this entire conversation is being tape recorded naturally. That includes your promise just now, so understand I will hold you to that…likely, Eric Pollins will too."

"I'm sorry, but who is Eric Pollins, Mr. Morgan?"

"Why—he's our corporate attorney Burt."

"Yes sir—I read you loud and clear."

"Good. Now here's the answer to your question."

I sincerely liked this kid—I instinctively trusted him, so I told him everything. I withheld literally nothing of consequence. When I was finished, he was visibly moved.

"You know Mr. Morgan, that 'is' some story…I'm not sure how I should feel about it you know. I can say this though, when you're ready to write your autobiography, I'd be honored to 'ghost' you, should you need one?"

"Thank you Burt, actually I never thought to write one. If I ever do, it would be more of a love story—than an autobiography. I'll assume that's still commercial enough these days, but back to your last comment before the book stuff. Burt, I can understand your reaction, as I felt the same feelings myself, believe me. As it all unfolded, I was aghast before becoming quite angry—yet full of angst too. At first, I couldn't get past those emotions, but once I did, the 'big picture' opened up for me if you will…with knowledge comes understanding Burt. So the anxiety and regrets passed, as I became at peace with the whole situation, rather than angry or bitter.

"Now, what's your next question?"

"Okay, here's the one you're likely dreading, so think of Ms. Connors—but I'll try to be more tactful than her. Some people find it just a little hard to buy into how this story is being portrayed. It's a little hard to swallow—that this went down entirely the way you say it has. What is your comment on that specifically?"

"My comment Burt is, that your people are absolutely logical in thinking that way. I could see myself even saying that, if I were an outsider in the press. In addition, that is what you are all paid to scrutinize. However I will assure you again—it's exactly what happened.

"In order to understand it Burt, you would really have to look for a moment at my late wife's values. Doing for others and the less fortunate, were the 'core values' of her entire professional life.

"Moreover, I now realize this was apparently not lost on our sons growing up either. I could not tell you myself, as you already know I was not around. I can say however, that when Taylor said those fateful words, he not only meant them…he understood he was offering his help with a full heart and commitment. Hell, thinking it over Burt, I think both of them were used to asking this very question of their mother too…countless times.

"The rest of it—meaning the ease in which it all came together from there, I'm really at a loss to offer any sound explanation honestly. I could attribute it to something preordained; magical or even divine in nature, but who the heck would believe that anyway Burt, really?

"Nevertheless, the idea that the boys came up with was so damn obvious—yet so incredibly brilliant too. You could actually contend—it was 'so obvious' that it was simply overlooked by the rest of us. I still can't understand how our entire staff seemed to miss an outside product like the Minis…but we certainly did!

"Listen Burt—let me be candid, my kids are ordinary eleven-year-olds, they are most definitely not rocket scientists. Mind you, they're sharp, but they're just kids, you know?

"In our marketing department at Verandas, we were focusing on stuffed animals and take home food products we already distributed. The boys looked from a fresh prospective, with a new and different foursome of eyes from outside our box. They took my advice to simply remember things they themselves had observed or knew on the outside—in essence they carried no creative baggage.

"Where they actually impressed me the most was their retail model to support the Minis' success. Their Minis' Dessert Court concept was aces. Yet, if you asked them what I just referred to by their 'retail model', they likely wouldn't have a clue what the term itself means—see? They just knew instinctively how to get people interested in buying the Minis by creating the right retail presence. Most people just wouldn't know how to do that—believe me I've been there—having tried to do it at times...myself!

"The boys' saw the Minis at one of our local resorts here, yet apparently many times before that, only back in England. But the boys didn't stop by duplicating those applications. They came up with an ideal way to get people drawn over to the stands, then—motivated to buy. Their retail model brought a dessert and coffee kiosk along for the ride into their mix, creating the dessert court concept to tie it together with some good old American schmaltz if you will. And with the kiosks right in the middle of our retail area, honestly Burt, it was brilliant.

"Truly Burt, that was their brilliant stroke, so believe me; I'm thrilled as well as humbled as hell to be their beneficiary...honestly!

"You know, in essence, two valuable years were lost for those folks at CPF. Yes Burt, I thank God for my sons' intervention—believe me...I do.

"Now; you have just heard the one hundred percent truth, out of one very embarrassed, yet humbled father—even as a successful executive."

"Amazing Mr. Morgan, okay—and yes, I can buy this explanation...so will the boys one day run your business, then?"

"I can't say Burt. I have no idea what their long-term dreams are—hey they're eleven, therefore nowhere near contemplating that yet. Right now, it's all the fantasy stuff still, but I will say this with full certainty. Their true talent, or gift if you will, is their music. Burt, they are really gifted in that way. Like any father, I am very proud of their many talents, yet honestly Burt, I'm not exaggerating this fact. I've recently encouraged them to start a garage band to get a little more confidence under their belt. Honestly, I think their potential is limitless—and yet, I'm quite aware I'm biased, in case I'm wrong."

"Mr. Morgan, getting back on topic, would you like them to run Verandas someday?"

"You know Burt, if you ask my ego that question, you already know the answer...we both do. But if you were to ask strictly my heart, I'd have to say—no, not really."

"Now, that's a very surprising answer Mr. Morgan—can you elaborate?"

"Sure, but only if you promise to 'can' the Mister stuff already. Burt, please call me Marc, hell my Dad's not even in the car—so there's no Mr. Morgan here...follow me? You know Burt, I can't be more than five years your senior, we're contemporaries, nothing more."

"Yes Marc...I do agree with you. Thank you for the informality...so what is your answer? You know I'm sorry, I don't mean to interrupt my own question, but you're simply nothing like I thought you'd be Marc."

"Really? Well how exactly did you previously perceive me then Burt—I'm just curious?"

"Oh, I don't know exactly. You know, the typical self-made, super rich, successful entrepreneur type, I guess. The kind of guy perhaps, we all saw back there earlier—thumping on Concepcion while turning her into mincemeat.

"You know Marc, I did my homework on you...I've checked you out. In the inner-circles of the food service industry, you're known as 'the quiet guy', yet a genius and skillful negotiator but brutal too at times—with your honesty. You are known as an industry innovator, a very hands-on CEO with a charismatic personality—plus a bit of a dreamer too. Your employees therefore, are super devoted and rightly worship you on the lines of a Dave Thomas, Ray Kroc, or Carl Karcher.

"Financially, you are extremely well placed—worth near one billion so I'm told, while playing in all markets; stocks, bonds, and commodities. You enjoy a phenomenal cash position, along with highly diversified assets. Your cross utilization of a B & B as your chain's test kitchen, is considered just one of your greatest accomplishments professionally, nearly equaling the brilliance of your food concept itself.

"There are extensive Real Estate holdings by the company, in addition to multiple homes. Add to that, three jets, prestigious auto collection, philanthropist, yata, yata, yata—shit—my God—I want your life, Marc!"

"Okay Burt, I follow you, but now that you've met me and spoken to me a little, how do I seem to you...now?" As I continued chuckling over his very candid remarks.

"Honestly Marc, I'm not shooting for brownie points, so please understand that; I could really like you as a regular friend. You have an 'every man' quality to you—and it's irrefutable, yet you're self-assured, but always a people person first. You are indisputably modest, but also straightforward enough that you do not hide your wealth, yet you feel no need to flaunt it...or deny it for that matter.

"One thing is certain; you're obviously a very caring father who hasn't had the typical fatherhood experiences yet...the ones, to either help you through this, or hurt you—either. In short Marc, you are super likeable...I can affirm that already by stating that I already like you just from my respect for you immensely."

"Jesus Burt, I'm really touched—thank you. You know, you're obviously a candid person—and certainly your mostly spot on too."

"Marc; do share with me though, what you meant by your last response concerning your wishes for Trevor and Taylor?"

"Certainly Burt, it's really simple, yet you must realize that it's also because of my sons' circumstances. Listen Burt, let me temper this; by asking that you don't change your opinion about how I feel about the value of money. Don't assume that I'm being arrogant or snooty now, because I'm not; it's simply the reality of things.

"You see Burt, even without my own financial involvement; my sons were born into substantial wealth, long before I knew of them. Whether it ends up being a blessing, or a curse, remains to be judged a long time from now. Had they remained in England, the boys would have grown into very wealthy Lords. They are by birthright, with the passing of their grandfather this last December; young Earls already, you see.

"They've always had the opportunity to grow up doing what 'pleases' them, rather than chasing the almighty buck. They will never have to worry about the rent or the groceries. As such, I really want them to do what will make them happy and whole, rather than necessarily simply adding to their personal wealth.

"They must get a good education though, even if they are students as a life-long pursuit. But if that becomes the case, I would also like them to continue to be sensitive to the less fortunate. I would encourage them to continue their philanthropic pursuits, even if it means lessening their net worth. It's a perfect alternative to a gainful career, just like their mother and grandmother before them.

"So in my heart, I really would prefer them to stay out of my industry altogether. Let them do what makes them feel 'whole', first and foremost. You know, hopefully they can make a difference, like what they're doing now—already. However, in the final analysis, it is all up to them—so that's it in a nutshell Burt."

"Damn Marc, you keep surprising me. I would have thought you had all these big plans for your sons?"

"Well Burt; whose life is it—mine, or the boys? Why should any parent try to supplant their own goals, whether realized or not, onto their children? But you know, in the process, they always invariably seem to supersede the child's own goals and dreams. I ask you, what gives any parent that right, me, or anyone else?

"Why are you a journalist Burt?"

"Because I wanted to be one—ever since I could remember."

"So, did your father and mother ever try to talk you out of that?"

"Never, both of my folks always just encouraged me."

"Sounds like you have great parents Burt—like mine?"

"I guess so Marc. I never realized it until now though, on how fortunate I was in the fact that they supported me. I guess it could have been different if I had chosen something they were against."

"Yes Burt, that's the real issue—isn't it? Take my folks for example; they had to keep an open mind with me, because I had challenges myself. This is off the record Burt, but I had A.D.D. growing up, yet we just didn't know it until years later.

"So my folks had their hands full, as they were hit with all the negative reinforcement from the medical professionals besides. They were told that I would never amount to anything at all…even as I mastered the piano within four years…I was a true enigma to the professionals, that's for sure. Faced with this reality, my parents simply refused to get caught in that philosophical trap at all, if you follow? So my parents just set me free to find my own road… whereby I did find one—didn't I?"

"Yes Marc, I would say you did, however, it's time for another confession. I already knew about you're A.D.D. from our researchers, but I will show you the data so that you know that it's true. I want to be forthright with you, so I can't speak for my producer on whether he will keep it out—or not? I will try though Marc, if that's your wish, but honestly, I feel it explains your great humanity, my friend."

"Thank you Burt, you're a gentleman, so I appreciate the sincerity of your words."

"You are most welcome Marc, however, let me ask you something else, because it was to be a question anyway. Is your substantial commitment to people with disabilities, rooted in your own past, or are there perhaps—other reasons?"

"Burt, of course it is…besides, I am not exactly hurting financially any longer, which you know. So I'm worth a fair bit of change now…big deal. Since it's my money to spend after all—I'd like it to do some good now…look at it as my own little recycling program of funds to help others.

"It all starts with the wonderful patronage of our loyal customers, year after year. They buy our food while they enjoy our ghosts and singers. They pay fairly for their stay with us, leaving me to pay the bills, along with pocketing some for future growth and the unforeseen. Afterwards, I share some of what's left—with people who can't do the same things I'm blessed with doing—end of story."

"Does this also explain your unorthodox work staff?"

"Sure…although I would never refer to it in that way. I prefer not to differentiate my employees in any way, they are simply my employees…case closed. I'll gladly work around little details or inconveniences to give any employee, who really wants to work, that opportunity…honestly they're often my most conscientious employees as well.

"You know Burt; a work ethic can be a very important 'goal' for everyone, not just the healthy or unchallenged. My employees are all empowered and challenged to contribute greatly to our company's success, so I'd say that's a true, win/win, wouldn't you?"

"Yes Marc, I would agree.

"Okay Marc, let's talk about you, what are your personal passions?"

I was chuckling as we were already turning into my company's parking lot. I needed to wrap this up in order to get to my own work, yet I was really enjoying Burt's company, so I wasn't going to boot him out rudely now. I would just have to offer to let him hang with me. I would allow him to observe my daytime work activities until he himself, had enough raw material to finish up back at his office.

"Burt, I'm going to have to answer that one inside the office if that's alright with you?"

"Thank you Marc, I'm truly honored to be invited inside your private domain as they say, I'd be thrilled to join you sir."

"Good. So let's go then…but can the sir stuff Burt. Listen, I have to take you by security for a visitor's badge…first. Now let me warn you Burt—go beyond 'the john' and you activate a passive alarm monitoring system with or without your badge."

"I wouldn't know Marc, but don't worry about me anyway. Hell, I never even read the tabloids." We both busted up at that crack.

"Burt, I'm going to break my golden 'press' rule with you…I'll give you a little more freedom. I trust you to do this piece fairly, as you seem very passionate on your interviewing along with researching it well, I believe. So forget my fifteen percent background rule. But Burt, please don't lose sight of the emphasis I've eluded too however, fair enough?"

"Thanks Marc, I promise you'll enjoy the piece."

"Okay Burt, I'll take you at your word, now let's get you through security—shall we?" I took Burt into security where I got him set up with his temporary credentials.

We went into the executive office reception foyer, then on to my office; where I immediately went to the phone for Robbie.

"Robbie, let me have my usual Hazelnut latte please, while Mr. Jacobs will have—what Burt?"

"Look, let me be honest here, if you stock all of the coffees you normally serve, do you have any of that incredible Blue Mountain Jamaican? I worship the stuff, but honestly, four bucks is too steep for my salary, except as a special treat."

"Funny you should mention that Burt, but I'll elaborate on that in a moment. Robbie; 86 the latte for me—just set us up a pot of the #23 Blue Mountain Special Reserve alright?"

"Yes Marc, right away, obviously this guy is 'A' list, isn't he?"

"Quit clowning Robbie—just get working on it."

"Okay Marc."

I turned to Burt, who was checking out the office with a fine-tooth comb now.

"Burt, back to our conversation—my passions include my family, first and foremost. The boys are at the top of that list now, as they should be. It's still too new of an experience for me to verbalize it to you though. So far, it's been awesome; I'm in heaven just being a Dad—Christ, who knew Burt?

"Next, would be what you just requested, the search for those singular, finest, coffees in the world. I admit that I am a hopeless and lost, coffeeholic. Then add in my cars, or flying in one of my jets—and certainly music. Yep, I'm one happy camper Burt."

"Might I ask, why in that pecking order, I never heard you mention a current personal relationship—or am I prying?"

"No, I'm not shy about that either, hell; I just buried my wife after all Burt...I'll assume you're taking our separation into consideration in your question and our unusual circumstances? You need to realize that while we remained separated, we did still love one another quite deeply—so I haven't fully grieved yet.

"You know Burt, there were not any other real serious relationships during our separation either,—four brief casual relationships, is all. I'll only consider myself truly available—once I finish working through my grief, if you take my meaning?"

"How about you Burt, are you married, got kids, anything?"

"First Marc, since you asked, I'm actually from the 'other school' of thought, so no, I do not have any children or a partner at the moment."

"Whoa...sorry. All righty Burt, I guess I just got a little too personal there myself—sorry?"

"Please don't be, I'm happy enough."

"Well, that's what's important, isn't it?"

"Yes Marc, it is."

"If you don't mind Burt, we'll take a little break so I can start getting some work done. As things come into your head from your observations, take some notes, save them up. We'll address your questions in-and-out of my other calendar items after I get Robbie in here—fair enough?"

"Sure, that would be great."

"Hey, no problemo" I picked up my phone again for Robbie.

"Rob, can you get in here with the coffee already...my God, I'm parched here pal. Please bring in my appointment schedule too, okay?"

"Sorry Marc, they're still trying to find the #23, seems it's not in its normal slot in the warehouse."

"Oh really, do we have a security problem here Robbie?"

"Too early to tell yet Marc, but it could be possible though."

"All right, keep me posted on that, but get in here just the same." As I hung up.

"Is everything alright Marc?"

"Sure Burt, it's just that our coffee seems to have gone A.W.O.L. in the warehouse. You know, at thirty-seven dollars, per pound wholesale—that's a serious concern. By the way Burt, Blue Mountain is the brewed coffee we've selected to sell in our Minis' Dessert Courts—exclusively. But here's the bigger news Burt; since it all goes to charity, we're dropping the retail price as well...I hope I've made your day?"

"Actually Marc, with the richness of that coffee—you've made my year!"

Moments later, Robbie walked in, where I introduced the two men immediately. I thought I detected a smile from the corner of Robbie's mouth as he turned back around to address me. My resolute loyalty to Robbie precluded me from tipping my hand to either gentleman in front of me now.

"Okay Marc, from the top, Bill needs in for a five-to-ten to give you an update. I can also advise you they are moving quite nicely along at the Minis factory. Forty-two freezers are already on their way as we speak."

"Damn, that is good news Robbie—wow, I most assuredly concur with you."

"Also, Vice Principal Riley at the boys' school wanted a word with you too. I'll call him when you're ready."

"I'm ready now Robbie, make the call please, it could be quite important."

A few moments later, Robbie had Mr. Riley on the phone for me.

"It's so nice to speak to you again, Mr. Riley, everything alright there, I certainly hope so?"

"Yes, Mr. Morgan. I just thought I should call you to see if there is anything else we can do for you or the twins? We feel we were caught off guard…we honestly didn't like that. You know, we don't really like being in the forefront of these kinds of things, as you can well imagine?"

"Yes I can Mr. Riley—but I can't control stupid people either, can I?"

"No Mr. Morgan, you can't yet you did an admirable job handling them as it is."

"I do try Mr. Riley. I trust that the boys themselves aren't complicating this situation any further?"

"No sir, they've been great Mr. Morgan, truly—although they inadvertently set off a brief stampede at recess this morning." This comment made both of us chuckle.

"I'm glad to hear that they're trying to help. If they give you any problems whatsoever, remind them that we talk regularly, will you Mr. Riley?" Now he was chuckling at my remark.

"Oh, I most certainly will Mr. Morgan, you can count on it,—but seriously, they've been great—and very modest. Good parenting is clear here sir, so you're to be commended."

"Thanks Mr. Riley, but I can't really take the credit for any of that…these two came totally house-broken you know."

"Yes, I remember that from your initial interview, so I'll assume then— that their Mother is mostly responsible?"

"Yes Mr. Riley, most definitely. Please call me again if there are any other developments, will you?"

"Yes sir, good day to you." Riley and I hung up, as I returned to my schedule with Robbie. Happily, he had been informed on the whereabouts of the Blue Mountain with a pot already brewing. Apparently we had merely been out of stock with our shipment literally sitting on our delivery dock.

My day whizzed by quickly, despite numerous breaks to answer Burt's many questions. He really was a very thorough and thought-provoking reporter, at least by the questions he asked. He finally left at 3:30 in Laverne, after making the ride over to pick up the boys with me so he wasted no time in interviewing them, on the spot…with my permission of course. So he left us with a full stack of notes—along with Robbie's home number, I think. It seems Robbie's gaydar must have been operational by the way those two were kibitzing on the way out of my office.

Riding back to our home alone now, I began a litany of questions leading up to hopefully getting their full report.

"So—I see you're both in one piece?"

"Sure, easy for you to say Dad, you weren't mobbed—but we were!"

"Alright boys—we've talked about all of this before, so what did you do about it?"

"We talked Dad."

"So, how did that go Taylor?"

"Pretty good".

"Is that all I'm going to be getting out of the two of you?"

"Yes Dad—for now. We're very tired from answering so many questions that we could really use a break now...I bloody swear Taylor...we go to school with a bunch of nutters...ay?"

"Bloody hell Trevo."

I was busting up from their exchange, but I also wanted to show my support too.

"Okay, calm down guys...just relax. I apologize T-men, you know-I didn't think about it from your perspective so, it's all right. You guys share it when you've recovered, fair enough?"

"Fair enough Dad, but thank you too, because we really need a break, you have no idea."

"No problem boys, hey it's me...remember? You guys just relax...so enjoy your ride home in silence, okay?"

And that's what we did.

I knew them well enough already that I could tell they were not saying something that was on their minds. Given what I knew about their day already, I wasn't going to push it, they were entitled to relax some.

We got home, where I sent the boys upstairs to hit their homework, which they actually seemed relieved to do now. I set out to warn everyone to give them some breathing room, rather than bombarding them with questions.

This seemed to work well with everyone except Dad; his curiosity was always on a full boil anyway. Naturally, I gave him no choice in the matter though, when he started to verbalize his desire to question them. I just gave him 'the look' as I quickly changed strategies for good measure too:

"Say Pop, did you see that Sofia left some Osso Buco out for you to finish off in the kitchen...Dad?" There he went, following the call of his stomach.

CHAPTER 6

▼

SOMETIMES, I COULD ALMOST KILL MY MOTHER!

WE ARRIVED AT OUR SUMMERLIN unit; right at crunch time…the restaurant was mobbed. There were more than twenty guests fishing, along with a dozen more or so—in paddleboats. Both the terraces were filled to capacity from the still running heat wave—while the 'haunted' workstations on each terrace, were currently putting on their little show for our guests which was delighting them all at that moment.

As we approached the entrance, a family we passed was whispering between the mother and her son. I could faintly hear pieces of their conversation.

…"Yes Peter, I suppose that's them, now quit staring, it's rude."

My wheels were spinning; this was going to be interesting. I wanted to see how my sons would handle themselves. Perhaps merely after this small taste of celebrity with the boys themselves, I'd have an easier time saying 'no' to Scooter's near constant assaults of turning them pro. With his relentless appeals on the telephone, perhaps I could finally build the case to him—to end that whole fiasco between us.

Dad, Mom, Sofia, and I were talking outside on the gazebo about the long-running, record heat wave. All of a sudden, we heard clapping coming from inside the restaurant. So like everyone else it seems, we turned around to walk inside to see what the situation was all about. Walking in, we immediately saw the twins getting an enthusiastic and spontaneous ovation from the entire group of guests in the General Store area. As more people entered from outside, along with the dining rooms, the applause continued to build. I watched intently. I wanted to make sure they were not only all right, but how they were going to handle themselves in this situation…would they keep quiet or try to stop them? In their current situation, they were out there all alone after all, so naturally I was concerned—and much more.

To my surprise though, they kept their cool to the core along with their modesty too. Trevor got them to stop their applause with hand gestures, as he then began speaking to the room full of people as calm as can be. I was surprised of course…unlike Taylor in our board meeting—Trevor was certainly quite assured of himself; I think he was actually enjoying it too.

"Hi everyone, thank you…but please, there's no reason to clap. You know, we just come here to have us a feed and stuff our gobs…but actually—the food's quite lovely here.

The little pisher had the room in hysterics with his British slang words and expressions…just before he turned into a novice huckster on the Crusade too:

"We're just glad that you're here, so we know we can count on you to help us raise this money. Our grand opening is next Saturday, right here at this very Verandas, at one pee, so please try to join us—thanks everyone."

Trevor's remarks generated more applause now—but I think some confusion too over the one—pee comment. Then he noticed me…watching him, as a wicked little smile came over his face. I instinctively knew what was coming next…I knew I didn't have a clear escape path to the door either, what with the packed room…I was therefore—toast!

"But, I can see someone over in the corner there, who knows a little more about the food here. When I can't get my head around something…I turn to him…that's our Dad across the room, the one trying to hide himself behind my Nan—come here Dad." There was another round of applause now-as I joined the boys…Trevor was going to be eating 'road-kill' for supper—I can assure you.

"Thank you folks, I appreciate your patronage this evening."

From quite a distance away I heard a voice:

"Hey; I just come for the food Mister." Everyone laughed of course including me.

"Whoever you are sir—thank you…and so do I.

I was now getting laughs too.

"We sincerely hope you enjoy your stay with us tonight, but again, thank you." I grabbed both boys as we walked quickly out of the room to more applause—as thoughts of waddling around in my full pants brought me back to reality.

When we finally made it to our private dining room, I purposely sat right next to Trevor,—you know—I just love payback.

"Gee T-1, I think you've got some 'splainin' to do, or am I mistaken here?"

"What do you mean—what's wrong? What are you talking about now, Daddy…you sound angry? You don't think Taylor or me made them clap on purpose, do you?"

"I really don't know son—are you sure you weren't seeking it out?"

"What do you mean, seeking it out—you mean on purpose—I don't think so?"

"Don't be coy with me Trevor, this is your old man, you know damn well what I'm asking. And you calling me Daddy, tells me you're guilty or scared… so which is it? Did you purposely walk into that room looking for folks to recognize you and your brother? I noticed you were together—no doubt to make yourselves far more recognizable being twins—or am I just mistaken on all of this?"

"Yes Daddy—you're mistaken. We just wanted to check out our spot by the Coffee Bazaar for the kiosks for Saturday—that's all…don't you believe me?"

His response instantly brought me out of my anger…along with the accompanying fog. But I needed this dose of sanity…because along with that came my own guilt for even having thought such ludicrous ideas about my own sons. So I went into damage control now:

"Oh. Well that certainly does make sense son…but is that all of it? Is this the one-hundred-percent-whole-of-it, Trevor?"

"Honest Dad, that's all we were doing, really."

"Alright then, let me apologize for blowing a fuse. I'm sorry for jumping to conclusions or else assuming the worst.

"You know son, let me also add—that you were pretty darn good up there on your feet!"

"Was I Dad, do you really think so?"

"Yes son, you were quite poised, I must say."

"You know Dad, it was kind of fun—is there anything wrong with it being fun?"

"No son, there certainly isn't…again Trev, please accept my apology. Sometimes even Dads can be wrong you know. I got a little confused with what motivated your behavior, so I erroneously jumped to some stupid conclusions—the wrong ones I'm afraid."

My greatest fear hit me right there at that very moment, these had all been my repressed insecurities talking—as usual.

"Its cool Dad—but you were good too…for a bloody old sod, that is."

"Gee, thanks T-1, but compared to you—I'm clearly second fiddle."

"What's that mean, Dad?"

"I guess it's an Orchestra expression, but I can't be sure. It just means that I'm in second position, like with your ability to speak so well to our guests. You're the master, while I'm the student in a sense."

"Oh. Well Dad, when we were driving home from school, I meant to ask you a favor. I wanted to know if we could sing a little for our guests after dinner—you know, that could be fun too."

"Are you kidding T-1, do you want to scare all the paying customers away?" I was busting up, so once T-1 figured the joke out himself, so was he.

"No seriously Dad, can we? You know, you still make us practice three times a week for some bloody reason. Can't we see if we like performing here in front of people we don't know—like we did at Toonland? Besides, you keep talking about that garage band thing."

"Okay Trev, sure…what the hell. You know, it would give you and Taylor a little feel for performing, like you said. So if you're really going to do this, what would you like to do?"

"I haven't the foggiest, do you know what our singers have for tonight, cuz we don't have our keyboards here anyway?"

"Hum—let me think…it's the second Thursday of the month so they're doing a Cole Porter tribute tonight, I believe."

"Right, well I only know one of his songs, Taylor too. It's called Night and Day—ever hear of it Dad?" Man did I laugh at his question.

"Yes of course T-1—it's my personal Cole Porter favorite…I believe it's still the opener to their tribute—it's good to own the place, you know!"

"Oh."

"If you want to join them Trev, I can arrange it, but I think you'd both probably feel pretty uncomfortable. You're not going to know their staging once they get out on the terraces, will you?"

"Yeah, I guess you're right Dad—well; how about the three of us play Amelia's piano—do you think she would mind that?"

"T-1, she's an apparition created with special film and lighting effects. Her piano is played electronically. A pianist sits in a small room behind the bar with a remote controlling second keyboard while watching the audience on a video screen. Sorry for having to burst your bubble son—but sure—I'd say she's okay with it."

"Oh, okay, so what should we do, I mean sing?"

"How about—what ever strikes your fancy; you're the one in the mood to sing—not me?"

"I know, Taylor and I could sing Consider Yourself from Oliver—we sing it real good in an upbeat tempo. But you know, we prefer rock music though—right Dad?"

"Yes, I do know that…I think that's great Trevor. I haven't heard you two sing any song yet that you didn't do well…I mean that son. Even though by the time I get home, you're always 'too tired' to play for me." I admonished my son a little with mock sadness accompanying the comment, while he seemed to get the intended message.

"Okay Dad, I get it—this is that Jewish Guilt shite again—isn't it?"

"Why son—I'm only speaking the truth."

After my laughter subsided, I looked at Trevor as he was definitely unconvinced with my answer.

"Look Trev, if you guys want to sing—you have my permission, alright?"

"Wicked, look; I'm going to ask Taylor, to see if he's cool with it, otherwise it's me and you Dad."

"Hold everything there Sparky,—count me out on singing son, but I will handle the ivories if you like…wait a minute…never mind that—Amelia will!"

"What are you saying Dad? Do you want Amelia to play instead of you?"

"Yes son, that's exactly what I'm suggesting. Look, if you're intent on doing this, we might as well give it some theatrical elements,—don't you think?"

"I never thought about that Dad, I guess that could be real cool…whatever theatrical elements means?" I was laughing at Trevor's honesty, when Taylor seemed to mosey into our conversation.

"Taylor, how would you like to sing with me at Amelia's piano while she plays for us?"

"Bloody hell Trev, I think that would be fun, especially with Amelia."

"Okay Dad, your idea is great—so what do we do now?"

"To quote two of my favorite Brits: We have us a feed…we eat son, that's what. After dessert, I'll sneak down to the piano player for the evening to have a little pow-wow. I'm also going to give this a little set-up too, so you guys will play after I get finished with the audience on that. And, you two will do one number singing while playing the piano yourselves before Amelia joins in for a finale…okay?"

"Sure Dad—but what's a set-up?"

"It just means we're going to make it look more theatrical for the audience, that's all. Trev, remember like the ToonCrooners at Toonland; more staged if you will. I'll be doing that before you both come up…I used to have to do it every night, after all."

"Oh—you did? Okay, but you're goin' tell us what to do, right?"

"Of course Trev, if we're really going to do this, we want it to look good, don't we?"

"Sure Dad." Trevor agreed as Taylor nodded his understanding as well.

We had a lovely dinner, but true to my word, after ordering our famous Key Lime Pie, I slipped downstairs. By the time I finished with Josie, Amelia's pianist for that evening, we had it worked out on a routine including a real upbeat tempo on 'Consider Yourself' for the finale.

I returned to the dining room where I filled the boys in on the overall set-up along with what they had to do…and when they had to do it. They loved the idea behind my 'bit' so they were excited in general to get started. I told them to slow down because nothing was coming between our Key Lime Pie and me…with my Dad agreeing…naturally as he sat there devouring his huge piece of our famous Coconut Cream Custard Pie.

We finished, as I had gone over the set-up one last time, quizzing them on all the cues…but they had it wired already…they really were pros! I then asked them what they had planned for their first song without Amelia playing.

"It's a surprise, Dad." Came naturally popping out of Trevor.

"Touché Trevor, now let's get going son."

We walked to the Birdcage elevator as we had to wait on it.

"Why is this lift so bloody slow Daddy, I want to get downstairs already?"

"Because T-man, it's supposed to be nearly a hundred years old, so when it's not haunted and going crazy in a performance, it moves like a real old elevator…silly boy."

"Oh, that does make sense, I guess, thanks Dad."

"Your welcome."

We got in and exited onto the main floor some twenty seconds later. The boys jumped right out, they were so excited. Mom turned to me now as she quipped:

"You know Marc, if this goes over well; there go your evenings off again."

I immediately cracked up…she was right of course.

"Don't worry Mom, we're just going to play a little music to entertain our guests a bit—let them have their fun Ma, it's nothing serious."

"All right Marc, but don't say I didn't warn you. Those two have finally got the bug real bad son…I notice it every time they practice now. I believe that they're ready honey…so what I mean is—you may never get them off tonight! Hum; I'm going to think on that a little bit myself Markie."

"Its fine Mom, really, just watch and enjoy."

With that, we headed into the restaurant's parlor, which in essence is a multi-purpose room that transitions its utility throughout the day. For dinner, it is used as a coffee bar, waiting area and of course Amelia's parlor—to perform hourly each evening.

I left the boys with the folks and Sofia as planned, while I walked up to Amelia with several children communicating with her at that moment.

Amelia Withers is the dead matriarch of the family that originally built and owned Verandas, along with her husband Jedadiah. That was—until the mysterious fire that claimed the lives of all of the guests and staff that were residing there in 1909. The story goes that with her dying last breaths, she pushed the old Steinway right out the front parlor doors to safety; just as a beam collapsed on top of her…she loved that pie-ana so.

So nowadays, Amelia's spectral half, communicates through her keyboard as her means of expressing herself. She answers questions with 'bars' from songs, and other communicative nuances. So if a child asks Amelia if she is mad about something, if it's yes, Amelia would typically bang on the bass keys. If the answer's no, she would typically hit a couple of high ones or cut into a happy song. While all this is happening, her spirit body flows in and out of appearing surrounded by frigid air for added impact. Forgive the pun—but it's a convincing parlor trick.

The kids hanging at the piano were really getting into Amelia so it was now my turn to intervene—as planned. I eased myself into the roped off area surrounding the piano. A young girl, with obvious body language indicating she would need a restroom shortly, also seemed concerned for my wellbeing—or Amelia's I guess, as she asked me:

"Hey Mister, are you going to get in trouble doing that?" I looked at her as I smiled before responding to her question. Meanwhile, she now proudly introduced herself as Tiffany, and then just as quickly, shook my hand.

"No Tiffany, honey, that's not likely to happen since this is my restaurant… you see, I don't like Amelia giving you kids a hard time—so is that all right with you Tiff?"

"Sure it is mister…I gotta go make tinkie anyway." She replied.

"I'll tell you what, honey,—why don't you go and have a tink—Tiff, but hurry back so you don't miss anything…too titillatingly terrific—okay? Is your mommy or daddy here to help you? As her mother came to her rescue and escorted her off to her intended destination. I meanwhile cracked up silently over my play on words, along with the rest of the audience I think. I now returned to my comments to Amelia.

"Amelia, stop teasing these kids this instant—do you hear me? And by the way, stop making them all go tinkie like poor little Tiffany.

Amelia stopped playing immediately, as the remaining children standing by, all sort of looked at one another, as if to say:

"Do you have to go, because I don't?"

Amelia meantime, answered me with the two keys on the piano that most closely resembled saying 'okay'.

"What's gotten into you tonight, old woman—you're as ornery as ever?"

Amelia answered by playing the lines of a tune from the musical; Damn Yankees. She played, "Whatever Lola wants, Lola gets", from the song of the same name. Her response implied in meaning; that whatever she wanted, she would get—no matter what I thought.

"Listen Amelia, if you can't play nice, I'll play this stupid thing myself."

Immediately Amelia ran a skipping scale from the bass keys up, simulating someone taking flight or running away.

"That's better; playing it myself, you won't mess me up—will you Amelia?" I said it loudly making believe I was looking at her up on the ceiling now.

I began preparing to play; cracking my knuckles, adjusting myself on the bench—all the things I actually did at home. As I sat there in front of that audience preparing to perform, I flashed back instantly to my earlier years when we only had our one restaurant on Flamingo Road. There I could be found nightly, performing just like this, but with all of our kids in their musical numbers and skits along with me for the ride. At that moment, I realized just how much a part of me missed that nightly interaction with our guests.

I began playing Gershwin's Rhapsody in Blue very dramatically, until eight bars into the piece, Amelia's spirit returned, pounding over my keys messing my performance all up as the surrounding kids all began busting up. Not surprisingly, so too were many of the adults that were present around the room, it was all quite humorous by design—while I was milking it besides.

"Alright Amelia, if that's how you want to play it, I'll get my boys up here to fix your wagon—but good!"

Amelia's response was to play the mourners' march, again making everyone crack up.

"Boys, get up here—show this ornery old gal how to play a 'pie-ana'."

At that moment—right on cue, out stepped the boys at my side, to a room full of applause. If they were nervous at all—it would likely only prove temporary. Out of the corner of my eye, I also saw Tiffany and her mother walking over too.

"Listen guys, she's never stopped you from playing before, has she?"

"Why no Dad" came out of my older, number one 'ham'.

"She's always been a proper lady for me too Dad…you must have done something to her!" This came from Taylor—oh; excuse me—my number two 'ham'.

"No, I didn't Taylor, but she sure made Tiff, have to take a tink! So listen—why don't you two take over—because she's not cooperating with me at all? I know she likes your singing—so why not give her a tink or two…I mean—a tune or two, to mellow her out, okay?"

"Sure Dad, whatever you say."

"Is that alright with you, ladies and gentlemen?" I asked, turning my attention to the children standing around the rope barrier.

"Sure Mister, let's see what happens…I'm tinkie-free now."

We all heard this out of Tiffany now, with a great big smile since her visit to the ladies room. It was clear that she intended to play the stand-up comic for the assembled young group, so the audience was rewarding her now with spirited applause as well. I already was use to this interaction with the guests, from many years before…it was a comfortable feeling…I felt home again, in a way, but I digress.

"Fine boys—let her rip." I yelled out now.

The boys then shared the eighty-eight keys by breaking into a very hip rendition of Elton John's Crocodile Rock as I quickly removed myself from the roped off area to leave. I rejoined my parents and Sofia. I noticed moments earlier that the boys had gone into one of their little trances for all of but a few short seconds. I had pointed it out as well for my folks benefit, but they only had a second or two to notice it.

After the boys intro, they really had to begin belting out the lyrics as there was no microphone for this impromptu performance…so I quickly ran for the wireless at the podium. Yet, with their big voices, they were undaunted as they wailed it out with tremendous passion, aplomb, and style. At first the customers seemed stunned into silence.

Moments later, when they were suitably amplified, you would have thought that someone had lit a fire under the entire place. People were stomping their feet to the chorus, drumming on the tabletops while singing right along with the twins. They finished the song with Trevor doing a full 'pass' across the keys, where the room then went bonkers.

You know, until that very moment, I don't think it had hit me fully. I truly never realized the depth of their talent…that they could create such a compelling sound in their 'Rock' personas. Honestly, they possessed their own unique sound…theirs alone for sure…it was something in their voices… that stereo speaking quality of theirs, came through as startling in their vocals too…clearly the guests had absolutely dug it.

I had goose bumps truthfully now, as the boys received a vibrant ovation! I had to wonder—what had we unleashed here tonight? All of the smaller guests surrounding the piano were jumping up and down and carrying on as well.

By this time, the room was filled to over-flowing with not only guests, but staff as well. They were either on their breaks, or just circumventing our rules. I honestly couldn't be sure at that moment. Christ, in all my experiences inside one of our units performing, I'd never witnessed a reaction anything quite like this from our audiences!

The boys got up, gave a little 'bow', and as planned, started to leave the piano. At this point though, the room erupted with requests for "more" and "give us another" comments.

Trevor held up his hand to quiet the room down.

"Thank you everyone—that was fun, wasn't it?" The room answered with more robust applause as Trevor then directed his question at me, as planned.

"Listen Dad, do you think you could talk Amelia into doing a song with us, would you like that everybody?" Of course the room applauded along with some catcalls, while I began walking back towards the piano even as I answered my son.

"Trevor I don't know about this—do you think it's such a good idea? How do you know she won't get all uppity on you two as usual, or make you or Tay need to go make tinkie...right Tiff?" I was still milking my tongue twister for more laughs from the room.

"Yeah, she could do that Mister...it happened to me." Apparently Tiffany wasn't finished either.

"Look boys, I'm just concerned that she will try to ruin your song like she did mine."

"Don't worry Dad—she won't, (the boys looked up together at the ceiling in unison, right on cue), as Trevor continued.

"Amelia knows that Taylor and I love her."

Whereby Amelia immediately recaptured the keys again, as she began playing the Wedding march as her acknowledgement, causing more laughter from our audience.

"Okay boys, but don't say I didn't warn you if she acts up again." At that moment though, Amelia played her own rendition of; "Nah, nah, nah nah nah nah."

I had been told where to go in no uncertain terms—much to the delight of the audience and boys it seems. I didn't have to be told twice, I quickly disappeared again, into a hole off to the side of the parlor. I rejoined Sofia and the folks moments later. They were honestly enjoying themselves immensely at that moment too, which was nice to see.

Trevor and Taylor each stood on either side of Amelia's spirit at the piano...Trevor then asked her:

"Amelia, do you know the song Consider Yourself, from the play Oliver?" Amelia gave him her response for "yes" as her spectral body nodded.

"Okay Amelia, let's do it."

And with that, Amelia began the introduction, but just before the verse was to begin, that song disappeared and switched seamlessly into 'chopsticks'. This got the room busting up again and egged the boys on a little, throwing them completely off. Amelia then abruptly stopped.

"Amelia, are we going to do this or not? You know our guests don't want to wait all night." Amelia scratched out "sorry" on the keys.

They began again, but this time Amelia cooperated fully. They did the song all the way through in a strong upbeat tempo—the audience just loved it all, I think especially the twins' wonderful British accents which they even embellished by portraying the cockney accent pretty darn well.

When it was over, the boys bowed, Amelia said "thank you" on her keys, and the audience ate it all up. The audience's applause told the story…of that, there could be no doubt. Finally nearly a minute later, the audience quieted themselves.

"Thank you so much everyone, we enjoyed this too, and we'd like to thank you for coming tonight—right Amelia?" This time it was Taylor doing the talking to which Amelia answered on her keys.

"And thank you Amelia for playing the song so beautifully—right everybody?"

Whereby everyone clapped for Amelia now.

I assumed the boys were now ready to get out of the limelight, but apparently Taylor was not finished. It appeared he was just warming up to dust off his soapbox to go into a crusader's mode. God; was he ever committed now I thought.

"Thank you everyone, we've really enjoyed this very much, so we'd like to invite you back here again. This next Saturday at 1:00 p.m., we're having a very special Grand Opening of our Minis Make Miracles Happen crusade… so be sure to tell all of your friends to come too. Our very first Minis' Dessert Court will open for business—right here in this very restaurant's General Store. Remember, all of the profits from this crusade go to help build a new home for people with Cerebral Palsy. We hope you can come to help us raise a lot of money…thank you and good night."

More applause greeted Taylor's comments as the boys walked back over to me as the clapping continued. The boys and I waved to the guests before leaving the room with our group in tow…but sure enough, the boys' both needed to stop at the loo first!

We immediately left the restaurant after their, twin-tinkie-stop-on-the-tinkle…tour!

We all climbed into Dad's Nav to leave, but not before I spied Robbie… there he was, sitting on the terrace with—you guessed it—Burt! My, he worked fast I thought.

Once inside the Navigator, Mom spoke right up as I got an uneasy feeling merely observing her excitement level. While she calmed down, her comments and questions that followed—did absolutely nothing to improve my mood—I can assure you. But I vowed to keep my mouth closed to hear out whatever she was apparently about to connive or hatch…for as long as possible.

"Boys, I want you to know that Gramps and I truly enjoyed your performance—we're so proud of both of you in fact."

"That goes double for me guys." My Dad added.

"Thanks Gram and Gramps, I really loved doing that tonight, how about you Trev?"

"Blimey Taylor, I think we all know I did—it was my idea remember? Heck bro, why have we waited so bloody long to do this? I had a blast—it was so much fun."

"Yeah Trev, it was fun. Hey, did you see how excited all the people got?"

"Yeah bro, God it was fab." Came from Trevor.

Mom decided to go on a fishing expedition of sorts now, as I became very nervous indeed. I could sense where her fishing boat might be heading… trolling her bait. I'd been down this river before with her as they say, while in choir myself.

"You boys are talented, you know that don't you—I mean really talented?"

"Do you honestly think so Nan? Like maybe we could become famous someday, and make our own CDs?"

"Yes Trevor, I do…I can think of four or five major stars that can't touch your talents already. Boys; what I want to know is how you feel, you know, about performing yourselves…what we think as your family, doesn't matter after all?"

"Gram it makes me feel great—I really love the applause and making the people happy—it's a bloody blinder. It was just like the contest at Toonland here tonight, so I felt really good about what I had done…I kinda feel proud of myself too for finally trying it out—how about you Taylor?"

"Yeah Trev, it makes me feel terrif to see how the audience really enjoys it…I mean, I guess we we're good—right?"

"Taylor; as your Gram, I want to be completely honest with you both. Boys, I'm sure that you know that I understand a thing or two, about talent already…don't you?"

At that moment, Mom kept pointing in my direction by cocking her head eliciting giggles out of the boys now.

"But honest about what—Nan?"

"Well Trevor, let me be honest enough to tell you both that you have the talent to be professional artists—right now...today in fact!"

"No way Gram!"

"Yes Trevor, absolutely—you do."

"Wow!"

"I'm bringing this up because I feel you've crossed a threshold this evening boys. I believe you both really need to start thinking about some things now. If you boys truly love performing as much as it appears you did tonight—then you've likely found your life's work! I would say it might be what God has in mind for you two to do throughout your lives anyway...perhaps its your destiny to sing. I believe you two could bring a lot more joy into this world... where we all know, it sorely needs it—but how does all of this make you two feel?"

"I think, it would make me feel real good to know I could make peoples happy Nan."

"Great Trevor, but honey, we say 'people', not peoples, alright?"

"Okay—I could make 'people' happy—got it."

"And how about you Taylor, how do you feel about all of this?"

"Okay Gram, it really makes me happy when I'm up there singing and I've always wanted to make people happy. But right now, I just want to raise this money first for the CPF people."

"So, is that your only hesitation then, Taylor?"

"Yes Grammy, it is."

"Gee Taylor; I like being called Grammy—why haven't you called me that before dear...after all, your brother seems to take turns calling me Gram, Grandma, or Nan?"

"I don't know Gram; it just sort of came out of me, but if you like it—I do too?"

"Yes sweetheart, I most certainly do...call me that anytime you want, you both can. Trevor you just go right ahead and add it onto your list of names too—okay baby. Now Taylor, have you considered how you and Trevor singing, while raising this money for the crusade, could actually go hand-in-hand?"

No Grammy, what do you mean? How could that work and still do both things?"

"Look at it like this Taylor—if you two recorded a CD like when your parents made their record years ago—you could actually sell your CD right on the Minis kiosks...you can raise the money that much faster that way, don't you see?

"Not to mention that doing this, would give you two the opportunity to try this whole 'professional thing' out for size—to see how it all fits. More important though, it's all for a wonderful cause at the same time—your cause in fact!"

"Grammy; oh my God—what a bloody Nora—it's brill! Can we Dad, can we, oh please Daddy; say yes?"

"Gee Mom, thank you so very much. Do you realize the consequences of what you're suggesting here? Damn; I was just getting excited over the idea of a 'garage band' for crying out loud. Now you want to bypass all of that already? One impromptu performance and they're pushed inside a recording studio for a fundraiser…just like that? And all of this without even discussing it in the slightest with me first…are you going nuts here, Mom?"

"My heavens Marc—aren't we discussing it now? Of course I realize the consequences of all of this. And don't look so damn shocked Marcus, I saw your reaction to their performance with my own eyes too. I'd say you were pretty well overwhelmed with the audience's reaction—so be honest… yourself!

"I know from our conversations regarding your friend Scooper's appeals that you're leaning against allowing the boys to perform professionally. Well, I'm going on record right now Mister, to tell you that you are so dead wrong—it's pathetic!"

"Cute Mother, but my nickname for him is; Scooter. God you are truly priceless—Scooper? Shit, he'd love that. Secondly, I am only trying to protect the boys from being hurt from any of this crap. And lastly Mom—I'm their Father, so I feel it's in my court dear—not yours?"

"Marcus Earl Morgan, you just shut that stupid mouth of yours right this moment so that I can explain. Or if you prefer, I'll shut it for you, you're being so damn infantile, now stop it—God.

"Look Marcus, since when has it been your policy to disenfranchise anyone's ambitions—let alone your own child's? Malcolm, I'm asking you seriously, so no jokes honey, didn't we teach our son better than this—all those years ago?"

"Marilyn I certainly agree with you on this point—we did, but that being said, Marc makes a valid point, himself, sweetheart."

"Mom, I would never do such a thing—you should know better than to even suggest that? I was just speaking of this very subject today. I don't believe in doing that, so I'm quite insulted at the suggestion. I'm quite confident that I do not resemble that remark, nor am I guilty of such a terrible act!"

"Oh, well let's just see about that, shall we?

"Trevor honey, would you consider singing professionally as something just fun to do—like someone playing in their garage…or would it mean more to you? In other words honey, have you ever thought of doing it as a career before, you know; performing professionally?"

"Sure Grammy…all the time. I think about it mostly during practice, but sometimes I just pretend I'm like; this big star. I'm singing on a stage where all the girls are screaming at me before they run up to start kissing me…that's my favorite part—all those girls screaming and kissing me."

"You see mom, now there's a healthy 'reality' to genuinely encourage isn't it, screaming girls indeed?"

"Sure it is Marc, now shut up—I'm not even finished yet and you're overreacting already; I swear; put a sock in it, son."

"Okay Trevor, but how do you feel in your heart about it…is it what you feel you really want to do, you know, as your life's ambition?"

"What's an andbition again, Nan"

"That's ambition honey—it means, more or less your 'dream' of what you want to do in life as your life's work, more or less."

"Oh yeah, I remember now; ambition, well, I guess I'd have to say—yes, then."

"Alright Marcus, that's one down, and one—yet to go. Taylor, baby, how do you feel about what your brother and I just talked about?"

"Honestly Grammy, I don't know for sure, but I think I sort of feel that way too. But I didn't see those girls screaming when I think about singing—is there something wrong with me? You know Gram, sometimes when we rehearse, I could go on forever…I feel the music inside me—is that stupid?"

"No Taylor, I most certainly do not think it's wrong, or stupid, you're just fine, and thank you boys.

"Alright Marc; I believe I've just illustrated my point—so what say you— but before you answer, I want to remind you of a certain conversation we had back in October regarding speaking for not only myself, but Miranda as well?"

"Mom, I say that I'll concede to you what the boys have shared with us. Its obvious they're passionate about all of this—right now, but you know Mom, with boys their age, they could change their minds tomorrow too. While I will consider everything said in coming to my decision naturally, this is also about protecting my sons, and nothing less important than that. Sure, I admit I abhor that industry, but this goes beyond that concern alone, this is a parent's preservation instincts in play. To put my sons into that whole environment as professionals scares the b'Jesus out of me Mom; you know what I'm talking about—get real. I'm not denying them an outlet—or a musical expression—I'd love them to start their garage band as simply a first step. I just don't want to see them go professional at this very moment, that's all, what's so horrible about that?"

"You know dear, I'm afraid that you've been hanging around your father too long."

"Can it Mom, you know this whole thing is impractical—even if I was okay with it—which I'm not. I mean, this could turn out to be a full time thing eventually, meaning someone has to manage them and schlep them everywhere. Beyond that—the boys just moved here, so I think a little acclimatization is prudent here too…before we turn their lives upside down… you know—some more!"

"Marc; I would argue their lives have already been turned upside down— enough! I believe son, that this will serve to ground them nicely—music has been the key constant in their lives after all, even beyond the issue of caregivers—hasn't it?

"I say, let's cement the twins new roots here with you in Las Vegas, through their musical expression being that focus. Look Marc, with proper parenting, you'll help them adjust on many different levels—this is just one more.

"While were on the subject Marcus—what's wrong with me handling the boys? After all, I certainly cut in my baby teeth on you in my kitchen… compared to that—they're a cakewalk?"

"Alright Mom, hold on a minute—let's just say your point makes sense— do you know what you'd be getting yourself into here?"

"You know honey, the last time I looked; I had a valid driver's license, along with a great head for business. Haven't I done a fair job marketing Morgan Winery? Now beyond these skills, I'm passionate about this…you know I'll soon be out of a job anyway, don't forget. I hope you don't expect me to hang around the stables to shovel horseshit all day, along with Roy Rogers—here?

"Marilyn, are you nuts? What about our dream of just slowing down to smell all of those roses?"

"Now just listen you two, I know exactly what I am saying, and doing,— so can the crap right now. Moreover Malcolm, I would not be throwing around that phrase any longer—'smelling the roses'. You know those roses better be a nice ways off of the stables, if you take my meaning—Roy? I know you only too well Mal, you'll practically be living down at the stable office… only pretending to be working on the books.

"Look, I'm more than aware of what I might be getting myself into with this. But I'm also remembering something else, something far more important to me personally—really, to all of us."

"Okay Mom, what are you talking about?"

"Miranda, of course, Marc. I'm remembering her words to me last October, when she told me her feelings clearly. She begged me, more than insisted, that the boys do something serious with their music." She said they had God-given talent, so she wanted to make sure they didn't miss out on that opportunity. Her only caveat was the boys themselves. If they were steadfast against the idea—we were not to force it. I should point out son, that Mir specifically referred to them being opposed to it—and not you!"

"All right Mom, Miranda, and I did discuss some of this too, but without any particulars, so I'd assume the garage band should cover her concerns as well. I never took our conversations to mean she desired to have the boys commercialized professionally, nor does her letter address it."

"So son, you admit that you two did not speak specifically about her ideas in your conversations together?"

"Yes—I mean no, we didn't honestly—why Mom?"

"Because Marc—Mir and I—did!"

"You're kidding me, what came out of that exactly?"

"Yeah Marilyn, what did Miranda say?"

"I want to know too Grammy?"

"Me 'four'—Gram."

"Wow, if the four of you will keep your traps shut for thirty stinking seconds, I'll tell you. Boys I asked your mother what she meant by her comments. She thought about it some, before she said: 'Anything' that would bring you two, personal happiness and a little more confidence too. She also hoped that both of you could bring some joy to those around you through your music.

"Oh my God, Mummy said that—really Gram?"

"Yes baby, she did. I know that whatever you two do, will always bring her much happiness up in heaven. However boys, I also heard from Mummy that you two are quite the 'rock and rollers' which we all saw tonight. She told me that you both practiced non-stop on your Rock music constantly. So much so, that she had to force you to practice your classical pieces as well—or am I mistaken?"

"No Grammy, that's true, but when Daddy came home; we weren't practicing as much as we were trying to get to know him better and Mummy was so sick too."

"Well Taylor, from the way you two played that crocodile song, I would not have known that. But why have you two always practiced so much, have you asked yourselves that question?"

Trevor responded first.

"Not really Gram, I never really thought much about it, but now that you're asking me, I think I know the answer.

"Grammy, I love the music, I love playing it—I really love singing it...but only when we do it perfect. And now I know that it's not scary to do it with others around you—I mean other people. I was always afraid we'd make some mistake...then look stupid. But now I realize we know our music real good, we won't probably mess up so much. I just can't believe it Grammy, Mummy telling you all this is so cool, what do you think bro?"

"I still can't believe it Trev, but I know Grammy would never say it, if it wasn't true, would you?"

"No boys, I would never joke about a thing like this. Your Mummy knew exactly what she was saying…but I think I know why too."

"Why Grammy?"

"Because sweetheart, if for no other reason, it's the way your Mummy and Daddy met themselves—don't you see? In her heart, Mummy knew that nothing bad could ever come from you two performing…whether for fun—or professionally speaking.

"And along those same lines boys, Mummy told me something else I just thought back on, from our talk. She said that when you're singing, its God's special way that her love for Daddy lives on to touch everyone else. Boys, I honestly can't believe I forgot about that remark now. Because as I look back on it, I think it's the most loving and touching thing from our entire conversation."

"Yes Grammy."

Mom's comments, along with the twins' responses, did not allow me to sidestep the subject any longer. I wasn't going to be able to continue sweeping this under the carpet with a garage band—that much appeared certain now. The revelations from Miranda were not lost on me either, how could they? I had heard some of this myself from her before reading her letter—while some of this-did come out as I read it, all those many times—now my Mom had added even more.

Just the same, I did not intend to give my mother a free pass either. She would have to convince me she could handle all of this while keeping it controlled. For me to consider it further, I would need her solemn assurances…I therefore put it straight to her.

"Okay Mom, I just want to ask you a few questions for the jury, if you don't mind?"

"Sure Marc, go ahead—I'm a big girl."

"Cute Mom, all right then: One, how will you assure me that they are always safe? I want them protected from every shark, leech, drug pusher, and opportunist? How, will you safeguard and protect their schooling, the B'nai Mitzvah training, not to mention the relationships they're establishing with their new friends? Three, assuming they get a break after the CD for the Foundation, what are you're plans for preserving their level-headedness? So how do you plan on keeping them grounded in reality, reasonably unaffected, or jaded?"

"My Marc, is that all you've got?"

"Isn't that enough Mom?"

"I suppose, but somehow I was expecting so much more—given it's you."

My mother was laughing at my expense big time at that moment. I simply chose to ignore her obvious crack, by again asking:

"Okay—let me hear it Mother, I'm all ears, really?"

"Yes Mar, I'd like to hear this myself, dear."

"Fair enough Marcus…you too Malcolm. Here are my answers, care to take notes son?"

"Mom—can it—this is serious. I'll promise to keep an open mind given the boys' desires along with Miranda's wishes. But that assumes you can satisfy me with your own answers first—fair enough?"

"Come on Grammy, here's your chance; Trevor and I are counting on you."

"Okay Taylor, you leave it to me.

"Alright Marc, first, concerning protecting them. I would never let them out of my sight unsupervised. If I were not to be with them personally on a rare occasion, they would of course be chaperoned. And by someone I pick… preferably Daddy, once he is here full-time of course…and providing he showers regularly after returning from the stables. As far as the drugs, the leeches, and the assorted other fodder out there—it's elementary. It all comes down to clear rules, no-nonsense consequences, and focused parenting— through these two good eyes.

"Secondly, considering their schooling, the B'nai Mitzvah training and their friendships, I don't see major problems, just flexibility issues really. We keep them limited when possible with any performance activities to the off months of school and weekends. When necessary, I tutor them on the road during those times they have to travel during the school week.

"After all, if I was able to succeed in tutoring you, I can easily handle two bright boys—now can't I?"

Mom purposely threw that little 'zetz' my way I'm sure, to make me realize she could truly teach anyone.

"Daddy of course, will handle the Hebrew training when on occasion; they miss their regular Hebrew classes. And given their displeasure over their Sunday school situation, maybe we leave the history of our people to Dad's talents at trivia and storytelling as well.

"Keeping their traveling to a reasonable amount, their friendships will not be adversely affected by any of this either. And honestly Marc, with four planes—I think that from time to time, the boys can bring their friends along with them, besides all of this.

"Lastly Marc, when was the last time you personally had a big head? Or a time you got so full of yourself that I had to put you in your place?"

"Not since my initial OSV days Mom that I can recall?"

"Exactly…but you are today—what then Marc? I'll gladly tell you what you are son—you're a grounded, yet highly modest man…despite your many successes and substantial wealth. I'd like to think—that wasn't happenstance.

"Your Dad and I had more than a little to do with that—we raised you well, don't you think? And to be a caring, sensitive and fine man too. Nevertheless, today you are a globetrotter, a car collector, and an aspiring young billionaire—yet all the while—a common man of the people too.

"Despite all of your many accomplishments, you still act like the salt of the earth—don't you…I wonder why? It's because we instilled in you humility, to always retain your modesty and level-headedness—throughout your life…and you have.

"Now, you just go right ahead and tell that to your damn frigging jury mister, because I've said my peace."

"Boy Grammy, you really told him, but you used some bad words."

"Thank you Taylor. I apologize for the bad words…really I do—but don't let me hear any coming out of you or your brother either."

"You know boys; your Daddy just wants the best for you two. He loves you with all his heart so he feels he needs to protect you from some things that could hurt you…that are out there—if you become professionals. You are both too young naturally to comprehend these things, let alone know how to deal with them yet. Grandpa and I share your Daddy's concerns too, as we love you very much, just like he does. But sometimes, even Daddies need to remember that the apple doesn't fall far from the tree."

"What does that mean Grammy?"

"It means Taylor—that your Daddy only need look at himself in the mirror first. His own reflection will illuminate that all of these same things could have happened to him when he was performing…they didn't though. Likewise, they're not likely to happen to you two either. All you two need is the same good parenting by your Dad that he benefited from by Gramps and I."

"Oh."

Trevor's question to me at that moment dislodged me only temporarily from my own personal introspection.

"Dad, so can we do it—please Daddy, p l e a s e?"

I was still silent—thinking, Christ, I just kept right on ignoring my kid… didn't I? I now realized that Mom was generally spot-on about everything she had responded with. Both her logic, along with her arguments to my concerns were sound. So I had to be honest with myself again…where was this aversion really coming from?

Honestly, it was my own repressed feelings once I moved past my real concerns for their wellbeing and adjustment. My feelings of inferiority to other men, carried over from my marriage, had reared its ugly head yet again. I knew if the boys were successful, my own inferiority complex with other men, especially my own sons down the road, would be painful to accept. And to a lesser degree, I wallowed in self-pity over being denied the boys, so I now felt entitled to hoard them to myself—forever!

I thought about all of this as I continued to ignore Trevor's evil-eye stare, for the moment.

Jesus; I could not allow my sons to suffer for my own warped feelings; I just couldn't! No matter how I felt personally, I would not deny them their own dreams; so I had to move past this crap already. I would have to deal with my problems without interfering in their dreams; it was that simple…in short I had to grow up and stop feeling sorry for myself!

Yet lastly, in light of these revelations of Mir's, along with Mom's steadfast stubbornness, I really couldn't decide otherwise—could I?

I finally burst out of my self-induced fog just in time to be rewarded with the evil-eye stare—getting beamed in—in stereo no less!

"Trevor, Taylor; I've decided that you had both better start—kissing up real good to your 'Grammy' right now. You might just want to prepare yourselves to worship her forever—for all the trouble she just made for herself. So, I guess if this is really what you two want…with her so willing—then hell—so am I. But boys, there's going to be some real serious rules, and I mean—super serious, okay?"

After the boys shouted their affirmative yeses to me, they continued screaming and jumping all over the truck. They were giving out kisses wholesale, mostly to their grandmother of course.

The rest of the ride home, they spent talking and planning between themselves non-stop. They were definitely 'jazzed' that I had relented, so they also took turns hugging me nearly the whole ride home. And they were thrilled as well; to bring happiness to others through their music—just as their mother had always wanted for them.

With all of these unexpected developments though, I on the other hand—was a train wreck now!

"Mom, I'll expect you to visit me tomorrow at the office for an extended conversation. You know, on just how you hope all of this is going to work out, along with what exactly your plans consist of. But please Mom; let's start out with the CD for the foundation as a starting point. Let's just make sure it's a quality recording so that we can see if we can get a contract for them out of that—all right?"

"Alright Marc, I can agree with you in principle with all that—so when should I be there?"

"Why not drive in with me? We'll get to it first thing as I'm positive my morning's wide open surprisingly…even Robbie was shocked."

"That works for me—how about you Malcolm?"

"Me? Oh—so now you consult me? Well, I'm fit to be tied Marilyn— by the way son, that goes double for you—for caving in."

"Dad?"

"Yes Marc?"

"When exactly was the last time you went against Mom; Mr. Macho?"

"Hey son, don't rain on my parade—I live for this stuff when it's not me she's tangling with. You're on your own boy—oh, and by the way, thanks again for the Nav."

"Thanks Pop—this is 'your' 'Captain' signing off, over, and out, thank you for all of your support…not!"

My Dad was busting from my last comments, as he then added:

"Just roll with the punches son, every dog has his day—even with your Mother."

"I'll try to remember that Dad."

"So will I Mal—now if you two have had enough, I would suggest you both shut up—try watching the road with your driving Malcolm…for a change.

"Yes dear…tomorrow morning first thing, will be just fine with me too." Dad offered.

I returned to my hugs from the twins, while sulking over this whole stinking turn of events and both of my parents' actions. Between my Mother interjecting herself into my decisions, along with my Father's total lack of supporting me with his comments—it was going to be a truly wonderful ride into the office in the morning, if I had anything to say—regarding the subject.

I know that speaking for myself, I would plan on really playing—the 'pout' on the ride in, tomorrow morning!

CHAPTER 7

▼

TWO PEAS IN A POD

THE NEXT MORNING, WE DROPPED the boys off at school before heading to my office. As expected, our drive into the office was awkwardly silent from all of us. Clearly we were all still reeling over the prior evening's conversations and disagreements...while my pouting was magnificent by the way.

As we passed by Robbie's office, I got into my office where I less-than-nicely demanded of my assistant to bring in two pots of coffee stat'...decaf for the folks, but Espresso Nuevo for me—the strongest coffee we imported. I felt I needed it today. I also made sure to ask him for lots of 'nosh' from the cafeteria. Surely when the food would arrive, Dad would act as if he hadn't eaten in a week...naturally—so he would likely begin to pig out. As a result, Mom would then explode as always. The altercation to follow would surely produce sufficient payback from me, for their prior evening's actions.

You see, in terms of the American Jewish Family dynamic, this was that special moment within the family, where everyone felt aggravated or used in some way, by the prior evening's trials...and so pouting became the accepted norm for the 'morning after'.

We were all still silent when Robbie came in with the 'The great American Jewish calling card'—food! And we all know what I hoped would come out of that...don't we?

"Okay Mom, let's start with your plans and ideas for the CD, shall we?"

I said these words—quite aware I was diverting her away from her otherwise assault on my Father's eating, just long enough so that her anger could stew a little longer towards a bigger explosion at him further into his noshing on the platter of goodies. Not surprisingly, I succeeded.

"Marc, first I want to talk to Scooter. By the way, wasn't he that nice boy who would come to visit over-night when you worked at Toonland?"

"Yes Mom, I'm surprised you remembered that—good memory, considering how much 'younger' you were back then…but can you remember his real first name?"

"Of course dear—isn't it Scott? But I can't say I recall his last name. I remember him well—like you, he never stopped eating for a moment…just like your Father is doing right now—Malcolm!"

Bingo! Marcus 15, Mom and Dad, Love…I felt vindicated already… somehow, so I spoke right up.

"Boy, Mom, you really do remember him—he can still eat too, believe me. By the way, his last name is Davis."

"Oh yes, that's it…well get him on the phone Marc, I'd like to ask him a few things now. It's regarding the conversation you shared with me about all the harping he did on you to wise up. Obviously I may have use for that very astute 'harping'. I could use a man of his many proven talents besides… certainly you and your Father—the glutton here, are of no help to me."

"Thank you Mom—I so appreciate your 'spin' on our situation."

"Can the crap Marcus—just make the damn call."

"Yes Mother."

I buzzed Robbie to attempt to track Scooter down at Toonland. He buzzed me back a few minutes later that he wasn't in; it was apparently his day off. I pulled out his info on my organizer as I dialed his home number personally. After two rings, the man of many proven talents—to quote my mother, answered the phone.

"Scoot, Marc here, are you still wearing your costume around the house while you dust?"

"Oh cute Morgan, real cute—now what do I owe the pleasure of this call bud? Are you coming down to buy me dinner, or have you finally come to your senses about your two talented off spring, who I saw on the news… oh, by the way?"

"Okay Scooter—don't gloat…you were right. Listen, I need to put you on speaker as my Mom would like to say hello—is that alright?"

At that moment, I activated the hands free speaker, just as Scooter responded (so call me pisher, I still enjoyed razzing him…he's a big boy besides which.)

"Sure Marc—absolutely. I'd love to say hi to your old lady—damn what a cook."

My Mother's eyes bugged out immediately. This was wonderful I thought…Scoot was simply marvelous, to quote Billy Crystal—he was doing my own dirty work for me!

"Hello Scott—this is the old lady here—just roasting someone's foot, so he can stuff it into his mouth later on." Dad and I were busting now.

"Jesus—oh Mrs. Morgan, you know I only meant it in the most endearing way? I'm like so sorry."

"Alright Scott—I can see you haven't lost that 'Eddie Haskell' kiss-ass quality of yours. Can the crap right this minute young man…now answer me a question."

"Sure…yes ma'am, what's your question?"

Scott responded with a fair amount of trepidation in his voice. Like all of my friends growing up, Scoot had already seen this side of my Mother's personality, once or twice before. I was actually pretty much convinced that most of my friends were just a little bit afraid of her shocking banter and bluntness at times, in calling them out.

"That's better dear—now here's what I want to know from your many years of production experience. We want to cut a recording of the twins for fund-raising purposes to benefit Marc's Foundation. So in your opinion, would you suggest in our situation to do this totally independently, or try to make some other arrangements?"

"Mrs. Morgan, does this have anything to do with the story I saw on the boys, day before last?"

"Why yes Scott, it does, the boys want to make a CD to sell at their Minis' Dessert Courts."

"Excellent, because that does make a difference given it's solely for charity, but a great cause at that. Listen, I'm sure I could get you a little 'gratis' help in your endeavor, like free studio time with an engineer. I am also quite positive Toon Media would gladly help for such a worthy cause too. Lastly, I'd be thrilled to assist you as well. I would be honored to offer executive producing responsibilities to the project—with one simple request."

"And what is that—Scott?"

"Look, Mrs. Morgan, can I be candid with you…while perhaps a little 'out there' too?"

"Certainly Scott, enlighten me…from 'out there'."

"Funny, Mrs. M. Look, no disrespect to Marc's concerns, as they are merited concerning the music industry…I can assure you. The thing is, your grandsons' talents from what I have experienced only once—are simply 'too' apparent to ignore!"

"I see—do you really think so Scott?"

"Are you kidding Mrs. M? Yes—I do. Listen, I don't know if you're particularly religious or not…but wait a minute—isn't there a sect of Jews that are specifically spiritual…don't they study the Kibitz or something like that?"

God, were we three laughing at that one now, before Mom finally calmed down enough to answer.

"No Scott, it's not a Kibitz…they study the Kaballah…but nice try, my sweet young gentile friend."

"Look Mrs. M.—not that any of that is my business, but I personally am religious, you know. Candidly, after all of these years in this industry—I can bear witness to those artists that enjoyed that 'divine' intervention too…I've seen it! I'm not ashamed to admit that either Mrs. M…because your grandsons are surely blessed with it in spades…and I haven't even heard them play the piano yet…so I'll just take Marc's word on that!

"As I see it, we are all on this little planet of ours for a specific purpose. Some of us it seems are given special talents or gifts beyond the norm. These special abilities are here to help create a greater good for all humanity—who knows for sure what the reason.

"So, I'm not trying to preach or anything else, but I'm also dead serious here. As far as I can tell Mrs. Morgan, Trevor and Taylor were given these gifts as a divine calling to music…I believe that they are only meant to sing and perform music. I believe this with all of my being—I'm certain of it actually.

"You know Mrs. M., if I'm right on all of this—it has to start somehow… someway, and certainly at some—point. So I want to have the boys cut a demo for me to see where we can take it. Three songs of my choosing from their song list with me alone, calling the production shots. With my belief in their talent, along with a little luck—'fate' will tell us all—soon enough. But if I'm right, they'll have a recording contract and stellar careers before we all know it."

"My word Scott, that was quite a sermon, but I do see your point. I agree with your logic wholeheartedly—Marc what do you have to say to Scott's ethereal explanation?

"What can I say Mom? Dang, but who am I to argue with you two— learned clergy…this close to Passover…I don't want to be visited by the ten plagues for disagreeing, now do I?"

"You're right son, so don't! But onto another subject Scott, what exactly did you mean by—you call the production shots?" Mom asked.

"All I mean by that is I would have creative control strictly in producing this one demo. I'm not trying to usurp anyone; I just want the demo done, as I believe it should be produced for its intended purpose…this is my area of expertise so I can assure you that you will not be disappointed.

"Honestly, the boys have an unusual phenomenon in their singing—I'm not even sure if they realize it themselves…they're harmonies come off in an organic stereo of sorts. I want to take advantage of that…not every producer knows how to capture that…let alone exploit it fully. Think of it as a sort of voice modeling. So does that seem fair to all of you? I hope I'm not stepping on anyone's toes with any of this?"

"No Scott, I don't believe it does, but I'm not prepared to commit further just yet, if you don't mind?"

"Certainly Mrs. M—should I also assume that Marc has deferred the boys' handling on this project, to you then?"

"Yes you may Scott…but call me Marilyn…Eddie. Now, just so I have an idea with their demo, can you give us an inkling of your ideas or plans on capturing their sound?"

"Sure Marilyn, I could, but I would much rather sit down face to face with you guys—instead, as these are all important considerations after all. Could I drive up there and meet with all of you—say next Friday?"

"Hey Scooter, what's your schedule like today buddy boy?"

"Today? Well Marc, I'm relatively open, but I had planned on going to the driving range later on—why? And hell, you know it's a little late to be hitting the road to get to Vegas today—right?"

"Yes Scoot, but I had a different idea. I was thinking that if we have an available plane, I could send it down to pick you up. We could knock this whole thing off by a little past lunch, if you like?"

"If I like? Listen, old buddy—if you've got the jet, I'll feign your—pet?"

"Oh my God, Scoot, I see you're still pushing the stupid rhymes and limericks aren't you…now I am depressed?"

"Nice crack Marc, but at least I grew up and stopped carrying out stupid practical jokes."

"Alright, you two knock it off right now!"

"Yes Mom." Came out in stereo from both Scooter and me simultaneously. This of course set all of us off nicely.

"Marc, in the time you've been running off that mouth of yours, we could have found out if you have a plane available!"

"Alright Mom, I get the message. Scoot, let me put you on hold for a moment, okay?"

"No prob, bud." I pushed the hold button as I next dialed the 'Wall' man direct.

"Wally?"

"No it's Sam, Mr. Morgan, but let me get him for you."

"Thanks Sam."

"Boss, what's up?"

"How are the girls Wall—and more importantly, where the hell are they at the moment—at 'finishing school' perhaps?"

"Cute boss, but no. They're all out on quarterly QA inspections all over the country at the moment."

"Great—just my luck. So which one of them is the closest inbound Wall?"

"We happen to have number III finishing up in Ontario, why?"

"Would that be Ontario, California or Canada, Wall?"

"California, boss."

"Good, it seems I have a hitchhiker in Orange County, I thought we could offer a ride to. What's the flight plan on number III after Ontario?"

"She's coming home to papa, boss—you want me to divert her to John Wayne or Long Beach Airport? Perhaps your hitchhiker would be agreeable though, to catching a ride to Ontario to save me the landing and takeoff fees, elsewhere?"

"Sure Wall, that's close enough. What time do you expect to depart, give, or take?"

"Bout eleven thirty, I would surmise—so do I call Bill?"

"Yep, tell him to be on the lookout for a slight built guy with a big goofy grin—that will be him."

"Boss, what in hell are you talking about?"

"Sorry Wall, just clowning, I'll explain later—but go ahead and have Bill keep an eye out for my friend Scott Davis. I'll tell him to get dressed and hit the road for Ontario. I'll instruct him to find number III at their Exec terminal."

"You got it Boss."

I hung up with Wally, while I also put Scooter back on the squawk box.

"Scoot, it seems you're in luck…so are we. We have a Lear at the Executive Terminal at Ontario; can you be there by plus or minus 11:30?"

"Ontario, sure Marc—I'll be there with bells on. Which plane do I ask for?"

"You know Scoot, forget the 'bells'—your costume's frightening enough!"

I laughed, as we all did, before I continued.

"Look, just tell them Verandas Inc. at the executive terminal."

"Okay, got it. Say, how's the weather there at the moment, what should I wear?"

"Dang Scoot, I'm glad you thought to ask, it's pretty cool and lousy here, haven't you heard,—better dress warm? It's like 48 degrees, windy as hell and overcast—they're predicting possible thunderstorms this afternoon."

"Really, thunderstorms? Alright Marc, duly noted, I'll see you around lunch time, so I suppose you realize this means—you're buying again?"

"Don't worry Scoot, there'll be a Happy Meal° waiting for you in the Limo."

"Fine Marc, good bye Marilyn and Mr. Morgan. I'm really looking forward to seeing both of you after all of these years."

"So am I—Mr. 'Haskell' but please make sure you bundle up real well before getting on that plane. I don't want to send you home to your wife and family with a cold—do I?"

"Sure thing Mrs. Cleaver, don't worry—I'll wear my new parka…how's that?"

"Good, see you in a couple of hours." Mom added.

We hung up, whereby we were all instantly on the floor in hysterics over our conversation with Scooter. Our current weather conditions were somewhat different from what we had just told him after all.

We could only imagine the look on Scooter's face when he would step out of number III, shortly after noon. Right into clear skies, eighty-one degrees, zero wind—in his parka!

"Marc, we have to go get him when he lands, I've got to see his face."

"Naturally Dad, don't worry, I planned on that. We'll see if he still thinks my practical jokes are stupid, after one of my classics has done him in but good. And kudos to you Mom—that certainly was a brilliant stroke of 'supportive' bullshit on your part as I've ever seen."

"Gee son, thank you. Let's just say, I don't think we'll be hearing much out of Mr. Davis—I mean, Mr. Haskell, as it concerns him referring to me as the 'old lady' in the near future—do you?"

We had a bit of time to go on Scooter's arrival, so mom filled us in on all her ideas. This took up considerable time, with mom insisting on my seal of approval on each issue.

Scooter's motives and his spiritual bent deeply impressed Mom. Her ideas on how to best utilize his talents were most interesting. Actually all in all, they were brilliant on many levels.

Eventually, Robbie paged me to inform us that Paul was waiting outside for our short ride to the airport. We continued our conversations once inside Laverne. By the time we reached McCarran, Mom had run off her final ideas to Dad and me. I was comfortable enough with her plans and suggestions on everything, that I actually found myself beginning to relax somewhat. Further, I had given up on all of my pouting as it never worked with these two anyway…you'd think they knew my every move—go figure?

Arriving alongside number III, we waited anxiously with bated breathe for our prey to deplane. As the hatch opened—the ladder came down. We could all see Suzie getting out of the way for Scooter. I think our three mouths dropped open in unison—there was Scooter…He was wearing a big and baggy parka:

Chapter 8

▼

Busted!

—ALONG WITH A BAGGY PAIR of shorts!

Busted! We were the ones now being played...how utterly disappointing. Down the steps he walked, dropping the parka to his side like a model strutting her stuff on a fashionable runway as he walked.

Wearing sunglasses, a Panama hat, along with a hand-painted t-shirt—he was a sight to behold for sure. You see, the t-shirt boldly proclaimed in 'air-brushed' strokes: 'I showed your ass up' on the front side. Then on the back of it, it said; 'Marc & Mrs. M. get theirs.'

Scooter was now drawing attention to his T-shirt by pointing to the front, and then the back in an exaggerated fashion. He was waving, reserving his middle finger for a one-finger salute, discreetly flashed to me as he stepped onto the tarmac.

If you think I was in shock—you should have seen Mom—she was nailed—along with peeved! There in one fell swoop, ended her big plans for a payback for the 'old lady' crack.

I just had to laugh though at my friend's obvious intelligence of 'smelling a rat' by verifying our local weather information for himself before departing. Mom was not pleased with Scooter, or for that matter—my reaction on this turn of events at all.

We all walked up to Scooter who was still losing it. He and I embraced as we shook hands, before he then shook hands with my Dad. Scoot now turned to my Mom.

"Well Mrs. M...Marilyn, it's certainly a pleasure to see you and Mr. Morgan again. I hope you took my joke in the manner in which it was meant, that being, with respect and love?" Then Scooter kissed her on the cheek along with giving her a very tender hug.

Mom knew when to throw in the towel, so she simply kissed Scooter back and just stood there in his hug for a moment.

"It's wonderful to be seeing you again Scott, after all these years, don't you agree Mal? My, you've grown into quite a handsome man, even with that asinine t-shirt."

So, at least Mom got some satisfaction with her crack, as we all talked animatedly now as we headed over for Laverne…Scoot especially.

"Marc, I must say that I've always wanted to know how the Jet-Set lived—so now I know. That's one hell of a plane you have there bud…but your stewardess was truly a riot to fly with, I have to tell you."

"Thanks Scooter, Suzie is a hoot. But listen pal, I'd hardly call myself a member of the Jet Set. Then again, wait until you ride in the new plane later. Seriously though, our planes merely get us to our many units more efficiently. That saves us valuable time, and therefore money on the bottom-line as well.

"Just the same buddy boy; it sure beats the hell out of my '89 Malibu for getting around."

"I see your point Scooter, but a man of your many talents could have done anything he wanted. You simply chose with your heart—I certainly respect that quality in anyone—especially you bud."

"Thanks Marc, that's true I did, but would you mind explaining that to Beth. You see, I never hear the end of that argument when she's trying to stretch our recourses and get all of the bills paid each month. Mind you Marc; this is all coming from a public school teacher—of all—super top-paying professions."

We were all agreeing with Scooter's commentary, as I began allowing some of my own reservations to escape.

"Scooter, you have to fight your own battles. Hell, I've got enough of my own, like with this whole situation with the twins. I hope you and Mom can work this out, because my terms of acceptance are mandatory for my continued support."

"Fine, I get the message Marc…I'm sure we can bud, once I hear them of course."

"We'll see Scoot; I wish I could share your enthusiasm though."

We drove out of McCarran, as Mom began going over all of my issues one by one while Scooter listened. As she explained how she saw things work out if the boys really got a shot, I saw that Scooter began actually taking notes—this impressed me to no end. He was concerned enough about my reservations and issues, to know the ongoing ground rules along with my concerns for the boys...smart man.

"Marilyn, I really don't see any major obstacles here, if we properly plan out everything. We can even keep 'old sour puss' over there, quite satisfied—now, more importantly, how can I be of help besides the demo duties?"

"Scott, how would you like to become involved?"

"I'm really not sure yet Marilyn, but if I get somewhere with the demo, I'd like some role with them in or out of the studio. You know Marilyn; I've been the one person berating Marc the loudest—for the longest time among all of us anyway, haven't I? Naturally I'm not dictating terms here, but does that seem fair to everyone in principle?"

"Yes Scott, I certainly agree. Listen, I've run a few ideas of my own by Marc and Mal. They agree with me that you would be ideal and perfect for the boys' Business Manager and Executive Producer while I'll serve as their Personal Manager—now how does that sit with you?"

"Fine, you see I have absolutely no doubt that these two are going to the moon professionally. But, I still have a job now, while I attempt to pay my bills in the meantime, so I would assume you all understand that...and I'd also like to know how the boys themselves would feel about me becoming involved with them? I don't want any 'bad feelings' from anyone naturally."

"Scott that's fine—we'll speak to them, but they voiced a desire to work with you again...anytime. Look, we've got an idea about your present career as well—would you consider a job change that relocates you here to Las Vegas?"

"What? I don't know Marilyn. You realize I've already got nearly seventeen years total invested with Toon Media? My earnings are finally in the land of the 'living' with all the side work they get for me. You know, it's quite possible to act as their business manager from another locale—it doesn't require me to quit my present job, so what exactly are you suggesting here?"

"Marc and I have talked at length Scott. If you would consider it, he'd like to talk to you about joining Verandas to create a formal Entertainment Department for his company?"

"Really...wow. Gee Marc, since you're letting Mom do all the talking here, care to enlighten me a bit on the job description at least, old buddy?"

"Sure Scoot, I'd be delighted to, but first, let me give you a little background, so you'll understand my reasoning. We have never had a producer...or for that matter, any head person for our entertainment. It has simply evolved more or less on its own, over all these years. I originally got it off the ground myself, but honestly Scoot...I would hardly call myself a producer. As each new unit opened, I would just turn it over to our managers to carry out our loose guidelines along with a library of rehearsal videos.

Over the ensuing years, with over three hundred units now, along with entertainment being a key element of the overall Verandas dining experience, you'd think I would have done something about that, before now...but I haven't—so it's time we give it the attention it deserves—don't you think?

"Right now, there are no two units anywhere, handling their entertainment quite the same. We have simply allowed our managers free-reign in taking the entertainment to whatever level they like beyond our basic guidelines and directives. Believe it or not, some of my managers are producing Broadway quality stage shows every night...while others could care less...which sometimes shows in a hit to their QC score for their lackluster entertainment...I think its about time to demand some consistency out of all of our units.

"Scoot, you could greatly enhance that consistency from unit-to-unit, as well as develop an incredible entertainment experience for all the units, I'm sure. There would obviously be a lot of travel with this job initially. You would also have very heavy responsibilities. The good news is that you'd be on a fast track to a Vice Presidency for the new department. I usually want someone in that position for each department before too long anyway. Most importantly pal; it would be your baby to impress the shit out of the board, along with myself. Naturally, I'll leave it to you to develop it into something stellar, that you believe to be our proper direction and style. Essentially Scoot...that's the job description.

"Concurrent to all of this of course, you would have your duties to help the boys and Mom with their situation. Both inside the company as it relates to their fund-raising efforts, along with the outside efforts with their commercial opportunities. Utilize your travel to cover the two directions simultaneously when you can.

"I of course, have to figure a way to keep your outside activities with the boys within the tax laws. Don't be surprised when I have to bill the boys' production company for a representative portion of their plane trips. But outside that one concern, it's your baby like I've already said. And if you stop to think about it Scoot, it makes a lot more sense for you personally, if you're going to end up working with the boys down the road anyway—see my point?"

"Yes Marc, of course I do...but damn, that's my idea of an opportunity, I'm really at a loss for words. What kind of compensation are we looking at here?"

"Scoot, my side of the equation is a base of eighty-four grand to start. Add to that, bonus potential, some exceptional management perks, fully paid expenses—plus it's a safe bet that we can retire the '89 Malibu with an appropriate company car as well.

"Beyond the Verandas opportunity, the boys' side of it is unlimited with the standard rate of 10% for managing the boys' career, plus your royalties and fees as Executive Producer. When would you be able to speak to Beth about all of this?"

"How about later today…when would we have to make a move?"

"As soon as possible, at least for your Verandas position. What's Beth's situation with her job—you mentioned that she's now at mid-semester in her teaching track—right?"

"Yes…good memory bud. I can tell you though; she has been solicited by your school district on more than one occasion. Given this opportunity, she would probably jump ship at the end of this current track, but not before… she is naturally seriously committed to her kids. With her Masters Degree and tenure, she'd start at around fourteen thou more with your district—than hers. So believe me, she should consider all of this quite favorably."

"Alright Scooter, let's sweeten the deal up a tad so that Beth signs on to this. Tell her we will provide you with corporate housing until she and the girls can all finish this school track out. Alternatively, if you prefer, you can stay with me at the house, or I can give you the houseboat at the Lake—if that suits you?

"One of your perks as a new transitioning middle manager is unrestricted access to the planes as well, so you can arrange weekend trips for either you or the family to be together every other weekend anyway. We will also compensate you under our relocation policy for your move. This will substantially help you sell your home faster and to find a replacement here."

"Jesus Marc, you're sure making it hard for me to say no—aren't you?"

"That's the whole idea Scoot—isn't it? So how do you think Beth and the girls will feel about these life changes, as I never like to screw up family harmony?"

"Marc, I have a pretty good idea that Beth will love the idea on the basis of the changes to our combined income alone. After all, you likely just more than doubled my present salary; with the factored potential from the boys' side included in that. She is also really fed up with lots of little things in Orange County, like the traffic, so that is a plus too.

"The girls on the other hand, will be impacted what with all of their friendships, Girl Scouts, and sports. We'll just have to see how they feel about it, although it's obviously our decision in the long run. It also doesn't hurt that both of them have serious crushes on your two boys. Given that, I'll be able to tell them that they'll be spending lots of time together with all of this."

"Fair enough Scoot, why don't you call Beth when she's through with her school day, so that you two can talk at length in private about it?"

"That's just what I was going to suggest Marc. However, I am curious about something else. Just what kind of an 'appropriate' company car does the job come with?"

"Honestly Scoot—I don't know for sure bud, what exactly did you have in mind? Obviously the car doesn't exist at this moment so I guess that gives us an opportunity to consider your ideas—within reason of course. We do have quite a variety already, but most of our company cars are actually Expeditions and Tahoe SUV's...I don't think those are appropriate for your situation, especially given the role you'll play as the boys' producer."

"Well Marc, it's just that Beth has always wanted one of those Mustang Convertibles. We've never been able to afford one on our pay, let alone dream of any new car. Assuming that request isn't beyond what you had planned to spend, I know it would add the icing on the cake for Beth?"

"Hum...you know Scoot, why do I feel like you're playing 'good-cop, bad cop' with me, while your own wife isn't even here to confirm or deny any of this? But really Scoot, I think that's an excellent suggestion, because it lends itself to your 'Business Manager image' enough too...so consider it done...I'll just forget the Jaguar I had actually thought of suggesting to you."

"A...Jag! Are you BS'ing me?"

"No, not at all Scooter. Like I said, I wanted you to have an 'image' car for the boys' side of this too. We can't have you looking like some pauper in that industry, now can we? But the Mustang will save us major cash as it still works as a sports car...making Beth happy as well too. Hell, with what you just saved me, you can go ahead and get the Cobra model if you want though?"

"Oh Marc, you're making me salivate now, are you for real about this?"

"Why of course Scoot...what color do you want it in?"

"Wait, let me recover first. I've got to let my heartbeat calm down a bit."

"Fine, we'll table the color until the end of our day then, meanwhile you and Mom need to put your heads together anyway on the boys' strategy, even if Beth says no to the Verandas offer."

"Certainly Marc, right after you buy lunch bud."

"Oh dang it Scoot—I almost forgot—here's the Happy Meal®...sorry.
I handed him the bag from McDonalds that Paul stopped for earlier.

"Which toy did you get-by the way?"

"Cute Morgan, but I think I'll save the Happy Meal for a snack later on if it's all the same to you bud. Now where are we really going to sit down to eat?"

"Alright smart-ass, let's go to the Cheesecake at the Forum, fair enough?"

"Now you're talking Marc—that's one of my favorites back home...no offense."

While still busting over Scoot's crack, I called Paul on the intercom to tell him to head over to Caesars...we were there mere minutes later. Naturally, I had Robbie call the Cheesecake Factory earlier in the day for me to make reservations. Upon arriving there, we were immediately seated at this wonderful, popular, Forum Shops restaurant.

I took a moment now to spy my Dad's expression—more like a scowl. I think my Dad was just stewing something fierce looking at the prices on the menu. He realized this meal could have been 'gratis' if I had only taken us to either of our units instead—but he just sat there...sulking.

Over lunch, Scooter did a very convincing job of explaining to me that all of my concerns were in reality—quite real and justified so at least I felt vindicated somewhat. And yet he believed, controllable with the proper handling along with 'focused' parenting of course. I was relieved to hear him describe in detail the many young entertainers he knew who were well balanced, grounded, but most importantly—drug-free, happy, levelheaded kids.

Scooter then laid out how to get the ball rolling with the boys' career. He laid out what would be the most logical steps to take if the bait from the demo or the boys' recording for the restaurants got some attention. For one thing, Scoot insisted on promoting the boys for the Foundation's CD by tying it into our grand opening for the boys' crusade—after all, the press would already be there.

By the end of this lunch meeting, I was beginning to come to a less ambivalent and concerned attitude over this whole going pro thing...which comforted me to no end. I was also very impressed with Mom's ideas along with her resolve to protect the boys at all costs—Scooter's too.

The only one out there who I couldn't read at that moment—was my old man. I honestly didn't think his silence was over the price of the lunch...but then again? He hardly said anything the whole time. I made a mental note to pick his brain later. It appeared another spa conference would be in order between us—later in the evening.

After lunch, while on the way back to the office, I directed Paul to stop at Spanish Trail Realty so Scooter could meet Natalie to see if she could give him some ideas on houses available in his price range. I thought this was prudent as it would further motivate Scooter.

When Natalie told him a few minutes later, how substantial of a home he could buy on his current four-hundred-thousand budget from Orange County, you would have thought he hit the lottery; as he was totally floored in the differences in the homes. Natalie then gave him some ideas to consider, along with some current listings to review with Beth later on. She went so far as to have one of her in-house lenders explain why Scoot needed to consider matching his new home's price range to his new salary as well, to maximize his tax planning. In short, all of this really got Scoot excited with the move's possible changes to his personal lifestyle...score one for the Markster!

At that moment though, my reflections were cut short by my cell.

"Marc here, hello."

"Hey Marc, its Robbie."

"Hi bud, what's up?"

"Marc, did you happen to have any cross words or perhaps a pissing contest with one of those reporters yesterday?"

"Yes Robbie...Jesus, didn't Burt mention that? I thought for sure he would...it was the lovely, pert...and ever-obnoxious—Condescension Connors...the girl everyone loves...to loathe."

Instinct motivated me to switch to speaker on my telephone at that moment...I already felt I might need witnesses!

"No Marc, I guess he thought it was privileged information. He seemed to take that issue rather seriously—poor boy. Hell, here he was with all this good gossip on you...so I could have had a field day...damn him.

"Great Robbie...but I've switched to speaker by the way. Listen—thanks for your support Rob, but what's up—or do I really want to know?"

"Honestly boss, this is one of those times that I would have to say seriously—no, you don't want to!"

"Holy Christ, alright Robbie—spill it."

"Well Marc, I just heard from Jessica in accounting. She just returned from the sandwich shop around the corner for lunch. She claims that you were certifiably crucified by your lovely Ms. Connors during her lunch hour segment. Poor Jessica was so upset; she said she started screaming at the TV in front of all the other patrons.

"Poor kid, make sure you tell her I appreciate the support—never mind, I'll tell her myself when I get back."

"Yes Marc, that would be an excellent idea, she was so shook up, I couldn't get much out of her at first."

"So, Rob, can you share with us, what you did get out of her?"

"Yeah, but are you sure you really want to hear it, it's pretty outrageous boss?"

"Yes pal, what do you think—of course, let me hear it already?"

"Okay Marc, but remember, I didn't hear this broad personally, so I'd suggest you not rely on my spin or Jessica's."

"Jesus Robbie, get to it already, you're starting to piss me off."

"Okay boss, I know when I'm screwed—believe me."

"Fine Robbie."

"Thanks Marc, all right, here goes. It seems that your Ms. Connors took some truly cheap shots at Miranda apparently."

"Miranda!"

I yelled out for all of Las Vegas to hear. I was so furious just hearing Robbie's words, I couldn't imagine how what she said, would actually affect me. I was soon to find out—unfortunately. As Mom jumped into the fruckus too.

"What kind of cheap shots." Mom demanded. After all, she was certainly Miranda's advocate now.

"Yeah, get to it Robbie—damn it." I now added.

"Yes Marilyn—okay boss. Connors has apparently launched an investigation on the boys' crusade—she still doesn't buy our story. She's dubbed it: the charade…crusade!

"Apparently, she sent two of her flunkies over to England to dig up dirt on all of you. According to Jessica's explanation, she naturally discovered your unusual familial situation. She then began a tirade by not letting up on what Miranda had done to you or the boys either. As Jessica tells it, she's made it out to look like Miranda's the diabolical heavy for not telling you about the boys for all those years.

"It really upset Jessica, because she knows the real story, so she said that what she reported was totally off-base. Worst of all, her team interviewed several people who lent their unknowing support to their inaccurate spin, by twisting their words through some of their questions."

"All right Robbie—I get the gist of it regrettably. You know pal, when I'm finished with that bitch, she'll rue the day she ever tangled with me. In fact, she'll regret the day she decided to leave the womb or enter journalism altogether."

"Marc, you have a right to be angry, but keep your head too, honey."

"I will Mom, don't sweat it."

"And justly so boss."

"Okay Robbie, we'll keep our heads…let's follow procedure. First and foremost, call the boys school to forewarn the administration on this latest development. Next, get Eric up to speed before you do anything beyond the school; have him interview Jessie for one thing. Let's get her take on all of it, seeing as she does know the facts herself. I think Eric needs to know how that affected her personally…not just as my employee. It becomes important from the damages standpoint.

"Lastly, arrange a copy of the report from the station; use whatever leverage you can—remember we have a large portion of our TV ad buy on their national network. We'll dissect her report; expose her lies, while we then issue a rebuttal with the true facts, via a press release."

"Yes Marc, I'll get right on all of it...boss—I'm so sorry this has happened to you all. It's unbelievable what good people have to suffer for their efforts to help others."

"Thank you Robbie, I do appreciate your words—believe me. Let's just hope I still have some friends in this town."

After hanging up with Robbie, I had to bring Scooter up to speed overall on the matter. Of course, this also necessitated me explaining the facts of my marriage's outcome to Scoot, for the first time as well. He knew little other than the fact that I was widowed. After explaining my wife's true motives, he was as incensed as the remaining three of us.

Given the situation that would now take me back to the office, I suggested we stop to retrieve the boys at school. We would then make a brief side trip to the house.

They would be out of school in around twenty minutes anyway, so I wanted to insulate them from this if possible. I didn't want them broadsided from any kid getting fresh gossip from their arriving parents.

We arrived at The Meadows School right as the kids were getting out.

When my two saw Scooter in our car—their eyes lit right up. Being bright eleven-year-olds, they knew something was afoot immediately...fortunately that was apparently all they knew. As such, we all knew better than to bring up what had just been shared with us, besides, their excitement with seeing Scoot, was a truly pleasurable diversion.

"Hi Scott, what are you doing here?" This came from Taylor with the subtlest of giggle thrown in for emphasis.

"Hey there guys, I'm here to see about making you two into major 'rockers' for real. That is, if my wife can be talked into moving here...would you like that?"

"Sure Scott, we're dying to, this is so brill, you helping us would be so cool...like can you really help us?" It was now apparently Trevor's turn.

"Certainly I can guys—by the time I'm through with you two, you'll both be heading for the top of the charts if I have anything to say about it."

"Wicked Scott, I'd like that—how about you Taylor?"

"Natch bro...sure I would—but we need to talk about a few things first."

This seriousness on Taylor's part, rather floored all of us, especially me—the car instantly fell silent now.

"Are you having reservations Taylor? You know son, if you are, you can pass on all of this right now. Taylor, no one—and I mean none of us, is going to force you into something you don't want to do sweetheart. You see son, Trevor can have a go at it on his own if you've changed your mind?"

"Not at all Daddy, I'm excited about all of this stuff; I just want to talk about something I've given a lot of thought to, that's all."

"Oh, fine then—so what's on your mind T-man?"

"Well Daddy, I'd like to know something from Scott since he's here anyway. If this works out, can we make a lot of money in this business?"

"Why yes Taylor, it could make both of you quite well set for your futures." Scott offered as his answer...I think he was as surprised by the question as I was.

Scoot's answer though, was perfect so I left it as it was, without elaborating at all on his comments. I did not intend to share with the boys the extent of their personal wealth at such a young age, as I would surmise that Scoot had a fair idea himself, having met Cedric before. Taylor, though, now continued his thoughts.

"Good, so here's what I'd like to do with my half Daddy. I want at least half of my money to go into your foundation. How do you feel about that Trev?"

"That's cool Taylor—I'll match you pound for pound...sorry, I meant dollar to dollar."

"Damn bud, where on earth did you get these kids? How is it Marc, that you deserve them in the first place? I told you there was divine intervention here...where else would that comment come from bud?"

Then drawing from our most recent traumatic events, I made a very poignant, yet true statement:

"Their Mother, Scoot...if only you had met her, you would understand... that's all I can say on the subject—isn't that right boys?"

"Yes Dad."

"Listen boys, if this is really what you two would like to do, we can set both of you up with your own joint foundation, or one for each of you, that way you'll be able to totally direct how that money is spent...and for whom. And on that subject, I can give you two suggestions, since you're obviously serious about this."

"We can do that Dad, our own foundations?"

"Of course Taylor, why put it into the Verandas foundation? You know, thanks to you two, we will have more than enough now in our foundation's treasury. Besides that guys, you cannot really control how your donations are spent in our foundation—that's essentially decided by our board. With your own foundations however, you can. But if you wouldn't mind, I'd still like to have you do your recording for my foundation's efforts since it's tied to the kiosks and your crusade?"

"Sure Dad, no sweat."

"Thanks T-1. I see you're still working on your American slang full time?"

Trevor was enjoying my commentary when he replied:

"You don't really mind—do you Dad; I mean you're like always bringing it up?"

"Not at all son, it's just that it always surprises me when all our most treasured slang words and expressions come out of that little adorable British mouth, flavored by that accent of yours, no less."

"Oh."

"Now, may I continue with my two suggestions boys?"

"Sure Dad—sorry we forgot."

"No problemo T-man, so here's my idea. First, have you two given any thought to Mummy's two Foundations back home in England? You know, with Mummy not there to keep everyone motivated, their treasuries could probably use a real shot in the arm about now—don't you think? Also, you know Grandfather's arrangements for the manor, in honor of Mummy. So why don't you two put these great causes at the top of your list of concerns to help through your joint foundation, or two individual ones?" And just so you know, I've also added Mummy's two foundations to our list of charities, as well as the Miranda Richards Morgan Cancer Research and Care Centre."

Both of my two sons, just lost it right there on the spot. Without so much as a word, I instantly had the two of them in my lap of sorts, hugging the breath out of me.

"I take it, that this idea meets with your approval, boys?"

"Yes Daddy—thank you."

I think everyone was just too emotional to say much else, so the rest of our ride to the house was mostly silent. Scoot in particular seemed quite overwhelmed with this very abundant view into the character of his future charges…that much was clear by how much he kept staring at them while shaking his head.

We got to the Trail to drop the boys off at the house to get started on their homework. It was still a mountain's worth each night, so I suggested that the folks hang around to assist them. I would return to the office alone, given what had happened, it only made sense. Besides, they would be far less distracted working with Scooter from home anyway for the rest of the afternoon. I also knew that Scooter would want to speak to the boys privately at some point before calling Beth on her cell too.

So I left Mom, Dad, and Scooter to plan strategy while I left for—the war room.

I arrived at the office where I immediately sought out Jessica. It was clear just seeing me walk up to her cubicle, unsettled her, but she was a trooper… so she smiled instead.

"Hi boss, I hear you know all about it now?"

"Yes Jessie—sort of. Without boring you to tears, I was hoping you'd share it with me personally."

"Yes sir, I'm not surprised really, I know I'd want to hear why someone insulted my poor dead spouse. Oh forgive me boss, if I'm being insensitive?"

"No Jessie, I understand what you mean exactly. Naturally I agree with you one hundred percent…it stinks—case closed."

"Yes sir, it does, but what really peeved me though, were those two supposed reporters on her team. Those two scumbags very carefully worded their questions just 'so'. They wanted to make sure that the people they interviewed would agree with where they were leading them. I mean, have you ever been interviewed by a pollster, Mr. Morgan?"

"No Jessie, I haven't—why do you ask?"

"Honestly sir, it was just like that—what these two reporters did with their questions. They were precisely worded to throw the people off. No wonder they appeared to be siding with the reporters' story—you would too!"

"Was it that bad Jess?"

"Yes sir, it was. Frankly sir, your poor late wife didn't stand a chance with those two. They manipulated the facts to make it appear that Mrs. Morgan's decision to keep the knowledge of the boys from you…was only made to look like it concerned you starting Verandas here. They contended the true reason—was Mrs. Morgan's bitterness that you had left her behind, alone in England.

"Then based upon all that crap from those two, Concepcion really went to town denigrating and bashing your wife. And you should have seen how she feigned her shock and surprise over the revelation of it all, it was so stinking phony, it was pathetic."

I knew at that moment that tears were silently slipping from my eyes, yet I was powerless to hide them. Employee or not, this was too hurtful, unwarranted, and unacceptable for me to do much else at that moment… hopefully she would understand and say nothing. And Jessie did seem to understand—she certainly was sympathetic.

"I'm sorry boss; I know how you must feel. You know, I read about your wife's story in the employee's newsletter. I remembered it you know—how she selflessly sheltered you here so you could build Verandas uninterrupted. I got so upset right there in that sandwich shop, that they all looked at me like I was nuts standing there screaming out my defense of your actions to the TV screen."

"Thanks Jessie, I thank God I have supporters like you out there."

"Yes boss—you do. I would guess that with what went down today, I believe you'll be hearing from lots of them too."

"Thanks Jess—is there more, or should I just get it from the report itself?"

"You know boss, I would try to get their report. Don't let me over or understate anything. You need to see it for yourself anyway. But let me warn you boss, it's biting and cutting-edge cruel—truthfully sir."

"I understand Jessie—but thanks again."

"No problem sir."

I left Jessica's cubicle to walk over to Eric's office. It was clear by the stares I received; that this horrible event had completely made its way throughout our office staff already.

I could always tell when the staff knew about a sensitive situation. My employees would unconsciously convey their empathy or sympathy through little non-verbal nuances. A nod here, a smile there, all to show me their unspoken support. I then remembered back to the very first time this occurred…over that horrible day in Dallas. I would never forget it then—or now…God how I loved the people that I worked with!

It was four years ago, that our very first Dallas unit opened their doors one beautiful spring Saturday morning, having no idea of what awaited them with their breakfast rush.

At a nearby low-security correctional facility, two career hoodlums had orchestrated and hatched an impromptu escape plan that went awry…it seems their stolen car broke down right in our parking lot entrance. Whereby the convicts naturally rushed inside our restaurant…seeking to gain the upper hand and avoid capture from the pursuing Sheriff's department cruisers.

Before anyone in charge had time to react, our unit was taken hostage by the pair. Almost immediately, one of them grabbed a hostage from among the staff, holding their improvised knife to her throat. This was all done to get an off-duty, deputy sheriff sitting at the coffee bar, to drop his gun that he was brandishing at them. Once the deputy realized they would likely stab the hostage, he gave up and kicked the gun over to them. The other convict now grabbed the gun deciding right there to shoot him…dead on the spot in front of our already traumatized guests…how totally unnecessary and cruel.

And so began an eleven-hour standoff that saw three others killed that day…including my lead manager…all while I eventually stood outside the unit, feeling helpless to do much of anything but watch in horror as the events unfolded.

Prior to that morning, I had never flown either of my Lear 60's at their maximum speed or at an altitude above 47,000 feet before…but I made it to

Dallas' final approach at DFW in a little over two hours. From the time I got the call on my way into the office, to the restaurant in Dallas, it took less than three hours total for me to be standing in front of the unit with the better part of the Dallas Sheriff's department and the swat team there too.

Eventually, I did redeem myself though. I knew where all of our security cameras were focused, so I knew that a small swat team could enter the rear of the third floor Veranda seating area that was always closed at breakfast, but more importantly…avoid being picked up on any of our cameras. They would hopefully be able to take out the convicts without further loss of life.

To run further interference, I then proceeded to join in on the negotiations themselves, as the swat team prepared to launch their assault. To my surprise, I eventually got the thugs to release all of the children in the restaurant to allow them to walk out of the restaurant to safety.

Only after the kids were clearly out of danger and off the premises, did the Captain of the swat team eventually give the command to move his swat team in.

Sadly for my manager Vince, one of the convicts had just enough time to get one more shot off from the dead deputy's gun as he himself was being gunned down by the swat team storming the ground floor. The bullet struck Vince in the right temple and killed him instantly.

Within seconds, both of the cons were dead along with one of my favorite managers…but my customers were saved at least, yet no one left that restaurant that day the same as they arrived…I can assure you.

Everyone told me that I should consider myself lucky that it wasn't worse, but it was no solace to me, or for many of our staff or guests. I was personally in therapy over the guilt I felt, for over two years. A few of the guests and employees were so traumatized, I couldn't be sure if they were ever 'right' again.

It was with these heavy memories, that I proceeded down the long corridor to my legal counsel's office…the very man within the company that had to oversee the fallout from the Dallas disaster as it came to be known around the office.

Walking into Eric's office now, I could see he was already on the latest case, if you will…talking on the telephone. I sat down, listened, and waited; it was our advertising sales representative at the CCC television affiliate across town.

Apparently they were already willing to allow our courier to pick up a copy of the tape. I couldn't be sure which suggestion of Eric's had done the trick, leave it to him though, he was masterful. I suspected it was either the one about a multi-million dollar lawsuit for slander, or the one about our television advertisements mysteriously evaporating off of the CCC network, nationally…for all time.

After Eric hung up, I could tell he was clearly upset himself…somehow that made me feel better already. He was not taking this situation casually or dispassionately, he was focused and therefore collected himself before speaking to me.

"Marc as they say so colorfully downtown in divorce court, you've been screwed, cork-screwed, and tattooed. I actually kind of thank God, this has happened now and not later. In a few more months, this could have damaged us on Wall Street with the I.P.O.—but now though; we're still relatively in the clear."

"How bad is it Eric?"

"Honestly Marc, it definitely was a hatchet job by that woman. There's absolutely no doubt about that. Hell, even our rep Toby in their sales department, had heard about her venom match with you yesterday. And now today, this investigative report gets launched coincidentally—whew. How stupid can one reporter be?

"Plus, I wasted no time in telling them your side of the story, such as it is. And that you had forbid her from speaking to the boys—she didn't tell them that little tidbit either. They didn't know much of any of it honestly; I swear the woman has no producer to answer too on an on-going basis."

"How did you get wind of my side of the story Eric?"

"Robbie, Marc. He called someone who was there, another reporter I believe."

"Oh yes, Burt Jacobs with Fox."

"Yeah, that's the one."

"So how are they reacting to it now…at this moment?"

"I would say quite cautiously Marc, while still defending her right to investigate anyone along with being armed with the freedom of speech. Apparently though, they contend the facts of your altercation are coincidental, as she had sent her crew to England after suspecting something afoul at the press conference from the day before, rather than what happened at the school.

"However Marc, enough of her venom had escaped her mouth and circulated within their offices, as I've said. Enough vitriol apparently, that her handlers are now feeling the heat from upstairs for her actions, acknowledging statements like she's on a witch hunt or a personal vendetta."

"Good, I want the story pulled from further broadcast, how can we go about that?"

"I'm way ahead of you—it's already done. They too, I believe, have agreed in principle. That's what came out of my inference to slanderous acts and minimizing damages to victimized parties."

"So what are we going to do now Eric?"

"Why don't you write a rebuttal after you've viewed the tape? Let me review it all, but once we're agreed, we'll let it out as a press release with a full court press. I certainly want to seal this woman's fate if possible."

"I'm pleased to hear you speak in those terms Eric, but I'll be candid; I want her dead...professionally speaking. I want her reporting the news 'live' from her trailer in the Moonlight Trailer Park from Bumf__k, Nevada!"

"I understand boss. While I can see your point, you must look at the bigger picture here for the moment. Right now you want to stop her venomous mouth—afterwards you can poison the bitch...hell—prepare a special buffet for her if you like—and then invite her down for lunch!"

We were both trying our best to be stoic over this situation along with our diabolical leanings, but Eric's crack was certainly testing our resolve at that moment.

Now; what have I done with that—hemlock I thought to myself before leaving Eric's office?

All in all, I was feeling somewhat vindicated now. I was also better from simply speaking to Eric. It was clear that Condescension's true motives had been exposed, thanks to her big mouth and supernova ego.

By the time I breezed by Robbie on the way into my inner sanctum, I was feeling so much better. I was already writing my rebuttal in my thoughts. Then a horrible thing happened—the damn tape arrived. I was stupid enough to view the thing...which wasn't too smart.

It was vindictive, thinly veiled, along with being dead wrong on all so many levels. It was truly nasty, so much so that even Robbie was railed by it...and he could be biting himself at times.

Now, I couldn't console myself at all. I was screaming at the images on my screen as I cussed like a sailor at that same time...did I mention—I was upset!

It took everything I had, not to sermonize the entire rebuttal through our PA system—nailing the bitch in the process. Somehow though, I got through writing my rebuttal, over the following two hours, until I was satisfied. Eric personally liked it so much; he suggested taking space out in our daily paper to run it directly to the public. I had Robbie call the Review Journal to arrange it for the first available day.

After Robbie and I had finished whatever else we had pending for the afternoon, I decided to call it a day...Lord only knows I had had enough! Before leaving though, I arranged for a dozen long stems for Jessica. I thought her unsolicited defense in a public setting was touching—and brave. It also called for a gesture from me personally. Now having seen the vile segment myself, I certainly could relate to her sentiments...Jesus.

I returned to the house at four-forty, where apparently, Scooter was still in private conference with Beth in my home office...this couldn't be good. Meanwhile on the sly, I programmed my VCR to record CCC's next newscasts as a precaution.

I brought both the folks and the boys up to speed on what had happened with our adversary. My explanation for my sons' benefit downplayed the nastiness of the segment, with simply sweeping that part of it under the rug as much as possible.

The boys of course seemed far more concerned for me than themselves—which always touched me. Like with their philanthropy, this tiny little glimpse into their characters was so enlightening and pleasurable to experience. After we all wrapped up from our conversation, I returned to the great room to await Scooter.

I was actually getting a little concerned that Beth did not much care for our offer at all. That worried me, as I did not know what to do if that was the case. When Mom first mentioned Scoot for producing for Verandas, the whole idea instantly clicked for me—it was brilliant, long over due, and really had been sorely ignored, given how anal I normally was about perfection in all of our firm's operations.

Then reality hit me—for the real reason why I had never hired a producer...came bubbling right up to the surface to stare me in the face...it was my own stubborn ego. To open our entertainment program to an outside producer—exposed me to accepting the mediocrity of my own past efforts to date...something I wasn't prone to embracing...but now I knew better.

You see, entertainment was a critical component within the Veranda's 'back-story'. The premise of the entertaining wait staff at the restaurants was simple. Our live cast was supposed to be keeping the more-rambunctious ghosts in residence...from attacking the paying customers with their song and dance.

Scoot could tighten things up—at all levels of our entertainment experience, while I realized that I truly needed someone like him for this responsibility—perhaps more so than even assisting the boys with their careers.

Another thirty minutes dragged by before Scooter rejoined our little party...finally.

"Are you still alive, buddy boy—you know, we were all beginning to wonder?"

"How long have you been back at the house, Marc?"

"About a half hour, but what in hell took you that long, or is it any of my business?"

"You can relax Marc. Sometimes, wives will surprise us…you know what I mean? For years and years, they complain and bitch about all the issues in their daily lives that annoy them. Then, the minute you give them a way to solve most of the problems in one fell swoop—they certifiably freak out. They instantly take stock of what they already have, where they're at, their children, the close neighbors, you know—everything. And all in all, I guess that it's a good thing that one of us rules with their head first, rather than just from the excitement or the possible changes it means."

"So what was the decision then, Scoot—are you in—or what?"

"Oh, I'm in alright Marc, but that was some conversation we just had."

"You know Scoot, I think I'm going to let it rest right there, I don't want to pry."

"Thanks Marc. I do appreciate your sensitivity in not pushing it now, but if you were worried, don't be—it wasn't anything earth-shattering."

"That's good bud, so care to stay for dinner?

"Sure…love to Marc, but then I'd better get home shortly after that."

"Great—let me call Sam at the hanger. Does eight p.m. work for you for a return flight?"

"That should be fine bud."

We now sat down to a wonderful dinner prepared by both Sofia and Gracie—who apparently was starting to miss preparing dinner each day. After a wonderful meal of a perfectly aged, Prime Rib standing rib roast with all the trimmings, including Gracie's awesome Yorkshire pudding, we settled into continuing the small talk at the table that began in earnest earlier.

"So what's your timetable now Scoot, after speaking to Beth?"

"Given Beth and the girls will be remaining in Orange until June, I'll start up here after giving Toon Media the required four weeks notice. Hell they deserve that after seventeen good years—don't you think?"

"I understand pal, but more importantly—I agree Scoot. I personally highly value someone who is that considerate to their current employer. To me, it illustrates your moral fiber…which says you're Vice Presidential material."

"Thanks bud, but I have to do the right thing by these folks, because they've been as good to me, when I needed them. Besides, we'll be talking regularly, at least your Mom and I will, until I start for you."

"This all sounds fine with me Scoot, but I'll need that color now for your Cobra Convertible?"

I looked at Scooter somewhat in shock as he had started turning red immediately at my comment. When he finally returned to his normal…pasty self, I asked him the obvious question, to which he answered:

"You know bud, about twenty minutes of my conversation with Beth, was dedicated to that very subject. You see, Beth had settled on that beautiful yellow with white interior and top, until I then stupidly admitted to her that I should have kept my big mouth shut. I confessed I could have had a Jag instead of the Ford. Boy was that a mistake Marc. It seems Beth would have loved a Jaguar, so I heard it from her—loudly and…repeatedly!"

"Oh really, well I'll tell you what then Scoot—let me fix everything. You just pick out a color for a Jag S Type…fair enough?"

"Jesus, that's great Marc. Thank you for redeeming me in my wife's eyes. And I suspect that their wonderful deep Indigo Blue with Palomino leather—will do just fine to please Beth."

"Nice choice Scoot, you're making me jealous myself…God that will be pretty.

Before we all knew it, our after dinner conversation had ended. Scoot meanwhile, had spent a good half-hour in conversation with the boys, which I thought was a great idea.

We were now saying good-bye to him at the hanger.

"Marilyn, I'll call you on Tuesday the latest, or I'll email Marc, to give you guys a rundown on my studio time efforts. I'm also going to courier over some arrangements for the boys to review for their demo and grand opening as we've all discussed from their repertoire of songs."

"Okay Scott. I'll take the boys clothes shopping this weekend as you suggested, along with overseeing their rehearsals."

We all said our good-byes as Scooter climbed the stairs to enter Cedric for his brief return flight home. We all heard him yell, 'wow' from inside the plane. Obviously, he really did like the color yellow…Cobra or not?

We returned to the house where the boys were just finishing their homework finally. I reminded them that our new friends, the Scotts, were coming tomorrow as planned for our barbeque which they were excited to remember. They finished their homework and headed for their computers for emails and instant messaging back to England to their mates. I'm sure they were among the longest ones written so far, with everything that had transpired this week.

I found Dad in the kitchen, of course scavenging for leftovers…my God—what a shocker! Mom foolishly had gone into the theatre where she had no idea what Dad was consuming in her absence. It was a good thing she had—for his sake. Though after all, it had been a whole ninety minutes since he had devoured a slice of Prime Rib that was easily twenty-eight ounces… while the bastard's cholesterol numbers were half mine!

"Dadio, would you care to take a meeting with me in the spa in around thirty minutes?"

"Sure Captain, thirty minutes…but you didn't see a thing—right?"

Busting still, I told Dad his secret was safe with me—even as the piece of Prime Rib hung in the balance…half on his chin at that very moment. So I left him to go into my office to check my personal emails, since I had not looked since the morning.

I was now stunned to find over one hundred and forty two new entries awaiting me. Once I began reading the subject lines, I realized why.

Without an exception, they were notes of support, sympathetic disgust, or anger over the Connors debacle. The outpouring of love and support from my many friends, colleagues, and employees—was so overwhelming; I was touched to the core. My response barely did justice to the feelings of love, thanks, and esteem I felt and held for each of these people. I sent each of them the following note back:

"What can I possibly say; I felt so honored to have received your note of support this evening. I thank you from the bottom of my heart for all of your encouragement and empathy expressed over today's events…the thoughts you shared within your email, have touched me profoundly…I am humbled and thankful—truly.

"As you know Miranda's story already…I don't need to elaborate that the report was patently false in its entirety. I'm pleased to tell you that the appropriate steps are now in place to secure a complete retraction of their story from the bogus investigation, as well as an apology from the reporter and her team…at a minimum. I have attached my open letter that will appear in tomorrow's RJ. And while I am not a vindictive man by nature, nothing would bring me greater pleasure than for this sad and tasteless episode to coincide with her permanent departure from the airwaves.

"Again, my warmest thanks.

Marc.

An Open Letter From Veranda's Founder and CEO; Marc Morgan:

Good Morning, My Fellow Locals:

I have often been asked in the past by many a Verandas customer; what am I most proud of with Verandas success? Honestly friends, it's not an easy question to answer for me so I have always answered this question essentially with the same response: The smile I see on a child's face as they catch their first trout in our pond, or watching anyone waiting with excitement for Amelia to appear at her piano…that's what makes me proudest, because it magical! And that's what Verandas represents to all of us in essence…magical moments. So I thank you, our valued guests, and supporters—for contributing your own magical moments to my company's great success…we could not have done it without you.

Yesterday, I'm sure that many of you may have heard the recent report from one of our local television reporters…and her team, concerning my late wife, Miranda.

I would like to take a few moments of your time to share my feelings with you.

First though, allow me to say categorically, that the entire report is false. It is rubbish not worthy of a tabloid, let alone a respected network such as CCC News.

It is my understanding that there will be a full retraction along with an apology to my entire family from the network, some time within the next forty-eight hours.

I hope that you can understand how pained I am to have suffered these vicious and slanderous lies from this reporter and her team…falsely accusing someone who is no longer here to defend herself…someone that I loved more than anything else in life.

So very few of us have been as lucky as I, you see, to have known the love of a woman so selfless and with a purity of purpose, as my lovely Mir.

Ask yourself this simple question: How many people do you know that would sacrifice their own personal happiness, while battling a life-threatening disease that would consume them by the age of thirty-one, to keep their spouse halfway around the world, unawares—just so that he could build his dream of a business uninterrupted and free of guilt?

It is a precious gift that my wife gave to me without hesitation, my friends. She knew exactly what we all had to sacrifice…my sons included, in order to keep me in the dark, while busy building these crazy restaurants that most of us here in town—along with the rest of America, seem to love visiting.

Miranda was one of a kind. Spirited, stubborn, loving, passionate… committed. My wife was inimitably unique in all of these ways. And yet my friends…she always had the most infectious giggle your ears were ever lucky enough to hear. I miss her so very much…that mere words can never convey that—so I won't bother trying now.

So my friends, from this day forward, when people ask me what makes me proudest about Verandas success—I will have a new answer…I will share this story:

That God made me the lucky one…he chose me to be blessed with her, along with our sons. Through their sacrifices alone…my dreams came to fruition…my dream is boldly alive today.

Thank you for your patronage and support.

Marc Morgan.

As I was about to shut down my email, a fresh one popped up in my inbox from my cousin Beth. She lived in LA and happily hadn't heard anything about my Connors crisis. Still, her news wasn't what I had hoped to hear either. She and I had talked about her coming up for a visit. Beth wrote to say they had to cancel due to a conflict that had come up with her husband Barry's job. He worked for a major airline, so sometimes had to move on a moment's notice to put out some 'fire' somewhere.

Beth was excited as she heard all about the boys' crusade on TV. She seemed very proud of their efforts. This was despite her mother's comments that she felt the boys were being used—by me of all people! Jesus…with an aunt like that, who needed Concepcion, I ask you? I would certainly have some choice words for my Aunt when she next 'graced' my home though, I can assure you.

In truth, Beth, had always been more like my Mom—than her own mother. I guess that's why all of us so enjoyed seeing her—away from Aunt June. She really came alive then, anytime she was out of her mother's evil influence…Attila truly had that kind of effect on you. Whenever they were here together, Beth always remained neutral—if not silent…smart girl!

I replied, lamenting her cancellation with the offer of a rain check anytime. In addition, I gave her a little info on our plans for the boys with their recording. I also told her about my folks moving plans. Lastly I told her of my earlier day, so as to forewarn her that it could reach her via the Yenta Hotline…assuring her not to worry—that things were solidly in control within our court.

My emails completed, I changed into my trunks to mosey on down to the bar where I poured out two Cape Cods. As I made my way out to the grotto, I could hear the boys practicing in their studio. At first, I was surprised they were through with their emails so fast; but then again, they were committed now, along with dying to get started with this whole 'pro' thing apparently.

I got in the grotto, only to find that Dad had beaten me there, yet again. But tonight apparently, he was seriously awaiting his drink…impatiently. He was singing along with the twins at the moment…sounding—quite pathetic.

"What's on your mind son? I see our two are practicing again."

"Yep Dad—they are…but let's leave it to just the two of them, okay? And you know Pop—you would do well to just sit—drink—and listen… silently."

"Funny son, you're a nice piece of work yourself, but what's up with this meeting anyways?"

"You—Pop! Listen, you've been real quiet with this whole thing, so I'm justifiably curious is all,—or should I be worried instead?"

"Very perceptive of you as usual, but no, I'm still just getting over the shock of all of this—that's my reason."

"What's on your mind most Dad...am I missing anything?"

"No—nothing. It's just your Mother's whole attitude, about jumping into all of this responsibility. I've known for years that she's wanted to seriously slow down—but now all of this—out of the blue...I just don't get it son."

"Dad, after Mom talked to Miranda, she made it clear she felt firmly—wait a minute—that's not a strong enough commentary—she felt compelled about following through on anything Miranda asked of her to do. I guess this is one of those things, so she's committing to honoring her promise to Mir, that's all."

"That's true. It's surely the case here—but it doesn't explain Mom's sincere excitement over these new responsibilities. I haven't seen her excited like this, since we first decided to purchase the winery. I think she may be more excited about it, than even the boys are—if that's possible?"

"Honestly Dad, I'd find that a bit hard to believe, but just the same, it's nice to see her so passionate on something again...I hope you're really okay with it—Dad?"

"Oh I am son; this was always what I wanted for you, if the truth be told."

"Really Dad, I never picked up on that?"

"No of course not, because I wasn't about to put any pressure on you son, you had already been through enough. I was just thrilled you had overcome your obstacles. I would have been satisfied if you were a contented custodian somewhere, honestly—I simply wanted you to be happy. Besides, going professional in that industry has to be rooted in the person—not simply suggested or being pressured into it. I wasn't about to do either...neither was your Mother, even though we both wanted too."

"Wow Dad, I never even had a clue. I suppose you're right. I guess then, that Mom handled the boys' situation quite well, although at the time, I was furious with her."

"Sure you were Marc...hell, I'm positive you really don't want to share them with anyone outside our family—now do you...answer up the truth son?"

"No Dad, you're right...I really don't. Being completely honest, now that I have them Pop, it amazes me sometimes. Somehow I feel like for all those years I never knew they existed—I was still missing them inside of me! Jesus; does that make sense to you Pop, cause it sure confuses the hell out of me?"

"Certainly it does Marc...that's a very natural reaction, believe me you're not crazy—it's called yearning son."

"Thanks Dadio, that does make me feel better about it."

"Hey what's a father for?

"So, what's on tap for our party with the Scotts' tomorrow, what are you barbequing for dinner?"

"Dad, you're not seriously thinking about food again, are you?"

"No son, I'm not—but it never hurts to be prepared."

"Okay Pop. Sofia, and Grace will take charge of most of our dinner; I'm just preparing the main entrée...BBQ brisket."

"Your brisket? Man oh man, I can't wait, that will be wonderful. I'm in the mood for your brisket anytime. When you slow cook it all night in that wonderful fruit sauce of yours, I go nuts...I knew I smelled something—sinful."

"Good, at least I can count on one person to scarf it down."

"Oh I don't think you'll have anything to worry about on that score—I'll wager even money. Son, there won't be any left by the time our combined group leaves the table."

"I doubt that Dadio, I started out with a twenty-two pounder at the butcher. But I guess we'll see in about eighteen hours, won't we Dad?"

"Yeah, you got that right son—Jesus...twenty two pounds?"

Dad and I talked a little more, but then decided we were properly 'cooked' for the night. We dried off as we then went into the house to get off to bed.

I crawled into my king-size bed, where as usual, I had to be very quiet so as not to disturb my two slumbering bunkmates. I treasured this closeness, but I would enjoy getting my bed back for my sole enjoyment and use as well. Once Dad leaves for the winery, Mom would be taking the foldout in my office, giving the boys their bedroom back...and me, my bed...alone.

I quickly fell into a deep sleep. I dreamed quite vividly that night of Miranda. In the morning when I woke, I was certain that I had not been merely dreaming. Our conversation had an unmistakable authentic quality to it...that we had been talking in 'real time'—I was certain of that now.

I distinctly remembered her talking about the whole Concepcion matter along the lines of how she felt about it. Not surprisingly, she was touched by my letter; while philosophical on the dispute itself...she more or less, actually brushed the whole matter aside.

My wife's reaction shocked the hell out of me. She simply stated I should consider the woman's stupidity—then just let it go. If I were truly only dreaming all of this, my own 'dream' thoughts would have been far closer to my actual feelings concerning this issue alone. Further, I certainly did not share Miranda's forgive and forget attitude by any means. I couldn't believe she was so damn forgiving herself.

More so, Miranda certainly didn't share my reservations about Vic

Tremmers—that also was a wake up call, explaining far more than I could have possibly figured out for myself…or naturally—from Vic himself.

Clearly, Miranda was taking Vic's motivations under 'her' wing. She shared with me—by what I can only call an instant immersion of this information, that Vic was in fact a very old soul. A soul in fact—betting the farm this time around…on humanity—of all things.

His current incarnation it seems, was nothing more than a lifetime hand of poker of sorts. His goal, was to try to win over the hearts of as many of his fellow mankind as possible…all in the face of various adversities…shit did I feel like a louse now.

After finishing with Vic's motives, Miranda focused on the boys. Like with everything else, it was always in real time, like when she asked if I noticed how much they had matured since being with me…along with how proud of me she was, for my strong parenting skills, although she claimed—not to be surprised at all.

All of this was too matter-of-fact to be a mere dream, I was certain of that.

I distinctly recalled as well, Mir saying that Mom was doing what she thought she would do from their conversation. No reservations materialized on her part, so I assumed it was an affirmation to continue onward with Mom's plans.

Being with her like this, made me feel closer to her in this new way too. I also noticed that she looked somewhat different during our conversation—she was a tad bit younger in appearance, yet radiated in a bath of light surrounding her. There wasn't any evidence of her past illness…which I think, was my first clue the conversation truly wasn't a dream at all.

After waking, I took a nice long steam in the shower before finally dragging myself downstairs to the kitchen. Gracie greeted me with a very contented smile on her face—herself.

"Morning Gracie, my you look very happy this morning."

"Yes Marc, I had a lovely evening."

"Good dear, nothing wrong with a lovely evening I always say…Grace?"

"Yes love?"

"I already know how you feel about Ms. Connors, but I'm more interested to ask you about the boys.

"What do you think about all this stuff with them turning professional, does it worry you too? After all, you've known them longer than any of us older Morgans—so what's your spin on it?"

"Honestly Marc, I think it's about bloody time. I never understood your qualms in the first place. And for that matter, I never understood why Miranda didn't push them a little harder herself. Although, maybe she recognized she would never have the strength to keep up with it, so rather than disappoint the boys, she didn't push it at all."

"Yes, that's possible I guess Gracie, but leave it to you in not mincing your words…but so you know, Miranda came to me last night…it was wonderful. I would assume not much different from you with Marisa?"

"Yes, but that's loverly Marc. So what did my darlin' little lass have to say for herself?"

"Oh, she's of the opinion that I need to forget about that woman's news segment, because she feels I should let it go, as she feels that Mom's on the right track. She also complimented me that she's convinced the boys have matured greatly under my tutelage."

"I agree love—haven't you noticed that yourself in the boys' demeanor… they're no longer our little lads you know? They're becoming very mature young teenagers and quite grown up, all of us have noticed it."

"Yes, I guess I have noticed it Grace, but what else do you account for it though?"

"My Marc, you really are modest, aren't you? It is rather simple; the boys have blossomed out of their fragile shells under your care. They have gained tremendous confidence thanks in part to your parenting, whereby they have lost most of their fragility for all intense of purposes. You've given them ample support, and of course unconditional love to draw upon, to branch out. With all of that comes—trust, confidence, self-esteem, and maturity Marc."

"Jesus Dr. Gracie—I did all that?"

"Yes love—you did. But if you honestly don't realize you possess these talents, do yourself a favor—please forget I ever said any of this. Whatever you do, don't change a thing, as you'll only screw it up by trying too hard from here on out."

We were both laughing now.

"Okay Gracie, I certainly get the message, yet since I honestly don't know how I'm doing all these things you attribute to me—I won't change a thing, believe me".

"Good boy."

"You know Gracie; I can always count on you to tell it just like it is."

"Good. Speaking of telling it like it is, Suzie called me to tell me she's hopefully moving her things in next weekend."

"Yes I know–I caught her for a moment yesterday at the hanger. She told me the same thing, although I guess it depends on her Dad's hip problems too. You sure you're still okay with her moving in, what with your relationship going so well with Fleming?"

"Don't you fret my dear boy, everything will be just fine. Reggie understands how I feel about Suzie."

"Oh—so its Reggie now, is it?"

"Yes it is, but I must say Marc—that he's a very kind man. He is very sensitive to my wishes and a caring man as well. I'm enjoying his company immensely. I dare say he's as good as my lovely Ronnie was to me."

"That's wonderful to hear dear, but can I ask you a personal question then?"

"Of course love, you're the closest thing I'll ever have to a son, I feel comfortable talking about most anything with you."

"Thank you Gracie, I feel honored to hear those words, especially coming from you. Naturally, what all of America is dying to know right now is—did your relationship with Fleming begin here or back in England?"

"Son, I wondered when that question was going to escape your mouth... but it depends on who you ask first. Honestly, I had no idea he had these feelings for me, as such, I was very shocked.

"When we arrived in Las Vegas, I was speaking to him about his lack of patience concerning Sofia. It just all sort of came out over that, but like I said, it was a shock."

"Do you feel comfortable telling me how it came out?"

"Certainly love. I made him realize that he wasn't being fair to Sofia at all. He didn't know the arrangement you two had concerning her responsibilities when you were away traveling, so I said he shouldn't judge her. He thought on it a tick before then agreeing with me. He looked at me and said, I understand now—why I've loved you so very deeply for all these years—you're always fair to everyone.

"When he said that Marc, I honestly thought he was saying 'love' in a platonic sense. That was, up to the moment that without warning, he kissed me quite passionately and tenderly. What was I to do then Marc, I was stunned naturally? But then I instinctively knew that I deeply cared for him as well. I then thought on it more—I realized it was truly love, not just caring for a friend—I loved the old sod—I really did. Now looking back on it, I realize that I've carried some feelings for him for some time already. I never stopped to really look at those feelings honestly, guilt had me trapped worshiping Ronnie's memory I guess.

I think my love and devotion to that memory kept me from honestly looking too deeply in any direction. And now that Reggie and I have shared our feelings with each other, it has been simply loverly.

"As a matter of fact, love, I'm quite sure that by the time we have the new home ready, Reggie will likely ask me to marry him."

"Really Gracie? My word that would be wonderful, if that's what you both want?"

"Look Marc, at our ages, it's just nice to have someone—you should try it sometime."

"Now Grace, are you trying to marry me off?"

"Why not Marc, it's not like you're the typical widower...right? You and Miranda had not seen each other for a dozen years. While you had a very wonderful and loving reunion, you still need to move on to seek love out again. I'm doing it Marc, and you know how I adored my Ronnie, so if I can move on, you can too."

"Gracie, it's somewhat more complicated with me, but when you next meet a woman you like—tell me. If you think I should take a chance with her, let me know so that I can ask her out."

"Certainly Marc, but will you?"

"If she passes muster with you Gracie, while assuming that I find her attractive too, then yes—I will."

"Then that's all settled Marc."

"See, but that wasn't so hard—was it Gracie?"

"No it wasn't—I believe that you're caving much faster these days love."

"Gee, thanks a lot." I said with mock scorn.

"Oh I meant it in the kindest way Marc, really"

"As long as you did then, I'll accept that."

"Good. Now drink your latte, its getting cold, love".

"Yes 'Mom'—as you wish."

I drank up and started eating my breakfast while I read the paper. My biological parents joined me now, but I could see that Mom must have been up half the night planning. Apparently she was thinking about her new 'project.' She had circles under her eyes, with them looking all puffy.

"Mom, you didn't sleep well—did you?"

"No Marc, I didn't. I found it hard to clear my head with so many thoughts and ideas you know...all of them competing with your Father's snoring and flatulence for a change."

"Yes, I can well imagine." As I cracked up royally at my poor Father's expense.

"So when are you taking the boys shopping then?"

"I guess, tomorrow after the interviews—what time do you suppose that will be son?"

"I would expect they'll be home from Sunday school by one, with the interviews concluding before three."

"Very well then...so you've decided that you want them to continue with Sunday school there?"

"Yes, but only for the time being Mom. I think it's a good idea for them to face their demons if you will, instead of running from them. I want to see how they deal with this young loudmouth as well…my gut tells me that this kid actually wants to make friends with them."

"Oh. So you're talking about that 'ferry' thing with that other boy still?"

"Yes Mom, of course, boy—you are tired aren't you?"

"Yes, I guess I am son, but very well then. We should be able to get a nice couple of hours of shopping in leaving at around three. Can you ask Paul to take us?"

"Mom, you know he's off on Sundays, why not let Dad take you all in your new Navigator?"

"Yes, that will be fine, won't it Mal?"

"Sure dear, whatever you say…say Marc, which mall has the best food court?"

Dad of course knew what he was starting with that crack…so did I.

"Malcolm, don't start with me."

"Yes dear."

Just then, my two sleepy heads descended into the kitchen, no doubt following their noses directly to Gracie's famous French toast.

"Morning everyone. Daddy, when will these new friends of ours be getting here?"

"Taylor, do you mean all of the Scotts, or just their boys, I'm merely curious?"

"Oh Daddy, you know what I mean."

"The Scott brigade should be here by one pee, if that is all right with you?"

"Sure Daddy that will be fine." Taylor added as I noticed for the first time that Trevor, who was standing next to his brother—looked troubled and distant.

"I'm glad that pleases you T-man…Trevor, why so silent this morning, son?"

"I'll tell you later Dad."

"Hum, should we excuse ourselves to go into the office now instead, son?"

"Yes sir, please."

I grabbed Trevor around the shoulder as off we headed towards the office.

Once inside, Trevor closed the door. After some embarrassing hesitation, my son informed me that Bartholomew appeared to be having a relapse of sorts. I took a quick look, but had to agree…the poor guy was all red again, as before.

"Jeeze Trev, I'm really confused here. Are you sure you're giving him a good wash in the tub?"

"Yes Dad, I am...I'm pulling him back real good in the loo too. I don't understand why it's coming back again?"

"Okay, why don't we go upstairs? If you're all right with it...why not let me see how you're keeping him clean in the shower?"

"Sure Dad."

"But honestly son, if you and your brother were circumcised...we'd likely never have to worry about this."

"Oh. Well Dad, let it go...because no one's touching my Bartholomew... bloody hell no way...not now...not ever!

"Okay T-1, I read you loud and clear. So let's get you in the shower and then we will give him some more of that ointment to calm him down again. However son, if this does not go away within another few days for good, I'm getting you to my doctor."

We went upstairs, where Trevor got into the shower. He showed me both how he cleaned Bart, yet hygienically protected him with retracting and shaking him properly too. I could not find fault in his method, so I hung up my metaphoric stethoscope from WebMD as he applied more ointment once he dried off. After he redressed, we went back downstairs to join the rest of the family.

All of the adults present were giving me the eye, as if whatever took us to our private conference was something of earth shattering significance...which of course it was...to Bartholomew, no doubt.

So I just ignored the looks by continuing along as if nothing had happened. Why I should say something that would have my son embarrassed—wasn't in the cards anyway. It was after all, a very personal matter for a young boy.

After breakfast, when the boys had excused themselves to go clean the pool, I shared what had happened discreetly with the adults. Everyone, but particularly my Mom, was concerned it had been something more serious, so she was relieved it was something of a personal nature instead.

..."I just hope little Bartholomew doesn't have a serious on-going problem here. What if there's another reason for it doing this? God damn it, why couldn't she have just had them circumcised like all the other Morgan men?" I said.

"It's quite uncommon in England love—but you need to get them a pediatrician anyway. So perhaps you'd better start that search sooner rather than later. I wouldn't fret too much over it Marc, the boys have had their share of this growing up don't forget?"

"I know that Gracie, Mir alluded to it, but it's alarming to me being so unfamiliar with an intact penis."

"Don't worry Marc, it will all work out." Grace added.

"Thanks Gracie, I think I'll run the issue of pediatricians past Lisa once she gets here. Let's see who she uses for her gaggle of kids—what do you guys think about that?"

"Son, I think that's an excellent idea. Lisa certainly has to have a handle on good pediatricians with her brood of six, don't you think?"

"Yes Dad, I would suppose she does."

I excused myself to tend to the brisket in the smoker box where it had slow-cooked for some fifteen hours now. Meanwhile, Gracie and Fleming went off to the market, while I left Mom and Dad to talk in the kitchen.

CHAPTER 9

▼

FRIENDSHIPS

BEFORE WE ALL KNEW IT, it was right after one pee, when the Scotts' were cleared through the gates. I went out to the pool where I informed the boys that our new friends were on their way in. They got out to quickly dry off as we began walking around the house to await them on the driveway.

The over-laden van pulled in a few moments later, with all of the Scotts' in their 'assorted' sizes quickly 'deplaning…after all Tom and Lisa arrived with the full platoon—their six kids plus Tom's mother, Lucille. This made their large GMC van conversion look more like a cramped two-seater, rather than the super-behemoth it was. I greeted our guests on the driveway where you could see that the exterior of the house was overwhelming their children now.

We got everything out of their van then into the house as we made all of the introductions with everyone from staff to children on down. After a quick tour, the Scott kids wasted no time in expressing their desire of getting in the pool, with my two boys leading the way.

While the folks and Tom took comfortable seats on the terrace, Lisa joined me at the summer kitchen island out by the terrace.

"Can I ask you a question Marc—a personal one?"

"Sure Lisa.

"I'm just a little baffled over your situation with your sons. Were you not able to see them much since their birth—or was it something else? I mean, from our conversation at Sarah's birthday, I got the distinct impression you were a new father—or am I just confused?"

"Lisa you're correct. I am a neophyte father, but trust me you're going to find the explanation difficult to believe and accept. You see Lisa; I didn't even know the twins existed until this past October, when my wife was dying."

"I'm sorry Marc, I should have kept quiet,—this is obviously something much too personal to discuss with a near stranger."

"No Lisa, I'm really okay with it. Besides, with all of these kids, I know that we're all going to become fast friends. You're obviously a caring, warm person so I'm comfortable sharing it with you if you would like to hear it?"

"Honestly I would…I just thought…"

…"Well don't think Lisa…just keep an open mind about it is all".

"Alright Marc."

I went on to explain everything from beginning to end…the whole sorted mess.

When I finished, I noticed that Lisa's eyes were misty.

"My word Marc, that is indeed a story…I don't know what to say to you—I really don't."

"That's okay Lisa—at least that's honest."

"I know one thing Marc. I would have loved to have known her—what an incredible woman she must have been?"

"You have no idea Lisa. She was one in a million—believe me."

"I can see that easily Marc.

"Boy oh boy—and I thought I loved my husband."

"Pretty incredible, isn't it?"

"Yes Marc. It's probably the most unusual yet beautiful love story I've ever heard in my life…I know it is.

"Listen Lisa, pick up tomorrow's RJ, you might find it interesting on the last page of the first section."

"Oh? Okay Marc, I'll do that. So Marc, how are you enjoying your two new sons; how's fatherhood treating you so far?"

"Lisa, I never imagined in my wildest imagination that it could be this good. It has changed my entire life's perspective really."

"No doubt, Marc."

"Are they easy boys, or tough?"

"Early on, I would say that they tested me just a little, but we've gotten nicely past that now. Mostly they're pretty darn terrific boys…much easier than I ever was for my parents."

"They seem so Marc. But how are they dealing with the losses of both their Mother and Grandfather?"

"It's a little too early yet on that score Lisa, but all in all, I believe they're adjusting pretty well. When you consider what we have all had to deal with, I'm actually amazed they're adjusting so well."

Lisa and I now walked over to join the folks and Tom under the terrace's misting system to cool off. It didn't take long for Tom and me to begin some 'shop talk' as they say.

"Tom, what exactly is your position with Caesars?"

"Marc, I'm the lead graveyard Food & Beverage manager for the resort… Lisa works directly with me."

"Really? But you spend your hard-earned cash in my restaurant—what the hell for?"

"Honestly Marc—your restaurants really are the kids' favorite besides McDonalds for fast food. Secondly, I steal some of my best ideas from you guys on a regular basis…only kidding." As we both had a nice laugh.

"Oh how nice—a spy from a competitor—and a thief." I was still laughing with my crack back at him.

"Yeah—that's me."

"Seriously though Marc, you run a truly peerless operation—so my hat's off to you and your team."

"Gee thanks Tom, but maybe I'd be doing Verandas a bigger favor by just stealing you from Caesars…if you're going to steal all of my secrets away anyways?"

"What, and give up working every other weekend along with nightly from midnight to eight am—are you crazy Marc?" He grinned sardonically.

"Alright, but if you ever change your mind, just let me know?"

"Marc, you hardly know me—but I'm not one to ask for favors from anyone…not that I really have any favors to call in mind you." He was laughing again now.

"Tom, isn't working those hours, hard on the family though?"

"Yes Mal, it is at times—but it's not without its plusses either. Besides, Mom here does a great job helping us out. She's been with us since she and Dad split."

"Yes I can well imagine Tom, especially the savings on sitters and the like." Dad commented now.

"That's true Mal. I guess you must be a financial analyst to see that angle of it?"

"No Tom—he's just cheap…very cheap in fact." We all laughed.

"Thank you for that son—that was just priceless…really."

"Yes Dad…you hit it right on the head. With you it always is—priceless."

We were all howling now.

"Sorry Dad, but I couldn't resist the set up—forgive me, will you?"

"Sure, I'll forgive you son, but I also plan on keeping score for a rebuttal later."

"I'm sure you will, Dad."

"Now fellas—don't fight on my account?"

"Alright Tom, we'll behave—can I freshen up your Scotch?"

"Yeah that would be great Marc—thanks.

As I was heading back from the bar, I spied Tom in action with his kids. There he was at the terrace, refereeing a fight between Austin and Sarah. Boy he took no nonsense from his kids. You could see they were not going to challenge him either. I decided right there—he was my new hero and role model!

Over all though, all of the kids were getting along fine, while having an incredible afternoon together in the lagoon. The Scott children were in love with the pool, especially the slides with their fog, music, and fiber-optic lighting...my two were just reveling in having some peers to hang with, for a change of scenery it seems.

Our day with the Scotts was turning out to be a great time for all. The kids were all very well acquainted by the latter afternoon with the two sets of twins continuing to build a friendship with one another. Yet it was also clear that my boys seemed closest with Austin for whatever reason, which surprised me...was it a maturity issue, I wondered?

Dad, Tom, and I hung around the pool with the kids going at it with the water cannon at that moment. We men were naturally—being men...we were drinking, grunting, not so discreetly—scratching, while of course—also BS'ing.

Later, I made my way into the kitchen, where lo and behold, I found all of the ladies discussing pediatricians. I knew I had been beaten to the punch again—by Mom no doubt...I never should have left them alone. It seemed that the ladies preferred hankering down in the kitchen talking 'girl' talk. They had been there I suppose, for the better part of the last hour. I guess while they were futzing around with the dishes to go along with the brisket—doctors had become the topic of conversation apparently.

"I can't speak highly enough about the kids' pediatrician, Deborah Steinberg—Marilyn, she's an excellent doctor."

"Gee Mother; I see you wasted no time...as usual?"

"No dear, I didn't. When it comes to the boys, you know I will not. Besides, as their new personal manager, I feel very strongly about this. I want them to both have complete physicals before we get started. You can never be too careful about these things dear."

"Marc, how do you think your boys would handle having a female doctor thrust on them at this age...are they modest?"

"No they're not, but I can't really say how they'd react to that Lisa. How do the twins and Austin feel about having to be naked in front of theirs?"

"Gee, they've been with her for so long now, I don't really think it bothers them. You would think that with the twins in puberty now—it would, but they don't even make a fuss...right Mother?"

"Yes Lisa, I actually think all three of them have a little crush on her." Lucille added.

"Candidly Lisa, I suppose I'll just have to speak to the boys about it. Do you have a male alternative if they should throw a tizzy fit?"

"I don't, but certainly any number of my girlfriends can help us out—wait...actually I do have a name. My girlfriend Julie uses a wonderful older pediatrician by the name of Sharif I believe, she swears by him."

"So we're covered either way then, that's a relief."

"Marilyn tells me that Trevor has some infection problems with his private?" Lisa asked. Whereby I proceeded to blow my top at Mom.

"Mother, have you cleared this subject with your grandson? You know; he would likely be very embarrassed over you discussing Bartholomew so casually. And may I also point out—not unlike I've come to learn you did with—ah—Freddie as well?"

"Bartholomew, Freddie—who are these boys Marc?"

"Oh, they're not boys per se Lucille; actually you would more accurately classify them as very specific male genitalia...oh forgive me...privates—belonging to Trevor—and if you must know—me."

"Oh, I see."

Lucille was carrying on something now with her laughter over my very candid remarks at my own expense. So were Sofia, Lisa, and Grace.

"But seriously Lisa, to answer your question from before I was compelled to admonish Mom, Trevor is specifically having infections on his foreskin of all places...and Mom, not another crack out of you—or I swear..."

..."Forgive me, but on his foreskin, Marc? I thought you were all Jewish?"

"We are Lisa, but we're Reform Jews. The boys had the ritual prayers and ceremony without the surgical procedure itself. My wife made the call on that; I would have gone the full procedure, personally."

"Oh, I didn't realize that was an option now in your faith. Being Catholic, we do not have any direction from the church, but we had all the boys done anyway. At any rate, I will try to get you some other doctors' names too.

"By the way Marc, would you all like to join us to attend a twin's encounter meeting that's coming up?"

"Sure, whenever you say Lisa, as far as I'm concerned."

"Okay. Well we have an Ice Cream social in two weeks, should I put you down for three or more?"

"At least four for now—Mom you'll want to come, won't you?"

"Absolutely Marc, I wouldn't miss a roomful of twins for all the tea in

China, at least—not once. Maybe Sofia, along with Grace and Fleming would enjoy it too?"

"There you have it Lisa; we're at least a party of four. Dad will be at the Winery in Paso Robles by then, so we'll see about everyone else in the Morgan family well in advance, fair enough?"

"Alright, I'll call you with all the details in a couple of days."

"Great. Now let's get this crew fed, shall we ladies?"

"Sure Marc, are you ready to bring in the brisket son?"

"Yes Mom, I am. Let me go get it as it has to 'rest' for a few minutes before we slice it. Gracie would you like to have the honor of carving, or would you prefer Sofe taking it?"

"I'd be happy to carve Marc, just bring it in. I'll start sharpening my knife now—you know how tough that American beef of yours can be since you blokes refuse to age it."

"Oh Gracie, it's not nice to demean American Beef, girlfriend. After all, at least ours tastes like beef—not gamey old English mutton, with or without the Mad Cow thrown in. I would venture a wager Gracie, that our Black Angus or Harris Ranch beef, like we serve, will stand up to anyone's for flavor, marbling, and tenderness, save for perhaps Kobe beef in Japan of course. And if I was raised on a diet of beer like the Kobe cows, I'd be more than tender—myself!"

"You know Grace; I truly understand these little games you and Marcus seem to play with one another. Still, I must confess dear, while we were in England, I never did find an English roast, or cut of beef that wasn't a little bit gamey, Grace. I really would have to agree with Marc on this one score therefore…I'm sure you know how that pains me dear?"

"Marilyn, don't you know that our beef is fed and aged especially to bring out its full flavor? Maybe to the American palate that comes across as gamey in taste, but to us Brits, it's the only way to truly enjoy beef."

"Listen Gracie, you Brits age your beef way too long for the rest of us, believe me. If it was aged any longer, it would be better off buried six feet under, along with its carcass." I had her now with that one.

Lisa's mouth dropped open from my verbal attack. The other ladies were somewhat shocked by the banter of insults, but not quite to Lisa's level yet!

By this time, everyone was completely captured by our argument. Gracie and I were in fact, beginning our very first US vs. Britain argument in Las Vegas. And we were by no means even really going yet. I was enjoying every moment of it as for once, we were in my country, my home…and in my kitchen,—so finally—I had the home field advantage of sorts…it was about time for crying out loud.

Now empowered, I left the ladies to retrieve the brisket from the smoker which would allow Grace a window of opportunity to develop her rebuke. I intentionally gave her this time to prepare another retort, because with my fruit-infused, BBQ brisket—she was certainly going to need it! I returned to the kitchen with pan in hand along with a big grin on my face just from the seeping aroma.

"Okay girlfriend—here it is. I dare you kiddo to find fault with this here Amerikin piece of steer."

I said it with my best Texan drawl. Then for added drama as I finished my statement, I pushed hard to slide the pan smartly across the entire island. It came to a stop directly in front of Gracie, which was my goal. The rest of the ladies were silent. They seemed genuinely shocked at how far this had already gone between us.

"I see Marc; well, let's have a look then…shall we?"

"Be my guest Gracie, but if you need to sharpen your knife to carve this baby, I won't sleep tonight waiting for the morning so that I can go out and buy you a whole new set of Henckels at Williams-Sonoma, just to prove my sincerity."

Grace chose to ignore my remark as she simply opened the sealed foil wrap, allowing the pent up steam and aroma to permeate the kitchen fully. Naturally this fostered instant reactions from around the island now.

"Oh my Lord God, that simply smells divine Marc." This came from Lisa.

"Well done son." Escaped from Mom.

"Marvelous, really Marcus." Added Lucille.

"Ay caramba." Came out of Sofia now.

"Nice aroma love." Grace herself conceded.

"Go on then Grace; let's see if you can cut a small piece with your carving knife without sharpening it—I double dare you?"

"Marc! Mind your manners, you're getting much too carried away with this whole infantile farce. This is Grace in front of you son—not Aunt June—behind your back."

"Mom I love you, but when my country's insulted, I'm insulted, so butt out of it."

"Good luck Grace, dear—he's all yours."

"Don't you fret Marilyn; I've seen this side of him before. He just needs a lesson in fine British manners."

"That's right Gracie, just keep living your denial. I don't see you jumping on that roast to see how tender it is—or am I just mistaken?"

"I'm simply allowing it to rest love, because in my presence after all, that influence alone—will make it melt in the mouth like butter—will it not?"

I didn't know why, but at that very moment, I was stunned and silenced by her poise contained within the comeback. It was her defiant, yet tender way of telling me she was conceding to me already. But—not before stealing a little of my own glory by taking indirect credit for the roast herself.

I immediately walked over to her, threw my arms around her, hugged her deeply as I gave her cheek a kiss for her valiant effort, not to mention—conceding with such finesse.

"Jesus, Gracie, do you realize that this was our very first fight here in the States?"

"Yes love, but I doubt that it will be our last, either."

"I guess your right on that score Gracie." Meanwhile, all of the ladies seemed to let out a collective sigh of relief.

After explaining to our guests the nature of Gracie and my past practical jokes and schemes, Grace then continued.

"You know Marc, I think it's time to carve this wonderful roast, don't you love?"

"Yes Gracie, I most certainly do. Why not go ahead and grab a taste for all of us too."

Grace carved off five thin slices as she commented:

"My Marc, it's heaven to carve…bloody hell—there went my new set of Henckels."

"Grace, the knifes are still yours, as I know that had to hurt."

We all took our piece of the brisket and practically put the meat into our waiting mouths simultaneously…almost with a sense of urgency.

"Oh my Lord, now that is heavenly. My goodness, I could swear I taste raspberries?"

"Thanks Lisa, and yes, you're not only tasting raspberries, but cherries and chipotle peppers as well in that sauce."

"Mom; how is it?"

"Sensational son—absolutely perfect as always."

"Lucille?"

"Simply wonderful Marc."

"Marko it is magnifico."

"Thank you Sofe."

"And Grace?"

"Loverly Marc, truly splendid—let me just fetch my white flag now—all right, so it's only a tablecloth—still, I surrender."

"Cute Gracie. Well now I am happy ladies. Shall we get everyone ready?"

"Yes son. Get everyone out of the pool, will you?"

"Sure thing Mom." I departed the kitchen to go outside.

In my best, old western movie, chuck-wagon cook's voice, I yelled out to the lagoon full of kids.

"All right you varmints, rascals, and youngins, get those fannies of yurz out of that there, cement pond, cuz chows on now, yee—hah!"

The lagoon emptied faster than Noah's Ark after it had reached dry land to dock in West Palm Beach!

Within minutes, our 'spread' was all laid out as we all began enjoying a wonderful dinner. There wasn't a word spoken for a full ten minutes or so. And only then because the telephone rang. Fleming went to answer it, advising me that Robbie was calling upon his return to the table.

"Fleming, could you tell him we're eating and I'll call him back in a half?"

"Yes Marc."

Fleming returned to the table, but more importantly to him—his plate.

"Marc, Robbie says he just got a call from a Mr. Jacobs telling him that his piece has been moved up to seven pee tonight, instead of tomorrow sir."

"Thanks Fleming, I guess due to Concepcion Connors, they want to keep their interview with me exclusive. We'll all have to watch it."

Apparently, either the Scotts hadn't heard about the Connors matter, or were purposely not commenting on it, so I briefly filled them in on that along with the boys' efforts.

"Marc, what exactly are the boys going to be doing with their music?"

"Lucille, first they're simply going to record a CD to sell in our units at their Dessert Courts. While they are recording that album though, their new Business Manager and Executive Producer will cut a professional demo as well with a more commercialized sound. If it all works out, they may have a shot at a recording contract, that's the abridged version."

"Oh my, that sounds wonderful boys, are you excited by all this notoriety you'll be getting?" Lucille asked.

"Yes Mrs. Scott, it's very exciting, but we're a little nervous too."

"Don't worry Taylor; I'm sure you will both do just fine, from what I hear, you two sing wonderfully—at least, that's what your Grandma told me earlier in the kitchen."

"You know Lucille, if you would care to hear them, perhaps Marc would turn on the recording made of the three of them at the piano from Miranda's service?"

"Sure Mom. Lucille, would you like to take a listen?"

"Gee Marc, if she doesn't, I know I would?"

"Okay Tom, you got it."

I got up to play the CD that Robbie had arranged of our performance. I quickly put it into the player as I turned it on.

I returned to the table just as my opening comments were ending on the CD. Within another moment, I had begun to sing Miranda's tribute, A Lady Like You. I started to explain the song but Tom immediately gave me the 'cut-it' sign across his throat with his hand to tell me to be quiet, so I did. The Scotts' were all listening intently right on down to little Hayley. Lisa, Lucille, and Sarah too, were all moved to tears by the song's end.

After the CD ended, Tom just looked at me for a moment before speaking.

"Markie old boy, what on earth are you doing frying chicken—you belong up on that stage with your boys?

"And boys, I am truly impressed with your talent; I do believe you've got a real shot at this."

"Do you really think so Mr. Scott?"

"Without a doubt son."

"Gee, thanks Mr. Scott—and I'm Trevor. We always know when someone can't tell us apart when they call either of us—'son'."

"Yes you're right Trevor, I couldn't tell, but you'd think with all of my own practice—I would have?"

"Marc, Tom's right, you should someday consider recording a song or two with the boys,—you might be surprised with a hit."

"Thanks Lisa, but it's their turn now, I had my shot."

"Yes, you told me how you and Miranda met; it must have been so exciting touring all over the world like that though?"

"It was Lisa, but it also was a hell-of-a-lot of hard work, believe me".

"I'm sure it was Marc, but would you 'not' do it all over again, if you could?"

"Yeah, I certainly would do it again, all of it. After all, how else would I have been blessed with first Miranda, and now the boys?"

"Well then, see, that's the true test, isn't it?"

"Yes it is Lisa."

"Look, if my watch is right Marc, I think we had better save our dessert for after the news, because damn, we've got two minutes to get in front of your TV, let's all get a move on, shall we?"

"Thanks Tom, for that two minute warning—you come in real handy old man."

"Old man—yourself?" All the kids were already gone from the table.

"Let's get in there Tom, before the kids steal all the good seats."

"You're right on that score buddy, but let me handle that, remember—I own six of them."

We all moved into the Great room where my hero, good old Tom, remanded all of the kids to the floor immediately. The adults all made do with the assortment of chairs and the sofa. I flipped on the big screen as we all waited for the feature story on the crusade.

After all the usual national stuff that Fox thrives on, they finally got into their featured stories. We were their top story of that evening's second segment.

"And now we go to Burt Jacobs in Las Vegas with his in-depth look at one very special—yet unusual family—Burt?"

"Yes Shep. I'm here in very sunny Las Vegas, Nevada, where only two days ago, I met up with one of this desert City's, most prominent and charismatic citizens. No, it isn't Siegfried or Roy, nor the City's colorful new Mayor, or resident comedian Jerry Lewis, either.

"His name is Marcus Morgan. At thirty-two years of age, he is the fourteenth wealthiest person living in Nevada today.

At that moment, my media kit photo was in the upper right hand corner of the screen.

"While he is by no means necessarily a household name outside of Las Vegas—his 347 restaurants are.

"You see, Marc Morgan is the founding force, and majority stockholder behind Verandas Inc—America's only ethereally-themed restaurants.

"Morgan originally hails from Los Angeles where he began to make his mark after overcoming his own early obstacles. You see, his early developmental years were burdened with the then-unknown learning disorder of Attention Deficit Disorder.

"His difficulties proved extremely challenging for his family. The only way he was finally able to grasp and learn school fundamentals was after joining his mother in her kitchen. Mom taught him how to learn—by teaching him how to cook. In following and understanding the mathematics of recipes, it proved to be the breakthrough our young future entrepreneur needed. He was finally able to get by in regular school classes, although still just barely.

"By the time Morgan was a mere ten-years-old though, he could professionally prepare a seven-course dinner setting…fit for royalty. Years later, he would actually live to see that honor to fruition while a chef at Toonland's World Famous 'the door at forty-four' restaurant where Morgan eventually grew a reputation as the most requested chef by returning royal guests from the world over.

"But getting back to young Marcus, it seems providence stepped in when he joined the choir at his High School at fourteen. The following semester, he was selected to join that choir's elite competing chorale; Our Sixteen Voices. This led him to travel the globe in international competitions throughout his high school years.

"While in Salzburg, Austria at the age of fifteen, he meets the girl of his dreams; fourteen-year-old, Miranda Richards, whose own choir was representing England.

"Despite the trials and tribulations of such a long-distance relationship, our young couple maintained their feelings for one another. Barely out of college, they marry and settle down in England where Marcus accepts a position within his in-laws' restaurant interests. Here Morgan gains valuable management experience to go along with his established culinary skills, as he tweaks his entrepreneurial passions as well.

"But our story only begins here; as our young restaurateur becomes disenchanted with his career in England…it seems that he longs to launch his own restaurant concept back in America.

"Our young couple realizes, that for at least the time being, neither can live happily—in the other's world, so Miranda sends Marcus home. While the couple goes their separate ways, it's not for the typical reasons. It's certainly not for lack of love, as they continue to love one another deeply, so they choose to not divorce.

"Our young Mr. Morgan returns to the States, where he soon settles on relocating to Las Vegas…he eventually hopes to build a successful life there, as well as to reunite with his wife. It is here that he will start his restaurant concept. He believes that starting a restaurant in Las Vegas, with its myriad of inexpensive buffets will test the waters sufficiently of his concept's viability in less difficult markets across the country, for our entrepreneur has big plans… indeed.

"Using the bulk of his family's life savings, along with government financing, he opens his very first Verandas restaurant. After some early struggles, the novel concept of dining with ghosts in a haunted Victorian mansion takes hold and is followed by tremendous success. This is thanks in great part, to Las Vegas' drawing power and word-of-mouth advertising as a must-see destination for tourists visiting the desert city…just as our young entrepreneur had planned all along.

"In short order, Verandas' begin popping up on all major interstates across the Country, but to this day, each is company owned, managed,—and haunted!

"Yet back in England, events are creating extraordinary circumstances and consequences when Miranda discovers she is pregnant shortly after Morgan's departure. The following July in fact, she delivers twins, first Trevor, along with Taylor, four minutes later…while still half a world apart from her husband.

The boys' pictures were now below mine on the right side of the screen.

"Initially you see, Miranda planned on surprising Marc with her appearance in Las Vegas, along with his sons, but sadly, fate stepped in, as it wasn't meant to be.

"During Caesarian delivery, her doctor discovered Miranda had uterine and ovarian cancer. She was given a mere year to survive.

"The last thing that Miranda wanted to do was interrupt any of her husband's business efforts with this earth-shattering news. Naturally, Mrs. Morgan realized that Verandas' success and future hung in the balance along with her husband's aspirations…so the situation called for a bold decision.

"Miranda came to the brave and pivotal decision—that she would tell her husband nothing about her fatal illness! Knowing she had only months to live, she wanted to spare Marc this knowledge in order to assure his continued business success. Yet as a necessary consequence, she also made the painful decision not to tell him of his sons' births either! Only under such a deception, could she be certain of keeping Marc where he needed to stay—at Verandas' helm and not looking after a dying wife.

"According to Morgan, she knew that he would sacrifice anything—including abandoning Verandas altogether, simply to support his family by her side.

"Therefore, Miranda Morgan vowed to herself to keep silent so that our hero could follow his aspirations back home, free of any knowledge or remorse.

"In the last few days regrettably, a reporter for another network has presented a much darker argument of Mrs. Morgan's motivations. This reporter has put forth the argument that Mrs. Morgan's goal was to deny her husband, the existence of his children to punish him for abandoning her.

"My team thoroughly investigated all of this story's facts, but we have found that reporter's conclusions wholly unfounded, as you will see."

Wait a minute, was I hearing this right? Can I believe my ears, even as I hear the very words? Yes! My late wife had just been completely vindicated by a respected national news network; Fox News, with Connors' full report characterized as nonsense and rubbish—in the process.

I now returned my attention to Burt's very well laid out story.

"Mercifully, Miranda didn't die within that year as her doctors had predicted, instead, she fought her battle aggressively for a decade longer.

"Ultimately, she waged an eleven-year battle with the dreaded disease quite privately until this last October, when she sadly—succumbed.

"During this same period of personal struggle however, Miranda succeeded in raising millions of pounds through her own foundations to help England's underprivileged, disenfranchised, and sick.

"Yet for Mrs. Morgan, the bigger and more painful struggle was Marcus himself…keeping him away from England along with the true facts. You see, all these years later—Morgan was still oblivious while back in the states, to what his wife had done selflessly to assure his personal success.

"Miranda never faltered to the end as she succeeded in remaining silent about her illness as well as, the existence of their boys. Four months ago, essentially through his father-in-law's intervention, Morgan finally learned of his sons' existence while sadly, his wife lay dying.

"Morgan was further shocked to learn that his eleven-year-old sons, were agreeable accessories to this deception continuing for all those years. And the boys surprised their father with a complete knowledge of his personality, likes and dislikes, along with their family's history. They literally knew every bit of pertinent information about his life through to the present time of last October.

"Marcus believes that the revelation of his sons' existence has made all of his pain and regrets far more sufferable.

"Which leads us to where our story is today Shep. Our proud father brings his sons' home to Las Vegas just a week ago, where their new life here begins.

"Being the proud papa, one of Marc's first joys is to give his sons a guided tour of his company's headquarters. This is where our story takes on an unusual twist, as you'll see.

"While touring Dad's packaging facility, the boys see an 'assembly room' full of Verandas employees working away packaging products. But some of these employees look somewhat different to the boys, as they're disabled, which surprises them. Dad explains that these employees have some challenges they deal with, but work all the same like everyone else.

"The boys are profoundly moved by the physical challenges faced by their father's employees, and yet, how he has attempted to assist them. So the boys ask how they can help too. Values no doubt, carried over from their late mother's work with her charities that the twins had been reared on.

"The boys offering to help their father, seems to be another bone of contention for that other reporter and her story. From the beginning, she doubted this offer ever took place on the boys' part, but initiated from Marcus Morgan personally, or was purely contrived to appear as such in order to garner favorable press. The reporter chooses to believe it is merely a marketing department scheme or some charade as she purports…but certainly nothing more.

"Her story's entire focus is based on this one postulation being correct and accurate.

"Her argument of doubt is fair enough on the surface, yet she never offers any evidence to back up her allegations except some hearsay, and instead chooses to unfairly attack Mrs. Morgan's character viciously in our opinion.

"What's fascinating Shep, is that something Morgan himself said, the day he and I met, led me to some very revealing video footage."

"You see, upon entering Morgan's offices the day of our interview, he forewarned me not to walk past their restrooms unescorted. Morgan informed me that doing so would trigger the company's passive surveillance system if I went nosing around their building, despite a clearance badge from security.

"Yesterday in speaking with his assistant, I remembered Morgan's comment and asked about it. That led to the videos you're about to see, ultimately being recovered."

At that moment on the TV, I saw the boys and I walking into the packaging room at my plant at about a twenty-foot distance. Christ, why hadn't I done this myself—days ago? I now knew I had Robbie and Burt to thank for saving all of us in the process.

Sure enough, the conversation with the boys' offer was captured clearly enough…and intact, along with—everything else on the video. In the second segment of footage, we were in the General Store where Taylor was explaining their concept to me. Jesus, I did have the goofiest grin on my face at the time, how embarrassing I thought.

"Shep, as you can see from these videos, there is no basis to the other reporter's contention. To the contrary, it unmistakably proves the two critical points that Verandas has put forward. One, the boys freely offered their help as they claimed—and two, this concept originated with Trevor and Taylor Morgan…and no other!

"I might also point out, that I had our video and body-language experts review these two pieces of film. They assure me that both pieces of footage are genuine. They are not altered, staged, or subsequently created, in their professional opinions.

"But more so, I don't know about you Shep, but as I watch both segments, I am moved by them profoundly. Isn't it amazing in this day and age to see such wonderfully caring and giving children, as these twin brothers?

"Incidentally Shep, the Morgan boys are not stopping here by any stretch of the imagination.

"Trevor plans a program to assist the homeless and working poor to get into apartments and homes with grant loans. Taylor would next like to assist the Las Vegas Special Olympics by building a world-class sport facility here in town.

"And if that isn't enough, I have just become aware that the boys are planning on doing a little more fundraising by recording a CD soon. Their album of music will be sold alongside their kiosks to raise additional money for the foundation. The boys are accomplished pianists having studied since they were five-year-old tykes in England, and they sing incredibly well.

"I had the pleasure of hearing the boys perform the other night at their local Verandas. If that audience's reaction is any indication, they have very bright futures ahead...indeed.

"So there you have our report Shep, part love story, part heartbreak, and all of it—truly inspirational.

"Mostly though, it's the story of how a successful man who once thought his life ideal and complete, learned otherwise. He came to realize just how much more to life there truly was, when he became blessed—with fatherhood...back to you Shep."

Everyone in the room thought that the piece was so moving, they all asked to run it again, so we did before returning to conversation.

"Marc, I never realized what you had all been through, your story is truly inspirational, but I'm confused, why would that other reporter try to malign your wife?"

"Lucille, it was a personal vendetta against me—I had the nerve, you might say, to stand up to her. So I put her solidly in her place—but publicly in front of her peers.

"Who was the reporter Marc?"

"Concepcion Silvia Connors, Tom."

"Oh Lord help you pal—my condolences."

"My sentiments exactly Tom."

"Marc, what are you doing about it?"

"Everything I can Lisa, that's why I mentioned to you to pick up a copy of tomorrow's RJ newspaper. Right now, we're putting enough pressure on CCC that they are definitely feeling the heat, hopefully that will do the trick. If it doesn't, our next move will be to seek relief in the courts."

"You know Marc, in all sincerity; you have many friends in LV, and not just these fresh ones sitting around this table. Your reputation is beyond reproach, yet so is your credibility here in town...but let's face it—you also obviously come from good stock.

"Thanks Tom, but the two deserving of the credit for that are sitting next to you. Without them, I can tell you—I'd be a different person today, and we wouldn't all be sitting here in this beautiful house, that much is certain." At which point both my parents started moving about somewhat embarrassed.

"I had no idea about the A.D.D. issue Marc; here I thought you simply were in the right place at the right time?" Tom added.

"Mr. Morgan, what was it like not being able to learn things, I get confused in school too?"

"Austin, it wasn't fun, I can tell you that—for my teachers or my parents."

"Mom, do you remember my breakthrough, when I finally 'got it' for the very first time, so it changed everything in one feel swoop?"

"Yes son, I remember—I'll never forget that day, believe me. We were making an Asparagus Bisque. It called for two tablespoons of heavy cream. I showed you how three teaspoons of cream equaled one tablespoon, by filling three separate teaspoons. Then one by one, I poured them individually into the larger measuring spoon, making up an exact tablespoon.

"You looked at me with tears in your eyes…my, you were crying hard. I remember that it really surprised me seeing you cry so deeply. But can you remember Marc what you said to me when I asked you why the tears?"

"Of course, I was still bawling but looked at you as I said—I get it Mommy, I understand."

Lo and behold, at the conclusion of this exchange, I heard the distinctive sound of my father blowing his nose. He did that with so much finesse and aplomb…not! It shook the chandelier—inside the dining room some forty feet away.

Looking around, I was shocked to see not a dry eye in the room though—with Dad leading the way. There he was, choked up while Mom walked over to me. She then gave me quite a tender hug, which created an odd sort of feeling that was unlike anything I had ever felt before. I honestly believe that Mom was trying to convey her feelings of pride towards me, or something of that magnitude.

Eventually as we all composed ourselves; we had a very delightful conversation that quickly ensued during dessert. It was becoming Tom's favorite subject, aviation and the merits of owning one's own plane.

It had been a wonderful day, but it was getting late with both Courtney and Hayley sleeping already. Trevor and Austin were close behind, while most of the adults were yawning and stretching some too.

"Tom, I think we have a bunch of tired kids here, what's your spin?"

"Yes Marc—plus a few older kids as well", pointing to Fleming, Grace and my Mom, who were all starting to fade out.

"Lets call it a night Marc; the kids all have Sunday school in the morning, so I'll have to fight them in the morning when we get home from work, just to get them all out of bed and over to Saint Ann's."

"Yep, it will be the same with these two, over here."

Within minutes, we loaded up the van with all the Scott children, then said our fair wells and good nights.

I was not surprised when everyone in our group immediately said good night as well, once we were back inside the house. It was off to bed for all of us.

CHAPTER 10

▼

ODE TO LARRY

I WOKE IN THE MORNING feeling truly rested, so I made my way into the steam shower to finish waking myself up. By the time I stepped out, I saw each twin pass me, while waving and running straight for the commodes. As I got dressed, they began their morning rituals, so I left to go downstairs to eat. I also wanted to finish reading the Sunday paper. Yesterday I had pretty much only read our rebuttal prior to its publishing to check it for errors on our end…this morning I needed to check the RJ's work.

I was almost through with my meal, when the 'tornados' made their entrance into the kitchen.

"Morning Dad, good morning Grace."

"Good morning my two loves, did you sleep well?"

"Yes Grace, thank you." Taylor offered.

"Lovely Grace." Followed out of T-1."

"How did you sleep Dad?"

"Fine T-1, but I think I ate too much brisket. Speaking of which, who was our own little trumpeter in bed last night boys…in such closed quarters?"

"Whatever do you mean—Father?" I heard from a red-faced Taylor. He then quickly attempted to move on to a new topic of discussion.

"Wow, yesterday was so much fun Dad…thanks a lot for having the Scotts over."

"Oh, you're welcome T-man, but you know, I enjoyed being with all of the Scotts myself, I guess just about as much as you seem to enjoy ripping off a nice ripe fart every now and then in bed. So there's no reason to really thank me, they're simply our friends, aren't they…my little chief—Brown Cloud?"

"Daddy!" My son said through a look of shock and mortification on his face.

"Alright son, let this be a lesson to you. Fart again in my bed and I will embarrass you even more so next time…do I make my point son?"

"Yes Father, you do." My son said this with his infamous undertone of independence and sarcasm, so I now moved on to my own reinforcing comments.

"And Taylor, sadly at the risk of fueling the fire even more so, young man, you need to eat your breakfast quickly now…so get a move on. Remember, we still have to make it over to Temple in time for School. Paul has the day off, so I'll drive you myself, unless either one of you has an objection?"

"Okay. Are you going to drive us in Laverne, I want to see you wearing Paul's hat Dad?"

"Nope—you can forget about the hat T-1. But I guess you guys are slipping."

"What do you mean—by slipping, Dad?"

"Oh, I don't know T-1; it's just that you two apparently didn't notice the car in the garage is all."

Without a single word, my two boys darted off in a flash to the garage. I heard them open the door from the house where they then yelled out in excitement.

Moments later, they returned with huge smiles on their face.

"Why didn't you tell us the Bricklin was home from England Daddy?"

"T-man, I'm surprised at you, do you think you would have been this excited if I had just told you—as a matter of fact?"

"Oh, you're right Dad, this surprise was much better, but can we take her to Temple?"

"Of course."

"Cool Daddy."

"I'm glad you're so pleased T-man."

"Sure I am…this way if we see that sod Larry Levison, you can stop right in front of him, okay?"

"Why T-man?"

"Because, it will make him bloody hell mad—he says his mum drives the very best car in the whole school."

"Now is that anyway to work out your differences T-man?"

"Maybe not Daddy, but it will make me feel better, since all he does is brag all throughout class."

"You know boys, it sounds to me that what young Mr. Levison really needs is two new friends…with British accents, I would suppose. And you know, the last I checked, you two could use some yourselves, isn't that true as well?"

"I don't know about that Dad, but I certainly don't care to find out." Trevor added.

"Listen T-men, just remember one thing; most kids who operate the way Mr. Levison is acting—do so for a simple reason. They feel like an outsider in their own group of peers. What they are really trying to do—is to simply get themselves noticed. They might not go about it in the right way, but they're actually just trying to make friends in most cases."

"Too bad Dad—no one is going to call Trev and me—poofs, then get our friendship in return—I just can't get my head around that…no bloody way."

"Alright guys, I'd be the last person to disagree with how upset that made both of you feel. I'm just trying to explain to you both, why Larry likely acts the way he does. Sure he screwed up, so what you two decide to do about it, is your business within reason."

"What are you saying Dad, we should just forget about what he said, act like it didn't happen—when it did, just so we can make friends with him?"

"Well maybe T-1. If you were to reach out to him by just acting friendly or at least neutral about it, who knows what he'll do? You might discover he's just a lonely kid without many friends…who's just crying out to make some—don't you see? And if I'm right, you two would have another friend yourselves, probably one you'll end up cherishing very much."

"Oh…what do you think, Taylor?"

"Only if he apologizes Trev—then he can be our friend…he is real funny when he's not too busy bragging."

"Natch bro…okay, that works for me too."

"Alright Dad, we'll see how it goes."

"Boys, it's your decision—so don't do it for me. Do it for yourselves—and Larry if it's in your hearts."

"Now finish up, we've got to get a move on."

I got up from the table to go into my office to check my emails while the boys finished. Ten minutes later, we were in the garage but the boys began fighting of course, over who was going to push the switch to open the Gull Wing on their side of the car.

"Stop it now, or we'll take the Navigator!"

"Yes sir, sorry." I heard weakly.

They got into the car as I fired her up. From the sounds coming from the engine compartment, it was clear that she was no less for wear from her trip back over the Atlantic. I had to let her warm up for the compulsory minute before then letting her rip…we were off in a flash as always.

The trip up to Summerlin driving this car, somehow took us only six minutes, so before I knew it, we were there. As I dropped them off, I was actually relieved that Larry Levison was not there now because I wanted the boys to think about what we had talked about without having my car start them off in the wrong direction again. Surprisingly, they didn't bring Larry up at all again before leaving. I wished them a pleasant morning, as they waved to some kids they apparently knew from the prior week, so I took off.

I decided to stop at our unit up the street to see how their Sunday traffic was, along with picking up some coffee for the house. I arrived at our unit about four minutes later, where I found the lot still sparse, so I knew things were going to be slow inside…Church wasn't out yet after all. Christine immediately greeted me as I walked in.

"Good morning Marc."

"It sure is Chris—so, how's business been this week?"

"Fine, our numbers were real strong, almost as good as number one's."

"Very good, how do things look staff-wise for next Saturday's big day?"

"Fine, we'll be at full staff plus five floaters for that timeframe, which should put us in great shape."

"Good, but remember you'll probably have a fair amount of press show up early as well. Remember that their number is a guess beyond our local group of eighteen. If you think you'll need more back up, don't hesitate to pull out all of the stops…do it now while you still can. I would prefer being a little too heavy on the labor ratio for the day, than too light." Remember, we're focusing on our crusade with this, but it is also a showcase for Verandas' service and hospitality as always…so we need to dress for success!

"All right Marc, I see your point. By the way, your little performance the other night with the boys was darling. I really can't ever remember receiving so many compliments from the guests—you should do it more often."

"Gee, thank you Chris, for putting me back to work in my old age like that."

"Is it true the boys will be recording a CD now as a result, did I hear that right?"

"Yep, to help raise more money for the Foundation, so we'll just see where that leads us.

"Oh, by the way, you're the first to hear this, so keep it quiet. We've hired a full-time entertainment producer who starts March 1st or thereabouts. So be prepared, you're unit and number one will likely be 'the guinea pigs' for his ideas first."

"Actually Marc, that's terrific news. I'm delighted to hear we're finally going to have something a little more formalized. You know, I'm sure all the kids will be as well, as I personally stink at production—so who's this producer?"

"His name is Scott Davis…he and I go way back. He has been heading up Toonland's entertainment and parade production for quite some time now, and he's very sharp. I know you're going to enjoy working with him; he's masterful at staging and has a great eye for production. He'll make a great asset to the entire organization I'm sure, besides he's a hoot to work with."

"My word, he sounds perfect. How did you two meet, if I'm not being too personal?"

"Not at all, he and I worked together at Toonland-California years ago where we were both in the ToonCrooners. That's their performing group made up of volunteer park employees. Scott was our unofficial producer and choirmaster. The kid had the talent even at eighteen, I swear."

"And he's stayed there all those years Marc?"

"Yes Chris, he has…that's actually more common with the park than you would think. Nevertheless, Scott quickly moved up the ladder of sorts. Now for the last eight years, he's the top 'bear' if you will, in their stage production department. He also consults for other Toon Media interests all over the world as well. He does a killer job at everything he touches in production."

"He sounds wonderful, so when will we see him first?"

"I'll bring him in the next time he's up here, which will probably be early in the week to prepare for next Saturday with the boys' big opening for their crusade. Later today, you'll be getting Jesse's email with some changes to Saturday's schedule; there will be some more performing that day to promote the boys upcoming fundraising CD. He's also going to be working with them on the side, to see if he can get them a recording contract."

"Wow Marc; I would have thought that would have been the last thing on your mind? I guess I don't know you as well as I thought…I'm really surprised to hear this?"

"No—you've got me pegged, that part of it wasn't my idea—I was dead set against it at first, truly."

"So what changed your mind then?"

"Their names are Trevor, Taylor, and Mrs. Malcolm Morgan, along with Miranda too, that's who."

"Oh, now this sounds interesting, care to share more about it?"

"It's nothing juicy, I can assure you, but it was interesting. Frankly, I can blame myself for the whole thing in a way."

"How so?"

"Simple, I allowed Trevor to act on his wish to sing here last Friday in the first place…that got the whole damn thing rolling naturally."

"Really boss—what made it so interesting then?"

"Oh, I guess you could say it was my Mother's conversation with my late wife just before she passed over. No one knew of my wife's position on this topic as completely as Mom, it seems. She then shared Miranda's feelings on the subject with us on Friday after seeing the boys' performance. Apparently, Miranda was not opposed to allowing the boys to pursue becoming professional, therefore, how could I argue either?"

"You know Marc; you're opinion still counts for something…after all, you're the sole parent raising them now."

"Yes, good point Chris, but understand that I would never stand in the way of another person's goals for themselves. Especially when it's my own sons. Apparently, they both do want to try this, so I won't refuse them…I know how important this is to a person Chris…hell, look how things started out for me. But just the same, they have to play by my rules. Meanwhile, I will be honoring Miranda's wishes besides. She deserves that, don't you think?"

"Oh yes, I do. It does make sense—still I'd watch them like a hawk."

"You won't get an argument from me on that score either, I can assure you Chris. Mom is taking on that responsibility, so 'she will be' watching them like the mother hen she is."

"That's good Marc, I believe your sons' have tremendous talent, I just wouldn't want to see them go down the wrong path. You know, like so many of these young stars who end up in trouble—or worse."

"Me either Chris—but don't worry, I've got their rules down hard and fast. Besides, I do trust my mother on carrying all of them through, believe me."

"Great. So what are they going to be doing on Saturday, as far as entertaining us?"

"Honestly, Scott hasn't enlightened me exactly; but he's talking to Mom daily, so I guess we'll have to wait and see. The boys have been practicing constantly, so I know something good's in the works."

"That's great, but if we can be of any help, just give me a call."

"Thanks Chris, as you'll need to set everything up. Listen, on another subject, I'm in need of a pound each of Blue Mountain and Espresso Nuevo, how's your stock?"

"Fine, let me get you a couple of pounds."

"Thanks."

Chris left me to retrieve the coffee, while I glanced around at our guests enjoying their meals as I waited.

Out of the corner of my eye, I saw a couple waving to me to come over, which naturally that seemed odd as I didn't recognize them at all. I went over to their table, not knowing who they were, or what they wanted with me.

"Hi, I'm sorry; did you want me or someone else?"

"No, I wanted to speak to you sir; you are Mr. Morgan aren't you?"

"Why yes, I am, but please call me Marc—and you are?"

"I'm the boys' teacher Marc…I'm Mrs. Geary, but please call me Susan, while this handsome guy next to me, is my husband Rick."

"How are you Susan, my—what a pleasant surprise, it's a pleasure to meet you face to face…and its nice to meet you too, Rick. Honestly Susan, I had to avoid going into your room to meet you on the boys' first day. I didn't want them to be embarrassed you know."

"I understand Marc—please join us, won't you? We come here about once a month for brunch on Sundays. Ricky has also made it a habit to eat lunch here on occasion."

"Susan, you certainly aren't going to get an argument out of me with that."

We were all laughing.

"I don't argue with her either Marc, but I've just have to say this without any patronization. The fact is, I'm in a marketing program at UNLV in food service. Your restaurants sir, are beyond compare on so many levels…believe me. I'll never grow tired of your concept nor stop being impressed with it—really.

"Marc, you have somehow managed to put all the right components and elements together in the ideal marketing mix. It's the perfect environment, top-drawer food, presentation, and entertainment in a unique multi-faceted dining destination and retail experience. Your execution lacks nothing. And the whole ghost thing is just another example of your brilliant execution on every level. I'll never forget my first visit, where I saw the fake 'family' scrapbook and photo album in the waiting area. What a little shot of genius that was. You give the guests the necessary back-story information to have a connection with the ghosts now haunting the damn house!

"All in all Marc, there is no better food concept in the country…which I think you, yourself—must know.

"You know, I had planned on using your business model myself for my Doctoral dissertation next semester—with your permission of course?"

"Really. Well, I certainly don't think I can refuse you after all that, can I Rick?"

"Sure you could Marc…but I hope you won't naturally."

"Will you be publishing it?"

"Yes of course, is that a problem?"

"I guess not. Now Susan, forgive my rudeness please, I didn't mean to steal away all of your husband's attention."

"You're just lucky you got the Readers Digest version Marc."

"I see, well whatever I got, I enjoyed hearing the information."

We had continued small talk, mostly about how well the boys were doing in class as we finished our meal together. After another hour or so, I needed to get going.

…"Good, now Susan, Rick, you two have a wonderful day, but thanks so much for calling me over along with all the helpful info Rick. I hope I'll be seeing both of you here next Saturday?"

"Sure, I'm taking a personal day, just so I don't miss it."

"Thank you Rick, that is very nice of you—as well as—your boss!"

"The heck with my boss, Marc, I wouldn't miss the opportunity of meeting all of Susan's kids, including your two. And we're very much looking forward to introducing them to her cousin Becky…she's very precious to all of us."

"Thank you, now you honor me, I look forward to seeing you then along with meeting Becky of course."

I got up, shook hands with both of the Geary's before returning to Chris at the podium.

"Someone you know Marc?"

"Yes Chris…now I do. That's Mrs. Geary and her husband; she's the boys' teacher at the Meadows School."

"Oh, well they're regulars—did you know that?"

"Yes, they pretty much said they're here once a month or so for brunch."

"I'd actually say a little bit more often than that. The husband eats lunch here quite a bit, he always complimenting us on everything."

"Yes, I guess after speaking to him and being in marketing, he would. And speaking of which, comp them today…along with sending them home with a gift basket of coffee—you know the one I mean, it has the large complete set of beans along with the French Press carafe and grinder?"

"God Marc, you are such a pushover."

"Am not…he shared some very helpful information!"

"Are so!"

"Okay cool it…just see to it alright?"

"Sure thing boss. I just think that of all the people I've ever had the pleasure to work for, you're the most unique—but I mean that in a good way—believe me."

"Thanks Chris, I very much think you're special too. When I think back to when you started with us straight out of LVA, I realize just how old I've become."

"Thanks boss." As she giggled for good measure.

"You're welcome, now if you'll pass me my coffee? Jesus, I've blown my whole damn morning here. I have to get my guys at Synagogue; they have a short session today, along with the press coming over beginning at one."

"Gee, good luck with the press, although I was blown away so far with the stories I've seen. You know that guy from Fox especially really hit it on the mark, I thought. And you remember my old man George—right?"

"Of course, George and I won the three-legged race at the last company picnic as I recall."

"Oh yeah, I forgot. Well, George told me all about that Team Concepcion report, I couldn't believe it…but God was he ever upset by it. He said their attack on your wife was nasty and seemed more like a set up…so George and I thought the guy from Fox buried her pretty good though, hopefully forever."

"Yep, me too, Burt did do a great job slamming her, but besides that, he pretty much respected all my wishes too."

"Anyway girlfriend, I'm out of here…see you Saturday, but make sure this place…sparkles."

"Don't worry Marc, we won't let you down."

"I know you won't, see you later alligator."

"After while, crocodile".

I left the unit, jumped into the Bricklin, as I took off back on the road to the Synagogue.

I arrived shortly. I got into a long line of cars ready to pick up the kids. I popped my gull wing, got out, to wait for my identical off spring. No sooner did I do that, than a man, two cars behind mine, got out of his car to apparently mosey on over to me.

"My God man, I can't remember when I last saw one of these in such great condition. It must be a hundred-point car."

"Thank you; she's one of my favorites—but an everyday driver despite her condition."

"Wow, quite impressive. So you collect then?" He asked.

"Yes I do, do you have a soft spot yourself?" I asked.

"Yeah, I restore and turn Corvettes mostly, but Cobras too when I can find them."

"Really, well I've got two Vettes myself, as well as a half-dozen of the AC's."

"Six AC Cobras…damn,—you must be Marcus Morgan?"

"Wow—I am indeed…but please call me Marc."

"Hell Marc, I'm pleased to meet you, I'm Rod Martin. I've seen a few of your pieces at shows. When you mentioned the six AC's, I just knew it had to be you."

"Nice meeting you Rod, how is it we've haven't met before at a show?"

"Can't say I can answer that Marc, but we have now, so it's a real pleasure."

"Likewise Rod, thank you."

"Say, I'm told you have an incredible Duesenberg, perhaps the finest West of the Mississippi—is that true?"

"Yeah, I would say I do Rod, but I'm putting her up for auction this summer. Before I do that Rod—if you have any interest in her, maybe we should talk if you're seriously in the market? After all, why pay all the commissions on both sides, if we can strike a deal beforehand ourselves?"

"I'm certainly not opposed to that Marc in the least, but I would suppose that you are going to reserve her somewhere between the 1.7 and 2 mil mark?"

"Yes…exactly…so when would you like to see her?" I inquired.

"Anytime you say."

"How about Tuesday then?"

"Sure, here's the address, I'll clear you with my men, but they're still working on the cowl at the moment. While you're there Rod, be sure to take a tour of the restoration facility itself, as we do a fair amount of outside work now, if you ever require it." I wrote out the warehouse address and then handed it to Rod.

"Great, I'll look her over on Tuesday with your facility as well. If the car is everything I've heard it is, I'll have my secretary fax you a letter of intent."

"Seems fair to me Rod, I look forward to your opinion of her, one-way or the other. Do you know the car's history?"

"Yes, I've been made aware its original owners were Al Jolson and Ruby Keeler, but I'll cover all of that with your men when I see it and if I'm interested.

"Fair enough Rod. I will hope to hear from you with some news on Tuesday or Wednesday then. Here are my boys; I've got to get running now."

"Sure thing, I hope my grandkids get out here as fast."

"Hi Dad."

"Hey there guys, so—how was it today?"

"We saw a real good movie, so it was much better today, especially getting out earlier."

"I'm glad to hear that T-1—I think.

"So, is there any news on the Larry Levison front?"

Taylor jumped right in with that question.

"Yeah, he was really surprised when we kind of tried to make friends with him, now he wants us to come over to sleep at his house, and all kinds of stuff. I guess you were right Dad. He really is a nice mate once you get to know him. And God, Daddy, he's so funny, he'll crack you up, I swear—he's brill. I really like him now, and he did apologize to us right after we became friendly to him…we didn't even need to say anything first, either. Can we call him later; I've got his cell phone number?"

"Hey T-men, I ask you, do you guys have a smart old man or what?

"And sure you can call him, but remember today is shot with the press coming over, along with shopping afterwards—but you could invite him to dinner I guess, that is—if you'd like to?"

"Can we—that would be so cool?"

"Sure, call him before we get started with the press, but don't forget to let Sofia know if we'll need to have an extra table setting."

"Thanks Daddy."

"No problem guys, I'm just glad this all worked out so well for all three of you."

"Yeah, me too."

"And me three" said Trevor.

The boys did not fight this time, as Trevor popped the Gull Wing. You could hear the surrounding kids 'wow' in the background as the boys opened it, then got in…but with Taylor now closing it…they were sharing it, which was good to see.

We got to the house at ten past twelve pee, with fifty minutes for the boys to eat, as I gave them some pointers regarding how we were going to handle the press.

As they ate—heartily I might add, I filled them in on the drill.

…"Okay Dad, we get it."

"Good Trevor, but remember—if you don't like a question, tell them so."

"Alright, I will Dad, but I didn't find any before that bothered me."

"That's great son, but remember these reporters have waited days to talk to us again. They've also followed what's been reported about the Connors controversy, so they'll be looking for their own angles on that alone, I'm sure."

"Oh, I think I understand, okay Dad." Trevor added.

Promptly at one pee, the front gate called through our first reporter. A few minutes later, the front door knocked, as I waited for Fleming to escort our guest into the office. This procedure repeated itself until every one of our reporters had come and gone. We really did not have any problem with any of them. It quickly became clear that after the recent Connors debacle and subsequent fallout, they were all satisfied with the authenticity of the boys' crusade now, which was great to see. Most all of them concentrated on that, rather than mentioning the controversy itself. If anything, they all seemed clearly content to go along with sweeping Connors under—the bus now.

Once we were finished, Mom immediately herded the boys into the Navigator and they left lickity split. I was a little surprised that Dad had not joined them as originally planned, but when I found him sleeping on the sofa in the great room, I understood why. I could never remember my Mom, ever waking anyone from a good nap, myself included. So I left my Dad to his catnap too, returning to my office for a little paperwork.

Opening up my email on my laptop, I saw one from Scooter, so I opened that one first.

"Hola Amigo, como esta?

"Marc, I can't begin to tell you all the excitement I've come home to. The girls are really quite jazzed over our move, while Beth is getting excited too… but I swear if Natalie emails one more picture of a gorgeous house that's in our price range, my damn wife will never be able to make up her mind. The news of the Jag also did not hurt; she does love that Indigo blue. At any rate, here is what is going on now.

"First, I gave my notice to my boss Stacy, whereby she literally went into tears, but she did wish me well too. She didn't blame me a bit when I mentioned the eighty four k, the perks, the opportunities, and of course—the Jag. She also advised me that I am entitled to my accrued vacation and sick time, which all slipped my mind of course. This essentially means, that my pay will continue on for several more weeks, even though I am free to leave the organization physically after a staff party tomorrow afternoon in my honor. And if you can believe it—she insists I name my own replacement, as she feels I'm the only one qualified to know anyhow.

"Now here's some other news that should please you and Marilyn. I have lined up the studio; engineer, back up musicians and vocalists—everything through a contact of Stacy's. She referred me to a friend at an outside studio where it won't cost the foundation a penny to produce this album; merely production costs for duplicating the CD itself, plus the packaging. And who knows, we might get that gratis too, by the time I'm finished calling in favors.

"Next, I've sent a Fed X up to your office with some arrangements for the boys to have a look at. These three are my selections for their demo, so I hope my choices meet with their approval. Please let me know if they aren't happy with any of them.

"I'd like to come up tomorrow if you have an available plane, for a few days of advance work…no time like the present to get started as they say.

"Lastly, I'd like to arrange for my three ladies to join me here, this next Sunday. The girls will be returning from a Girl Scouts campout and starting their final track break in Orange, so I'd like to show them around town. We can also look at these houses that Natalie sent to Beth, during the week. Is this too soon for you, or should we arrange a visit for them at another time?

"Well I guess that does it, let me know when you have a moment…Your old amigo, Scott."

My I thought—that was certainly a mouthful. I replied immediately, letting him know I was fine with everything. And I was pleased and thankful with his efforts on the boys' and foundation's behalf.

When I was finished, I hit the send button, then began opening up my remaining mail one at a time, doing whatever was required. Once I finished, I left my office for the kitchen.

I found Sofia working in the kitchen where she was grinding up a batch of the Blue Mountain Jamaican coffee I brought home.

"What's for din-din Sofe?"

"Oh Marco, you're just like your father when it comes to food, where is Senor Mal, by the way?"

"Last time I looked Sofia, he was catching some 'Z's in the great room, why do you ask? Moreover, can't you hear that lovely trumpet section of his, coming out of his nose?"

"No I didn't, but he asked me to make him a sandwich earlier, but he hasn't been in to get it. That's really not like him Marco; I hope he isn't sick with something?"

"It isn't Sofe, but it's also not like him to take a nap, so I guess his need to sleep overruled his stomach—for once…wait a minute—he must be sick! Hurry call 911." I then laughed as she started for the phone, thinking I was serious.

"So what are you preparing for dinner—are you holding out on me girlfriend?"

"No, sorry Marco. I'm preparing blackened Orange Roughy, green beans almandine, a wedge salad, and my family's recipe for flan as dessert."

"Your flan—hell, I hope you made a double recipe, you know how that custard and I get along? And Lord help you if the boys take to it like I do, you know, I think it's in the Morgan genes to love your flan."

"Gracias Marco, but I'm surprised at you—I made a triple recipe, especially with a guest joining the boys."

"Oh, so the infamous Larry is coming then…great, I forgot to ask the boys that."

"You must be going loco en la cabesa Marco?"

"Afraid so Sofe, I guess I am."

"Say, just what kind of sandwich did you make for Dad anyway?"

"Guess.

"Now don't toy with me Sofe, I could do with a bite to go with this coffee that's near ready, so stop holding out on me."

"Fine—it's a roast beef, pepper jack, avocado, all on Panini sprinkled with smoked sea salt and garlic…if you 'must' know?"

"I must, I must,—maybe I should just spare Mom, Dad's wonderful garlic breath by eating it myself—how's that?"

"Pretty weak excuse Marco, but after all—es su casa."

"A very wise, astute answer Sofia, I think I'll just follow your retort to the letter—where is this infamous Panini?"

"In the refrigerator…you can't miss it. There's a note attached—reserved for Mr. Malcolm Morgan only." Sofia was barely holding it together at this point.

"Hey Sofe, if you snooze—you lose." I went to the fridge where I stole the sandwich without hesitation.

I sat down with my Blue Mountain, as I bit into the aforementioned sandwich. Damn, it was good. Yet at that very moment, who do you suppose came sauntering into the kitchen…groggily I might add? Not being a total idiot, I quickly wadded up the piece of paper with the warning message that was lying out in the open next to me on the table.

"Sofia, I had a wonderful little nap, but I'm ready for my sandwich now. Where is it dear?"

"Oh Senor Mal, I forgot all about it, when I saw you taking a siesta—I'll make it for you now." Sofia then threw me a wink.

"Gracias Sofia, no problemo.

"Say son, what have you got there?"

"Oh, just a sandwich Dad. I asked Sofia to fix me one, just how you like it. Want to start on my other half?"

"No son, I can wait it out, but thanks all the same—that's very considerate of you though."

"Hey you know me Dad—I'm Mr. Considerate, hell, I'd love to share my sandwich with you."

I could not help myself with my obvious sarcasm, which was not helping a drop either. As such, none of this was lost on my old man…groggy or not.

"You know son, I'm beginning to smell a rat here, or am I just mistaken?"

"Gee Dad, this is roast beef, the mystery meat Panini was—yesterday's selection, so whatever do you mean?"

"Oh I don't know. It just seems a little odd to me, that's all. You know, I requested a sandwich three hours ago, and then I walk in to find you eating one with the same exact ingredients…just sayin'."

"Just coincidence Dad, really."

"Hum."

"Really Dad, why not start on my second half while you wait then?"

"Alright—maybe I will." And with that short take on a comeback, Dad grabbed the remaining half of the sandwich, wasting scant time in sinking his teeth into it.

"Gee son, just the very exact way I take it."

"Yes Dad, I told you that already."

"Oh yeah, you did."

I heard the automatic garage door opening at that moment.

"Seems the troops have returned Dad."

"Good, I hope your Mother followed my instructions to park away from all the other cars?"

"You must be joking Dad?"

"No, not at all son. I warned her if there's a single ding on that Lincoln, she's dead meat."

"Whose dead meat Malcolm? These choice words escaped from my Mom as she walked in just at the right moment to catch Dad's last crack."

"Oh—nothing dear."

"Listen Marc, thank you again for the truck…I can't believe the pick up nor how civilized it drives—it handles like a dream."

"You're most welcome Mom, I'm glad you like it."

"Marc, now that I have driven it some, I love it."

"That's great Mar, so did you park her in a safe spot like I asked?"

"I parked, where I parked Malcolm, and that's all you need to know about it!"

"Honey, what did I tell you about always keeping it at a safe distance?"

"Mal dear, your idea of a safe distance would have been in 'Reno,' sitting in a two acre vacant lot! The mall was packed, so we parked very carefully… case closed. Oh, but we never once went near the food court, so you really didn't miss a thing—satisfied?"

"Mar, it's not all right. I asked you to do me one small favor, yet this is what I get for my simple request?"

"Yes it is Mal—sorry."

Mom left us as she started climbing the stairs.

I yelled out to her to ask where the boys were.

"Oh, you'll see shortly Marc—you all will." Then she was up the stairs in no time flat.

Meanwhile, all this time, our two lovebirds, Grace and Fleming, apparently had been in the grotto, as I now saw them emerging, hand in hand. After wrapping themselves up in their robes, they joined our little group in the kitchen.

"So how long have you two been in there?"

"Why love—is there a time limit?"

"Honestly—yes there is Gracie. You see that water is not safe for older folks for longer than give or take thirty minutes without a break."

"Fine Marc, when I next see some bloody older folks go in there—I'll be sure to warn them." Way to go Marcus! I thought to myself.

"Sorry Gracie, I didn't mean it the way it sounded, forgive me?"

"Certainly, just remember you're only as old—as you feel Marc. As for me, I 'feel' with my hands, so thank you love!"

I was thankful to be off the hook. Over the years throughout all our insults at one another's expense, we never touched on the subject of age. I knew for a fact, that it was a very sensitive subject for Grace, you see.

I now heard a cat call coming out of Dad, as I reacted by turning to look upon my boys in their new performing costumes—wow what a remarkable sight they were.

"Oh Mom, damn…you did great. Listen guys, you two look incredible, so how do you like your new clothes, dudes"?

"Aren't they bloody wicked Dad?"

"Yes they are, you guys look so awesome, really Trevor."

"I think so too Dad…they're a bit of all right, aren't they?"

"God boys, how I love your English slang. And Taylor, you would be right about that too. I really dig the black leather vests with those t-shirts; they look real cool as well."

"Thanks Dad, Grammy really knows her clothes, doesn't see?"

"Yes T-man—she most certainly does. Hell, I'm even all right with the jeans that short, exposing your socks like that. Mom, I'll say it again; you did a superlative job dressing them. I'd say you're off to a great start as their personal manager."

"Thank you honey, that means a lot to me, to hear that from you, and the short pants are an interesting story too."

"How so mom?"

"Marc, would you believe those pants the boys are wearing now, are the same exact length as the ones I bought them in Paris over the holidays?"

"Are you pulling my leg Mom—that would mean the boys have grown like at least an inch or two?"

"Yes…well they are dear, so I guess someone's been pulling on 'their legs'. I suppose we've just missed them sprouting up—haven't we?"

"Dang, I guess we have, you know, now that I think about it, I had noticed something different, but just didn't put my finger on it."

"Boys, you're going to need Bobbies by the dozens, just to keep all the young ladies away." Fleming offered.

"Gee, I hope so Fleming. Do you really think so?"

"Yes Master Trevor, I do."

"Bloody hell."

"Alright boys, now go on upstairs and change out of your new threads. Why not get into your trunks. Maybe Larry and you two can swim a little before dinner, did you tell him to bring his 'bathers'?"

"Dah—yes Daddy of course." Taylor said with a little too-much attitude.

"You know, I was just asking Taylor, you needn't get snotty with me."

"I'm sorry Daddy, I didn't mean it to sound bad,—I was just trying to be funny like Larry…would."

"That's alright son, but I insist on a kiss to make up."

"Anytime Daddy, except for when our mates are around." And with that, I had first Taylor, followed by Trevor, giving me sloppy wet kisses.

When the two had totally covered me, they got up, kissed Mom again for all of her efforts, before starting back upstairs to change.

Moments later, the gate phone rang.

"Allow me Marc." Fleming answered and cleared a Mrs. Levison through the gate.

I quickly called the boys on the intercom to tell them that Larry was inside the gate so that they should hurry. Moments later it seems~our intercom responded.

"Roger, over and out Dad—sounding like the RAF with those accents of theirs."

I went out onto the drive only moments before Mrs. Levison and Larry were to appear. As they reached the inner gate on our street, my mouth dropped open in awe. There they were, driving up in the most truly incredible…Coral Pink, 1957 Thunderbird—damn! The top was off; it had a Continental kit on the rear bumper, with Kelsey-Hayes wire wheels—it was simply stunning to behold—and that was just the car!

Mrs. Levison was drop dead gorgeous in her Ray-bans, a coral scarf matching the 'Bird' along with a very hot dress. Since Miranda's death, she was the first woman who actually raised my radar…believe me—I was open for business.

I immediately walked over to her door to offer her an exit. I had not even noticed Larry yet, who was invisible in the lustful fog I was in.

"Hi there Mrs. Levison, may I assist you?"

"Why thank you Mr. Morgan, but its just Carol now…there is no Mister Levison at home any longer."

"Oh, I'm very sorry."

"Please don't be. Divorce can be a redeeming experience, trust me—I know."

"Fair enough, but please call me Marc."

"Oh, I intend too...Marc. Larry, where are your manners—introduce yourself to Mr. Morgan, how's he suppose to know who you are?"

"Hello Mr. Morgan—I'm pretty sure I'm Larry—as I guess you gathered too?"

I liked the kid instantly...his humor and timing were impeccable for a twelve-year-old.

"Hey there kiddo. You know, the boys told me you were a riot—now I know what they mean." I extended my hand over the narrow seat to shake Larry's hand. I was honestly surprised by the strength of his grip...yet he seemed happy to meet me as well.

"Carol, why don't you and Larry come in for a moment or two, to meet the family before you leave?"

"I would love that Marc, thank you so much; my, your home is quite lovely."

"Thank you. Why don't we go inside then—shall we?" I helped Carol out of the car as we headed towards the house and walked inside.

"My word...now this is a house Marc—but who did your decorating, it's stunning?"

"You know Carol, my decorator just happens to be in the kitchen—the last I checked."

"My God, you're not trying to tell me that your wife did all this; heavens, I hope she's got an opening for a new client?"

"No Carol, not exactly. You see, my wife passed on last October, the decorator believe it or not, is my Mother."

"Oh, I am truly sorry Marc, I didn't realize. But I would really love to meet your Mother then."

"Sure. Let's go into the kitchen, shall we?" I could not take my eyes off of her, while I continued to more or less disregard Larry's presence, but at least he was checking out the living room while keeping himself entertained.

"Come Larry...but don't you dare touch a single thing, or it will be no Playstation again...for the remainder of the month."

"Yeah Mom...I know...it's barely out of hock."

We walked into the kitchen, where I introduced everyone around. It was obvious to both Mom and Gracie, that I was smitten big time, so they were eating up on all of my fumbled words and remarks. Dad on the other hand, was oblivious to that, as he was actually talking to Larry now I noticed.

"Mrs. Morgan, do you decorate professionally?"

"Why no dear...I just love to shop with other people's money."

"Honestly Mrs. Morgan, I love to shop too, but you should seriously consider it, this house is absolutely gorgeous. I'm overwhelmed by it, which doesn't happen too easily."

"Would you care to see the rest of it dear?"

"Yes absolutely—if you don't mind, that is?"

"Not at all, Marc honey, would you care to join us?"

"You know Mom; I've seen it once or twice already. Let me join you both in a moment, I'll be right up." I fumbled out. As Carol rewarded my efforts at comedy with a laugh.

"Very well then Carol—let's do it."

The two ladies left the kitchen, as I immediately ran for the two doctors. I poured myself a stiff one as I took it in one pass—damn she was so hot.

I called the boys on the intercom to inform them that Larry was in the kitchen. They replied they would be right down so they asked me to show Larry where to change in the cabana. I followed their suggestion as I escorted Larry into the rear yard.

"Dang Mr. Morgan, this is some pool you have here, I bet it cost more than my whole house…okay, so I'm exaggerating, but you understand."

"Larry, you are truly a riot. As I continued to laugh at his crack"

"Thanks sir, but just the same, I've never seen a pool like this in someone's house before—only at the hotels, but they're bigger of course."

"I'm glad you like it Larry, but just you wait bud, soon you'll see the new one I'm going to be building…that one will make any strip hotel jealous, I can assure you."

"Really? Well what's wrong with this one Mr. Morgan, it looks real cool to me?"

"You're right Larry, but you see, we're going to be building a new home, that's the reason for it."

"Oh, now I get it—that's cool too."

"Anyway son, you can change in this little dressing room. There's a bathroom next to it there through that door, should you have a need of it later on."

"Thanks Mr. Morgan—but mostly for having me over for dinner."

As his head dropped into the imaginary cellar, he confirmed everything I suspected about him already…this kid reminded me…of me during my A.D.D. years! I felt an instant connection, what can I say, the kid got to me.

"I don't have a lot of friends, so Trevor and Taylor are real cool to invite me over to swim. I like them a whole lot, especially the way they talk…but they said dinner was your idea, so thanks again, sir."

I was surprised to see him get a little choked up with his remarks, so I tried to be as tactful as possible with my next comment.

"Yes, their accents get everyone Larry. Listen, I'm just glad you were able to make it over tonight…I've been sort of waiting to meet you." He instantly looked scared.

"You have? Why? Was it my big stupid mouth and what I said? You know, I'm really sorry about that, gosh sir, it just sort of slipped out of me, sometimes it happens."

"Lar, they told me you apologized, so it's over, but if you wouldn't mind, could you just try to be a little more sensitive in the future to those kinds of hurtful words?"

"Oh sure I will Mr. Morgan. Jeeze, I just got jealous of all the other kids talking to them when all they do—is ignore me every week…what's a guy got to do to, you know?"

"Like I said Larry, its history now, but let me share something with you. You know kiddo; I think you're just using the wrong sort of bait, if you want my opinion?"

"How do you mean sir?"

"Son, you're a very funny guy…and I mean that pal. So I think that's what you should be using for bait…use that to your advantage".

"What do you mean Mr. Morgan?"

"Larry, it's like this. Up until high school, I really was just like you, although in a completely different sort of way. You see son, I always had trouble making friends myself because I had a learning disability. I really wanted the kids to notice me, but all they did was ignore me because I was different in class…sort of slow or special-needs, you could say."

"Yeah, that's sort of like how it is for me too Mr. Morgan; I ain't mental or nothing…sorry sir, I didn't mean that. It's just that hardly anyone will talk to me. Like your problem, they just ignore me completely…like I'm not there or something."

"You see Lar; we do have a lot in common, don't we? You know buddy, when I told my Dad about my problem, he reminded me that I could play the piano great and sing well too. He suggested I ought to try focusing on that to help me get noticed, so I did.

"With making that one little change—it all worked out son. I joined the high school choir and from then on, I had lots of friends in school, I even became a popular kid if you can believe it. I'm thinking that might work for you too."

"Gee thanks Mr. Morgan, but I can't sing all that good, even though my Cantor says I do."

"You're missing my point Larry—you're funny—very funny in fact. People love to be around funny people. Start using that mouthpiece of yours for humor, instead of insults. Try that comedy of yours out to see where it will get you...understand?"

"Oh—I get it. Cool. I'll give it a try. Hey thanks Mr. M., I appreciate the advice. I'll try it—and you can take that to the bank."

"Gee Larry; I don't ever remember a boy your age using that expression before."

"Oh, well, you see I kind of learned that one from my Dad; he runs a bank."

"No I didn't know—hey, but come to think of it, I do know Rob Levison over at Southwest Bank here in town—any relation?"

"You do? Yeah that's my Dad, Mr. Morgan. How do you know him?"

"We met when I needed a loan for business expansion. Your Dad was one of the bankers I was referred to."

"So did he give you the loan?"

"Honestly Larry, no he didn't. He felt it was too risky backing any restaurant in Las Vegas of all places. Your Dad, like many bankers, believed there was too much 'cheap food' available from the hotels, which was a valid point. There is tremendous competition in Las Vegas. But in our case, as one of the country's first true dining destinations, you could say that all that hotel competition worked to our advantage, as my restaurants were so unique... while family-focused that money was far less of an issue altogether."

"Yet I was so desperate for the cash as I recall; that I actually offered your Dad some ownership interest in my company."

"Are you still in the restaurant business Mr. Morgan, did someone else, finally loan you the money?"

"Yes Larry, I found another banker. But I guess the boys haven't mentioned it to you yet, but I own Verandas."

"Verandas! Holy sh...oot! Boy that's my Dad for you...the rocket scientist of banking. My God, what a schmuck...right Mr. Morgan?"

I could not contain my shock and subsequent laughter at Larry's candid remark, but I did try to.

"Now Larry, just because your Dad made a business decision that you might not agree with, doesn't make him a schmuck by any means. And especially when you're evaluating his decision strictly in hindsight...see my point...but remember what we said about insults too, right pal?"

"Yeah, yeah, I get it...but this is different, this was a bad decision! Tell me something then, will you Mr. Morgan? Just how much would Dad's ownership in your restaurants be worth right now, if the rocket scientist...oh, excuse me, I meant to say my father—had made the loan?"

"Oh, I don't know, maybe around thirty million."

"And how much money were you asking him to loan you?"

"If I recall correctly Larry, it was around five million at that time...my—you sure know a lot about business for twelve...where did you learn all of this?"

"From the rocket scientist of course, Mr. M...and—you don't call that a schmuck?"

I was dying now, and ready to soil myself with this kid's candid commentary.

"My Larry, you certainly say what you feel. You're going to love our cook Grace who you met a few minutes ago—you're just like her."

"That's fine Mr. Morgan, but it doesn't change anything my Mom says about Dad—he's a real schmuck!" Oh, now this is making more sense, I thought to myself.

"Gee Larry; do you think you should really talk about your Dad like that?"

"Why not, Mom always does, shouldn't I tell it like it is too?"

"You know Larry, for one thing, your Mom was married to him, and so she may have reason to feel the way she does. You on the other hand were not, but you are his son, so I therefore think you should form your own opinions—and fairly...without insults too. It should be based on your relationship and experiences with him—not your mother's. Lastly, I feel you should try to respect your father, until you yourself, know otherwise."

"Oh. Well I guess that's only fair. Okay I'll try, but believe me—in a nice way then...he's a real putz...how's that?" God was I losing it over this kid's pisk (mouth).

"Are those your words again Larry—or your Mom's?"

"Yeah, yeah, yeah...okay, I get it Mr. Morgan, let's move on...sir."

"No problem Lar, just remember that your Dad most assuredly loves you very much. You might want to think about how he would feel at this moment, if he was standing right next to you—catch my drift?"

"Yes sir, you're right—but this will never work with Mom, I can tell you that."

Again, he was getting emotional, so I thought I would just try to end the whole damn conversation.

"Somehow Larry, I believe you're right on that. Listen, why don't you go change while I send out the boys—but no swimming until they're here, got it?"

"Got it and thanks again Mr. Morgan. You know, I understand why the guys think you're so cool now...you're all they talk about pretty much. You might not get there fast—but you sure make sense...once you do!"

"Well thank you Larry. Considering your recent commentary—I'll take that straight to the bank myself. As I walked back to the house, I would be less than honest if I did not admit I felt deeply troubled by my conversation with Larry. Boy, out of the mouth of babes, I thought—but was he ever a riot. I knew right then, I loved having this kid around, he was such a natural comedian…but there was more to him than that too.

I returned to the house, as the boys were walking out of the elevator. No doubt they were hoping to find Larry back in the house so they could impress him with it.

Meanwhile, I assigned pool patrol to Sofia, as I spotted Mom and Carol leaving the Master. I quickly made my way up the stairs to join them.

"Hi there ladies, sorry I was detained. How's the two-cent-tour going?"

"Wonderful Marc, but your Mom has definitely missed her natural calling."

"Trust me Carol, she hasn't. She's just gifted in so many areas, that she was forced into making choices."

"That's sweet dear, thank you."

"So how do you like my suite, Carol?"

"Oh, it's heavenly Marc, and the bath—I thought I had died and gone to heaven…that was my first Japanese bathing garden."

"Well I'm so glad you liked it. Perhaps you can consider purchasing it in the fall?"

"You're selling—what on earth would possess you?"

"I will be breaking ground in six weeks on a new home. I have thoroughly enjoyed Spanish Trail, but it isn't particularly kid-friendly as you know…"

"…So you're giving up all of this and Spanish Trail—just for your sons?"

"Yes, does that surprise you?"

"Honestly…yes it does. I love and adore Larry, but he's my son. I'm entitled to live too, am I not; there should be a natural order of things?"

"Certainly, and I would never pass judgment on anyone else for how they feel on the subject, as that's not my style. I only know how I feel about it…as the boys are suffering for it."

"Marilyn, I would suggest you give Marc here, a little reality check before it's too late…he might actually sell this place."

"Carol, one thing I've studied thoroughly about my son, is his character. He has that quality in spades, so I for one, will not take issue with it. Candidly, besides those sentiments, I must admit that the boys do lack friends here, he's right about that."

"Alright, well I guess I just see it differently, but to each—his own, I always say."

"Me too Carol, and thanks Mom." I replied.

We finished the tour after introducing her to the boys, as I began to walk

Carol out to her Bird. A truly magnificent motorcar, which now appeared—sadly, far less flawed in my opinion, than the woman that owned it…if Larry was to be believed.

"You know Marc; I would love to go out for a drink with you sometime, or have you over for dinner, how would you feel about that?"

"Carol, that could be very nice…I'll keep it in mind, but not right now. You see, I'm still mourning a woman I loved very much, while getting my boys adjusted to their new lives with me. I think it would be awhile before we could do that."

"I understand Marc, so take your time. It's nice to meet a man who really loved his wife for a change—it's refreshing. So call me when you're ready, meanwhile when should I pick up my little brat?"

"Oh, don't worry about Larry; we'll drop him home by nine, if that's alright?"

"Sure. See you then."

She started up the T-bird and drove off. The sounds emanating from her classic glass packs were no doubt about to leave their mark throughout my neighborhood as she drove by…how ironic, I thought.

I walked back into the kitchen. I suppose that Mom seeing the three boys horsing around in the pool was enough incentive for her to open her mouthpiece now. After all, we were in an all-adult environment for a change.

"Now Marc, I would say that you we're perhaps a little taken by Carol, or is that my imagination?"

"Yes Marc spill it, you were like a stupid little school boy waffling on back there."

"Thank you Gracie, that was so very special. Okay, listen up you two yentas—should I give you the whole story, or just the abridged version?"

"Whatever makes you happy dear, we're all listening, right ladies?"

"Yes." Came out of the ladies in no particular order.

"Good, now someone pour me another cup of Jamaican, will you?"

"Sure Love, here you are."

Grace filled my cup back up, as Dad walked into the room. I downed a couple of sips of the wonderful brew, before beginning.

"First Gracie, I hope this situation puts to rest for you, the idea that I'm some dried up old prude who would never think to look at another woman?"

"Let's just say, it gives me hope, love."

"Fair enough Gracie, but here's the 'rub' because I went absolutely bonkers when I first saw her drive up. Especially after she drove up in that car of hers, it was autophile love at first sight…while my mojo went into overdrive."

"What was she wheeling son?"

"Dad, just the most frigging pristine, Coral Pink, 1957 Thunderbird—you ever laid your eyes upon is all. Hell I figured, we had to be a match made in heaven: You know, 'male' car nut meets 'female' car nut, seeking mutual fulfillment and engine balancing on the grease rack? Then, when she mentioned there was no Mr. Levison in her life, I really got excited if you follow me…hell, she had my motor running Dad?"

"Comprende mejo." I got from Dad.

"So, here I was with this drop-dead gorgeous woman, stunning car, and no Mr. Levison—I was in gaga land, big time. Everything was going incredible in my mind until—Larry stepped in!"

"Oh Marc, please don't tell me that you of all people, have a problem with a step-child situation down the road?"

"Hell no Mom, of course I don't. I'd go for the Brady Bunch scenario any day—as long as it was with the right—Carol!"

"Thank God, you had me worried for a moment, so what's wrong with young Larry, do you still dislike him over his previous comments?"

"No—quite the contrary Mom, he's a great kid—a super kid…you're going to love him Mom, but if you would let me finish, you'd understand already?"

"Okay, sorry, go on son."

"Thank you Mother. You see, it was my conversation with Larry that snapped me out of my lustful 'fog', if you will."

"Oh. How so love, what happened?"

"Gracie, it was Larry's unabashed candor about his parents' relationship and how he referred to his father so callously. It didn't take a genius to figure out it was wholly influenced by his mother's distain for her ex-husband."

"My word, what did the young scamp say that was so bad Marc?"

Gee Reg—say, do you mind me calling you that Fleming?"

"No, not at all Marc, I'm honored, we're all so informal here; I would actually prefer it with everyone."

"Great. Reg—this is everyone, and everyone, say hello to Reggie."

"You see Reg, little Larry—who's quite the comedic pistol, kept referring to his father as both a schmuck and a putz."

Mom and Dad understood, while Grace and Reg were obviously lost on these words as they looked towards Mom for an explanation. Naturally she jumped in.

"Alright, my dear gentile friends, it's time for your first lesson in Yiddish 101. A schmuck and really a 'putz' as well, are both less than endearing terms to refer to a person's character. In short, they imply the person is an idiot—at a minimum."

Our neophytes nodded their heads in understanding.

"So, there's Larry's spilling his beans about the Levison home life, where the more I heard, the more I cringed. I quickly realized that Carol would never make the grade in my book, so that's pretty much the story."

"Oh, come to think of it Marc, I wasn't crazy about some of her remarks in the master bedroom myself."

"You see Mom, that's as good observation as any, because that's pretty much what I got from Larry's conversation…only multiplied twenty fold.

"And outside on the drive, as she was leaving, she of course asked me out. So it was mutual lust…at first I guess, and yet—I wanted no part of her by that point."

"So how did you answer her son?"

"Honestly Dad, that was easier than I thought it would be. I simply said I was still in mourning, so that with getting the boys all settled in; it just wasn't the appropriate time. Then she wanted to know when she should pick her 'brat' up, that became the final straw for me.

"That kid was almost in tears, telling me how happy he was—just to be invited here. As I suspected, he admitted that he didn't have many friends— gee, now I wonder why?"

"Oh dear, that poor boy."

"Yes Mom, my sentiment exactly.

"I hope I succeeded in setting him straight on his Dad as well…but believe me that really pained me too, as his dad was that banker who actually laughed in my face for the expansion loan I went for…remember, back in '91?"

"Oh no, you don't mean the one who told you Verandas could never compete with the cheap hotel buffets in the long run?"

"Bingo Dad—the very one. As you'll recall, I even offered him ten points of the business! Of course, I softened the story for Larry's behalf, but not totally."

"How so Marc?"

"Well Mom, Larry's very sharp, so he peppered me pretty damn good with questions on how much cash those ten points were worth today. I told him the truth but didn't include the value of our real estate holdings."

"Alright, I don't see anything wrong with that—do you Mal?"

"No dear, not really."

"Thanks for the vote of confidence guys, but I do think I'm capable of handling one, very funny, twelve-year-old after all?"

"Yes Marc, you most certainly are. Sorry if I made it sound like you weren't."

"Its fine Mom, don't sweat it. I just feel so bad for Larry; you know he really is a sweet kid."

"So what's the problem love, he can visit here whenever he wants. In the meantime, you'll be a good influence on him I'm sure."

"Gracie thank you, that is very kind of you to say."

"It's simply the truth Marc. You know it too love."

"Just the same, you are too kind."

"Marc, do you think that Larry has real problems?"

"No Dad, at least I don't think so, but he needs to get a wake up call. He needs to stop believing everything his Mother says about his Dad—even if it turned out to be true, which it probably isn't.

"Hell, I remember this guy well, mainly of course because he literally laughed at my expansion plans. Yet it wasn't as if he was a jerk as a person—in fact I recall him being quite likeable. He was just a typical banker...had I flopped; Verandas' loss would have possibly buried his little bank right along with me. Today, he's the largest and most successful independent chain in Nevada—so he's no dummy either.

"And I remember something else about him from a few years back. He came up to me at a Chamber of Commerce mixer we hosted. The man had the guts to ask me if I remembered him...so I feigned that I didn't. He said: I was the 'idiot' who turned down 10% of your business as I told you your restaurants would never make it. I owe you my sincere apology Mr. Morgan, because you've made a believer out of me—and the rest of America too. I love your concept sir, good for you...you showed me but good.

"As I recall, that's what he said Dad or something to that effect. I mean the guy was honest—he owned up to his decision, yet sought me out, mind you, just to tell me to my face. Doesn't that sound like a stand up kind of guy to you Dad?"

"Yes son, it most certainly does."

"At any rate gang, let's just try to set a good example for our young guest while we can, and enjoy his sense of humor as well, because he is a little pisher, believe you me."

"What's a pisher Marc?"

"Reg, that's an endearing Yiddish term for a kid with an adult's sense of humor beyond his years, if you will."

"Oh my—I'm learning a whole new vocabulary around all you Jewish folks...do you think I'm ready to negotiate my first discount yet?" We all busted up at his joke.

"Who knows Reg, one day we might even invite you into the tribe all official like."

"Oh no Marc, I could never do that, I haven't had the 'operation', and it's too late for that now."

"But Reg, wouldn't you really like to stop paying retail for everything?"

This got us all laughing, but it also brought me back to reality too.

"Gracie, what's our ETA on dinner, I see Dad starting to salivate while you rub Sofia's Orange Roughy in the cayenne and spices?"

"We should be ready in another 25 minutes or so Marc, I'll go relieve Sofia. I'm going to send her in to finish up her recipe here...I'll likely just destroy the blooming thing."

"Fine Grace, go get her. Now for everyone else, let's all go outside and you can all get a little taste of our young comedian...shall we?"

"After you dear." Mom said, as she got up from her chair with everyone following suit.

We all headed outside as we found seats on the terrace, just minding our business as the boys played in the lagoon. All three boys waved to us, but other than that, they were into their own world as they paid us—no mind. After all, they had their choice between talking with us—or playing in the Lagoon...the Lagoon won naturally.

I was almost convinced that Larry was not going to say much of anything funny until Taylor seemed to get the ball rolling inadvertently.

"Grace, what's for dinner tonight?"

"Love, Sofia is making her famous black fish."

At which point, I think Larry spoke up out of genuine curiosity now.

"You mean, the fish is like a 'swartza?'"

Mom, Dad, and I were astounded...and close to busting, but I think Grace and Reg were just trying to figure the word out. Mom responded to our young, definitely politically incorrect guest.

"No Larry, we never say 'swartza' in our home, it's disrespectful to African-Americans dear. We would say 'black' person, or African-American, or person of color. And the fish is blackened from a spice mixture; it is not 'black' fish."

"Oh sorry, Mrs. Morgan, I'll remember not to say it, okay?"

"Yes Larry, that's a very good idea, after all don't you have any friends yourself that happen to be African-American?"

"Oh sure, I know two guys in school—even one more in our Hebrew class at temple."

"So Larry, in school, would you call them a 'swartza', when you're in their company?"

"No—of course not—why?"

"Then why would you call them that, when you're not with them? You see, if the words you use to describe anyone aren't nice enough to say to their face, well then..."

"...Oh I get it now, I guess I should never call them that—right?"

"You got it champ. Remember Larry, bigotry begins with differentiation, so avoid falling into that trap. Don't focus on thinking someone's different for any reason—were all just people...with no two people totally alike—not even twins, see what I mean?" My Dad added.

"Okay. Gee, you guys are pretty dang picky; a kid has got to watch every word around here...I hope I can make the cut!"

We all enjoyed Larry's retort, but his remark did warrant a serious response too.

"Larry, you will always be welcome in our home, but when you're here, we would appreciate you understanding what we feel is appropriate, from what isn't, that's all...but don't worry, we'll help you out when you need it."

"I get it Mr. Morgan, don't you worry about me. As long as you feed me, and let me swim with Trev and Taylor in this pool, I'll do whatever you say—promise."

We were chuckling as I thought of having Larry over one night for a sleepover just for the laughs. Not only with my boys, but little Mordy from the new neighborhood too. Oh would that be a foursome to remember I thought to myself, as Dad's comments interjected into my own thoughts.

"You know son, when you are right, you're right, he's quite the little pisher, that's for sure."

"Thank you Dad, I'm glad you agree. I'm also sure we can count on a few more zingers before he leaves as well, trust me on that."

At that moment, Gracie and Reg took Larry's mention of the food as their cue now. They both excused themselves to see about dinner and getting the table set.

"I think he's darling dear, simply darling...he's also very much reminiscent of a certain two ladies you hold close to your heart, Marc."

"Damn Mom, nothing slips by you, does it?"

"Not much—including the smell of garlic on your father's breath—Malcolm! I dare not ask what, or how much, you ate in my absence earlier?"

"Just a snack Mar, I swear."

"He's telling the truth Mom, I was there—and so were you, it was just that one sandwich as you got home."

Meanwhile, Mom kept up her interrogation of Dad's eating habits.

"Alright, but if you ask me, his weight has been doing a nice little climb up since we've been here. Thank God, I'm booting him out tomorrow."

"Oh, so it's definitely tomorrow then, when were you going to tell me?"

"What's the big deal Marc, I do have to go back sometime, don't I, and tomorrow's just as good a day as any?"

"True, but I'm just a little shocked to hear it like this so matter of fact?"

"Don't be son; I was wondering though, if I could ask a favor?"

"Sure Dad, shoot."

"Did I ever mention to you that Reg expressed in conversation with me, that he had a desire to tour the wine country sometime? You know, I was quite impressed to hear that he had been trained as a Master Sommelier, as well as a wine steward in his youth. So I thought I would extend an invitation to him to join me on this trip, if you can manage without him son?"

"Sure Dad, that would be wonderful, I think I can do without Reg and Grace for a bit."

"Why did you mention Grace—do you think she would want to see the winery too?"

"Maybe Dad, but more than likely, it's just being along with Reg, if you take my meaning?"

"Oh. Yes—I guess you're right—how stupid of me...so may I invite both of them with your blessings?"

"Absolutely Dad. You know, that helps me out here too. You see, if they go, I'll be able to move Scooter into the office instead of Mom—he's coming up tomorrow."

"Yes that's right Mal, he is."

"Alright—it's all settled then, providing of course Reg and Grace would like to come with me."

"Right Dad, when will you ask them?"

"During dinner I suppose."

"Okay."

Just then, Sofia called us from inside to eat. I got the boys out of the pool, but told them to change first. They all headed for the cabana, as I went inside the house to join the folks.

I poured out some of the folks' very nice Chardonnay to go with the fish, along with some sparkling apple cider for the boys' glasses. Gracie and Reg had done a beautiful job setting up the dining room table for our dinner. I was a little taken aback at first by the gesture, but didn't say anything. I was not to be in the dark long about their intentions. As Gracie came in with the platters to place on the buffet, she filled me in.

"Reg, Sofia, and I thought it would be nice to do this for Mal, since he's leaving tomorrow, while young Larry is our guest after all."

"Yes, I agree with you Gracie, this will be most pleasant, so thank you dear."

"My pleasure love."

We sat down now as we waited—and waited on the boys...along with Mom. I knew Mom was upstairs on an important call, but what in hell was taking the boys so long outside, I thought to myself? Apparently, I wasn't alone.

"Marc, this waiting is ridiculous, why don't you go check on them?"

"All right Dad, good idea."

I went out to the cabana, right as the boys were then departing the changing room…all three of them laughing hysterically. My two were in their robes, while Larry was in apparently Dad's or mine.

"Well now, that's better. I was honestly getting a little concerned on what was taking so damn long?"

All I got for my question were more giggles along with three flushed faces; I decided not to take it further. There were just some things a father should not ask with pre-teen boys…I'd been there myself after all. We went inside to join everyone else in the dining room.

Taking in the formal setting now, Larry seemed fired up.

"Dang, I never ever get to eat in the dining room at home, except for the holidays, you guys are so lucky."

"Larry, we don't normally either—Dad what's going on here?"

"Taylor, we thought it would be nice for both Larry as our honored guest tonight, along with Gramps, who's leaving in the morning."

"Oh no, please Daddy, don't let Gramps go, he can't leave…not now."

"Honey, he has to get back to the winery, but he'll be back for your big day on Saturday, so don't worry."

"But we don't want him to go Dad—can't you make him stay?"

"Trevor he must—that's all there is to it."

"Okay I guess—as long as he'll be here for Saturday, I guess it will have to be all right." Trevor then conceded with a scowl still present on his face.

Meanwhile, my Dad was fighting his own faucets now, from his grandsons' outpouring of adulation for him. He managed to respond as he wrapped his arms around both boys to comfort them:

"What's this all about boys—you two know I'll be back soon enough, let's not fuss over it…let's just enjoy ourselves now, okay?"

"Yes Gramps." He swatted them lightly on their bums as they sat down on each side of Larry.

Meanwhile, Larry continued to surprise me. When Mom returned from her call and entered the room, Larry immediately stood up as he pulled out her chair. She sat herself down, whereby he then gave her chair a push, before returning to his seat, as Mom thanked him. I was shocked but had little chance to say anything because apparently, Larry was confused about some things himself.

"Hey, anyone care to fill me in? What's all this stuff about Saturday… that's my only day off? What's happening this Saturday, dang it guys—I'm waiting?" The boys seemed somewhat unsure about sharing Saturday's events with their new friend…so I spoke up.

"Larry, didn't the boys tell you?"

"Tell me what—dang will someone tell me already?"

"Okay Larry—boys it's all right, you can tell him."

"It's like this Larry; we're going to be having a lunch at Verandas for our TMS class. That's why we didn't mention it; we didn't want to upset you, because it's only for our class from TMS, right Dad?"

"Yes that's true, but I don't know Taylor; I don't think it would be a major problem if Larry came along too . After all, he could come as your personal guest and good friend."

"You mean our best friend, Dad!" Trevor blurted out.

Larry was sitting there with his mouth agape now—as he started to choke up from Trevor's comment. It was clear he was shocked by this honor so early into their budding relationship. This kid had to be far more fragile than I had surmised—that much was clear. Nor did he realize just how friend-starved my two sons were, despite knowing they'd only recently moved here.

"So it's alright then Dad?" Taylor now asked.

"Sure sport, I'll speak to Mrs. Geary…but if it's a concern for her, Larry will simply sit with the rest of our family. And of course, we also need to ask his mother for her permission too."

"Great Dad thanks. Okay Larry—you're in."

It would appear that a little of Larry was rubbing off on Taylor now.

"Anyway Larry, we also will be introducing our new Minis Dessert Court this Saturday, it's all part of this crusade we've been working on for Dad's foundation, so we're singing there too. It's all for charity to help build this residential home for people with Cerebral Palsy."

"I wouldn't miss it Trev, it sounds cool, but when were you going to tell me about being singers? Do I have to drag everything out of you guys—jeeze you guys are tough?"

"Well Larry, actually there's still a little more, right Taylor?"

"Yeah Trev—Larry there is more. We're going to be making a CD to help fundraise for Dad's foundation, but while we're doing that, we're also going to be making a demo, to see if we can become professionals."

"Professional what?" Larry asked.

"Singers and musicians Larry—what else?" Taylor responded.

"Oh. You mean you two want to be like some rock and roll band, oh—now that is cool, dudes."

"So what are you two going to name your band?"

"Gee Larry, we don't know yet, Grammy do you?"

"No Taylor, if you don't have a name picked out, I certainly don't have one either. I guess we will ask Scott for some ideas about that tomorrow."

"It's okay Grammy, Trevor and I will try to think of one too."

"Now who is this Scott guy, I'm getting so confused trying to keep up with all these people?" Larry asked.

"Oh, he's just our producer Larry."

"Dang, you've got your own producer—for real?"

"Yes Larry."

"And you guys just let me see you naked and everything? God—dang, thanks guys."

"Your welcome Larry, after all, you are our best mate here you know?"

That shut Larry right up, again; clearly he was having a problem dealing with his new best friend status. I decided to change the subject quickly to calm Larry's emotions down.

"Dad, when are you heading out in the morning?"

"Marc, that all depends on the answer to my next question?"

"Alright Dad, shoot."

"No son, the question is not for you."

"Oh yeah—sorry pops, almost forgot."

"Reg, Grace, how would you two enjoy seeing some of California's wine country and visiting a working winery first-hand? It would be my pleasure to have both of you join me for the trip home for the week. You know, it's not likely that we'll have another opportunity before we sell the property and business."

"Oh my word Malcolm, I personally would be honored, but how about you Grace?"

"Reggie, if you're going, just tell me when to be ready love, but thank you Malcolm, you are too kind for including me."

"You're most welcome Grace, now how does about ten in the morning, work for the two of you?"

"Sure that would be fine Malcolm, but you're positive we won't be in your way?"

"Not at all Reg, we'll have a great time, trust me."

"Love, are you sure you want us going on holiday so soon after arriving, this is all so sudden?"

"Gracie, don't worry about it, go. Have a great time the both of you, we'll miss you, but we'll be just fine."

"All right love, you don't have to tell me twice, I love a crackerjack holiday anytime."

"Good Gracie, but trust me, Dad will put you to work besides."

"I certainly hope he will Marc. And Malcolm, thank you so much again, for your invitation, it is most gracious of both you and Marilyn."

"The pleasure is ours Reg; just remember the old battle-ax will be here with Marc, so at least—we'll eat well."

"Oh, thank you dear, I just love being the battle-ax of the house—who can't boil water—really Malcolm!"

"Mar, can't you ever tell when I'm funning?"

"Certainly dear, but no one said it was funny—it was just—'funning' after all."

"Touché Mom, good comeback, right Gracie?"

"The best Marc, I see where you get it now, I really do."

We served everyone around the table, as we were soon all complimenting Sofia's culinary skills on the meal. She really had done herself proud; everything had been prepared to perfection.

When Sofia brought out the flan for dessert however, our little comedian, feeling suitably recovered no doubt, was the first to speak.

"My God, would you look at that weird jelly-like stuff? Dang, look at how it shakes guys, like what's the deal with this stuff? Seriously, Sofia…what the heck is it?"

"Larry, this jelly stuff, as you call it, is not jelly at all; it's Mexican custard with a caramel sauce. In Mexico, we call it flan, it's a very popular dessert… it's quite delicate. I'm confident you will enjoy it."

"I'm sorry Sofia, but I'm more like a meat and potatoes and ice cream, kind of kid. No offense, but I never once had nothin' Mexican for dessert— except gas. So, are you absolutely sure I'll like it?"

I now jumped in to apologize to Sofia for Larry's innocent comment in my own way.

"Larry, we can't be sure until you try it, but I would say you most likely will love it. Go ahead, give it a taste, but don't worry—Sofia insists it won't give you any gas, I promise."

God this kid was too much…while it proved that no one in our home was immune from a little ethnic humor. Thankfully, Sofia was enjoying all of the attention from our young comedian.

With my coaching, our young bigmouth, took a tentative spoonful, closed his eyes and put it into his mouth. His reaction was immediate and totally Larry though.

"Holy sh…… I mean shoot, this stuff is totally awesome. What's it called again?"

"Flan, Larry, and I am so glad you like it, the recipe has been in me familia for six generations."

"Thank you Sofia, it's wonderful, may I have seconds when I'm finished?"

"Sure Larry, but you'll probably have to fight the twins off; they've never had it either."

"So now it's time for you two to try it, here, now go ahead." Sofia prodded.

Trevor and Taylor both took their first tastes quickly, taking in Larry's reaction to the slimy stuff. Moments later, they were smiling and gobbling it down too.

"Gee Sofe, it seems the flan is the hit of the day, at least for three young gentlemen we all know and love.

At this remark, Larry dropped his head and started choking up some more. Mom noticed it right off so she flashed me her famous look.

That look said it all.

Why did you say that, this kid is obviously having some real emotions tonight already, without your two cents mister?

True, I was only thinking these lovely thoughts, but it was her intent I was sure, yet I knew she was right. I decided yet again, to try to change the subject this time for Larry's and my benefit.

"So boys, what do you all say we take a nice dip in the spa tonight?"

"Okay Daddy, I'm in, how about you Larry?"

"Sure Taylor, I can dig it, how about you Trev?" Larry composed enough to get out.

"Yep, me three Larry." Trevor chided in.

"Okay then, it's all settled then, isn't it?"

"Alright boys, you help the ladies with the clearing of the table, while I turn on the spa. By the time we've all digested our dinner some, the spa should be ready for us."

I got up, as I thanked Sofia for the wonderful meal, before heading over for the pool controls.

I then went upstairs to change into my trucks, yet quickly noticed I had a shadow right behind me.

"Larry, what's up?"

No sooner had I said those three words, than I was wrapped in an embrace by our guest. He was bawling full steam ahead now.

Knowing that I was dealing with a very fragile kid…one who was as shaky as my two had been last October, I thought things out. He was hurting big time, yet I knew I had an obligation to play the parental role in his folks' absence. So I led him into my suite, where I closed off the world outside of that room. I sat on the bed with him, as I gently put my arm around his shoulder so that we had a physical connection while he cried it all out.

I knew I had to choose the words carefully, but say them all the same.

"Now what's this all about buddy?"

"I'm sorry Mr. M, but I haven't seen this many happy people in one room—that really love each other, in a long time…too long. Things have been pretty tough at home…I don't ever want to leave here, I really don't!"

He had said it through a paroxysm as he spoke, so I just hugged him and spoke calmly. I needed to make sure he would remain calm, as I now felt obligated to verify there hadn't been any sort of abuse at home while still feigning the appearance of someone clueless to his situation.

Once I had assuaged that concern, I kept right on talking to prevent giving him the opportunity to figure out what I had just done with all of my indirect questions.

…"Oh, I see how you feel Larry, I do, and we all love one another, just as you've said. Hey but don't worry, as their best buddy, you can come over as much as you like, you just need to ask your Mom. But you know Larry; you also have a pretty big responsibility yourself in all of this now, don't you?"

"I do, what do you mean?"

"Sure you do Larry—most certainly. You see, both of the boys have chosen you to be their best bud—without wasting any time either…but not just one of them, its both of them. Do you think that is always going to be easy, being the best friend in the middle of twin brothers—who always love to fight? Believe me, it won't be. I know how they can be at times—trust me it's a big job—but you know what?"

"What?"

"I know you can handle it Lar—you've got the goods to pull it off."

"I do—are you sure?"

"Sure I'm sure. You see buddy, you like them just the same; you don't pick sides, or favor one of them over the other. And Larry, that's the truest test of a best friend."

"Am I your friend too Mr. M.?"

"Yes, of course you are Larry. I mean, I'm not a friend like Taylor or Trevor per se, but I'm still most definitely your friend, everyone here is, but do you know why that is?"

"Why?"

"Because Larry, first the boys have chosen you. Nobody else but you can be their true best friend here in the states now! That's saying something Larry. It means a whole heck of a lot to the rest of our family too, because they mean so much to us. Secondly, you get all of us laughing and you make us happier just from having you around—you're special bud. That's why Grammy said you were always welcome here, which she really meant. You could say that you've already made yourself a part of our big extended family here, more like a big brother to the twins."

"I have, for real?"

"Yep, I wouldn't kid you buddy, I'm speaking from my heart here."

"So, why do I have to go back home then, I hate it there? No one loves me at home…couldn't you just foster me?

"First Larry, if you think your Mom doesn't love you, you're wrong, she said so today in fact—in this very room for crying out loud!"

"She did…really?"

"Yes Larry, she most certainly did…you ask Gram if you don't believe me."

"Cool."

"Look son, I'm honored Larry that you'd like to live here with us, but I doubt your folks would approve of such an arrangement, besides I'm sure things will calm down some, now that your folks are divorced. You have to realize though that divorce is tough on all of the participants Larry, and in a way, it changes everyone.

"Yeah, well that part I get, believe me, especially with my Dad. I've only seen him twice since he moved out. It's obvious he doesn't care about me anymore, but I don't get it. And Mom's changed too…she never laughs anymore, its sad."

"Look Larry, when your Dad was living at home, did you two ever do anything together, you know—just your Dad and you?"

"Are you kidding Mr. M, sure almost every weekend? That's why I'm so mad; it's like he doesn't care anymore. He just left me to my Mom because she's got custody…so he just dumped me with her! Sure, I get it Mr. Morgan… it was like good riddance for little old Larry as he was walking out of court… then he split—and I haven't since him since…just like that."

"Larry trust me, he hasn't dumped you off at all, believe me on this. Its impossible bud, that your Dad would do all of those things with you consistently, and simply not care any longer. No, your Dad is just trying to come to terms with this divorce is my suspicion. And he hasn't found his 'old' self yet to come see you…that's all it is—I'm sure of it."

"His 'old' self?"

"Yes Larry, sure. My guess is, your Dad is probably having a rough time of it himself, but mostly because he's missing you so much. Yet he's still too upset with your Mom and the divorce, that he just can't quite face her yet… so she stands in the way of him getting to you, don't you see?

"He probably feels he's let you down as well, but he can't yet see your Mom without either getting angry or sad. You know bud, after a divorce, it can be very depressing for the absent spouse, just to walk back into their old house from that point forward.

"So you see Larry, you just have to give him some time to come around is all, so don't worry. I'm sure he will…don't forget I know his character— believe me Larry, he's a good man, son. And I do know something else that will help though."

"What?"

"You should write or email him to tell him how much he means to you, as well as, how much you miss him. Talk about all the things you did together, while telling him you understand why he can't be there now.

"Larry trust me, your Dad will appreciate all of this, but more so, you forgiving him for what's happened since he left the house. This will let him know you're okay, while it will help him to alleviate his guilt some for not being there everyday for you. Once he knows you understand, he'll also feel more empowered to know that it's time to face the music—by talking to your Mom...for you. Your love for him Lar, will allow him to feel strong enough to put up with facing her, at least long enough to pick you up and drop you off."

"Do you think it could really work out like that?"

"Yes Larry of course I do—but I also know something else about you my boy, so here goes..."

..."What Mr. M.?"

"You didn't mean a single word you said to me in the backyard about your Dad earlier—not one word! That was just your anger talking...but you know what, you're entitled to be angry with him...it's only fair."

Larry's faucets were again open big time. Yet through his continuing tears and spasms, he asked the obvious.

"But how did you know I was lying, Mr. M? Yeah, I really do love him; you should see us when we go skiing. We have a dang blast and so much fun together, but that's what I miss Mr. M. I want my Dad back. God I need him so much, and I miss him—it really sucks. That's why I cried at dinner. I see you and your family with the love and fun you all share with one another. I used to have that, but now that I don't, it hurts so much Mr. M., it really hurts.

"You know sir, you'll probably think this is weird, but I just never thought my folks would ever split up—not them, they were so happy together for such a long time.

"The whole thing seemed crazy at first, I mean, they had been really, really happy, I'm positive Mr. M."

"I know Larry; sometime it's hard to figure out, even for us adults. But I really hope this little talk has helped you pal. I'm sure your Dad is feeling the same exact way right now, as you are. You just have to give it some time...it will get better Larry, so don't fret. Besides, you're always welcome to use me as your surrogate dad until then, fair enough?"

Larry said nothing now, he just hugged me. I was actually startled by his strength. I did something by simple instinct, which completed our little 'pact'; I kissed his forehead, as he finished his crying.

Larry regained his composure much faster, as I jokingly suggested we had better get a move on—or all the good seats in the spa would be gone. He laughed as I handed him some tissue for his nose. Once he looked 'all right', we went into the bath suite where I grabbed my trunks and another robe, as we left for the grotto suitably prepared.

We found the whirlpool packed with Morgans of all shapes and sizes, along with some other crashers, namely Gracie and Reg. Mom and Sofia had passed on the group tub-in apparently.

"Well, there you two are—we thought you ran to the market for something?"

"Nope, Larry and I were just getting a little bit better acquainted, that's all. How's the water Dad?"

"Perfecto, mejo."

"Dad, do me a favor, stay away from Scooter when you get back here from the winery. Honestly, Scoot could be dangerous with all of his limericks—I won't be able to stand two of him around, okay Dad?"

"Yes son, but I'm surprised at you all the same. Don't you know I was doing rhymes and limericks, before Scott was even born?"

"No I didn't, but please—let's keep it that way for my sake, will you?"

"Fine, fine."

I went into the changing room, but was soon in the tub myself. With all of us sitting crammed together—inside, it must have been quite a sight.

Actually, sitting there in this bubbling water, reminded me instantly of a clean, but cute joke I remembered from years earlier. I heard it unbelievably one evening in the Enchanted Forest, when I was greeting the real Carol Brady, Florence Henderson. It was Florence's joke, but she told it incredibly well, although I suppose, I had embellished it some over the years of retelling it.

"Say Dad, did I ever tell you the one about the two cannibals who were best of friends?

"No son you haven't, but I have a sneaking suspicion you're going to?"

"You're so right Dadio…I am. You see, they were sitting around their big bubbling caldron kind of like this hot tub, as they were talking. The cannibal cooking the meal, was lovingly tending to the cauldron constantly…clearly Dad, he was giving it his all as the chef.

"It seems that his best friend, the other cannibal, said to him: You know Murphy—that was his name Dad, I swear to God. You know Murphy, he said, I'm a nice guy, just ask anyone. If you ask them, they'll all say the same thing—why that Harry, he likes everyone…he doesn't dislike anyone at all.

"And it's true Murph, I don't bother anyone, and hardly anyone ever seems to bother me. But as my best friend, Murphy, you already know the one exception don't you? That's right Murph—I still can't stand my mother-in-law. Honestly, she disgusts me…I guess she always will. She's so horrible, that I hate her with a passion. Sitting here now—just thinking about her, is making me sick—and on this of all days, no less. So Murphy, what do you suggest I do?"

"Murph now turned to his best friend as serious as he could Dad, as he literally began screaming at Harry at the top of his lungs:

"Damn it Harry—I'd at least eat the frigging noodles! Listen, I've slaved over this stupid meal for six stinking' hours and why you ask? Because you're mother-in-law was no damn, pork-shoulder-picnic, getting in this pot, that's for sure.

"Harry began laughing so hard now Dad, that even Murph began to calm down, seeing his friend so happy with the news of his—now, late, Mother-in-Law's active participation in the evening's special meal. Murphy began laughing too, as he said to his best friend now: Well Harry…all I can say, is happy birthday pal…sorry I ran out of the gift-wrap."

Everyone was pitching a fit big time, the three boys especially, Reg too.

"Oh son, now that was a 'gooder' a real 'gooder'."

"Thanks Dad. I thought you might like it."

"Yeah Daddy, that was too funny."

"Thanks…Taylor."

"Call me Tay, Daddy. Do you like my new stage name Larry gave me all official like?"

"Sweetheart, if it came from Larry, you know it has to be good." As I gave our guest a nice hug of his shoulder, since he had insisted on sitting next to me.

"Thanks Mr. M., but I've got one for you too, if you won't get too mad, that is?"

"Oh my Lord, I'm afraid to ask—okay, what is it?"

"How about Harry Bear?"

My boys, along with everyone else really, were nodding their heads in agreement already. It certainly was a very fair descriptive name for me after all. As I myself had commented often, I wasn't a hairy man at all—I was more like—a balding gorilla!"

"You know what Larry, that name is fine when it's just our little grouping here—you know, the family. But don't call me that outside of our present company, okay?"

"Sure thing Hairy Bear. Hey—I could always call you HB in public… right?"

"Yes that's works—but one more thing young man. What's good for the goose is good for the gander, so you are now known in these here parts as—The Lar-man!"

"Gee, you won't get an argument out of me—I like that name, really HB, but so you know, I gave Trevor a stage name too, he's now Tre."

"Good, it's all settled then." I said.

"Grace, while you and Reg are away, might I impose on using one of your bedrooms for someone, although I'm not sure who yet. Either Scott or Mom, obviously?"

"That would be fine, right Reggie?"

"Of course, I'll change the linens in the morning before we leave."

"Thanks Reg, I appreciate that."

"It will be my pleasure Marc, so not another word."

"Boys, I do believe we should be getting along, so that we have the Larman home by nine as promised?"

"Okay Dad, I'm getting water logged anyway."

"Sorry to hear that T-1, will I need to wring you out?"

"No Dad, but I'm starting to feel all wrinkled."

"I know that feeling too bro, look at my fingers?"

"Yeah Taylor, you're starting to look like a prune."

"Thanks Daddy—but so are you."

"I guess I am at that."

We all started to get out, as the boys offered to speed things up by changing into their robes together—again. I had to laugh at their reference to 'speeding' things up. True to their promise though, they were out in a flash this time.

I sent the boys up to my bath suite for a fast shower to rid them of chlorine, Larry insisted on joining them. I went into my closet to put on some slacks along with a shirt for the drive to Larry's house in Summerlin. When I was done, I left the bath suite as I waited for the boys to finish. I finally heard the water die off as the steam pump ceased.

I grabbed the keys to the Navigator from Dad, as I began waiting what seemed an eternity for the boys to come downstairs. Finally, they showed up. Larry gave all the adults hugs and thanked each of us for having him. I thought that showed real good parenting, given his present circumstances. Minutes later, we were on our way to the Lar-man's house.

Larry gave me excellent directions in between clowning with the twins, so we were soon at his very nice home in the Tournament Hills subdivision of Summerlin. Carol buzzed us in, and met us on their expansive driveway. Homes in this community were right on par with Spanish Trail.

"So did he behave for you Marc?" Larry was looking at me with pleading eyes, which rather surprised me honestly. After all, he had been an entertaining guest, if not a perfect gentleman.

"Carol, you can be real proud of him, he's a fine young man."

"Thank you Marc, I do try, but it isn't easy sometimes."

"Yes, I can relate to that."

I was about to leave, when Larry decided he needed to give me a hug, but as he did so, I think that Carol was a little surprised at his obvious strong attachment to me already.

"My Marc, you must be the pied piper, I haven't seen him do that since Rob left."

"Carol, like I said, you have a wonderful young man here, so the feelings are definitely mutual, so please let's have him over again real soon, fair enough?"

"Thanks Marc, I can see you really mean that, so if you don't mind, I may call you tomorrow, I'd like your opinion on a business investment I'm considering?"

"Sure Carol, here's my card. That's my private direct number; it gets you straight to me."

"Thanks Marc, and good night boys, it was a pleasure meeting you—good luck with your crusade."

"Good night Mrs. Levison and thanks." The boys responded to Carol.

We left the Levison home, but stopped for gas before heading back for the 'Trail'. By the time we were in the garage, both of my guys were down for the count. I called into the house on the cell, where my Dad agreed to come out to assist me. We got the boys into bed, along with into their PJ's…they never even moved once, talk about instant slumber.

I went into the theatre where I found Mom and Sofia watching the credits to their movie.

"Hey there dear, did you get our young Mr. Gleason home to Brooklyn okay?"

It always amazed me, how my Mother so adeptly referred to certain people we knew by their 'TV' counterparts in personality—this was yet another example. Of course, she was right 'on' the mark with Larry, like she had been with Scooter as Eddie Haskell from Leave It To Beaver.

"Yes Mom, but I have to tell you, he's one very sweet, yet troubled kid, right now."

"Tell me something I don't know Marc…but did you believe the table manners that came out of that kid?

"Amazing Mom. You know, the boys have been trained in all of that, yet it seemed far more shocking to see it in Larry for some reason."

"Yes it did, by the way, how long were you together with him?"

"Jesus, you really don't miss a thing, do you?"

"No I don't, I saw him chase you up the stairs. And all the better for our own two young musicians, don't you agree?"

"Yep, that's for sure. And to answer your question, I think around a half hour, but who's counting?"

"Try like around fifty minutes Marc."

"So why are you asking me Mom, if you already knew the answer?"

"I don't know, what's it matter, obviously the boy is hurting. I know there had to have been a fair amount of crying."

"I suppose there was, he did bawl quite a bit, but I just comforted him with a logical explanation, as he is very hurt over his folks splitting up. His dad is no longer around and it's obvious that he is far closer to him, than his mom.

"He's such a sweet little guy—you can't help but love him, I just hate to see him have to go through this, so I did what I could for him."

"What did that entail?"

"I don't know really. I just explained to him how it must be for his dad...I suggested that things would work out in time, hopefully, but until they did, I promised he could count on me to be his surrogate dad."

"My word, as always, you never fail to make me proud of you Markie."

"Thanks mom, but you know, I really understand why the boys embraced him so fast now, as their best friend.

"In my opinion Mom, there's just something special about him—he somehow invades you and worms his way into your heart...with his humor alone, he's an astonishing child Ma."

"Yes he is Marc, but hell, aren't my grandsons a good judge of character besides? But what a 'pisk' that kid has."

"Yep; he does have quite the mouth, doesn't he?"

"Yes Markie, but he's really adorable too."

"Listen Mom, how would you feel about being in Reg's room for the week? I'm going to put Scooter in Grace's guesthouse, so the boys can have their own room back?"

"That's fine son, besides I've never had the pleasure of staying in a real English butler's room before. Damn, even though the butler will be gone—mind you."

"Hey now, do I need to warn Grace and Dad about you?"

"No dear-you don't. Reg is a handsome man, but if it's all the same to you, let me be honest—I'll just stick with the old windbag a little longer, thank you."

"Glad to hear that Mom, say where did the old wind bag go anyways?

"Gee, he was packing his suitcase when you called him at the truck...I'd suggest you check the boys' room."

"Alright Mom, I will."

I went into the boys' room, where I found Pop packing his suitcase in his boxers now—in all his glory.

"Hey, what do you say there Captain?"

"Nothing really Dad, except I filled the Nav up for you, it was a quarter tank low. By the way, did I mention I used to run at least mid-grade in her?"

"No, I don't believe you did, but I use hi-test."

"Boy, you really do love that truck, don't you Dad?"

"Son, as much as any man, can love a mechanical device, I do.

"Dad, I'll leave you to your packing, have a safe trip."

"Sure thing Captain, I read you loud and clear."

"Oh, I almost forgot, you all need to be at the Baketown airport, Friday by two, for the flight back, alright?"

"Two p.m. You got it, anything else?"

"Nope, that's it. But listen; can I give you a few hundred to take Grace and Reg out to a nice dinner or two?"

"Absolutely not son—they'll eat hash and beans like the rest of us."

"Funny Dad."

"Don't fret Marc; I've got the entire itinerary worked out already. I called in a few favors, so they're getting a private wine cellar tour every night, including all the wining and dining two person can handle—fair enough?"

"Wow…thanks Dad, but are you sure I can't chip in a little?"

"No, don't insult me son, this is my treat,—it's my pleasure, not yours."

"Okay Dad, thanks."

"Don't mention it."

"Hey, I'll see you before I leave for the office, okay?"

"Sure thing Captain, get some sleep."

"Night Dad, I love you."

"Night kiddo…right back at you."

We hugged deeply, before I then left to go to my room. I undressed quickly; just as I threw myself into bed with my bunkmates…I quickly fell asleep.

I awoke at four fourteen by the clock, to a truly startling experience. At first, I thought the boys were simply awake while having a conversation. Then I realized how wrong I was…they were not awake at all.

"Yeah, okay, I'll remember…okay, love you. Yeah, of course good night, I miss you." Mumbled somewhat out of Trevor.

"All right, I will…you too. Sure, I understand." Followed now out of Taylor.

I had no idea what I had just experienced, was it more of their twin communication skills with one another? Whatever it was—had ended now, yet leaving me to ponder what it was all about as I drifted back into sleep myself.

I awoke again to more talking, this time more animated, as I noticed that the clock was at two minutes of seven. The boys were definitely awake now.

"I can't believe it bro, can you?"

"Sure I can Trev, it wasn't the first time for me, but I do understand you getting your head around it."

"Good morning boys…care to share?"

"Dad, Mummy came to see us."

Oh, so that explains it, I thought to myself.

"Yeah Daddy, I must say, it was really amazing, but she kind of looked different too, though."

"Son, would you say that it looked like she had a halo of light around her?"

"Yeah, that's it Dad, but there was something else too—wasn't there Tay?"

"You're right Trev, but I can't remember what. Look, who cares, it's her, and she's awesome. She's watching us Dad…Mummy says that were becoming 'men'; ain't that great Dad, but she knew all about Larry and Scott too, it was so awesome…blimey."

"That's cool boys; it sounds like she's really following you guys with everything that's happening too."

"Yeah she is, but how did you know that Dad?"

"Because you guys were talking last night with her so loudly—you woke me up, right as you were ending it…but I heard enough."

"Oh wow, so you must have heard my confession then, right Dad?"

"Ah, no son I didn't. And since you are in a pickle here, I'll pretend I didn't hear that, if you prefer Trevor?"

"Thanks Dad, but no, I'm all right with it. You see, she knew I had been sneaking off a lot and crying from missing her so much…that's why she came. So now I feel much better about all of it. Especially knowing, she could hear me crying for her."

"I'm sorry Trev, I didn't know you were so sad, forgive me".

"Forgive you for what? For loving Taylor and I like you do? I don't think so Dad, you know, you're a pretty incredible Father…I love you Dad."

In the following moment with all three of us still in bed, I had Trevor in my embrace, soon thereafter followed by T-Man too. And we had a wonderful little cry, just the three of us.

Chapter 11

▼

The Crusade Begins

The following weeks saw the boys and I getting into somewhat of a normal familial pattern of activities. Each weekday there was regular school, with Hebrew as well, on Tuesday and Thursday afternoons. Then there was dinner, homework—with lots of rehearsing afterwards, so you get the drill. And I had my own bed back for a week, so I was happy.

I had a pretty 'free' week set up by Robbie, so that I could help with all of the planning and arrangements, although I specifically left the restaurant details to Christine alone, as she was the true pro at that. In short, my week was going to be exciting with the big upcoming event, but mostly quiet, otherwise.

As it turns out though, there were three exceptions to my quiet week. The first of these began with a call from Carol Levison, Monday morning as I was downing my fourth cup of coffee at around nine forty.

"Hello, Marc here, who's this?"

"Marc, its Carol—Levison."

"Good Morning Carol, what a nice way to start my day off."

"That's sweet Marc, but I need to speak to you, have I caught you at a good time?"

"Sure, so what's on your mind?"

"Larry of course Marc, it doesn't take a genius to figure out that he worships you. All morning, you and the boys, and your entire family really— were all he talked about."

"Great, I'm most flattered Carol, we all love Larry...I mean that sincerely."

"Thanks Marc, but yes, that's why I've got to speak with you personally. You see, I have a real dilemma concerning Larry, that I need some honest, straightforward, advice. Call me crazy, but I can't think of anyone, whom I would trust more now with my problem—than you Marc."

"Thank you Carol—I'm honored. Now what seems to be the matter?"

"Marc, my ex-husband Rob, hasn't been able to see Larry but twice since he left. You see, Rob has suffered a complete breakdown, so he's naturally hospitalized. Candidly, I don't know how to go about telling Larry. He believes his father has stayed away because of the divorce. If I told him the truth, I believe he'll suffer more because he can't visit him, which he won't understand why—as the kid worships his father. And being completely honest with you Marc, I will tell you that Rob has always been an exceptional father to our son, so Larry is really suffering…they're super close. What would you do in my situation Marc?"

"Alright Carol, let me be frank, but do you want the truth, or just what you can handle—which is it?"

"Marc, you're not catching me in the best light, but I need to hear the truth, please don't sugarcoat this."

"Fine, I won't, but first let me ask you, how is Rob doing, as that should be one of our first concerns?

"Better Marc and thank you for asking, even though I shouldn't care, I still do—of course."

"Carol, I understand your dilemma completely—but so will Larry! Jesus Carol, give the boy some credit, he's a super sharp kid—rest assured…he can handle this. He will actually have an easier time dealing with Rob being sick, than simply ignoring him, believe me.

"Sit down with him calmly. Explain the real reasons why he hasn't seen Rob. Just make sure first, that you assure him emphatically, that his father is getting better. Explain why he can't have visitors just yet, but not to worry, because he won't be going anywhere until he's recovered, or more back to himself.

"Once Rob is allowed visitors though, get Larry there first thing—and often, before anyone else in his family. In the meantime, encourage him to write to Rob, this will help Larry vent his pain and loss, while it will help in Rob's recovery too, down the road. When his father is up to reading, the outpouring of love from Larry in those letters will be a great subliminal shot of medicine adding further incentive to Rob.

"Make sure you tell Larry often, how much both you and his father love him, he's fragile now Carol. Frankly kiddo, he's told me that there's no love at his house anymore, so he'd prefer not to be there."

"Oh God, no!"

I waited for Carol to compose before I continued; I had vowed to be honest, even if it was brutal, but I couldn't bring myself to say that 'all-telling' word—foster. Moments later, I continued.

"Carol talk to him about Rob in the present tense, rather than the past, despite the divorce. But for heaven's sake, decide right now that you will not malign Rob again within earshot of that boy, be careful everywhere, kids are famous for listening in.

"I know it will be hard for you, but messing this up could be very damaging to Larry. And more so, disastrous to your relationship with him in the long run later on as adults.

"Now Carol, you had better take a deep breath here, because this is all about to get much worse.

I heard Carol take a breath through the phone.

"Okay kiddo, here goes nothing. Despite how unfair this is to anyone in your position Carol, you are now forced to absolve Rob, at least temporarily, through this crisis—for Larry's sake. You have to remember, that his father is sick and therefore defenseless…so Larry will likely champion Rob's cause, if you provide any negative feedback. Larry will rightly seek—to protect his father—from you!

"Trust me Carol, if you don't handle this compassionately today, there will come a reckoning between you two later on. Kids always hold their parents accountable to take the high road during times of crisis—you're at that fork right now, kiddo!

"I realize you are all in a family crisis right now, but this is truly critical Carol. Don't use the divorce as a motivation to lash out at Rob; because you do so at your own folly while he's sick like this. Carol, believe me, every action that you take forward of telling him of his father's situation, will be watched and judged.

"Look at my circumstances for a moment, because there is a lesson to be learned there, believe me. My boys only met me last October, yet immediately they expressed their undying love and respect for me unconditionally. Only by carrying no guilt or baggage was Miranda able to manage such a Herculean effort throughout an eleven-year separation. So my advice to you is—lose any baggage now, that you may be carrying against Rob, until he's well at least!

"Carol, as you can see, I don't mince words when it comes to those I love or care for."

"Yes Marc, believe me I see that, but I'm a big girl—I'll take it any day, to help my baby."

"Good Carol, because that's the exact attitude you need now. And your little guy, from our one evening together, already owns a piece of my heart, what more can I say Carol. So I feel I have a compelling and vested interest in helping you get through this, don't I?

"I know that this is none of my business, so yes, I'm being candid, blunt, and perhaps a bit unsympathetic to your feelings. As such I apologize, but damn it, I only care about one important someone at this moment, so are you following me on this?"

"Yes Marc of course, I've heard every word—I'm taking notes in shorthand no less. I truly appreciate your candor, I have been hard on Rob, some of which he deserves, and some things—that I already feel guilty for.

"The thing is Marc, I have been in a crisis—we all have…for the last thirty months. You see, everything you've observed about Larry and I, is a summation of the entire trauma we've experienced throughout this two and a half year mess. Look I don't want to bother you with my dirty linen, but the whole circumstances leading up to our divorce was unusual to put it mildly.

"Honestly Marc, Rob, and I had an exceptional marriage for nearly fourteen years—truly a wonderful, loving, and caring relationship…honestly. Yet he suddenly changed a little more than thirty months ago—it was like he had a completely different personality, I don't know. He became convinced my constant flirting was something ulterior—when it never was, or mattered before to him. The relationship was never the same again—it eventually imploded over his specific distrust of me—he became almost paranoid…those are the basic, honest, facts."

"You know Carol, if I may be so bold, have you spoken to Rob's doctors at all, wherever he's staying?"

"I've tried Marc, but I'm in legal limbo with them at the present time. I'm still Rob's partner at the bank while we continue to structure the buy-out that began before his absence, so I've seen to it that the bank's paying for his treatment. Yet the clinic will only talk to me about finances and nothing more, since we're divorced—why do you ask?"

"That's a shame; you've got to figure out a solution to that, even if you do it indirectly, so who committed him?"

"His brother."

"How was your relationship with his brother before the divorce?"

"It was excellent, but doubtful now, however his wife Trish and I are still close, but Rob's brother is naturally angry. If not for Trish, I wouldn't know anything about Rob's circumstances."

"Carol, have you given any thought to the possibility that Rob's breakdown has its roots in another issue—perhaps an earlier undiagnosed issue? I mean hell; I'm not a shrink, but even I recognize delusional behavior from what little you've told me. If your marriage was as strong as you say it was for that many prior years, aren't you just the slightest bit interested in that possibility?"

"Well yes Marc, of course I am. But honestly, I'm also so hurt and devastated by everything the man said and did, I'm not sure that I can look at any of it impartially anymore…does that make sense?"

"You know Carol, I can accept that—that's fair and understandable, just don't forget we had this conversation."

"Alright Marc, I'll keep it in mind completely, but thanks for all of your advise too, really, everything. You know Marc, you're quite painless to talk to—I so appreciate that. Can't you just make this all easy, by falling madly in love with me so everything will work out, one way or the other?"

"I wish life were that easy kiddo, but it isn't, at least not for me, but I'm honored Carol, so thank you as well."

"You are welcome Marc—anytime.

"And Marc, thank you again for being so candid with your help with Larry."

"It's just my way Carol, but I should tell you something else, before we end this call. I more or less promised Larry I would be there for him, kind of as his surrogate dad. I realize I don't have that right, but given his emotional state last night, on top of what I know now, I couldn't help myself then, so I don't feel the need to defend my decision further. I want you to know right now, when I make a promise, I do keep it.

"Please call anytime you need someone to keep him company, or he's bored whatever. And don't be surprised if I call you as well to pick him up from time to time?"

"My Marc, I had absolutely no idea, but yes of course I will, and thank you for that extra kindness. That reminds me, Larry mentioned something about Saturday?"

"Yes that's right, hell, I almost forgot, Christ—where's my head? We'd like Larry to join us at our Summerlin restaurant; you know where it's located, right?"

"You must be joking Marc, of course I do, everyone in Summerlin certainly does…what are you thinking?"

"What do I know? Listen, have Larry bring his trunks and clothes for Sunday school—and a warm jacket. We'll have him sleep over, it's part of my surprise for them, and you can pick him up Sunday evening. That will give you Saturday night to rejoin the single party scene without any complications, fair enough?"

"Oh. As Carol sighed deeply.

"Marcus Morgan, I would marry you in a minute if you asked me—you are a prince."

"Fine, Carol—but don't ever kiss me, because I turn into a frog." I finally had her laughing.

"How can I ever repay your kindness Marc?"

"You mean, besides selling me your T-Bird someday?"

"Marc, I'm surprised at you, Pinkie is my second child…can't you see that? Rob bought her as a wedding present for me; so I could never do that to him, or consider parting with her besides that. And you know, what else do I have to entice any man out there, without her; I'm damaged goods after all? So I guess that's the one way for you to get your hands on her?"

"Cute Carol, but stop that BS this moment about having nothing to offer a man—Jesus, you're drop dead gorgeous, with legs that run from LV to Laughlin, and you've got a brain. Trust me; you don't need any car to meet a nice guy."

"Marc, that was too sweet—thanks."

"Don't mention it, but have my surrogate son at the restaurant at twelve straight up, alright? Oh listen, I'll need a note from you that states he has your permission to cross state lines with me along with a consent to treat paragraph as well."

"What on earth are you talking about, crossing state lines—you do plan on returning him, don't you?"

Carol wasn't sure I was serious I guess, as I could hear genuine concern in her voice as well.

"Yes Carol, I promise to return him, though it's very tempting, believe me. Actually, we'll be eating in California on Saturday night, that's all. Heaven forbid, should there be any problems, I want that for his protection and mine.

"Lastly, we'll be flying there; so I need to know you don't have a problem with that?"

"Flying? Just where in California are you going for dinner, Marc?"

"Toonland, Carol—that's their surprise, so keep your mouth shut about it. I reserved a table at 'the Door at Forty Four' to celebrate their success, no matter how it turns out on Saturday. What they're doing with this crusade of theirs deserves something big—this will definitely be special to them. You know, you're welcome to join us too?"

"Thank you Marc, that is most kind of you to include me, but somehow, I think I should stay away for—Larry's benefit…what do you think?"

"I think you're one smart cookie, that's what I think Carol."

"Good, then we're agreed. Listen; just give me the bill for the airfare so that I can reimburse you, all right?"

"That won't be necessary Carol."

"Marc, now really, I must insist. You've already been so kind to both of us; I will not have you paying his way."

"Look Carol, so you know, it won't be necessary because we're flying there—on one of my planes."

"Oh…one of your planes, just how many—do you have Marc?"

"Four, and with plenty of extra seats on this particular flight, I'm putting Larry's name on one of the extras—any objections?"

"No—only are you sure you'll turn into a frog if I kiss you?"

"You know Carol; I wondered where Larry got his brilliant sense of humor…I'm not wondering any longer, believe me".

"That's sweet and thanks. Alright Marc, he'll be there, but thank you as well for my evening out, in addition to all of your advice really, I'll follow it all to the letter."

"Great. You know, it will be the twins' and my pleasure to have him, the whole family's actually."

"Clearly Marc, with the way he's being treated by you, I'd like to live vicariously through him myself! But I'll remember to be mums on Toonland too, it will do my heart good to know how happy that will make him, he lives for the stupid place."

"Don't we all, Carol?"

"Yes, I suppose you're right. See you later Marc, and thank you so much again for everything."

"You're most welcome, but I will expect a full report Sunday on your Saturday night coming out—again, party."

"That's only fair Marc, bye."

"Bye kiddo."

That was all the drama I had for the remainder of the day, until Robbie advised me that Eric insisted on a half hour meeting the following morning, first thing.

Bright and early Tuesday, with only three cups of 'preparation'—Eric proceeded to walk into my office as he surprised me with his 'opening salutation', that much was certain.

"Well Marc, here's my draft complaint against CCC."

"Your complaint? Damn Eric what's happened, I thought we had reached a consensus with CCC? I didn't realize you were going to recommend litigation this early?"

"Honestly Marc, I'm just going on a fishin' expedition with this—as the bait."

"Fishing, hah? Are you shooting for a big mouth bass to mount on your wall, or something else Eric?"

"No, but I'm hoping to beach a barracuda—permanently."

"Hum, I see.

"Alright Eric, spill it, what's your strategy to hook this fish of yours?"

"Simple Marc, as you know, it's a common practice to send a courtesy notice to the opposing party in any pending lawsuit. Exposing the intended complaint often motivates the opposing party to attempt some sort of an immediate settlement."

"Certainly Eric…great, so now we know the lure you're using, what's your intended trophy—beyond our little shrimp's apology?"

"Well naturally boss, I would like Condescension's termination in my net while I mount her head over my fireplace!"

"Wonderful, but for myself, I want something more, I want her ego violently crushed in a matter of speaking, by something huge—like maybe that humongous Ford SUV—what's it called again—isn't it the Sturgeon?"

"I believe that's—an Excursion boss."

"Whatever Eric…work with me here—will you? Listen, I want that red herring along with all of her feeder fish colleagues at CCC to pay dearly for this. Still, let it be a fraction of what I could take from them if we prevailed in court. They need to know they're vulnerable right now, just like those other feeder fish hanging around too long in the tropical fish department at Wal-Mart.

"They should have to buy air time on every network they compete with, to run their apology to the boys—plus all of the newspapers too. Then after the bitch apologizes Eric, I want her condescending ass—fired, case closed! Those are my terms Eric…but read my lips—they're non-negotiable. The little minnow fries! I want her reduced down to a plate of cerviche. Let's see…first I'll filet her, then I may sauté her, lastly I'll flambé…

…"All right Marc, I get your point".

"Look Eric, it's this, or your complaint moves forward for ten million dollars…the Barracuda can rest in the balance if they're that suicidal. You know, they can limit out now, by saving themselves with her head—or flounder by supporting her. Either way in the long run, it will be a—fluke, if she survives this!"

"My word Marc, you are quite the poet this morning…aren't you? Jesus, thank the Lord I went with the fishing theme Marc…at first, I had planned on using an 'Enema' theme…that wouldn't have been pretty, I'm afraid." As Eric busted up now—so did I.

"No, you're right of course. Look, I'm a sour, old octo—puss, with this barracuda in my tentacles, along with a side order of retribution flowing from my red—snapping lips Eric."

"Alright Marc, I think you've made your point—crystal clear—so don't overkill…allow me.

"You know Marc, by the time you're finished, she'll cut like a butterfish, holy mackerel. Seriously boss, you know you shouldn't cry over spilt milk—fish, but all the same, perhaps she should consider a career as a monk—fish?

"And with her out of work, who's going to take care of her tadpoles; Marlin and Oscar?"

"All right Eric, now I'd say that you've made your frigging point too, for crying out loud. You're like a pregnant sturgeon at this point, who's laying nothing—but eggs!"

"Honestly boss, I wouldn't know…but he who lives in a glass—fishbowl, shouldn't throw the first stone—crab!"

"Have you had enough yet Eric?"

"My God Marc, you're in such a crappie mood today, damn it, stop your carping!

"Eric!"

"Alright, I'm going. Boy someone didn't get their morning dose of Cod Liver Oil, did he?

"Go already!"

"You know boss, are you alright? Honestly, you're as white—fish, as a ghost?"

"The door Eric—close the damn door on your way out."

All of this, made me realize you never want to do anything—fishy with any lawyer—especially those that you employ. They'll swallow you whole like a minnow, filet your sole, while you end up getting kicked in the butt… halibut, that is!

Thank God that's over; it all seemed just a little bit too smelly.

Wednesday was a better day, as it was profitable too. Early that morning, I received a fax from my new 'best' friend—Rod Martin. It was a letter of intent to purchase the Jolson Duesenburg for $1.8 mil. I could not believe how easy that had been, but just the same, I countered him on principle.

We ended up cutting the deal at $1,875,000. With that number, sans any commission costs, I broke my old record, so I was truly beside myself—but I did cry just a little when the transport company loaded her up to move her across town the following day.

Thursday, brought the last of the three exceptions to my quiet workweek. I was to meet Vic Tremmers for lunch. In keeping with Miranda's comments to me on the subject of Vic, along with my own chewing of the cud, so-as-to-speak, I was actually at least looking forward to the reunion now.

As I've said, Vic was a very likeable guy. Yet now that I knew a little bit more of his ethereal motives, I was certainly impressed of his goals—even if Vic himself didn't know anything about it consciously. Now, if he could only work a little bit on his social skills, I could relax a little.

As Robbie escorted Vic into my office, I stood up to greet my old friend.

I noticed that clearly Robbie was already one of Vic's new fans; even if he'd never admit it to me...it was that obvious. I extended my arm as my old 'pal' from my Toonland days walked up, shock my hand, before grabbing a chair. He was still tall and lanky, wiry yet strong, but most of all—he looked—old!

His first words were classic 'Vic' though:

"Well brush my teeth, shit Marko, what's wrong with you boy...you're wasting away...where'd you go?"

"I went on a diet Vic, I dropped over fifty pounds years ago, but it's nice to see you looking so well yourself."

"Me...looking well? Are you sure we're both lookin' at the same— skinny—scrawny—shit-kicking—sickly-lookin' body? Shit, if I didn't load my drawers with twenty pounds of buckshot—a good wind would blow me right over, I swear."

"Nonsense Vic, you look great, so how have you been, it's been nearly fifteen years?"

Vic looked at me now, as if I was patronizing him more so, than just being polite. And in keeping with his past inability to socialize comfortably within normal situations like these, he chose to overreact instead. This too, was classic 'Vic'!

"Look Marko, let's slice through this horse shit to get straight to the innards, okay? We both know why I'm here...I'm in between, while you're sitting flush, so it don't take no genius to figure this situation out. The question is, can I call in my favor...or not?"

I knew that trying to explain things to him, like one would speak to anyone else, was out of the question...this was after all...Vic! I had to put my 'Vic hat' on before going further, thereby risking,—pissing him off some more.

Drawing on my memories, I realized my mistake now. I had forgotten to talk to him in 'Vicspeak'. This was a critical error on my part, so I quickly rebooted my internal computer—I chose my words carefully before continuing.

"Damn yes Vic; you can call in the favor...I owe you." With those magic words, I had a different Vic appearing right in front of me now, but we were both much happier for it, too.

"Sh.........it, you don't owe me nothin'."

"Sure I do Vic, but it's going to be my pleasure to pay you back, old friend."

"Well Marko, what have you got in mind?"

"You were right in your email Vic; I need you for my ponies. Thank God you saw them at the airport and thought to hook up with me. Really we're doing each other a major favor here, believe me Vic…I'm going to be needing a Stable Master for fifty head, and a personal trainer for my eight Belgians."

"Really? Great Marko—it will be my pleasure to help you with all of it, but I'm afraid I can't take less than $1,200 a week. What are your plans, I saw that the manifest called for Logandale as the final destination for the horses… so what's the deal with that, have you got a spread out there?"

"Temporary housing only Vic, that's the deal with Logandale. Until I get my stables built here in Las Vegas, they'll need to stay put—along with you with them, so are you okay with relocating for the time being?"

"Shit, sure I am, I got no bones buried here, holding me to Vegas—of all places."

"Great, so when can I count on you getting your butt up there?"

"Gee, how 'bout we say tomorrow, I'll catch the morning bus up there?"

"That's perfect Vic, but how would you feel if I fly you up there on my plane so I can introduce you to Lex at his ranch and show you around some?"

"Fine friend, that works for me—what time you want to leave?"

"I don't know, let's talk about it over lunch, how's that sound?"

"Perfect Marko. Listen, I also brought some pictures of my work with all of the T.A.R.D.S. that I told you about, riding with my horses to show ya."

"So Vic, what's that stand for again? You know, some folks might misunderstand that one."

"I know, that's why I love it, I can teach people a whole lot about these good T.A.R.D.S. using that word and then drawing out their fire against me…see?"

"Yes I do Vic, but what's it mean again?"

"Shit, sorry—almost forgot. T.A.R.D.S. stands for Tireless-Always Ready-Devoted-Staffers. Remember Marko, these kids bust their behinds taking care of these ponies right along side me, like."

"Got it, Vic. It's fine. T.A.R.D.S. it is then."

"Told you so."

"Yes you did."

Vic and I left for lunch, both of us understanding the other—perfectly now!

Over lunch, Vic showed me all of his photos which I must say, were very impressive. More so, they illustrated something far more important. Vic was still 'Aces' working with the physically and mentally challenged. Of that, these photos clearly showed how happy these special riders were for the experience… especially with him, one on one. As I sat there listening to all of Vic's stories about all of these riders, I was convinced this was the right thing to do for all parties concerned, especially his T.A.R.D.S. I was going to have to get used to that acronymic name…because damn—it was pushing it. However, I felt good with hiring him on, for the first time now.

Yet I was also confident that the honeymoon stage would only last so long for Vic and me, for when it came to Tremmers…he could be a true ball buster too.

Meanwhile, Scooter had been up all week as he and Mom were a beehive of activity themselves. Poor Scooter, he nearly about choked when I told him I'd hired Vic for my horses. I swear he never looked at me the same—all night.

All week, Scoot had been rehearsing the boys from after homework to up to their bedtime. They were sounding truly incredible with their performance material, so much so, we took it for granted already. Mom also confirmed they would include one of their demo cuts at Saturday's performance as a possible encore, Unchained Melody. In between all of this, Scooter had been previewing homes with Natalie, while burning up his cell phone back home to Beth with his efforts.

The week felt like it flew by very quickly. The house definitely seemed quieter with the absence of Dad, Grace, and Reg. After tucking Vic into Logandale in the morning though, I flew to Baketown to pick the three of them up myself. Both Grace and Reg were still carrying on to me on how much they had enjoyed themselves, as we walked into the house. According to the boys, they had already finished their dress rehearsal with Scoot, so he left for an evening out at a casino. The poor guy was still chasing a C-note he'd lost on his first day.

The twins then informed me that they had been trained earlier in the day on handling the Minis as promised by the Netherys.

At dinner, my boys ate for a full RAF squadron, before leaving me to watch some TV. Sometime later, I heard them head back into their studio. At around nine thirty, they were still going at it as I joined them there.

"How'd we sound Dad?"

"Trev, you guys were so good, I can't even begin to tell you, but I think I'm getting spoiled."

"Thanks Daddy, I know you mean that."

"I most certainly do T-man. I just can't get over your little transformation. You know, with those big voices you're blessed with, you guys are awesome rockers, while your ballads sound wonderful too."

"Gee, thanks Dad."

"So, are you two ready for tomorrow?"

"Yes sir." I heard sung to me in beautiful two-part harmony now."

"Wow!" Well I'd say you guys are ready after that little taste, aren't you?"

"You bet we are Daddy—but can we ask you one little favor for tomorrow?"

"Of course T-man, anything."

"Would you remember to call me Tay, when you talk to all the guests?"

"Sure thing son, Tay it is."

"And me Tre—Dad?"

"Whoa, I get it now—Tre and Tay, hey that does sound great as your stage name guys."

"Honestly Dad, actually we're thinking of going with: Tay 'n' Tre… The Morgans. It sounds best to us this way, what do you think…we went alphabetically with our names?"

"Sounds fine to me guys, really, interesting name in the way it flows, I really like it."

"Cool, it was Larry's idea—he's been helping us with a lot of things."

Naturally, but that's good of him to help you—remember to thank him. Look, you guys just knock one out of the ballpark tomorrow. I know you'll make Mummy proud of you all the way up there in heaven, as you'll do for me too, of course."

"We will Dad, we'll do our best. Scott has been real good at helping us Dad, so thank you for asking him here."

"Yeah Daddy, that goes for me too—Scott's the best."

"I'm glad to hear you say that guys, I know it will please him to hear it coming from you two personally. Please speak to him at some point tomorrow boys, so he'll know how you feel—okay?"

"Sure Dad, we were going to anyway, you didn't have to tell us. We did have the best Mum and Dad in the world teaching us—didn't you know?"

"Thank you Trevor, I love the both of you more than anything in this world, but tomorrow, I'll be the proudest Dad in that audience… while we already know how Mummy will feel about it, don't we?"

"Yes Dad, we do know." T-1 added.

"Boys, I think you two ought to think about hitting the hay, what do you think? Tomorrow is a big day…heck, it might just turn out to be your biggest! I'm sure you don't want to be yawning while you sing, do you?"

"Okay Daddy, but can all three of us sing a song tonight for Mummy and Grandfather and Grandmother first?"

"Taylor, I think that would be an absolutely stellar idea—let's do it!"

"Great Dad."

"Alright boys, what are we going to sing?"

We decided quickly on our selection. So as the boys were changing into their PJ's, the three of us started singing Miranda's song in harmony. Doing it Acapella, made it sound that much nicer and tender. After that, we did Cole Porter's, Night and Day together as well, which I personally loved how we sounded as a trio. Our harmony was kind of eerie-sounding somewhat, I wasn't sure just how the boys did that, but it was incredible.

I hugged the guys good night, then got them situated, before leaving the room. I had been thrilled to have my own bed back during the week, but a big part of me missed them too, not being there. Moreover, I was not the least bit upset, having to bunk with them again now that everyone was back at home.

Saturday morning came early at EuroMorganland that day. The house was buzzing again, with every one of us on 'pins and needles' just trying to kill time. Like the rest of us, I could not count the minutes fast enough.

"Scooter, is everything set?"

"Sure Marc, damn, chill out bud—they are so ready for this, believe me."

"Oh, I'm just the nervous Dad; so don't pay any mind to me."

"Don't worry—I won't."

"Gee thanks Scoot, Christ, that sounded so—hum, I don't know—like—so sincere."

"Anytime bud, no sweat."

"Mom, would you happen to know, if Paul is outside with Laverne yet?"

"Yes honey, he's in the drive."

"Hell, you know what, let's just go then, I can't wait any longer, I'm too excited, how about you guys?"

"Sure Dad, we're ready, let's go."

"Alright Trev, lets!"

We all got into Laverne, who obviously had a new beau, as she was sporting some serious fragrance in her interior this morning. It was subtle, but it was intoxicating in its bouquet. I complimented Paul on it as we quickly made our way over to Summerlin. I could not believe my eyes when we entered the parking lot, it was jammed everywhere,—boy was it packed. Every local television network had a satellite van there, eight of them total. At my suggestion, Paul took the long way around to avoid the press. It appeared, Connor's execution by Fox, had brought out the vultures to seal her fate with their final follow-up segments.

And Jesse's last press release, had obviously worked well too.

It was abundantly clear to everyone inside Laverne except the boys perhaps, that maybe the 'stakes' had just gone up considerably. Scooter was the first to comment.

Guys, I think we need to make a little change in strategy, given the obvious size of this crowd. Instead of opening the way we planned, let's reverse the order. We'll run with the ballads first. I want to go for every one of the press' jugulars with your killer finale first, that's all it's going to take, trust me."

"My word Scott, you seem quite confident of that."

"For sure Mar, just you watch what's going to happen here today."

"Scott, I am excited along with confident—but I just hope it finds its way to the right people who execute recording contracts, if you take my reservation?"

"That's an excellent point Mar."

"Thank you dear, it's finally nice to have you back home."

"Mar honey, were not exactly home-free yet, pardon my pun."

"Yes Mal, I do understand, but it's really the fact that Las Vegas feels home to me already, deep down—I truly just love it here."

"It's nice to see you so happy Marilyn, that alone is worth it to me."

"So Scoot, Mom makes a valid point, what say you?"

"Christ…would you all just relax! Just leave this stuff to me, I live for this stuff; it's what I do for crying out loud."

"Okay bud, we will. Won't we gang?"

I got an assorted group answer of yeses and yeahs.

We snuck in the back kitchen entrance by the smoke pits and BBQ's. We then followed a serpentine route through the kitchen and into a makeshift dressing room. It was there that we found Chris waiting for us.

"I can't tell you how happy I am to see you all here; earlier than planned… it's a madhouse out there."

"Now Chris, you promised me you would have everything prepared, do we have any problems we need to discuss?"

"Certainly not Marc, we're running just fine, thank you."

"Great. Listen Chris, I'm a bit nervous, so please understand if I'm not myself."

"I understand papa. You do have reason to be proud, but I can't speak for being nervous—those two troubadours of yours will pull off a repeat of last week's performance here, you can bank on that boss. Chris then continued.

"Now let's go over a few things, shall we? First off, I have sealed off the West Terrace completely into two half-tented sections.

"The kids from school will be in their half to enjoy their luncheon in peace. I will see to that personally. We have extra security on the exterior parameter so there shouldn't be any 'lost lambs' from the press corps either. The boys' guests have started arriving, so we have discreetly escorted them onto their half of the terrace.

"Behind the curtain in the other section, we have the high rollers of government, along with our other assorted guests and dignitaries from our company, Minis, our IPO bankers, and elsewhere. I set up a complimentary full-service bar in there; I hope you don't mind my initiative?"

"No, it all sounds very well planned and executed. Congratulations Chris, first-class job."

"Thanks Marc. I would suggest we all go into the twins' side, unless you think the boys would enjoy meeting our Mayor and Governor now, it's all up to you and them, after all?"

"How about it guys, would you like to meet the Mayor and our Governor now?"

"Let me at 'em Daddy. I'll make sure they're first in line to buy the Minis with their money…nothing else is more important. Mummy always loved taking money from the politicians…she was brill at doing it. She always said it served them bloody hell right too."

"I'm sure you will as well, Tay. Alright guys, let's go say hello, shall we?"

We walked our group through a maze of rooms and areas to bypass the guests. We went through a final door where we were right out on the other half terrace. The tent was adorned beautifully with large posters of kids eating their Minis. There was loads of collateral decorations. Bob and Katy from Minis had gone all out…it all looked wonderful. I had to remember to thank them afterwards.

The Governor's attaché now approached us as he introduced himself. He seemed taken with the boys right off, as he began explaining a bit of how these types of things ran. Afterwards, he signaled another man to advise the Governor. Moments later, the Governor of Nevada joined us.

For the ever-present press, it was all a field day of camera shutters and flashes.

The Governor was most cordial, while sincere in his praise of the boys' efforts. That became evident in his remarks from the get-go.

"Boys, what you two have done, will so greatly benefit our State and its' citizens, we are all humbled by its enormity, honestly. I know that I speak for all Nevadans today, when I say we're very proud of you both. And more so, we thank you sincerely for your efforts, on behalf of all the very deserving people you're helping today, as well as in the future."

My two were a little overwhelmed by the Governor's comments, as they were quiet for a change. Finally, Taylor opened his little pisk.

"Thank you your honor, on behalf of my brother and me, we are really happy to have you with us. We also would be honored if you were our first customer today?"

"I too would be honored young man, no—most honored, to be your stand's first customer."

At that very moment, a teenage girl in a wheelchair who I believe had CP, moved her way over to us as the Governor was taking his leave. No doubt, we were all about to meet Becky.

The young girl, stopped in front of the boys now. I could see that she already had tears growing in her eyes. She made an excellent effort in speaking her words clearly.

"Trevor and Taylor, I'm Becky; your teacher Mrs. Geary, is my cousin, I am very happy to meet you both. I want to thank you from the bottom of my heart. What you are trying to do for people like me is wonderful. I really appreciate you inviting me here today."

The boys were moved by her comments, yet I think more so, because she truly was a peer of theirs and not some adult from our factory. They became choked up themselves now. But they quickly composed, realizing I think, that no one wants to be taken upon with pity either. I didn't know how the boys managed to do it, but they calmed down so that they could simply thank her. Trevor spoke this time.

"Thanks Becky, we're so glad to meet you finally. I'm Tre, and this is Tay. That's Dad, Gramps, Grammy, Grace, Reg, Sofia, and Scott.

You had to give the kid credit; he wasn't going to leave anyone in our inner circle out of the introductions.

"Mrs. Geary said you would be here, so we sure wanted to meet you too."

Then both of my boys kissed a cheek, which was so precious and sweet that all of our ladies got choked up.

This time though, Becky lost it, as I quickly offered her my handkerchief, which she gladly accepted. She could not have been more than fifteen, and she was quite attractive. I think the boys' open demonstration of friendship, simply shocked her. Yet it was clear it satisfied her to no end as well.

"Becky is Mrs. Geary here already, do you know?"

"I don't know, I haven't seen her because my parents dropped me off at this tent so I haven't seen any of them yet."

"Dad, could Becky be our very first person, I mean, even before the Governor~to try the Minis...can we ask him?"

"Sure Tre, I'll see to it with his attaché, I'm sure his honor will agree... but you'd better ask Tay first, he did mention how important it was to have the Governor pay first...remember?"

"No Daddy, Becky's more important, I see that now...Tre's right. So after Becky, it will be the Governor, and let's ask the Mayor next, can we meet him now?

"Yes Tay, there he is now."

With Taylor, Trevor, and Becky leading the way, we all made our way over to the Mayor, who caught a glimpse of the boys walking over. He quickly dropped his conversation and excused himself; as he now met our group half way.

"My, just whom do we have here—let me guess? Could it be—two outstanding six-graders from the Meadows School?

"Hello Sir, I'm Tay Morgan, and this is my brother Tre. This is our friend Becky, and our family. It's an honor to meet you, is it true you started our school?"

"No Taylor, actually my wife did, but with what you boys plan on accomplishing before you two graduate, you've both made us very proud of that association, I can assure you."

The Mayor truly had a way about him…he had true charisma, the adults were all impressed, yet the boys seemed enthralled.

"Thank you Sir." Tre proffered this.

"Did I hear right boys; is it also true that you two plan to sing for us today?"

"Yes Sir, but we have one request of you as well though?"

"Now boys, if you expect me to sing with you two, you had better get a shower running right now so I can warm up." We all laughed of course, before Taylor clarified things for the mayor.

"That's all right sir; it's just that we would be honored if you were the third person at our kiosk after Becky here and the Governor, to buy the Minis today?" Taylor said.

"Of course Taylor, I love Ice Cream even without a great crusade like yours, although my wife says I need to learn to love it—a little less."

We chatted with his honor for a few minutes longer, before excusing ourselves to meet and greet everyone else.

We had made our way around the room, but before we realized, it was noon straight up. It was time to move next door to the other half of the terrace for the boys' luncheon with their classmates who were now all assembled along with the Geary's.

The first one to run up to us was Larry of course, who we were all glad to see there. The boys insisted that Becky join them, while Mrs. Geary had insisted that Larry join the class party too, which delighted both the boys and I. Larry quickly pulled me aside first though.

"Don't worry HB, I won't say nothin' 'bout sleeping over. I got my duffel under my table."

"Great Lar-man, but remember, you're sworn to secrecy too—you know, there just might be a surprise or two for you too, buddy boy."

"Really, that's cool, but you can count on me Hairy Bear, I won't say nothin'." Larry whispered to me as we broke apart afterwards.

All the kids talked, ate, talked,—and ate some more, as everyone was having a great time…it was all going wonderfully.

The kids were all still talking as I glanced at the time, it was now five before one—crunch time.

Chris began escorting all of our guests, into the General Store, where a special area was cordoned off, waiting for all of us.

Meanwhile, the boys and I had a little pow-wow.

"Jeeze guys, I guess this is it. You know, I love you both so much. Whatever way the chips may fall today boys—you guys share the number one spot on the top of my list.

"Thanks Dad, we love you too."

At that moment, Robbie arrived.

"We're ready guys, follow me. Marc, you're being introduced by someone close to you and the boys."

"Really Rob, I didn't realize I was to be getting any surprises today myself?"

"Yes you are, so just enjoy it—but shut up, we're ready to start."

We walked into the General Store where the room erupted for the boys. We had employees standing by the kiosks that made up the dessert court… standing ready to unveil them as both kiosks were still hidden under canvas covers. The boys would work the Minis kiosk naturally, with additional employees standing by for the coffee and dessert kiosk along with relieving the boys potentially should they tire.

I couldn't wait to see the recent renovations to our coffee kiosk we previously used out on either terrace; this one had been completely retrofitted to match the Mini's kiosk to create the Minis' Dessert Court theme.

Now I turned to the podium where I was stunned momentarily. At the microphone ready to speak, was my dear friend, and unofficial Uncle to the twins—Bill Sklar. He was adjusting the microphone for his abundant height, while also trying unsuccessfully to clear his throat out of obvious nervousness. He began with a normal introduction for an event of this order, followed by introducing himself:

"My name is Bill Sklar. I fly alongside that charismatic gentleman over there, wrapped in twin boys at this very moment. Those two clones of his, are my nephews—Tay and Tre…the Morgans."

"I personally asked for this high honor, of introducing my employer today, as he is surely that. But more so, ladies and gentlemen—he is my dear friend, so I know more about this fellow, than most. More so though, I know how happy our two twin tornados here, have made him. And I have seen the wonderful changes they have brought into his life, in such a short span of time—and now as they say—all of this.

"However folks, what most people fail to realize, is what an incredibly caring and generous man, Marc is. It seems that he has spent his entire professional life, not only building an incredibly successful and honest business, but in helping those around him as well along the way. Helping countless persons in need, both inside and outside of our company selflessly, has become second nature to him. And always quietly without any fanfare or desire to be recognized for his efforts. I can honestly say that the transparency of today's festivities is a first for our modest host.

"Marc's friends and co-workers have seen this generosity of his first hand on numerous occasions and situations. You know, we are always told nicely, to just keep it a private matter...so they will tell you proudly, what kind of a man that Marc Morgan is...how much he genuinely cares. And they will agree about something else as well—that it takes the great States of Nevada, California, and Utah—just to hold his huge heart. Quite honestly friends, truer words were never spoken about any man...that were so richly deserved.

"Therefore, on behalf of our 21,000 employees worldwide, along with his many countless friends, may I with great personal pleasure and honor, introduce our founder, and the CEO of Verandas' Inc—Mr. Marc Morgan."

I walked up to the microphone to spirited applause, as Bill immediately captured me into a profoundly deep embrace before I could begin my remarks.

"Hello everyone, my word, I'm overwhelmed. Thank you Bill, for that much-undeserved introduction.

"Folks, it is my belief that we are all here today as witnesses to something wondrous and monumental. Yes, truly we are. Today, we will experience the selfless power of giving, the joy of discovery, along with the promise of better things to come. And all of this, mind you, emanating from the love, determination, and commitment of two fine young gents—who just happen to be—my two sons. Tre, Tay, please come up here and join me, won't you?"

The room erupted as the boys walked up to join me. I looked at my sons, as I was already losing the battle with my emotions. With a cracking and overtly broken voice, I strained over my emotions to continue.

"Guys, when I think back to the joy your moving here has brought me, I had no idea, that reality was going to bring forth such wonderful fruit. Not merely for me, but for others as well—those that you alone, sought out to help—at least according to Concepcion Connors. There was an undercurrent of sedated laughter at my crack.

"So today, we will all bear witness to your love, compassion, and caring. Your wonderful crusade, will forever affect the lives of those around you, all of us really, and will likely motivate others as well. People will want to pick up the torch that you two have lit, so that they can carry it even further. No father anywhere could be prouder of his sons, at this moment. My love for you both is limitless, as such guys, it simply knows no bounds."

I now had two choked up sons, one tucked under each arm, as we hugged.

We composed ourselves as best as we could, before I continued.

"Now Ladies and Gentleman, boys and girls, I give you, one of the masterminds of the Minis Make Miracles Happen Crusade, the co-creator of the Minis' Dessert Courts—my son, Taylor Morgan—Tay to his many new friends."

You could hear the boys' entire class screaming, as I lowered the microphone for Taylor's more abridged height.

"Hi everyone. Gee, thank you for being here for this very special day, but hey, wasn't my Dad a mean old bloke, for choking us up like that, in front of all of you?"

"Tre and I thank each and every one of you for coming here for this, but there are some persons, we have to thank especially."

"First, we want to thank the Mayor and our Governor for coming.

"And you know that we have the best friends in the whole City—even though we just moved here.

"But we also want to thank our very best Las Vegas mate, Larry Levison for being here too."

Larry began hamming it up naturally. He was taking bows, pointing to himself, all while busting up the audience…mostly at his own expense, mind you.

"Now, when you're a Morgan—you can't be one—without a Gramps and a Grammy Morgan that loves you a lot…and you love right back. We want to thank ours, cuz they're the very best—how was that Gramps?" Dad quickly stood up.

"Taylor that was great, Grammy, and I love both of you very much." Dad sat down to applause while Mom just smiled as she blew kisses to both boys.

"But we also want to thank the other members of our family too, who help take care of us every day."

By the time Tay finished thanking everyone else, including all the Minis folks, I had yet to be mentioned:

"Now—we don't need to thank our Dad—because bloody hell—he should be thanking us…right?"

Nevertheless, apparently Trevor disagreed with his brother's assessment.

"You know Tay, that's not really a nice thing to say, so go ahead and thank Dad anyway. Dang it, he must have had at least something to do with us being here today?"

"Alright Tre, you're right, I'll say something, so relax bro. Dad, we thank you too, but dang it, don't choke us up again, okay?"

But before I could have answered him, he turned serious, as he was beginning to open his faucets. His words were catching now, as they became full of his young tears as he spoke.

…"And everyone has to have a Mum to get them born and raised up. Our Mum was wonderful. She taught us how to be good and to always help others who need our help. And that's why we're all here today, isn't it? She's with Grandfather and Grandmother in heaven now, but we love them all every day, only from here."

At that moment, Taylor covered his heart. Well, I just lost it right there—I think most of the adults present did.

Once Taylor composed, he continued.

"You know everyone, I think Dad's right, we are all here to be witnesses to something good at work…it will help a lot of nice people like our new friend Becky."

As Taylor waved to his friend.

"But you know what? The best thing about all of this is—all we gotta do is eat some dessert! Now I ask you, how brill is that? Blimey! I bet even as I keep waffling on, that we can all suffer through that—what a bloody Nora—right?

I think the audience was lost on some of Taylor's British slang, but he seemed undaunted anyways.

"And after we sell a whole bunch of Minis, and Dad's coffee and desserts too, lots of good things will start happening. In every city that has a Verandas Foundation charity; money will be available now for things we couldn't do before. And Verandas Foundation charities benefit people that need help around the world too, not just here in the States. But first, we want to start needed projects here in our new hometown—Las Vegas, the greatest city on the planet! Both Tre and I, love it here real well—its fab, although Dad keeps saying that he wants to see if we'll feel that way in August…whatever that means?"

"Well everybody, thank you very much for helping us with all this ice cream and the desserts we have to sell, but no holding out neither, we all have to eat at least one—cuz we're going to be counting."

"So on behalf of me and Tre, we are now ready to open for business… welcome to the Minis' Dessert Court at Verandas!"

At that moment, our employees quickly removed the canvas covers off of our Dessert Court kiosks. As our staff worked to wipe down all of the beautiful stainless steel ... they looked terrific. It all tied in beautifully into the General Store's livery theme esthetics, ambiance, and flow...yet it definitely caught your attention...the boys were especially thrilled.

The floor stanchion sign told their Crusade's story, which was graced with their caricatures as well...it all looked perfect. The coffee kiosk was loaded with its goodies too, and it would likely give the Minis themselves a run for the business too, as we were going to pass out samples of everything to all those waiting in line to pass the time.

Everyone was on their feet as the boys proudly gave the area a final, quick, once over, before moving into place.

"So, let's all help the Minis Make Miracles Happen everyone. Now, if you would all let Becky, the Governor, and our Mayor come up first, the queue starts behind them." Taylor added.

The press got busy with their cameras, as the boys put on their Minis' serving caps and matching aprons over their costumes, along with washing their hands. Moments later, Trevor served Becky a cup, while Taylor refereed a battle of bills between the Governor and Mayor.

They were fighting animatedly, over who could treat her as everyone looked on, then Taylor got a little brave, as he simply took both bills to settle it. He along with everyone else, giggled away...it was priceless.

The Mayor, then seeing our Governor refusing his change out of his one hundred dollar bill, quickly seized on his own brilliant idea. He turned to address the audience as he held up a second, fresh fifty-dollar bill that he had quickly removed from his wallet.

"Alright folks, I for one, know I speak for not only his honor, but all Las Vegas now. Young men—please keep the change...lets get this home built already, boys!"

The Mayor then handed his second fifty to Taylor, while the room full of customers were applauding yet again. People now began taking out larger bills in mass, readying them in line to buy their dessert item of choice.

Later, everyone became moved once more, seeing some of the youngest guests in attendance, literally surrendering their piggy banks to the twins. The first time this occurred, it hit home for the twins, as you could see that it affected them both immediately.

The boys began really moving along quite quickly, once we wised up to add a separate cashier. Meanwhile, the large bills continued to overflow.

The number one spoken line of the day had to be—please keep the change.

When the last person in line was finally served, the boys gave each other a 'high-five' as those paying attention, applauded the boys stamina, if nothing else. I then insisted they take a break, as I got our actual employees in place to handle the ample line for seconds and thirds. It had taken the boys over forty minutes to serve everyone in line. I wasn't shocked to see that they were seriously pooped now.

There was no doubt that everyone genuinely enjoyed the Minis—particularly the Mayor. Lucky for him, his wife was out of the country, so she wasn't there. As such, a strange phenomenon occurred—the Mayor was magically transformed—and began to act just like...Malcolm Morgan!

As the boys enjoyed their own cups of Triple T as they relaxed some, I once again went to the microphone.

"Ladies and Gentlemen, on behalf of all of us here at Verandas, thank you for your outpouring of support today for this very worthwhile cause. We now have a little surprise for all of you. We want to invite you to stick around for a little entertainment, right at two pm. Tay and Tre, want to thank you in their own special way...through their music.

"By the way, the boys will be recording a CD of songs to offer for sale at all of our kiosks to speed along our fundraising efforts with their crusade. Today is their very first professional performance of some of their music, so we hope you enjoy yourselves. If you like what you hear today, please look for their CD around mid-June, the sales will benefit the boys' Minis Crusade exclusively.

"They will be performing outside on our Gazebo, so everyone is welcome to mosey on outdoors to get comfortable. Thank you again, and may God bless all of you for your support and generous contributions. And most especially, we thank our younger guests, who came with their life savings in their piggy banks. There is no brighter example of giving, than that, so we thank them all."

The guests started for the exits out to the main Veranda and pond area. True, they had been generous towards our foundation, but they were now vying for the few shady spots to view the performance from. It seemed their concern for their fellow philanthropists, went right out the window—if you catch my drift.

The boys were still enjoying their dishes of Minis as they continued resting, when Chris came up to us. She had a very big smile on her face.

"Guys, we just finished counting the booty you two collected today. Take a guess how much you two raised for your crusade thanks to all these very generous people?"

"How much Chris, come on, tell us?" Taylor was in no mood to wait this out.

"Boys, how does $13,755 dollars sound? That doesn't count the seventeen piggy banks we haven't opened yet, or what's still being sold by the way."

The boys were jumping and screaming at this news.

"God, that's so good, isn't it Tre?"

"Yeah bro, that's unbelievable."

"Boys, we're so darn proud of both of you."

"Thanks Grammy, were proud of you too—and Gramps, aren't we Tre?"

"Yes Tay, and you were brill too, Dad, even with all the mushy stuff."

"Thanks Trevor, but listen, I think it's time that you guys stir up all those nice folks some with your music, don't you?"

"Yeah I'm ready Tay—are you ready?"

"Oh yeah, I am so ready for this Tre." The boys stood up to remove their aprons and hats.

CHAPTER 12

▼

SAYING THANK YOU WITH A SONG

SCOTT WAS TESTING THE MICROPHONES and amplifiers on the electric keyboards, as we walked out of the front doors of the restaurant. Scott went back to a microphone where he quieted everyone down as he spoke.

"Ladies and gentlemen, boys and girls, Verandas is pleased to introduce in their first professional engagement, Tay 'n' Tre...the Morgans."

The large audience erupted as the boys made their way out to the gazebo now.

After the crowd quieted down, Trevor started to speak.

"Hello everybody, thank you all for coming out today to support our crusade and the grand opening of our Minis' Dessert Court. And for helping us to raise some much needed money.

"We're going to start out with two songs that we have blended together. One was a favorite of Mum's, while the other one is Dad's. We perform them as one, because music brought our parents together a long time ago. Here are, In the Still of the Night, together with Stardust—for your pleasure."

"And now the purple dust of twilight time, steals across the meadows of my heart."

With that introduction from Taylor of Stardust's opening bars, the boys each began playing an overture of the songs.

"In the still, of the night, I held you, held you tight."

Trevor followed in his rich alto.

As they continued right on down through the two tunes, alternating the lyrics of the songs blending them beautifully...it was moving. The audience's reaction, as judged by their response, was gratifying. Even the staid journalist press reacted when the boys finished and took their bow.

Once everyone was quiet, Trevor spoke again to the crowd of guests and dignitaries. He spied Gloria Dehane over to the side. While pointing to Gloria, he spoke to the crowd.

"Everyone, here's the wonderful lady who is building the CPF Residential Center. Thanks to everyone's generosity here today, we've all helped raise over $13,755 dollars towards CPF's new home. Mrs. Dehane, would you wave to all these nice people, so they know who you are?

Gloria did as Trevor had asked, before throwing kisses to both the boys.

"Now everyone, in a manner of speaking, we're going to pick up the tempo a tick. Here is Elton John's, Funeral for a Friend."

The boys cut into the full version of this Elton masterpiece of classical and rock music and lyric. They skillfully used their keyboards with Taylor on the synthesizer and Trevor handling organ and piano leads. They were creating a full and dramatic rendition of the requiem portion of this piece which was masterful. As they made their transition to the song's upbeat vocal movements, guests began tapping their feet, while pounding on our railings. One couldn't help it, especially with Trevor's energy level on his piano lead. He was jumping up and down as he was pounding out the notes, which was amazing just to watch the kid's fire at his keyboard. Those knowing the lyrics sang right along with them—including me.

They ended the song to a tremendous ovation from everyone, as Taylor now addressed the audience.

"Ladies and Gentleman, and all us kids, here's our final song today. We would like to say that even though we've only moved here recently, you have all made us feel so bloody welcome. We feel like local blokes already, so this song is for all of us. We dedicate it to the greatest City on the planet...and all the wonderful people that live here. Here's an Elvis Presley tune, you may have heard—perhaps once or twice before."

The crowd was wise already as they began going nuts in advance for our city's unofficial anthem—Viva Las Vegas. The boys laced right into it with tremendous energy, along with a super arrangement courtesy of Scooter. The audience got carried right up with the excitement coming from their vocals along with their keyboards. Within moments, every person in the audience was singing right along, even some of the smallest kids knew it.

The audience loved it all—we all did. Scooter, standing with me, was particularly pleased.

The boys bowed, and then started out towards the main veranda. The audience however, was having nothing to do with that apparently. They started building their own momentum for an obvious encore, which they were not taking no for an answer at that moment. They stomped, yelled for more, to otherwise make it clear to the boys that they liked what they had heard. I saw that many of the adults were just shaking their heads in disbelief apparently.

Trevor was whispering in Taylor's ear, as they both now just turned right around to head back to their keyboards. They received a tremendous ovation as their reward for that decision. Trevor spoke into the microphone as he quieted them down from their roar of only moments before.

"Okay, okay, here's one more, but then we really have to go. We're sure you'll know this one by the Righteous Brothers."

The boys jumped into Unchained Melody, as they began belting it out with a passion. Trevor's vocal with that big voice of his, actually shocked me, it was so strong.

When they finished the tune, the crowd went nuts. I was frankly unable to stop myself now as I began alternating between screaming and cat calling. I looked at Mom who was surveying the crowd, as she looked at Scoot who winked. We were all ecstatic for the boys' success. I was certain that if this crowd had not been standing already, the audience would be now, for sure.

I walked down the dock to the boys, where I grabbed Taylor's microphone as I addressed the crowd, preparing myself to lie my ass off:

"You know folks; I don't even have to tell them to clean up their room!" To which the parents in the audience reacted as expected—hysterically, followed by a resumption of the sincere catcalls and screams.

"Well ladies and gentlemen, on behalf of all of us at Verandas, thank you for coming out today. Tay 'n' Tre personally thank you as well, for making this, such a successful and memorable day for their terrific cause. Please come back often to help support our 'Minis Make Miracles Happen' Crusade. And be sure to keep your eyes out for the boys' upcoming CD for this wonderful effort as well. Thanks again for being with us today, good bye and God bless all of you."

The boys came out from behind their keyboards a bit awkwardly, as they bowed again. And then something, I would have never expected before this day, began happening spontaneously at that moment. The crowd began rushing the boys for their autographs, it was startling.

I looked at Scooter, who was shaking his head. He then stopped long enough, to grab his microphone as he signaled to our security team to 'circle the wagons' around the boys. Then he began mouthing some words to me from across the dock:

"I told you so buddy."

That's what I made out from reading his lips. The boys meanwhile, were too busy signing away autographs, to recognize they were becoming surrounded with a large contingent of 'new fans' from all around them.

Before I was able to mouth something back to him, Scoot was being hugged by Mom. They were certainly two peas in a pod now. The rest of our crew, were all sharing their excitement with Scoot and Mom.

At that moment, I saw the entire Scott gang had walked over to our group on the veranda. They were hugging and congratulating our family, as I looked on. I decided to give the boys their first moment in glory alone, so I began walking over to our friends and family instead, but kept an eye on the boys as I did so. I also noticed that I wasn't alone in that concern with our security…I also noticed Mom as well.

"So, bud, still think I was over confident?"

"Don't be a gloat Scoot. Okay—you were right, I was wrong—satisfied?"

I now grabbed my close friend as I hugged him deeply—within an inch or so of asphyxiation, as he responded.

"Bud, with a reaction like this, how can I be anything but satisfied?"

"Good point Scoot…you can't!"

"Now Scott, all we have to hope for, is to get this kind of response in front of the recording Labels." Mom threw in her two cents too.

"I'm way ahead of you Marilyn, you let me handle that, have I been wrong about anything thus far? Trust me, the press corps here today, will undoubtedly see to that themselves."

"No Scott, you, my dear boy, have not been wrong. And as for you, Mr. Marcus Earl Morgan, have you ordered this boy's new Jaguar in that sporty blue color, as promised?"

"Why yes I have Mother…but thank you for blowing Scoot's surprise. It will be at our local agency on Tuesday morning pal."

"Good, and not a minute too soon dear." Scott was shocked, but pleased, as he hugged Mom.

"So Dad—what say you?"

"Marc, I don't know what to say honestly. This was incredible, fantastic, but certainly a wake up call as well."

"A wake up call Dad?"

"Sure…are you kidding Marc? Look out on that dock at your two sons! The wake up call, that our two little guys are no longer—just our two little guys—they're potential rock stars, son. Jesus Marko, look at the mob out there, clamoring for their autographs—don't you get it?"

"Oh yeah, I guess I follow you now, gee I sure as hell hope that we can handle all of this?"

"We'll be fine Markie, you watch and see."

"Okay Mom, but I hope you're right, because all of this seems somewhat overwhelming to me at the moment."

"Sure it is—now. Soon though, it will normalize as it settles down to a quiet roar."

"But if it doesn't Marilyn—what then?"

"Don't worry Malcolm, Scott and I have everything under control."

I wasn't convinced they were right, but I would keep silent for the time being.

I now turned to Bill, Grace, Reg, and Sofia, along with the Scotts.

"So—were they great or what?"

"Marc, they're a hit, that's for sure."

"Thanks Tom, but thank you all for being here, to share this with us."

"Wouldn't have missed it buddy for anything—you know that."

"Thanks Tommy boy."

"I want an autograph too, Mr. Morgan."

"Okay Hayley, they'll be up here shortly."

"Bloody smashing Marc, first rate."

"Thanks Reg—but well said too."

"Will they still talk to us when we get them home?" Sofia asked while laughing.

"If they want to eat—they will…it's their Achilles heel." Grace said to the laughter of all of us present.

"Actually guys, they're not going home, right now. I've got a surprise for them—isn't that correct Scoot?"

"Absolutely Marc."

"What are you doing Marc, you haven't told me anything?"

"Relax Mom, Scoot and I have to get Beth and the girls anyway, so we're taking the twins and Larry down to Toonland for the afternoon and dinner at 'the Door at Forty-Four'. Scoot is hoping to drop off the video he shot of the boys today, to his old boss Stacy, to pass it on to their A & R department. He wants an informal opinion of their potential from all the suits at Toon Media Records; it's really no big deal."

"Fine, but in the future, please make sure that everything goes through me first Marc. We always want to be on the same page son, this is the only way to assure that—agreed?"

"Why yes Mother—dear. My goodness Scoot, have I just been dis'sed by my own—Mommy?"

"I'm afraid you have Marc, you'd better keep your ship straight in the future…sailor."

"You're darn right he better." Mom admonished me yet again, as she bellowed…then cracked up.

At that moment, I turned to find the Geary's walking up to me.

"Hi Marc...congratulations to you all."

After introductions with the Scotts, I asked an obvious question.

"Susan, Rick, did you two survive the lunch okay?"

"Wonderfully, Marc."

"Susan, are all the children accounted for with their parents?"

"Yes Marc, except the ones waiting for autographs, which I think is hysterical, but their folks are here, so I'm pardoned in either case."

"You mean—we've been pardoned, don't you dear?"

"Sorry Ricky, yes, you were wonderful with all the kids."

"Marc, those sons of yours were incredible. I can't believe how polished they are, they were awesome, congratulations again." Rick said.

"Marc, I couldn't agree more, but all the same, we may have consequences in class Monday. If this hits the news, which it appears it will, it may take some adjusting in our classroom. Why don't you leave a few extra minutes to check in with me after class on Monday?"

"Yes, I think that's an excellent idea Susan, I'll make a point of picking them up myself on Monday then, alright?"

"Great. Now if I can just get my cousin back home to her mother, I'll be all set."

Susan and Rick said good-bye, as they left us to retrieve Becky. Moments after Susan got to her, it became clear she was in no mood apparently to be going anywhere at that moment.

From across our trout pond, I could make out a small disagreement between the two cousins...I decided to approach them. Perhaps I could be of some assistance, as I had my own suspicions of the problem at hand, anyway.

As I suspected, Becky wanted to speak to the boys personally to say good-bye to them, before she was willing to leave.

I walked up to the boys who were yapping away with everyone, as they signed their autographs. I whispered into Trevor's ear, explaining our little problem.

He whispered to T-man, before he then addressed their many waiting fans.

"Guys, we have to take a break for a tick. We want to say good bye to our friend, please give us a minute?"

Damn, I thought to myself, they handled that well, no complaining or anything, as they walked over to Becky.

"Look at the great luck you brought us Becky, being our first customer and all; we can never thank you enough for that." As Taylor said this, he bent down and hugged Becky. It was clear that she was touched.

"You're welcome Taylor—at least I think you're Taylor?"

"Good eye Becky, you're right, I'm Tay—but we would have never been this successful without your help. I can't think of a better person to receive the very first copy of our CD—what do you think Tre?"

"You're right Tay, Becky; you get the first one, even before we get ours. And we'll be real upset, if you can't come over to visit us at home sometime?"

"Oh, I would love to Tre."

"Okay, well listen, we gotta sign some more autographs.

"Great and thanks Tre, and thank you too, Tay."

The boys both gave Becky matching kisses and hugs as well. They said their good-byes, as Becky left with Susan and Rick—quite happy and content now.

The boys now went back to their patient autograph seekers. Damn, I was proud of them at that moment. My God, were they really only eleven? They had been sensitive to their new friend's feelings—yet knew their other guests were waiting as well. They had actually succeeded in keeping everyone happy.

It seemed that with this 'pro' persona transformation of theirs, they had matured some, as well. Not just on stage, but also with meeting their new fans, along with everything else, afterwards. I wondered how this was possible; maybe I didn't have as much to worry about as I thought?

With all the autographs signed now—the boys were now free. I walked back over to them, where we hugged immediately as I reached them. It was our renowned group hug again; that we had recently perfected, unconditionally conveying our mutual affection for one another.

"Damn guys, I can't even find the words—it was unbelievable, no bull. You two were brill, as you like to say. But all I want to know is—did you have fun?"

"Did we? It was wicked Dad—bloody wicked. I can't remember when I had this much fun. Well maybe that night singing with the ToonCrooners was close, but this was even better than that."

"Well Tre, I would say that you enjoyed yourself then."

"Yeah Dad, I think what I just said, says it all—doesn't it?"

"Good. So how about you Mr. Tay?"

"Me too Daddy, it was 'the bomb'."

"Oh, so now you're starting with the slang too?"

"Sure Daddy, why not?"

"No reason T-man, I just naturally assumed you were going to be my hold-out is all."

"Oh."

"Now listen guys, you've got to be tired, and so we should be leaving.

Before we do however, I need you two to go find Christine and her staff for a moment, to thank them all. Let them know how much you appreciated all of their contributions and help okay—but don't forget to find Bob and Katy too."

"Sure Dad. Dang—Chris knows her stuff, doesn't she?"

"Yes Trevor that she does. You can be sure, that I won't forget it either believe me."

We walked up the dock to the veranda now. All the assorted Morgans and close friends, were there to congratulate the boys with kisses and hugs.

Hayley walked up to the boys first as she succeeded in getting her autographs from the boys, which pleased her immensely—they were her first autographs after all. This gave all of us adults a nice warm feeling I think.

While the boys found Christine inside, I made a point to go around and thank everyone myself. Surprisingly, I found his honor the Mayor, still enjoying a cup of coffee at our kiosk.

"Marc."

"Your honor—did you enjoy yourself?"

"Marc I did, I had a wonderful time. I also must share with you, that I am humbled by your sons' commitment to their crusade. We all need to look at what they can accomplish with this. Isn't it amazing what our young can teach us old farts sometimes?"

"Yes, your honor it is. And listen, I don't think I have to tell you, how much the boys enjoyed meeting you today. But your gesture with the Minis was wonderful, your honor. You're little suggestion to our guests, according to Minis, added close to four grand to our efforts today, based on the number of cups sold. We can't even begin to thank you enough."

"Well, it was my pleasure. And, we have the Governor to thank for that one too, much as I hate to admit it."

The Mayor and I shook hands as we parted, whereby I now continued my rounds thanking everyone. All of our wonderful staff had managed to keep an incredible mass of guests satisfied and happy throughout the afternoon—that isn't always so easy. I think it came as a surprise to my staff, when I also slipped each of them, an envelope with a more material expression of my appreciation. I next found Chris at the reception podium.

"Christine, how are you doing...you look a little exhausted from all of this?"

"Tired—are you kidding me Marc? I'm exhilarated. This was a fantastic event, for a wonderful cause, and it all came off without a single hitch. I wish they could all go this smoothly."

I handed her an envelope now.

Chris looked at me somewhat surprised, but opened the envelope all the same. She read the note as she began discreetly jumping in place. She now ran around the podium where she gave me a death hold of a hug accompanied by a kiss.

"Marc, thank you, I don't even know what to say. Wait till I get home and show this to George."

"You are most welcome Chris, but thank you for everything…also let's try to keep this to ourselves, alright?"

"Sure Marc, no one else needs to know, do they?"

"No they don't, but you and George enjoy yourselves. Aloha and Mahalo, Chris."

"God—thanks again boss."

"De nada." I left Chris to her celebrating her bonus of ten days in Maui at our B&B, as I finished thanking our staff.

I returned to our entire group, where we loaded into Laverne now. Paul already knew our destination, so we just drove off as planned.

"Are we dropping Lar-man off Dad, or is he staying for a while and hanging with us at the house—please Dad?"

"Oh, didn't I mention it guys—the Lar-man is spending the night with us."

My boys started jumping and whooping it up with this news. What was amazing though, was how unaffected they now seemed by the whole event they had just finished.

Naturally, they were excited for their success, yet they were also back to being just our regular guys. They were not even rehashing or talking much about the whole thing, just little bits and pieces. To tell you the truth, it blew me away a bit, I must admit…were they a little shell-shocked themselves?

They had not even noticed we were on the freeway. I think they would have realized this was not our normal route home, even being newcomers.

When Paul stopped Laverne at our hanger at McCarran, only then, did they look around long enough to comment at all.

"Hey Dad, you're not going somewhere on business right now, are you?"

"No Tre I'm not, don't worry."

Like my parents, the boys' were now used to my little short trips that I took most every week.

"Good, you had me worried for a moment there, so why are we here Daddy?"

"Oh, I thought the Lar-man would enjoy you both showing him your planes, I knew today was the only day they'd both be here together. Why don't you guys take him on a tour?"

"Great idea Dad—thanks, let's go Larry, I want to show you mine first."

"Hey Tre, wait for me, but let's show him Grandfather's last since it's the newest."

"Okay bro, let's go."

As the three boys approached Tre's plane, I explained to the folks how I was going to pull this off. I asked their indulgence of not saying good-bye to the boys, which they understood.

Once the boys had all boarded to tour Cedric, Larry got inside our newest plane's cabin where he started going nuts by the screams we could all easily hear now.

After Paul took off, I boarded the plane as well; following Larry's carrying on to its source.

"Christ, this is beautiful, sorry guys, but your Grandfather's is the best one, no offense."

"Yeah, it is nice, isn't it?"

"Nice, you call this—nice? Jesus, this is much better than nice Tre."

"You know Lar-man, since you seem to like it so much, why not come up to the cockpit with me? I'll show you the wonderful Playstation® I have up there."

"You really got a Playstation® HB?"

"Yes Lar, in a manner of speaking, you could say...that I do."

"Okay, I'm coming Hairy Bear."

Larry walked into the cockpit where he rewarded my efforts.

"Wow. May I take a seat HB, please?"

"Sure Lar-man, start her up if you want."

"You're kidding me right?"

"No Lar-man, when have I ever kidded you?"

"Really HB?"

"Sure Lar, go ahead—push that red button there." As he did, Larry started up the number one G. E. fanjet.

"Wow, this is like so cooooooooool."

"Now this button Lar...yes that one."

With that done, number two fired right up.

I now pushed my PA button on my headset.

"Good afternoon gentlemen, this is your pilot speaking; Mr. HB Morgan. On behalf of your co-pilot, Mr. Lawrence 'Lar-man' Levison and I, welcome aboard Cedric. It is our duty to advise you that FAA regulations require us to shut down our engines properly, once they are started. We will therefore commence with that procedure, by circling the tarmac once to blow out our fuel lines."

From the main cabin, I heard my two laughing—they knew better—but Larry did not.

Mr. Scooter Davis, would you assist your flight crew with your best impersonation of Suzie, by please closing our hatch for this brief excursion? Moments later, my 'hatch open' indicator light, stopped glowing.

Larry was still checking everything out, as I started turning the plane onto the open tarmac. I could hear the boys laughing with Scoot in the back as I nonchalantly made my way for our taxi. Through the PA, I reminded the boys that FAA regs required them to buckle up, just like in a real flight plan. I heard the clicks seconds later, including Larry's.

Now I had them—where I wanted them, as I approached the westbound runway. The tower had moments earlier, cleared me for take-off into my headset, which was my cue. I now returned to speaking into the PA.

"Gentlemen, we have been advised by the tower that this exercise is now completed satisfactorily. Thank you for your cooperation and relax while I quickly get us back to the hanger."

I now opened my throttle, as we were soon doing 110 miles an hour, approaching lift off.

"Daddy, what's going on?" I heard Taylor yell from the main cabin.

I looked at Larry for a split moment, as his eyes were bugged out…for once, he was dead silent. This was his first cockpit experience, so the view alone was a wake up call difference for him.

Before I answered Taylor's question, we were airborne.

I pushed on my PA again.

"Gentlemen I apologize, but our co-pilot is new at this sort of thing. He insisted that we see what this new baby of ours can do before he would agree to turn back. I guess we're going to have to go along and humor him now guys."

"Oh Dad, knock it off—what's going on?" Now my older twin was yelling at me too.

With the PA on, I answered him.

"Would someone tell Mr. Trevor Morgan that nothing is going on—that six hours in Toonland—won't fix right up!"

Well that did it. You would have thought my two had just received their first Grammy awards, with the Lar-man not far behind them. They were screaming and carrying on so, I felt bad for Scoot who had to listen to all of it.

Once I leveled off, the boys ran into the cockpit.

"Are you kidding us Daddy, are we going to Toonland for real?"

"No Tay, I'm not kidding, we're in the air, aren't we? We have the park until ten pee, before we pick up Beth and the girls to head back home. We're having dinner at 'the Door at Forty-Four at 6:00, while we even have Hilary to avoid the traffic. So boys, how does this all sit with you two?"

"Oh, this is so cool Dad, but do we have to go back tonight, can't we stay at the hotel again?"

"Sorry guys, no can do, don't forget, you three have Sunday school tomorrow."

"Oh Dad, what's the big deal? We'll still be Jewish next week—if we miss it. I don't think it will rub off, you know." Trevor said it with just a tad too much attitude.

"Trevor, if you're not happy with my arrangements, I can just turn this little baby right around now and..."

..."Oh no, don't do that Dad, I'm okay. Its fine...I'm sorry."

"Very well, that's more like it, but I better not hear another word. Larman, what's your favorite ride, because as our guest of honor, you get first pick?"

"That's an easy one Hairy Bear, my favorite is Mt. Splashdown."

"Oh, I love that one too, Larry."

"Me three, Lar-man." Tre was getting into a new habit with this response.

"All right guys, we'll be starting our decent in fourteen minutes. Get back into your loungers. Larry, do you want to join them, or stay up here with me?"

"I want to stay up here so I can see you land this thing—you do know how, don't you?"

"Oh, I've got through it once or twice now."

"You are kidding, right?"

"Honestly Lar—no, I'm really not. Heck buddy, you know it's a new plane; I'm still learning how to fly it some. In fact could you hand me that—how-to-do-it book, over there in that pocket? I need to get started reviewing my landing stuff, God it's so confusing, I swear."

"Now Mr. M., please don't joke about this junk—I don't want to ruin my pants. Heck HB—they're not even brown, I can't hide a load in here you know!"

Larry was now pointing to his yellow and blue trimmed painter's pants. I of course had to try to avoid busting up from his usual candor.

"You know Lar; we do have a complete bathroom aboard...would you care to use it?"

"That depends."

"On what Lar-man?"

"On whether or not, it will be my final visit Mr. M. If it's all the same to you HB, I don't want my last 'dude' to be at thirty thousand feet up. You know, in some plane in a nose-dive trying to land."

I was busting now, but could not resist carrying this further with my diminutive, comedic, friend.

"Don't worry Lar; if you got a go, you got a go. While you're in there, I'll be studying real hard on this book, besides…I promise."

"Listen HB, do you want me to quiz you or something, would that help you—my dump can wait you know?"

"Well, if you're sure Lar, I would appreciate that. I know that I've got about half of it down right already." Larry opened up the flight manual that I handed him convincingly.

"Gee, HB—which half, the landing part, or the—we're-all-dead part? I'm just sort of curious you know."

"I don't know Lar; I always seem to get confused with all these gosh darn buttons and sticks. God, I don't like buttons and sticks they bamboozle me Lar—like, what's this stupid one for?" I pointed to the flaps, which are critical in take-offs and landings.

As if on a critical mission, my able-bodied co-pilot, now skimmed through the flight manual on my suggestion. Eventually, he found the schematic of the instruments I had directed him to—just in time…he was starting to break into a sweat. It was a good thing the boys were not in the cockpit. They would have clobbered me soundly for sure, not to mention blowing my gag, long before now.

"Jesus, where is it, damn, oh, here it is—it's your flaps HB…but it doesn't say what any of this stuff is supposed to do, now what's up with that?"

"The flaps Larry? Oh yeah that's right, I remember now. Okay pal, we'll figure it out. Listen; let me turn this switch once, how do you feel about that—think its ok?"

"Gee HB, how do I know…but do you think you ought to be doing that?"

"Why not Lar—what's the worst that can happen to us?"

"Gee I don't know HB—like maybe we could all die in a big dang crash…or worse—we could end up landing in Cleveland! Just don't touch it—okay?"

"Hey, don't sweat it Lar-man, we won't die, that's impossible bud…dang, thank God for that."

"It is—why is that impossible HB?"

"Because, I'm carrying my lucky rabbit's foot—want to see the little sucker?"

"No, I can't even look at it, or we'll all be killed, I just know it; look HB, I'm sort of, kind of…I think—I may be a jinx—there, I said it."

I looked at Larry, but realized I had already pushed him too far, as he was now starting to prime his faucets up.

"Okay Lar, I guess the jig is up. Come here, come on."

Larry got up and stood next to me, but he now had his floodgates open,— Christ I had pushed him too far.

"I guess I owe you an apology son, I've just been joshing you. I wouldn't be in this seat flying this Jet, if I didn't know exactly what I was doing—now would I Lar?"

"I don't know HB, you did have that DDD thing as a kid—I thought you might be having a relapse, what do I know? Besides, it's true, I am a jinx, just ask my Dad." I was trying hard not to laugh at my dear sweet co-pilot's remarks.

"Lar, that's A.D.D. but it doesn't work like that. Don't you worry yourself one bit, but please forgive me, okay buddy? Oh and if you're a real jinx—why aren't we already dead...answer me—that one?"

"All right, I guess you're right, we still are alive. Besides that, I guess you're forgiven too, but you're a real mean guy for doing this to me...I believed you HB...I trusted you like you were my Dad."

"I'm sorry Lar...you can trust me, but you also have to understand something else about me. Ask the boys if you don't believe it. I never play any of my jokes on someone who I don't like a whole lot...a real whole lot, son. So what do you suppose that tells you—Larry old boy?"

"That you like me HB?"

"Bingo bud, yet I don't merely like you, I like you something fierce Larry. Hell, nothing would make me happier, than if you were one of my own...I really mean that Lar."

The Lar-man was once again in tears, yet this time really in overload.

"Mr. M. I have to tell you something about my Dad." He was bawling buckets now.

"What Larry, what about your Dad?" I was acting oblivious to get him to open up.

"I messed up Mr. M., Dad wasn't ignoring me at all; he's been stuck in some hospital. He's got something wrong with his brains. His brains have broken down real bad."

"Larry, are you trying to tell me he's had a breakdown bud?"

"Yeah, that's it; he's had a nervous breakdown."

"Oh, well that's a relief Lar."

"It is?"

"Sure, lots of people have those, he'll be fine in a few months, I'm sure of it."

"You are—I wish I was? I'm worried bad about him HB, you know, maybe I did it to him…maybe I jinxed him?"

"Don't do that to yourself Lar, you couldn't have caused his breakdown—this was not from a jinx…even if you had wanted too. Breakdowns are caused by a lot of factors. But loving a wonderful, funny, twelve-year-old boy has never been known to cause one that I'm aware of…even one who's a jinx! Don't you fret on it again, okay?"

"Alright…if you're sure?"

"Oh I'm sure all right Lar, they're caused by being overwhelmed by lots of things all at once. But he'll work through it, I'm confident."

"Thanks HB; I knew you'd tell me straight."

"Hey; what are surrogate Dads for?"

"Oh yeah that's right, you promised to do that, okay I'm definitely cool now."

"Good, now if you don't mind, I need to get on with the tower for real, to get us cleared for landing."

"No sweat HB, do what you got to do, I'm in no hurry."

"It's a good thing you're not Lar, because we're going to be in a holding pattern for a few minutes yet, by all the chatter I'm hearing from the tower."

I waited through the chatter before finally getting on with the tower. I confirmed my assumption. We held to our current altitude for another eight minutes, before they cleared me to begin my final approach.

On the ground several minutes later at the Executive hanger, we deplaned and found a shuttle making its way over to us. It took us into the terminal where we caught a cab to the park.

Scoot directed the cabbie to the employee's gate, east of the main entrance, where we got out moments later. Scoot went into their little security building while he arranged to get us all cleared to enter with his credentials…how nice I thought.

"I hadn't realized you came in quite this handy Scoot? Am I mistaken, or did you just save me at least a 'c' note or two?"

"I did indeed Marc, but then again, you're now buying me dinner…so I thought I'd do my little part too."

"Works for me Scoot—but thanks pal, I really do appreciate it."

"My pleasure bud, but listen, while you four are at the Tour Center, I want to drop off this video. It's still early enough that I may get someone to watch it, even though it's Saturday. I will meet you all at Mt. Splashdown in twenty five minutes, so wait for me there."

"Why Scoot—are you afraid to go on that ride alone?"

"No Morgan, and eighty six your crap already. I may have some honchos with me that's all, if any of them are still working. They'll definitely want to meet the guys, if they're impressed with the video, that's a given in this business."

"Oh alright, but we'll only give you five minutes to arrive after we get there ourselves. If you haven't arrived by that time, we'll do the ride without you."

"Fine, but trust me, I'll be there before you, the way you move. And I'm going to call Beth too…let's see if the girls want to come by and hang with the boys for the afternoon, like I don't know the answer to that one."

"Yeah Scott, that would be great, we'd love to do the rides with them and let them meet Larry."

"Okay Tre, your wish is my command, see ya Marc."

"After while crocodile."

The three best friends and I made our way over to the Tour Center. As we walked in, we saw Hilary waiting for us. My two ran over to her lickity split, while I was further surprised when they gave her twin hugs and kisses.

"Hey men, it's nice to see you again too, and hello Mr. Morgan, but where's Grandfather today?"

Immediately, I cussed myself out for being remiss to warn Hilary about Cedric's passing.

"Grandfather died Hilary; he fell in his bath and got a stroke."

"Oh boys, I am so sorry to hear that—I truly am. Your Grandfather was such a fine man. Please accept my condolences as well as my apology for mentioning it."

"It's okay Hilary, anyway he's with Mummy and Grandmother now. Probably Grandfather's busy with them, don't you think?"

"Yes I do…I'm sure you're Taylor, too…am I correct?"

"God Hilary—you're good."

"And who is this fine young gent standing next to your father, then?" As Larry walked over to the hugging trio.

"My name's Larry, I'm the best friend—and you're not so bad yourself there sugar…nice to meet you too."

"Well—hello Larry, Mr. Best friend. I'm Hilary, your personal Tour Escort today, so it's a pleasure to make your acquaintance."

"Dang, I never had my own tour escort before when I came here—how come?"

"You see Larry; I'm one of our VIP special services escorts. I help make it easier for our very special guests to get around the park, that's all."

"Oh I get it, which makes you kind of like a big shot tour guide, for the big shots—is that it?"

"Gee, I guess that's true Larry, but never has it been put that eloquently before."

Hilary was laughing herself crazy with Larry's candor and wit.

"All right men, what's it going to be? Where in Toondom do we go first today? Let me guess, Wrong-way Murphy's Adventures?"

"Nope Hilary, today Larry gets first pick—he's called Mt. Splashdown."

"Alright, what are we waiting for then—let's go?"

We headed down Americana Avenue. Once the boys got ahead of us somewhat, Hilary started speaking to me.

"Mr. Morgan, please forgive me. I am so very sorry to hear of dear Mr. Richards' passing. What a horrible thing to have happened to such a fine gentleman. It truly saddens me, I hope I didn't upset the boys too terribly, after all, they only lost their Mother a couple of months before that...right?"

"Yes Hilary and thank you. Actually, I believe they're adjusting to the losses reasonably well. We're averaging about one outburst—or bad moment, each month now; I think that's good all things considering. I have an enlightened opinion on the afterlife, so the boys seem to have taken comfort in that, as do I. We're really holding up okay, over all.

"But let's not allow these three out of our sight right now, or we may never find them again, alright?"

"Sure thing, I'm keeping my eyes open. Right now they're staring into that gift shop's window, see?"

"Boy, you don't miss a trick Hilary, do you? I was panicking already."

"Not to worry Mr. Morgan, we're trained to see through the crowds, you aren't."

"True Hilary, but might I take you along with me to the mall the next time I drag them there too?"

Hilary was chuckling at my joke, as we joined up to our wayward charges.

"Boys, what did I tell you last time about getting so far ahead?"

"Okay Dad, sorry." This escaped from Tre.

True to his word, we arrived at Mt. Splashdown, to find Scooter waiting at the entrance...alone.

"My Hilary, don't tell me you got stuck with this detail again; doesn't anyone else ever draw the shortest straw anymore?"

"Hello Scott, nice to see you too. I guess you're off today—by your attire?"

"No Hilary, he's off—his rocker...permanently, to put it concisely."

"Thanks bud, but trust me; you're going to pay for that one."

"You mean beyond paying for dinner, which at the moment could amount to a greasy cold corn dog along with a warm Coke® chaser?"

"Oh forgive me, oh great one, for my jest."

"Can it Scooter—you never did do Hamlet well."

"Why do I get the feeling that you two know yourselves far better than meeting at the ToonCrooners contest?"

"Didn't you tell her Marc?"

"You know Scoot, I didn't, I must have assumed you would. Hilary, Scooter, and I go way back; we were both in the ToonCrooners ourselves."

"Really—do you sing too, Mr. Morgan?"

"Yes Hilary he does. Rarely now, thank the Lord, and pathetically— always!"

"Gee Scoot, that was so nice...thank you...really."

"Alright bud, then don't mention the corn dog and warm Coke®, old buddy—ever again! Beth and the girls, will meet us here in around twenty minutes tops I would guess. Beth will call on her cell when they're inside the back lot."

"So boys, are you guys going to get up that mountain or what?"

"Yes Hilary, may we go now?"

"Sure Trevor, we'll be at the exit as usual, go on—get in there."

With that, Hilary opened the VIP gate for the trio, none of which was lost on our young Mr. Gleason.

"Holy Sh...oot, dang—do we get to do this on every ride? Cuz if we do—I gotta get me—my own Hilary?"

"Yeah Lar-man, isn't this cool?" Trevor answered his friend.

"Cool? Are you kidding me Trev, with Hilary here, you can name your own price back at school with all your mates, the moment you tell them you can line pass them at Toonland."

"Really Lar, I never realized?"

"Well Tre...realize it dude."

"Okay."

We watched the boys make their way into the mountain's interior as they continued gabbing away. When they had all but disappeared, Scooter's demeanor changed immediately—why did I feel like a priest sitting in a confessional right at that moment?

"Bud, would you kill me, if I confess something horrible to you?"

"I don't know Scoot; I guess it would depend on what you told me—along with the capitol crime laws of California. But on the whole, I don't care for the sound of this already."

"Okay—never mind then."

"That's it...never mind? Do I look like an idiot Scoot—spill it Davis, while you're still vertical? You know pal—death rarely comes when we want it to!"

"Alright Marc, it all started when I tracked down Stacy to give her the tape. She remembered the twins from our contest, in addition to my resignation naturally. I also suggested she check the news channels while watching the video. She agreed to that, but since she already remembered them from the contest, I'm of the opinion she would like them to do a crowd test for her.

"Fine, we'll have her get with Mom, when does she want to do it?"

"Bud, don't kill me but—tonight at eight o'clock…here in the park."

"What! Are you going bloody crackers Scoot? I brought them here for some R&R for putting up with all the rehearsals and performing this afternoon. Now you want them to stop their fun and do some stupid test… tonight? What have you been smoking Scoot—I'll assume that that was the last of it hopefully?"

"Marc, the crowd test wasn't my idea, so don't beat me up, but it's not any old test pal, believe me. In my opinion, it would be a critical benchmark for the twins to pass."

"What in the hell do you mean Scoot; what kind of benchmark?"

"Marc its simple, the boys have thus far performed either as amateurs or in an ideal and unusual situation, correct?"

"All right, I'll concede that fact, so what's your point Scoot?"

"Marc, we have totally unbiased and raw audiences here in the park, they're disinterested third parties if you will. If your boys can accomplish with our guests, what they did earlier this afternoon, we know we truly have something tangible. Stacy suggested the idea I'm sure, strictly out of personal consideration for me, not to mention, our longstanding association. She's going way out on a limb doing this unauthorized, so just say the word buddy boy, if you really don't want to consider it?"

"Damn it Scoot, why do you always complicate my decisions—with such sound logic?"

"Damn, Marc, someone has to, what do you think about the idea now?"

"Honestly Scooter—I think—I had better call Mom!"

I picked my cell out of my pants' pocket to begin dialing home…Reg answered.

"Hi Reg, its Marc, everyone well?"

"Yes Marc, are you—and our fresh rising stars, having a good time then?"

"Yes, but damn Reg, that's a funny way of referring to the boys…still jazzed about the concert?"

"You know Marc, I'd love to garner credit for that quip, but I must defer to the news on the telly sir."

"Are you saying it's already been mentioned on the news?"

"Oh yes Marc—on all your stations as a matter of fact. I'm afraid that poor Malcolm has been going bonkers keeping up with the VCR. I thought we finally had him trained…but alas, apparently not."

"Jesus, what was I thinking Reg? I never thought to prepare the TV's and VCR's to tape?"

"Malcolm's fine—now Marc. Of greater significance is what's being said by the press, it's very upbeat and positive."

"Great Reg, listen—is Mom free?"

"No Marc she's not, but by her own admission—she's—reasonably priced."

"Good show old bean, now may I speak to her?"

"Certainly Marc, let me fetch her."

"Careful Reg—don't throw her bone too far this time."

I thought for sure I would have Reg busting with my crack, but he was undaunted.

"Marc, might I be so bold as to suggest, that you leave the humor to the experts, while we leave you—to your soufflé."

"Oh Reg—that hurts, oh the pain…"

…"Save it for a rainy day Marcus, I've been down this road with you before, let me get Marilyn so I can end—my suffering". I swear to God; someone was rubbing off on him.

I was still in shock from his cracks moments later, when I finally had the 'reasonable' lady herself, on the telephone.

"Hi dear, what's up?"

"Gee Mom, why don't you tell me. I mean, according to Reg, the boys are getting more airtime on the performance already?"

"Honestly son, I presumed that's why you were calling me?"

"No Mom, it wasn't my reason, but now that you mention it…look, never mind, here's the reason for my call. It seems that Scoot may be able to have the boys perform here tonight in Toonland. It's what they call a crowd test, and it would take place at around eight, if it materializes. Do I have your go-ahead to proceed with it, if the boys agree to it?"

"Marc, thank you. I appreciate your sensitivity in asking me."

"You know Mom, when you bark out the orders, I do usually listen."

"Yes son, whatever you and Scott decide, has my approval of course."

"Now let me fill you in baby. All of the local stations, along with Fox and MSNBC so far, have carried the grand opening today for the crusade. But they are all spinning their focuses now to include and promote the performance by the boys, it's been real gratifying Marc.

"They panned the audience's reactions, along with more than a decent pick up of the music. Their stories were strong and flattering of the boys' talent, exceptionally so. One reporter suggested that they could stop selling the ice cream anytime they wanted. He suggested just putting them on a street corner with their keyboards and an empty ten-gallon hat, to raise the money instead!"

"That's great Mom—and funny, but listen; did Dad figure the recorders out okay?" Mom started laughing at my question.

"Oh, I would say he did dear, your tutorial finally came back to him, but I don't know if poor Sofia will ever recover from it."

"Mom, what on earth did Dad do to her?"

"Son it's not what he did per se, it's more what came out of his mouth— while he was doing it. He was trying to figure out all that hi-tech equipment of yours. And as usual, his mouth got away from him where unfortunately, Sofia was the one to find it."

"Oh, say no more, I follow Mom. Listen I'm going to get back to Scoot, he's waving at a woman; it must be his old boss Stacy, the woman who's calling the shots here."

"Alright honey, let me know what happens, will you?"

"Of course Mom."

I hit the end button on my phone; Scoot seemed relieved that Mom had agreed in principle, as I watched the mystery lady walk up to us now.

"Stacy, this is Marc Morgan, the twins' father."

"Hello Mr. Morgan, it's my pleasure to see you again."

"Again—Stacy, have we met?"

"I'm not sure we met per se, but I saw you and the boys the night of the contest."

"Oh yes, of course, so nice seeing you again too."

"Mr. Morgan, may I call you Marc?"

"Of course, I was going to suggest that myself, I hate sir names."

"Great, me too. Marc, at the same time I was watching Scott's tape, the boys were being featured on a piece on MSNBC. It appears they're getting some great responses from their performance for their charity effort earlier today."

"Yes, I heard it got some airtime on some stations from the boys' personal manager. Naturally that's wonderful to hear, as my foundation is the beneficiary of their charitable efforts."

"Marc, given that, I want to give the boys a short twenty to thirty minute crowd test at the Futureworld Quad at eight pm tonight. If you give me the word, I'll call in some of our people to hear them."

"Scoot, you're the doctor, what say you?"

"Of course Marc, this is an incredible opportunity for them. Stacy please understand though, that I cannot speak for the boys' personal manager as far as anything beyond tonight's test. She likes to mull things over…she's likely to digest all of her options. In short, there would not be an opportunity, I'm afraid, for any deep conversations or negotiations tonight."

"That's fine Scott, but if that's the case, let's not bring in our people, we can just film it instead."

"I'm okay with that, how about you Scoot?"

"Sure I agree, why disturb their weekend, and jade him or her into a negative mindset over a long drive in, on a day off—anyway?"

"Good point Scott, I never thought about that angle."

"See bud, that's why you're paying me the big bucks to handle the boys."

"Cute Scoot, but we also have to take into consideration that possibility with the twins themselves. I brought them here after all, to relax and have fun. I plan to respect their wishes on the subject. I would suggest we avoid getting too excited therefore, until they've signed on to this little idea anyway."

"Marc I wouldn't be too worried about that, I spoke to them aboard Cedric. While I didn't have a clue about this naturally, I asked in general terms when they wanted to perform again. I wanted to gauge their responses to try to get an idea of their excitement level."

"What did they say Scoot?"

"Tre said the sooner the better, Tay was less anxious, but wasn't negative on the idea by any means. He simply commented that he hadn't recovered yet from signing all of those autographs."

"The boys were approached for autographs Marc?"

"Yes Stacy, and far more than approached, I'd have to say they were mobbed! And not just by the girls in attendance either. They must have signed somewhere near seven to eight hundred in all, wouldn't you agree Scooter?"

"Yes easily, I'd guess you're close with that number Marc, don't forget they were at it nearly an hour and a half."

"All right gentlemen—scratch my prior commentary. I'm going to call in an executive, Saturday or not—I want one here. You gentlemen should have mentioned this before; I'm surprised at you Scott—are you losing your instincts?"

"You know Stacy, I did say something to you, but it was when you grabbed that other phone call—remember? Perhaps you only heard my comment faintly?"

"Oh yes, I think I do remember something now, sorry Scott. But hey, let's not belabor it, at least I'm listening now, but this changes my entire perspective."

"How so Stacy, if you don't mind me asking?"

"No Marc, of course I don't mind. You see, initially your local crowd may have been simply motivated to show up from the press coverage for the fundraiser itself, as it's certainly for a good cause on a nice Saturday afternoon…get the picture? But people won't wait up to an hour or so, to have just any two, eleven-year-olds sign an autograph, I'm certain of that. That audience knew better after hearing the boys perform—in a sense, they were foretelling the boys' future, don't you see? Candidly gentlemen—but Scott, you correct me if you disagree—you should never second guess an audience's reaction!"

"Yes Stacy, you're certainly right—I agree." Scott responded to his soon-to-be—former boss."

"So Marc, here's what we're going to do, first we'll ask your boys how they feel about doing this. And no pressure from you Scott Davis or you will have me to reckon with. You know, Marc is a pussycat compared to what I will do to you.

"If the boys do agree, we don't change a thing to screw up their next couple of hours. What were your intended plans if any, for dinner Marc?"

"I made reservations to take them to 'the Door at Forty-Four'; Rudy promised them a crack on the harpsichord there. With these changes though, it might be smarter to stop in route—pick up something fast—you know… like a corn dog. We'll find a stand somewhere convenient to the Futureworld Quad. This will allow the boys their fun…besides—Scooter loves corn dogs. And after all, dinner at 'the Door at Forty-Four' takes two hours on a good night. I also have to fly us all home tonight."

"Marc, why rush home? Can't you all just spend the night at the resort as my guests? I can arrange a suite, clothing, and toiletries for all of you."

"I don't know Stacy; the boys have Sunday school tomorrow. And they have their friend with them who also attends the same school. I'm not sure his mother would be too keen allowing him to miss that?"

"Fair enough Marc, but why not call her to confirm that assumption?"

"Alright Stacy, I have her cell number, I'll call her…damn, I'm already breaking one my own cardinal rules to allow this Scooter."

"That's mighty big of you bud. I know how much this one must hurt. But what the hell Marc, no one knew this was going to happen, did we?

"And we're merely considering this to extend the boys' good time, which is an admirable trade off as well. Besides, didn't Marilyn mention you were considering having your Dad tutor them instead of Sunday school?"

"Your right Scoot—so I guess on that basis, I'm okay with it, if Carol agrees too."

While I attempted to find Carol's number, Scoot's cell rang as well. It was Beth…she and the girls were making their way to Mt. Splashdown, as Scoot announced their impending arrival.

Meanwhile, I found Carol's number and called it.

…"Carol, its Marc, has the coming out party begun yet?"

"No Marc not yet. Listen I caught the news, and my little ham along with the twins. Say, they are wonderful Marc, aren't they?"

"Yes and thanks, but that's more or less why I'm disturbing you."

"Oh Marc, you could never be a disturbance to any woman, at least not one with a bare ring finger."

"Cute Carol, but listen, how would you feel if your little ham missed Sunday school manana?"

"Is there a problem Marc—is he behaving?"

"Carol, he's been great, while having a ball—it's that something's come up with our plans. I may want to extend the trip into an overnight here, but only if you're okay with it."

"Oh sure, he gets to sleep in the same suite with you, before I do—is that it?" Carol's momentary silence following her joke, had me wondering if there wasn't a 'spot of truth' in her mock jealousy. But I had to say something.

"Honestly Carol, I have no comment to that one, I'm a proper gentleman after all."

"Fine Marc…avoid the subject, suit yourself, but tell him that I love him, and to mind his manners—not that he really has any!" I was splitting over that one, I can assure you.

"When do you foresee getting back to Las Vegas?"

"I'd be kidding you, if I told you I knew for certain, at the moment Carol. Right now, I'm not sure of any of this. We may yet still return tonight, although I doubt it now. Can I answer that question later tonight, or should I just keep him either way until tomorrow afternoon?"

"Oh bless you Marc, I get my night out, as well as my beauty sleep tomorrow too,—you've just been elevated to sainthood!" As I laughed.

"Good Carol, I'll call after twelve, or should I say later?"

"Twelve is fine, have a ball Marc, but thanks for everything."

"It's my pleasure Carol, talk to you tomorrow."

"Bye Marc." Carol hung up as I turned towards Scoot's probing expression.

"I guess this makes it official buddy boy?"

"Nope—not yet it doesn't, we still have two young rockers to ask, Scoot.

"Alright, well I guess we're about to find that out too, I just spied Larry I think—yeah, there they all are bud."

"Hey guys, man that line still had some distance I guess?"

"Yes Dad, it was still a ways to go inside the mountain, but it was sure worth it…we're soaked too."

"Yes I can see that, but listen; do you two remember Stacy from the ToonCrooners contest?"

"Oh hello Miss, it's nice to see you again."

"Thank you young man—and what manners—now are you Tay or Tre?"

"Tre, Miss, and this is our best mate—Larry Levison."

"My, well hello Larry, I guess you're planning on managing the boys'—right?"

"Look lady—I'm twelve…I still got my own life to mess up, you know?" Stacy was shocked with Larry's quick response I think.

"Oh Stacy, I apologize for being remiss, Larry is our resident stand up comedian. He has also offered to write their stage material too…he's brilliant."

"Marc please don't apologize to me—but I'd put him on the payroll immediately. I'm sure I'll have ample opportunity to get to know Larry—I'm so looking forward to it…actually."

"What's that suppose to mean lady, hey—are you sweet on Mr. M or something?"

"No Larry—I'm sweet on you—does that worry you?"

"Me—naw…but can you cook?"

"Why yes, Lawrence, I'm a fine cook."

"Oh, so it's Lawrence already? Well, what time's bedtime at your place then?"

"Oh I don't know, around eleven-thirty after the news, I suppose."

"Okay—I'm in."

We were all going crazy with our laughter, the twins especially.

Before our laughter had even ceased, Beth, Embeth, and Halley joined us. With the way that family was hugging and kissing now, you would have thought they had been apart for a year—or more!

"Marc, how are you?"

"Great Beth, thanks for joining us—and hi girls."

"Hello Mr. Morgan."

"Now Embeth, I think we had better drop that formal Mr. Morgan stuff around here, why not call me Marc, or better yet—Uncle Marc?"

"Okay Uncle Marc, gee that does sounds good, doesn't it?"

"Yes sweetheart it does…and how are you this fine afternoon, Halley?"

"Oh I'm fine, how are you Uncle?"

"I'm great dear, now that's my idea of a question." I bent down to hug my new 'pretend' nieces as I received kisses to boot in return.

"Listen, would you three guys say hello to everyone?"

The boys and Larry got with the program quickly. After 'hello cousin' all around, including Larry insisting on the faux title, we sent the kids off for some ice cream.

Beth and Stacy were long-time friends since high school, so they were chatting away regarding Lawrence, Stacy's new beau. We listened and laughed as Beth was not making the connection yet.

When the kids returned, I grabbed the boys and Scoot to join me in a huddle of sorts.

"Guys, Scooter and I, have a situation we need to run by you."

"Is something wrong Daddy?"

"No son, nothing's wrong, it's very exciting honestly, but we don't know how you guys will feel about it? I want to go on record as being in favor of whatever you guys decide, it's up to you two. And Uncle Scooter won't talk you into something you don't want to do either."

"Jeeze HB, is there possibly something you want to get out to the guys and say—by maybe—next Tuesday?"

"Sorry Larry, I didn't mean to make you wait this long, but this does concern you to as well."

"Really—well if I'm included too HB, get to the point for sure—hell I'm practically finished with puberty already!" God this kid was something else but my laughter showed it.

"Scoot, why don't you lay this out for our three amigos."

"Sure bud."

"Guys, what your Dad, and HB to you Larry may have eventually said by Tuesday next—is this. You two, have the opportunity to perform a twenty-minute set here at eight tonight on the Futureworld Quad. No one's going to force you boys to do this, if you prefer to go on the rides instead—or would rather not—tonight…we know you're tired from performing once today already."

"Cool Uncle Scott, I'd love to—how 'bout it Tay?"

"No problem here bro, I'm in, as long as there's no two hours of autographs afterwards, my hand's still aching from all the signing."

"Boys are you sure about this?"

"HB, cool it! My buds have spoken—we certainly don't need a whole new build up from you—again!"

"Oh, forgive me Lar, I had no idea I was such a bore?"

"You're not a bore HB; you just talk too dang much without getting—anywhere…fast."

"My word, thank you Larry, I think?" God this kid was killing me.

"Now listen you three, I did promise you six good hours here, which I meant. What with stealing away an hour for your preparations on top of playing, I'm rearranging things a bit. I cleared it with Carol that we are going to stay the night here—after all. Now, was that succinct enough for you Lar?"

"Hell no HB, all you had to say was: boys we're spending the night! But not you—no way. With you, it's just not in the cards; with you it's—talk until someone shuts you up—what's wrong with you anyways?"

After I recovered, I continued.

"Gee Lar-man, maybe I should just hire you to write all my speeches then?"

"Hell's bells, HB—if you did—we'd all get to bed a whole lot earlier!"

That did it. I was now rolling with hysterical laughter, as were Scoot and the twins.

"All right guys, any objections to us spending the night—or Larry serving as speech and stage writer?"

"No."

"Okay Scoot, I guess it's now decided."

We all rejoined the ladies and girls. As the kids took in another two and a half hours of rides, Uncle Scoot and Stacy talked some. They covered the equipment needs, while Stacy forwarded it on to her production staff and techs.

Meanwhile, Scooter sent Beth back home to pick up his set of Taylor's prerecorded synthesized instrument tracks. That alone would save nearly an hour with only minimal additional tracks needed to lay down, as a result.

Time flew by, as I looked at my watch to see that we were now at six minutes to six. I suggested that the whole group join us at Forty-Four, if I was able to increase the party's size.

"Marc, you let me handle that, but yes, I would love to join you all. I do have one request though; I insist that Lawrence escort me there, of course?"

"Sure lady, are you kidding? At this point, as long as there's food at the end of the escortin'—I'll put up with anyone."

"Now Lawrence, wouldn't you prefer calling your lady by her given name of Stacy?" I chided.

"Now see HB, there you go again—why couldn't you have just said: Lar-man, call her Stacy?"

Meanwhile, Beth had now realized the connection of Larry's transformation to Stacy's—Lawrence so she was getting a good laugh herself now.

"I'm sorry Lar; I'll try to do better next time, alright?"

"Well see that you do! Stacy it would be my pleasure to escort you—see how it's done—HB?"

Larry extended his arm to Stacy in mock fashion, as she took it, but wasn't able to stop from busting up either.

We got to, 'the door at Forty-Four' three minutes past six. Stacy approached Rudy at the podium. After a scant minute conversation, she returned to inform us that we would be seated imminently. Within seconds, we boarded their elevator up to the second floor then were escorted to a private dining room.

While we awaited our wait staff, Stacy excused herself to call her production office to conclude her arrangements. She returned in time to order, while I was hanging up on Mom filling her in on everything as well. I had also called Carol to confirm we were indeed spending the night.

Larry was super attentive to Stacy at our table, as he had been before in my own dining room. He had me in particular—impressed again now. Getting up to assist Stacy with her chair, along with standing when she left and subsequently returned. These were exceptional manners...evidential of great parenting at play here, despite Larry's candid style of conversation. I would definitely make a point of bringing this all up to Carol tomorrow, as I'd already been remiss.

Larry was also giving the boys tips on working the audience; I found his comments intriguing, as his suggestions would have likely been my own... although—honestly—shorter!

"Dad, will you ask Rudy if we can play the harpsichord, we'll be real careful with it—promise?"

"Stacy, do you think Rudy would oblige their request, he did promise he would consider it on our last visit?"

"Marc if he won't—I will. Besides, I for one would love to hear some of the classical roots of Tay 'n' Tre...the Morgan's, while I wait to be served."

Stacy and I got up to escort the boys over to the priceless instrument, which originally came from the Romanoff's palace in Russia. The placement of the harpsichord was ideal. Its sound carried throughout the entire maze of dining rooms without electronic amplification being necessary.

The boys sat quite gingerly on the bench for kids their age...here we witnessed great respect in play. They took a few moments, as they acclimated themselves. According to Trevor, they had only played on a harpsichord around a half dozen times in total.

Once they were set, they took turns with a marvelous assortment of classical movements. They played Mozart, Rachmaninov, and Bach. As each piece was completed, polite applause followed, coming from distant unseen diners. Most had no idea that they were listening to, two, eleven-year-old pishers taking turns at the ivories.

All the same, over the ensuing minutes, a sizable group of on-lookers did start to amass around the harpsichord while they played. Most anyone who opted for the stairs for instance, stopped for a listen. Once seeing the two diminutive musicians sharing the keyboard yet playing so expertly, they became entranced naturally—so none of them moved further.

When the boys finished their performance to the generous applause of the restaurant, we went downstairs to thank Rudy personally. He was delighted, as he complimented them repeatedly on their wonderful playing and selections.

He refreshed his memory on their names again, along with some basic facts.

As we reached the mid-point of the staircase, we heard the restaurant's pre-recorded music track stop.

"Ladies and gentlemen, boys and girls, please join me in thanking our two talented harpsichordists, Tay and Tre Morgan. And no, they are not with the London Philharmonic, they join us this evening from Las Vegas, Nevada. And believe it or not folks; these twin brothers are only eleven-years-old—thank you boys.

The restaurant reverberated now with thundering applause. As we reached the top of the second floor landing in the main dining room, guests naturally noticed us. They put two and two together quickly, as they all stopped their conversations long enough to give the boys a rousing ovation again. By the time we reached our private dining room, the applause was near deadening. Beth and the girls rewarded the boys with kisses, as Larry and Scoot congratulated them as well. Scoot also had a devious smile on his face now, which bothered me the moment I saw it.

"Scoot is there some reason why I shouldn't be alarmed with that smirk on your puss?"

"Yes bud—it's for a good reason, so believe me—just relax."

"Fine, what is it?"

"You'll see, that's all."

"Moments later, we heard the piped music track stop as Rudy came on again.

"Ladies and gentlemen, but especially you boys and girls, I have been remiss. It seems that young Tre and Tay will be performing again this evening. They will offer a more contemporary selection of music promptly at eight pm, at the Futureworld Quad."

"You know Scoot, you do have major cojonies, you know that don't you—I thought we wanted a raw audience?"

"No sweat bud, but believe me, you'll be thanking me when it's standing room only later. And don't worry; this is a private dinner club, the audience will still be quite raw overall. Damn it man, relax, will you?"

"Jesus Scoot, isn't this dinner thanks enough?" I was laughing at my friend now.

"I don't know bud; I guess we'll see about that, won't we?"

Owing to our upcoming performance, Rudy had arranged our meals expedited, so we were able to finish by seven-ten. This had to have been record time for the place. At least during the time I worked there, it was.

As we exited the private dining room, the boys received more polite applause as one teen cutie even stopped Tre in his tracks to speak to him.

"I'll be seeing you at eight, so please look for me."

"Thank you, we will." Tre gave her a wink as we were leaving.

We boarded two large golf carts waiting for us at the entrance to the back lot next to the exit. I got the opportunity to reminisce now with Scoot and Stacy, as I remembered the back lot route well. So well in fact, that Stacy asked how long I had been out of the organization. When I told her over a dozen years, she was impressed.

We arrived at an underground passageway that led to Futureworld's Quad stage. This quadrangle stage rises out and breaks through a futuristic sculpture like a giant transforming toy, as the performers begin their set. The boys were blown away by this fact when Stacy explained all the mechanics of it and how it worked.

We quickly walked down a long hall to a make up room. The boys received the full 'make-up' treatment, while Stacy continued her instructions. When Taylor was satisfied she was finished with her instructions, my own little crusader spoke right on up himself.

"Say Stacy, may I ask you a question now?"

"Sure Taylor, go ahead."

"Are we possibly getting paid anything here tonight?"

Stacy honestly appeared shocked by my son's question, but eventually responded.

"Taylor, I hadn't thought about that, after all, this was to be a crowd test—remember?"

"Hey Stacy, its okay if we weren't, I guess it doesn't matter."

"What doesn't matter Taylor?"

"Oh nothing, I was just going to ask you to give my half to Dad's foundation that's all. It's for charity you know."

"Oh?"

I couldn't believe it, but I caught a glance of Trevor, as he stood there, looking totally ticked off at his brother at the moment.

"It's okay Stacy; you don't have to pay us anything. God Taylor, I can't believe you sometimes. Bloody hell bro, she's trying to help us out here."

"Yes boys I am, but you know, a wonderful gesture like that, shouldn't go ignored either. Tell you what; I'll arrange our standard performance fee to be paid to the foundation, now does that seem fair?"

"Yes Miss, and thank you from both of us. I'm sorry Trev, you were right and I was wrong."

Meanwhile, Taylor got up and gave Stacy a kiss on her cheek. Immediately, Stacy blushed—obviously touched by his gesture.

"Marc, what on earth did you feed these boys growing up?"

Stacy looked at me as she laughed, but in a way she was serious too.

"Don't give me credit Stacy, my late wife Miranda raised these two to have huge hearts—but it shows, doesn't it?"

"It does…hell; I'll even kick in my ten percent too." Scoot interjected.

"Now—who said anything about ten percent for you Scott?" Stacy said it and was now busting up.

"Damn it, never mind then, I just thought it would be nice, that's all."

Once the boys were finished with their make up artists, we went over to the stage itself. It had been set up according to Scoot's instructions to Stacy. He had also worked with the technical people, who naturally he knew quite well anyway.

The boys took their seats behind the keyboards, with Taylor taking the one that accompanied the adjoining synthesizer and computer. They adjusted these 'house' instruments now to their own liking.

Scoot did a check on the sound, but as he did, he went over the set with the boys as Taylor checked the synthesizer and computer out. He told us all, that he was satisfied they would suffice for the majority of their set. He loaded Scoot's set of discs into the computer, as he began laying down the limited additional tracks on the synthesizer that he wanted.

They would open with Pin Ball Wizard.

"Uncle Scott, do you think it would be alright if we didn't do Viva Las Vegas, but replaced it with something that really swings?"

"What are you two thinking about doing instead, after all—'Viva' has a great beat?"

"Have you ever heard of a song called 'The House of Blue Lights'?"

"No, I don't believe I have, what's so special about it?"

"We love it Uncle Scott, it's a mix of bogey-wogey, country swing, and a bit of Ragtime—its brill and wicked—and we go into an awesome duel, the audience will love it. Both of us get to wailing on our boards, which makes it real hot."

"Boys enough said, let me think a moment."

Scoot thought on it for a moment before agreeing. The final song would be the medley of Stardust and In the Still of the Night.

"Boys if we have enough time at the end of your set, your engineer will flash these two stage lights twice. This will let you know you may add an encore, all right?"

"Sure Stacy, but what should we sing if that happens?"

"Whatever you want Tre."

"Listen guys, are you ready?" Stacy asked.

"Right, all I have left to do is finish laying down these synthesized sound effects tracts for Funeral." This came out of T-man as he slid back on a pair of cans (headphones) he'd been wearing.

"Do you want us to stay down here, or should we go up top where we can see you from the crowd?"

"Upstairs Dad, we'll want to know how it looks from there. Besides, we've got our hands full, just getting ourselves psyched up before this bloody stage goes up."

"You got it Trev. Listen it goes without saying that we're all proud of both of you so—break a leg."

"Break a leg? What in bloody hell is that suppose to mean Dad?"

"It's a tradition in American theatre Tre, to avoid jinxing any performers. To wish someone 'to break a leg' therefore, is another way to wish them good luck…without saying it"

"Okay, I get it."

As the remainder of our group wished the boys well, Stacy wrote out a short introduction on the boys. She handed it to the announcer who was standing by her.

We went upstairs and found an employee holding two patio tables for us.

The terrace surrounding the quad on three sides was now about a third to a half full, at the most. At five before the hour, Scoot pointed out he was sure that he recognized a few guests from Forty-Four arriving. It appeared that not many more of them would make it in time, but I didn't think that mattered anyway. I was interested in seeing a raw audience react without experience or impressions, as Scoot had promised.

Right at eight, the lighting changed just as the announcer began to boom out:

"Ladies and gentlemen, boys and girls, we're pleased to present two of the winners from last fall's ToonCrooners contest. Please join us, in giving a warm Futureworld welcome to: Tay 'n' Tre…the Morgan's.

As I sat there listening to the announcer's introduction, I had to stop my thought process for a moment to realize, that this man was just speaking about my sons...not someone else's—these were my two little pishers.

These were my boys, beginning only the second, of what could become perhaps—thousands of performances in the years ahead of them. I had no way of knowing naturally at that moment, but I did know that I was excited, yet frightened for them at the same time. And most obviously, their lives would likely never be the same again—under any circumstances.

What would happen here tonight? I wondered.

Final Questions

Will the boys see the efforts of their crusade and their music fulfilled? Will they find happiness living in Las Vegas with their Father and becoming Americans?

What other surprises and life changes, are in store for the boys and Marcus?

Will Marcus find fatherhood as wonderful as it has been up to this point, or will there be heartaches too?

How will Marilyn and Mal fit into these family changes?

What does Scoot have in store for the boys?

And—will Larry ever shut up?

The boys, Marcus, and everyone else, will be back—watch for their continuing saga and escapades in Blessings of The Father—Book Three–The Boys Break Out!

Thank you friend, for your read.

Mitch Reed

Comments to: mitchreed@hotmail.com. Please include the word 'blessings' in your subject line. Please visit me on facebook to sign up as my friend. Visit me on booktalk.org, where I have my blog: In As Many Words. Booktalk.org is a leading online book club for literary lovers the world over, and it's all free to register and post your thoughts on your favorite books…mine or otherwise. But while you're there, if you've enjoyed the saga so far, please recommend my first two volumes for the Fiction Book Discussion Group Forum, I would greatly appreciate your support.

Thanks much, Mitch